A LITTLE PLACE IN PRAGUE

JULIE CAPLIN

One More Chapter
a division of HarperCollins*Publishers* Ltd
1 London Bridge Street
London SE1 9GF
www.harpercollins.co.uk
HarperCollins*Publishers*
Macken House, 39/40 Mayor Street Upper,
Dublin 1, D01 C9W8, Ireland

This paperback edition 2024
1
First published in Great Britain in ebook format
by HarperCollins*Publishers* 2024

A catalogue record of this book is available from the British Library

ISBN: 978-0-00-867081-8

This novel is entirely a work of fiction. The names, characters and incidents
portrayed in it are the work of the author's imagination. Any resemblance
to actual persons, living or dead, events or localities is entirely
coincidental.

Printed and bound in the UK using 100% Renewable Electricity
by CPI Group (UK) Ltd

Part I

Chapter One

September

'Honey, I'm home,' called Leo through the open door of the top-floor apartment, stepping past the suitcases left inside the doorway.

There was no response but Leo heard a muttered curse, so he walked to one of the open doorways to find a large man, his own sort of age, squinting down at the instructions for a flat-pack construction.

'Hello, you must be my new flatmate,' he said, dumping his rucksack on the floor and looking around the light airy room with Velux windows tucked into the sloping roof. At first glance, his home for the next six months didn't look too bad at all. Hopefully his roomie would be okay, too, although Leo's immediate impression was that he seemed a little taciturn – but then, who wouldn't be when they were surrounded by little packets of screws and the pieces of a half-completed bed frame?

His new roommate glanced up. 'What?' he mumbled through a deep frown, his mind clearly on what bolt went where. 'Yeah, right.'

'Leo Knight.' He waved as the other man clearly wasn't in any sort of position to shake his hand. 'Sorry to barge in. Looks like you've got your hands full there. Need a hand?'

'I'm all right. Steve Munt.' He lumbered to his feet. 'You just got here?'

'Yeah, I flew into Václav Havel this morning.' He got a kick out of saying the Czech name with what he hoped was the correct pronunciation.

'What?' The man frowned, leaving Leo with impression number two, that his new room-mate was either a bit slow or a bit dull. The jury was out.

'Prague airport,' responded Leo. Maybe the guy needed a bit of tickle. 'Great transport links. I only got off the plane an hour and a half ago. Looks like you've been here a while and had time to go shopping.'

'No, drove here.' The other man nodded towards the bedframe in pieces on the floor. 'Brought it with us. My girlfriend's gone out to do the shopping. We only got here half an hour ago.' He gave Leo a careful and slightly suspicious study which almost had Leo checking himself over. Did he look that threatening? Or odd? They were both wearing T-shirts and jeans, although Leo's Armanis had put in a few miles and the fashionable rip was actually genuine – the result of a close encounter with barbed wire when a very displeased boyfriend hadn't taken kindly to Leo kissing his girlfriend. Not that she'd complained or even mentioned said boyfriend.

'Looks okay, doesn't it?' Leo ploughed on, determined to give the guy the chance to warm up.

'What?'

'This place. Not bad at all.'

Leo turned and surveyed the hallway and the smaller, empty room opposite. Someone was very organised. His plan was to nip to the nearby Ikea, grab a mattress, bedding and the basics and come back in an Uber. The store was open until eight. Plenty of time. When you were offered a very low rent on an unfurnished flat, you weren't going to turn it down, especially when you were going to be living on a bursary for six months.

'Fancy a beer?' he asked. 'I picked up a couple of cold ones from the shop down the road.'

'A beer?' Steve looked at his watch and then down at the instructions he was following and then scrunched up his face. 'Why not? This is doing my head in. It's a two-man job, so I can't do any more at the moment.

He rose to his feet.

Leo grinned. 'You'd better tell me where the kitchen is. All I've had time to do is dump my bags.'

'Up the stairs. This place is upside down for some reason.' The other man scowled. 'The kitchen and lounge are up there.'

Leo thought it sounded fun. 'Cool. Great views, I'm guessing, as we're top of the building.'

'Not my idea of fun, traipsing up the stairs all the time but I'm not the one who'll be living here.'

'Oh.' Leo, following him up the stairs paused, suddenly grateful for this news.

'It's my girlfriend. I'm helping her move in. Staying the weekend. Took the shuttle. Drove through. France, Belgium, Germany. Took fifteen hours.'

'Oh, right. Well, nice to meet you.' That explained the suspicious look, thought Leo. He wasn't vain but he also wasn't stupid.

Steve carried on, 'She's here on a cultural placement with some brewery. It's a bloody long way to come to learn how to make lager, if you ask me.'

'No sympathy, mate,' said Leo with a forced grin, feeling solidarity with his unknown flatmate, delighted to find he'd have something in common with her. 'I've got the same bee in my bonnet. I'm doing a placement, too.' All he'd been told was that he'd be sharing an apartment with another European who was on the same scheme to further knowledge of Czech culture, produce and industry. If they were also into beer that was a big tick. There was an induction meeting on Monday, where he'd meet his brewery sponsor and find out where he'd be working for the next six months. Although securing the placement was pretty prestigious and had been fiercely contested, he was actually more interested in the prize that was up for grabs during the placement. There was an amazing opportunity, at least amazing to him, to win a couple of brewery tanks as well as all the equipment to fit out his own small, craft brewery. On paper it sounded relatively simple: create a bespoke beer, along with a marketing and distribution plan that needed to demonstrate how he would raise the profile of Czech beer in the UK. The winner would be the headline beer at the newly established Christmas Beer Festival. It would be an amazing publicity opportunity. He wondered how many of the other people who'd snagged a placement would be interested in winning their own brewery kit.

He stopped dead as they walked into the lounge area, grinning when he spotted the unexpected roof terrace. 'Now that's a bonus.'

Steve shrugged his heavy shoulders. 'S'pose, if you like looking at roofs. Be better with a decent view. Like the sea, or a beach or something.'

'Bit difficult here. I'm pretty sure the Czech Republic is landlocked. Although, cool that you can visit four different countries crossing the border.'

Steve looked at him as if he were talking gibberish.

Thank God Steve wasn't staying, thought Leo as he carried his smaller rucksack into the kitchen. Maybe he took a while to warm up.

'Watch your head,' warned Steve. 'Why anyone would put a kitchen in here, I don't know. Every wall has a sloping ceiling. Complete botch job and a bloody nightmare. I'd have stuck the kitchen at one end of the lounge and made it open-plan.'

Leo bit back the words 'I'm sure you would.' He rather liked the quirky kitchen with its wood-framed Velux windows. It felt rather like an eyrie at the top of a mountain, with views from every window. He opened a couple of cupboards before finding some suitable glasses. At a push he wasn't averse to drinking out of the bottle, but a true aficionado knew it didn't do the taste of the beer any favours.

Taking the glasses and separating a couple of bottles from

the ones he put in the fridge, he moved out to the roof terrace, keen to get back into the late August sunshine after being cooped up in an airport, plane and cab for most of the day. Sitting in one of the bistro chairs, he took a deep breath and pulled his keyring with its bottle-top opener from his pocket to flip off the cap of one of the bottles of Pilsner Urquell. A safe, standard choice for day one here, but he was looking forward to trying some of the craft beers in the local brewpubs.

He handed a bottle and the keyring to Steve.

'Thanks.' Steve sank into one of the chairs and flipped the crown cap off his beer.

Leo carefully poured the beer into the glass, watching the foamy head froth up, already anticipating the flavour of the golden brew.

'Cheers,' he said and took a long, thirsty pull, before slapping down his glass with a grin. 'Absolute nectar.'

Steve wrinkled his nose, 'Not so sure about all that head.' But he took a sip.

Leo closed his eyes to savour the cool, refreshing flavour of the beer and the sun on his face. This was heaven right here.

He opened his eyes and squinted into the sunshine. Holy shit!

His hand clenched on the condensation-covered glass and the sudden grip forced it out of his fingers, so that it landed with a crash on the table, sending a spray of beer up his arm.

'Anna, you're back.' Steve jumped to his feet, ignoring Leo's mishap, and went over to the woman who'd stepped through the French doors onto the terrace. He wrapped his arm around her in a proud, proprietorial embrace, as Leo brushed ineffectually at his wet arm, all the while staring at Anna.

'This is Leo, the guy you're going to be sharing with.'

Leo's mouth turned dry and his stomach dropped to his feet. Fuck. Fuck. Fuck. What the— He grabbed his drink and took a quick slug of beer to give his hands something to do.

'This is my girlfriend, Anna. Anna Love.' Steve actually puffed out his chest as he laid claim to her in that and-you'd-better-remember-that-mate, territorial-gorilla way. Which was an effing joke because he clearly had absolutely no idea who Leo was.

'Anna,' said Leo, swallowing hard.

'Leo. Nice to meet you,' said Anna without so much as a pause, not moving from Steve's protective hold. She stared at him with the sort of smooth, bland poker face that gave nothing away.

He blinked and waited a second. Had she really said that? Nice to meet you? Did she not recognise him? Of course she bloody recognised him. How could she not?

He could feel his upper lip curling in … he wasn't sure what. Disbelief? Amazement? Disappointment?

Seriously? She was going to pretend she didn't know him?

Even after all this time, it was a kick to the stomach.

'I got you some milk. So you can have a proper cup of tea,' she said, turning to Steve. Her boyfriend.

B-b-boyfriend. Sharp acid soured Leo's stomach like curdled milk.

'Would you like one … er, Leo?' she asked, as if she wasn't sure of his name.

Ouch, that hurt. His heart crumpled, with a crisp, cellophane crunch.

'Uh, er, no. Uh…' Incapable of finding consonants, let alone words, he held up his beer in response as if she spoke a different language.

She nodded, almost dismissively, and turned to her … to Steve. 'Want one?'

Steve gave her an apologetic grimace. 'I'm on the beer, too. It's not bad.'

'Mmm,' said Anna, and, if anything, she looked a little disapproving. As much to annoy her as by natural instinct, Leo immediately offered her one. 'There are a couple of Pilsners in the fridge, if you'd like one. I'm looking forward to trying some of the local brews while we're here. I was thinking about visiting BeerGeek tonight. Do you two fancy coming?'

Anna's eyes brightened as a spark of enthusiasm lit up in them, and then she glanced at Steve and her mouth straightened – a little, but the change was enough to tell Leo that she'd seriously considered his idea for a moment.

'No, mate,' said Steve. 'We're going to be apart for the next few months, so we'd rather do something … just us.'

Anna nodded. 'I've bought a few bits to cook with.' She paused and Leo very nearly laughed as he saw her natural good manners warring with her desire to do the right thing by the boyfriend. 'You could … er … join us, if you want.' It was possibly the most grudging invitation he'd ever been given, and Leo could guarantee that his presence would be as welcome as a Siberian blast of winter in June.

'You're all right. I'll leave you two lovebirds to it. I need to get a bed sorted.' He picked up his phone and began to tap details into his Uber app.

'How are you going to do that?' There was a slight sneer in Steve's voice.

'Cab to Ikea. I ordered a load of stuff online, including one of their magic mattresses that come vacuum-packed. I need to go and pick it up.'

Feeling as if he'd had the last word, Leo stood up and took his beer and glass. 'I'll see you guys later.'

Downstairs he shut the door of his room and said out loud, 'I don't effing believe it.'

He was going to be living with Anna flipping Love for six months. What weird alignment of the stars had created this mess?

Chapter Two

Anna closed the bathroom door and leaned against it. A fine sheen of clammy sweat had broken out across her walking-dead-hued forehead and her heart skittered all over the place, banging frantically against her ribcage like a frenzied bluebottle against glass. Even though Leo had left the apartment an hour ago to go to Ikea to 'secure supplies', the sensation of panic hadn't subsided.

She took an inordinate amount of time unpacking her shopping and finding homes for everything in the kitchen. Thankfully, Steve, who'd returned to bed-building, hadn't noticed her distraction.

Huffing out a sigh, she sank onto the toilet lid. Panic had made her pretend she didn't know Leo. Why hadn't she gaily greeted him as if he was an old friend? But if she had, there would have been too many explanations required and inevitable questions from Steve. How did she know Leo? Where did they meet? And she couldn't control Leo's answers. What if he'd told Steve the truth?

Steve was everything Leo wasn't – reliable, solid and steady. He wouldn't let her down, flirt with another woman or make her feel she'd never be enough. Mostly importantly, she knew Steve loved her. With yet another sigh, she rose wearily to her feet, chewing her lip. At least Leo hadn't given her away. Could she trust him not to say anything in front of Steve before he left on Monday morning?

And when the hell had Leo developed an interest in beer? That was definitely new. And weird, she decided.

'Hey, Anna. I could do with a hand here,' called Steve.

'Coming.' Scowling at her reflection, she turned on the tap and splashed cold water onto her face. Nothing she could do now. Hopefully Leo would stay out of the way. Crossing her fingers, she uttered a quick prayer and hurried out to help Steve.

She knew he was being helpful and wanted to make sure she was settled before he left, but these days she found him a little overbearing. And now she was being a brat. He'd driven all the way across Europe for her, she reminded herself. When she'd first met him, she'd been so grateful for his attention. The local rugby hero. Everyone at home loved him and she'd been flattered that he'd taken an interest in her.

But, if she was brutally honest with herself, she now realised it had also been politic. Steve had slotted seamlessly in with her adopted family from day one, as if his presence made up for her shortcomings. He conferred upon her a status she hadn't previously enjoyed, particularly among the rugby-mad male members of the family and her village peers.

Steve was 110 per cent reliable. He would never let her down. She could guarantee if he so much as looked at another woman, she'd be the first to know because he'd tell her. There was a lot to be said for reliability and honesty, especially when the head of your own family was a blatant flirt and philanderer. She shook her head. She was being silly and ungrateful. Maybe they'd both stopped making much effort – but wasn't that what happened in long-term relationships?

Just as she was about to join Steve in what was to be her new bedroom, the intercom buzzed.

'Hello,' she said hesitantly.

'Hello. Taxi. Ikea.'

'Sorry?'

'I have shopping. From Ikea.'

She opened the door and, hearing the rustling of bags coming up the stairwell, stepped forward and peered over the railings in time to see a man depositing several blue Ikea bags through a slim gap in the doorway in the hall at the bottom, right in front of the door.

'Where's Leo?' she called down. The taxi driver looked blankly back at her.

'The man with the shopping.' She made gestures as if that might overcome the language barrier.

He shook his head. 'No room. He go.' The man indicated walking with his fingers.

The door closed, and then … nothing. She stared down at the blue mini mountain and then back at her apartment door. Presumably these were Leo's purchases. After waiting a little while, she ventured down the stairs to find a rolled-up mattress along with bags of bedding, towels, a bedside lamp, a mirror, a couple of pillows and two flat-pack boxes. A reluctant smile touched her lips. She could imagine it all too well: Leo getting carried away with his shopping and there being no space left in the taxi for him.

The door to the ground-floor flat opened and a petite, very elegant woman stepped out wearing a glossy fur coat and neat little heels. Anna tried not to stare at her immaculate, soft grey hair, which was piled into a stylish chignon, anchored with a diamante pin.

Her mouth pinched in disapproval at the sight of all the bags dumped in front of the door.

'Sorry,' said Anna and moved to grasp one of the bags.

'These are yours?' asked the woman in low, radio-voice quality, flawless English, poking at them with a highly polished walking stick.

'No. Not really. They're … well, I think they belong to my flatmate, but I don't know where he is.'

'They need to be moved,' said the woman, fluttering the bejewelled fingers of one hand with an imperious wave as if that might remove them from her sight.

While Anna agreed with her, it seemed pretty unfair that she was going to have to take responsibility for Leo's bloody stuff. But then, wasn't that so typical of him? He'd probably arranged the delivery and then been diverted by something brighter or shinier elsewhere, because that was what Leo did.

To Anna's surprise, the woman's face softened. 'Let's ask

Jan if he'll help.' With surprising agility, despite the stick, the woman trotted up the next flight of stairs to the middle floor and rapped on the door. There was a brief conversation in Czech and then a man about Anna's age, with a mop of dark curly hair, a closely cropped beard and sharp brown eyes appeared at the top of the stairs.

'This is Jan, he's going to help,' said the woman with a beatific smile as if she'd solved all the problems of the universe.

'Thank you,' said Anna, more than a little disconcerted by the turn of events.

Jan came down the stairs. 'Hi, you must be the new neighbour.' He held out a hand. 'Jan.'

'Anna.'

'And –' Jan nodded and mouthed three times, as if he were counting '– this is my girlfriend, Michaela.' And sure enough, a pretty elfin, blonde woman materialised at the top of the stairs behind him. 'Gorgeous but nosy,' he whispered, his eyes twinkling with quick, bright humour.

'Hello, new neighbour,' said the woman in perfect English, but with a slight American accent. She might have been pint-sized, with a petite, delicate frame, but she exuded energy from her flyaway hair to her sparkling brown eyes. 'Welcome to the neighbourhood.'

'Thank you,' said Anna shifting her weight, conscious that she was nearly a foot taller and twice as broad as the tiny fairy in front of her.

'Are you settling in?' Michaela asked. 'Do you need anything?'

'She wants to practise her English,' said Jan, shaking his

head, a mournful smile on his long-suffering face. 'Don't be fooled.' Despite his words, it was obvious he doted on the woman next to him.

'I like meeting new people,' said Michaela indignantly, elbowing him in the ribs before adding, 'but improving my English is always good.'

Anna nodded, wishing she could be as bright and breezy as the happy, confident Michaela. It struck her that Leo would have known exactly what to say. He was always good in social situations, with that same easy charm. She tried to think what he might say in this situation but remained tongue-tied.

'Shall we?' Michaela picked up one of the bags.

'Thank you. They're not mine,' Anna said hurriedly.

'Oh, who then?'

'The other guy that's going to be living in the flat as well.'

'Don't you know him?' asked Michaela.

Anna opened her mouth and then closed it, pinching her lips tight before her innate honesty could give her away. She shook her head.

'I told you, Michaela,' the older woman interrupted. 'The apartment has been rented by the trade attaché department for people coming here on placements.'

'You did, Ludmila. I forgot. Ludmila always knows everything,' whispered Michaela. 'She owns the flat.'

Ludmila, who was only slightly taller than Michaela, drew herself up, her fine eyebrows arching in haughty disdain. 'Of course I do. Now I'd like to leave the building. I have a date at the ballet and I shall be late.'

'Sorry,' said Anna, grabbing one of the bags blocking the doorway.

'Have fun,' said Michaela as the woman slipped out.

Jan went to pick up the mattress, but as it was packaged like an outsized Swiss roll in slippery plastic, he was unable to get much purchase on it.

'Two men for this job,' he said.

'Oh, I'll get my boyfriend to help. He's upstairs,' said Anna.

Michaela had already set off up the first flight of stairs, so Anna followed her.

Steve was less than impressed, ten minutes later, when he and Jan lugged the vacuum-packed mattress up the last flight of stairs.

'Would have served him right if we'd left it there,' he grumbled as they dumped it in the other bedroom alongside the blue bags now lined up against the wall.

'Thank you so much for helping us,' said Anna to Michaela, who despite her size had cheerfully carried one of the big bags up all three flights of stairs without pausing for breath.

'It's not a problem. I wanted an excuse to have a look in here for ages. Can I see the roof terrace?'

'Michaela.' Jan nudged her.

'You don't mind, do you?' She beamed at Anna, who found herself smiling back.

'No, come up.' Anna hesitated for a moment. She didn't really do spontaneous invites but on this occasion it sort of felt like the right thing to do. After all, the couple had dropped everything to help. They'd probably say no. 'Would you … would you like to stay for a drink?'

'That would be lovely,' said Michaela. 'Can we sit outside? It must be great to have that space.'

Anna smiled. 'I wouldn't know … yet.' She turned to lead Michaela up the stairs and caught Steve's quick glare as he mouthed, 'What are you doing?'

Ignoring him, she ploughed on up. 'I've only got beer.'

'And what is wrong with that?' asked Jan, a lilt of amusement in his voice. 'It's our national drink.'

Anna relaxed a little, grateful that she could offer them something suitable. 'That's why I'm here. To learn all I can while I'm at the brewery.'

'Which one?' Jan sounded genuinely interested.

'I'm not sure yet. I find out on Monday. There's an induction meeting where we meet our brewery sponsors.'

'There's plenty of choice in Prague, the old traditional brewers and the young craft beer makers.'

'I know, that's what makes it so exciting.' Anna let some of her enthusiasm spill out even though she heard Steve's barely audible harrumph from the back of their little procession trooping up the stairs. Poor thing, he really didn't understand her passion for beer, even though she'd tried to explain. It was a last link to her parents, who had died in a car accident when she was fourteen and she'd gone to live with her aunt and uncle. Her father had been the head brewer at Talbot's – the family-owned brewery set up by her great-great-grandfather. Although she worked there in the office for her Uncle Henry and her cousins who ran the company, she was desperate to make beer. Not that anyone would listen to her.

Michaela rushed to the French doors and beckoned Jan, speaking in rapid-fire Czech.

'I'll get the beer,' said Anna. 'You go out.' They stepped out and even though she didn't speak the language she could tell they were impressed.

'What did you invite them to stay for?' Steve hissed, following her into the kitchen.

'To say thank you for helping,' she whispered back, suddenly regretting her impulse. It would have been so much easier if Leo were here. He knew what to say to new people. It was his superpower.

'They didn't help you, they helped that idiot flatmate of yours.'

Anna acknowledged the truth of this with a nod. 'They're also neighbours, and it's not going to be that easy making friends here. I don't know anyone apart from the idiot flatmate.' And she definitely wouldn't be spending much time with him.

After opening a couple of cupboards, Anna found some glasses and took the beers from the fridge.

'Do you think you're going to be okay?' asked Steve. 'I don't like the thought of you being out here on your own, especially not with him.'

'I'll be fine,' said Anna, having already decided that she'd be looking for alternative accommodation first thing on Monday.

'Bloody cheek expecting us to sort his stuff out. I hope he's not going to take the piss. He seems like the laid-back type, a bit too cocky and sure of himself. I hope for your sake he's going to be tidy.'

Anna managed to bite back her snort just in time. The word 'tidy' didn't exist in Leo's lexicon, let alone his world. He was the messiest, untidiest person she'd ever come across, guaranteed to leave a wake of detritus in his wake.

'I'm going to have a word with him before I leave.'

'About what?' asked Anna, trying to tamp down her alarm. What if Leo said something? She wouldn't put it past him.

'You know – being respectful of you and not shagging loads of girls here, or at least being discreet about it. I reckon he's that type.'

'Steve! You can't do that. What he does is his business.' Behind her back, Anna clenched one fist. *Thanks, Steve, for putting the worst-case scenario into her head.*

She swallowed hard, stuck now with the image of Leo bringing someone back, but managed to say, 'Besides, what makes you say that? He might have a girlfriend.'

Her stomach hollowed at the very thought – but then he was bound to have one. He was Leo, after all. Women loved him. He loved them. Everyone loved Leo. He was like a sodding half-grown Labrador puppy.

'I know the type. Bet you anything he's a player. He's got nonstick all over him. The sort that doesn't do commitment. At least I don't have to worry about him coming on to you.'

Anna raised a brow, wondering whether to feel insulted or not. 'And why's that?'

'Because you're probably not his type.' Steve pulled a

face of disbelief as if puzzled that she'd even had to ask, which, to be frank, did sting … a lot.

'Thanks,' she said, folding her arms. Steve's words made her feel like a wilted lettuce well past its sell-by date.

'I don't mean that you're unattractive. You're gorgeous.' Steve wrapped an arm around her and kissed her on the mouth, laying a hand on her cheek, smiling down at her. 'But you've got more sense. He's not your type, far too flaky.' Steve kissed her again, giving her waist a squeeze. 'I mean, I guess a lot of girls would find him attractive but he's … well, he's too laid-back, a bit free and easy. Off to Ikea in a cab, arriving and starting straight in on the beer. I don't know, he strikes me as the sort that's out for a good time.'

'And you could tell all this from ten minutes' acquaintance,' said Anna with a quick smile.

'You can tell the type. He's probably chatting someone up as we speak. I'm not that comfortable with you having to put up with someone like him.'

Out on the roof terrace, Michaela and Jan were leaning on the metal rail that ran along two sides, pointing to local landmarks. Beyond them, Anna could see the nearby creamy yellow buildings with terracotta-tiled roofs.

'This is wonderful,' said Michaela, taking one of the seats at the bistro table. 'You have a great view. I would love to have some outdoor space in the city.'

Anna nodded as if she understood but she had no idea. She'd not lived in a city since her parents died. Although Prague was probably one of the most beautiful cities she'd ever visited. Michaela smiled at her and took a sip of beer.

It was one of those awkward and-now-you-ask-a-question moments.

'Have you lived in the building long?' asked Anna, thinking it was so obviously an attempt to find something to say. Steve wasn't helping, he was staring at his beer bottle – but then he'd never been great at small talk.

'We've been here for just over two years.'

'And the lady downstairs?'

'Ludmila!' Michaela's eyes brightened. 'She's a honey. She's lived here a long time. But she used to live in London, that's why her English is so good. She was a ballet dancer with the Royal Ballet and then a choreographer here in Prague with the Czech National Ballet.'

'She's in charge,' said Jan with a quick smile. 'When she tells us to do something, we do it.'

'But she's very nice,' said Michaela with a fond smile. 'We're a long way from our homes and family. She is the *babička*, the grandmother, of the building. She is a baker and brings us treats: *vánočka* at Christmas and *velikonoční bochánek* at Easter – they're both types of sweet bread with fruit in them. And she makes the best *kolach*, doesn't she, Jan? That's a typical Czech cake.'

'Hello! Are we having a party?' Leo bounced into view. 'Hi, I'm Leo.' With the ease of someone who always knew they were welcome everywhere, he strode over to Jan and held out his hand.

'I'm Jan.'

Michaela bobbed up to introduce herself. 'We live on the floor below.'

'Yes, they helped carry your shopping spree up here,' said Anna, her voice tart.

'Oh, has it arrived already? Great. I'll have a bed tonight.' Leo flipped open the cap of the bottle he carried.

Anna glared at him. Unbelievable.

'That shagging mattress was bloody heavy,' said Steve. 'You're welcome.'

'Amazing that they can roll them up like that, though,' said Leo, clearly impervious to the implied criticism. 'And the way they *pouf* –' he emphasised the word with his spare hand '– up when you break the plastic wrapping. Amazing! Thanks, though. You know what it's like in Ikea. You grab a couple of bits and before you know it, you're having trouble steering the trolley.'

Michaela laughed as Jan groaned. 'Every time,' she said with an empathetic smile.

As the four seats around the little bistro table were taken, Leo sat down on the terrace, his elbows resting loosely on his open knees. 'So, Michaela and Jan, give us the lowdown. What can you recommend about the neighbourhood? Where's the best pub? Places to go? I've got no sense of where we are.'

'We're in Kore. You know the city is divided into districts?'

Leo shook his head.

'This is Praha 5 and it's a beautiful suburb, lots of parks and families. Some parts are quite hilly. There is a supermarket on Pod Školou and a really good pub. We can take you there. We visit at least once a week, usually on a Monday evening.'

'Sounds like a great idea to me,' said Leo with enthusiasm. 'Get the week off to a good start. I'd love to join you.'

'We're busy this week but come knock for us at seven, next Monday,' said Michaela, the smile highlighting her sweet little dimples.

And just like that, Leo had made friends already. Anna couldn't help feeling a little nip of jealousy that he found it so easy. It cast light on her inadequacy.

'This is a cool apartment,' he said, gesturing with the beer bottle.

'We're very jealous of this roof terrace.'

'Oh, come up any time,' said Leo with a blithe wave, oblivious to Anna's quick glare. They didn't even know these people and he was already inviting them to drop in. 'It's a real bonus. In fact, the whole apartment is. Not what I was expecting from the outside.'

'Yeah, it's an ugly building,' said Jan. 'You find that a lot. Old communist practicality on the outside, Czech love and skill on the inside. We take pride in making our spaces our homes. Musílkova is a great street to live on, there's a good mix of the old and the new. And it's very safe.'

'Very,' interjected Michaela. 'The Czech Republic is one of the safest countries in Europe to live.'

Now that Leo had appeared, the conversation ran smoothly, with none of the false starts of trying to get to know someone. He had that ability to befriend people. Anna gritted her teeth. It was so annoying.

Chapter Three

A nna poured herself a cup of coffee from the cafetière and tensed at the sound of footsteps coming into the kitchen. All weekend she'd successfully avoided being on her own with Leo, but now it was Monday and Steve had left half an hour before to make the long drive back across Europe.

'Morning,' said Leo, full of cheer.

'Morning,' she replied, her vocal cords constricting her voice. She deliberately kept her back to him.

'Don't suppose there's one of those for me?' he asked, as if this was the most normal thing in the world.

'Sure,' she said, through gritted teeth, as she reached up to grab a fresh mug. She could feel her pulse racing in her neck but she doggedly poured the coffee and added milk before turning to face him. Maybe she should take a leaf out of his book and play along as if they were two strangers.

That was before she turned around.

Every drop of moisture in her mouth evaporated. OMG.

Whoa! Where the hell had these Greek god proportions come from? Leo had filled out considerably since she'd last seen him … but then again, they had been a lot younger.

He stood there with a pale blue towel wrapped around his hips, emphasising the golden tones of his skin and the white-blond hairs on his muscular legs. He had pecs, biceps and – she almost gulped – a darker track of hair leading down below his belly button.

She knew she was staring but Leo, being Leo, seemed totally oblivious. That blithe, insouciant confidence for some reason irritated her even more. How could he pretend that everything was normal? And how did he manage it, when her flipping stomach churned with the heaviness of a concrete mixer?

'That for me?' asked Leo nodding to the coffee that she was still holding.

'Er, yes.' She held it out, focusing on the white mug and the dark liquid, taking great care not to look at his face or to touch his fingers.

'Where's lover boy?' he asked, looking around as if Steve might be hiding in a cupboard somewhere, amusement curving his lips as if he were laughing at a private joke.

Anna drew in a breath, feeing prudish and wrong-footed by Leo's golden glory. It was so bloody unfair.

'He's gone. He had to get back for work tomorrow, so he left early.'

'Just you and me, then.' Leo grinned with a touch of malicious triumph. 'How long has he been on the scene?'

Anna's nerves, stretched to breaking point, finally

snapped. 'Two years, not that it's anything to do with you. And will you put some clothes on,' she snapped. 'There's no one here to impress.'

He grinned at her and finally took the coffee from her outstretched hand. 'Missed me?'

She glowered at him. She might have known he wouldn't take this seriously.

Leo's lips curled into a cheerful grin. 'I take it from your rapturous greeting yesterday he doesn't know about us?'

With a swallow, Anna shook his head. 'No. He doesn't need to. It was a long time ago. We were still children. And this is very unfortunate.'

'Mmm, nice coffee' said Leo, although he appeared amused by the situation. 'Fate's a funny old thing,' he observed, leaning back against one of the cabinets, stretching one arm. Anna tried hard not to register the way his skin rippled over the smooth muscles.

'I don't believe in fate. It's bad luck,' she snapped. 'But don't worry, I'm going to ask for alternative accommodation at the meeting today.'

'That's up to you,' said Leo with a nonchalant shrug, which drew her eyes to his chest again. How could anyone be that bloody gorgeous? But then she knew what he was like, which ought to have been enough to dampen her hormones, but they didn't believe in common sense and had suddenly leapt into life. Frisky, curious and completely out of control. She hoped Leo had no idea of the effect he was having on her. Shame helped douse the feelings. She had a boyfriend, for God's sake.

'Don't feel you have to move out on my account. I'm sure we can be civilised.'

Anna stared at him, at the deep blue eyes, guileless and sincere. 'So you won't do the gentlemanly thing and move out yourself?'

A slight frown creased his forehead. 'Me?' he asked with a touch of incredulity.

'Yes, you.'

'But why? I'm not the one with the problem.'

'Leo, be serious.'

'I am. I like this apartment. I like Jan and Michaela. I can tell they're going to be friends. It's a nice neighbourhood. I don't want to move. I just got here. We're grown-ups, we can live amicably together. I'm sure we can stay out of each other's way.'

'And since when have you been interested in making beer?' Unable to hold it in any longer, the curiosity-loaded question shot out.

He gave her a long considering look and held up his hands in a surrender gesture. 'I met a girl once who really liked beer. She got me interested. Then I lost interest and did various things for a few years … and then, eighteen months ago, I was at a loose end and got chatting to a guy who runs a micro-brewery in Richmond. He needed some help…' Leo shrugged. 'I started doing deliveries for him to start with and gradually got more involved. But it's too small an outfit to take me on full time and I don't have the experience yet. In the summer I met a couple of Italian guys who were also running a micro-brewery and helped them out as well. I just decided that I'd like to set up my own, if I could. And here I am.'

Anna refrained from voicing her thoughts. 'Just decided'. That said it all. Brewing was in her blood – that's why she was here.

Leo lifted his coffee mug in a quick toast, shot her another cheerful smile and ambled out of the kitchen.

Gritting her teeth to stop herself growling at him, Anna glared at his back, acknowledging that it was a fine back, and a very fine backside, his pert buttocks outlined by the fabric of the towel.

Why did he have to be so bloody reasonable? Surely he could see they couldn't share this place. Not with their history.

———

Half an hour later, she gathered up her bag, ready to leave. She checked her reflection one last time in the mirror and deemed herself ready for the day. The journey timings, which she'd checked and rechecked, would get her to the venue in plenty of time – it would be awful to be late the first day she met her sponsor and the scheme organisers. It was important that she impress her sponsor from day one, because she'd need all their support to help her win the brewery equipment, which was the main reason she was here.

Despite her best efforts, she'd been unable to persuade her uncle to allow her to be involved in the brewing side of things, let alone brew her own beer. If she could win this equipment and use her own savings, she hoped to persuade him to let her have a small part of the building to set up her own line. She was, after all, a shareholder and on the board, even if technically she owned only a tiny percentage of the company.

With a sigh, she stepped into the hallway, noting that Leo, who'd always been a last-minute, fly-by-the-seat-of-his-pants merchant, must have already left. His bedroom door was wide open and he'd obviously already left the apartment, early. That was a shock. Spontaneity ran through him like the proverbial stick of rock. Routines were anathema. In the past he'd always left everything to the last minute.

Ensuring she had everything, she left the apartment and took the stairs slowly, a mix of fear, nerves and excitement rattling through her. 'You're doing this for you,' she told herself. 'It's something you wanted to do.' She'd stuck to her guns, despite everyone at home thinking that she was quite mad to move to another country to gain work experience, when she had a perfectly good job working in the office of the family brewery. Wondering with some satisfaction what their reaction would be if she won the equipment and put her plan into action, she turned the corner … and ran smack into Leo.

The hand he put out to steady her was gentle, as was the expression in his eyes. Both immediately exhumed fluttery feelings she'd thought long buried. Her heart softened in quick recognition as she remembered those bright, joy-filled days when she'd first got to know him.

'What are you—?' she blurted, taken aback to see him.

She'd assumed he'd be aboard a tram already trundling along to the centre of Prague.

'Hello, again.' In his hand he held a bamboo reusable coffee cup. 'Really good coffee here. You have to try it. I stopped for breakfast.'

'Breakfast?' she asked, still nonplussed at seeing him and shaken by the flutters.

'Yes, *kobliha* – at least I think that's what the girl called it. Bloody lovely. Like a doughnut but with a tangy marmalade. I might have to stop here for breakfast every day. You taking the tram to *Dělnická?*' He repeated the tram stop name, which she recognised from poring over Google Maps when planning her route last night. 'I love saying these words out loud. Do you think we're pronouncing them right? Did you know that "hello" is *ahoj* but you pronounce it "ahoy", like "ahoy, sailor"? I love that. And "thank you" is *děkuji*. And "please" is *prosím*.' He grinned delightedly at her, like a small boy who'd gained full marks in a spelling test.

As always his wide smile was infectious. 'Very good,' she said, trying her best not to be sucked into his good humour. 'You'll be fluent in no time.'

Clearly what had been said earlier had not affected him but then he'd never been one to bear a grudge.

'I'm not sure about that, the doohickeys and thingamabobs over the letters are quite tricky.'

'Diacritics,' said Anna, unable to help laughing at his worried frown. 'That's what they're called.'

'You see, you learn something new every day. Are you excited about meeting everyone today?'

Excited wasn't the word she'd have chosen – curious rather than anything else – but with his positive outlook on life Leo tended to view anyone new as a potential friend. Anna, far more reserved, preferred to sit back and let others talk, so that she could weigh them up. Although one of his many superpowers had been to give her the confidence to push herself forward a little more and occasionally take charge of a conversation. He'd been like her very own social-power bank.

As soon as they arrived at the tram stop, Leo immediately got into conversation with an older woman who'd once lived in London. Before the tram had arrived he'd elicited vast chunks of her life story – okay, that was an exaggeration, but he did know exactly how many grandchildren she had.

When the tram arrived, it was so busy they were separated in the crowd of people hanging on to the poles. Like the world over, everyone was absorbed in their phones.

They arrived at the designated meeting spot, *Vnitroblock*, an old brick-built warehouse-type building which had been turned into a super-cool venue with a coffee bar, offices, a dance studio and a cinema as well as meeting areas and clothes shops. Exposed brick walls, shiny, industrial pipework and heavy, black-painted iron ladder-beams were lit by stylish black-framed windows high up in the walls and contemporary lighting. The spacious area was filled with funky furniture interspersed with lots of indoor greenery and arranged in different zones. People had already set up camp at some tables with their laptops, phones and cups of coffee.

'Over there,' said Leo, pointing to a sign on one of the tables in one of the alcoves. *Sdílená Kultura* was printed in large red letters on a folded piece of card. Anna already knew that this meant 'Shared Culture', which was the rather appropriate name of the trade delegation scheme that had organised everything.

A young man with pipe-cleaner legs encased in jeans and a pale blue T-shirt stood at a table filled with an enticing selection of cakes and pastries.

'Hi, I'm Leo Knight,' said Leo, immediately extending a hand. Buoyed by his effortless approach, she followed suit. 'And I'm Anna Love.'

'Hi, guys. I'm Jiří, the *Sdílená Kultura* co-ordinator. We've corresponded by email. '

'Nice to meet you in real life,' said Anna.

'Great to meet you, too. I'm so excited, this is our first cultural exchange and I'm really hoping it's going to be a big success. Someone from the British Embassy is joining us this morning, plus my boss and a couple of other people from our department, and of course the sponsor brewers and the brewery machinery manufacturers who are sponsoring the main prize.'

'How many people are on the scheme?' asked Leo looking round the room.

Jiří's beam faltered a little. 'Ah, well, erm … just the two of you, this time. Obviously this is a new scheme and things are growing all the time. And this is the pilot. It is all new.

But,' he said, brightening, 'we have three very prestigious sponsors.'

Anna had assumed there'd be more people on the programme. That it was just her and Leo felt like a lot of pressure. Like they were guinea pigs. It would have been nice if there had been other people on the programme she could have got to know and share the experience with. She didn't like it that the only other person on the scheme was Leo, or that they were in direct competition with one another.

'Can I get you a coffee?' Jiří asked them both.

When he turned to walk over to the counter, Anna, grasping the opportunity for a private chat, followed him, saying to Leo, 'I'll go and see if he needs a hand.'

Leo was too busy looking around, drinking in everything, to take much notice and he was already pulling out his phone and taking photos when she approached Jiří at the coffee counter.

'Er, I wonder if I could ask you something,' she said to him.

'Sure.' His bright smile encouraged her to continue.

'This is a bit awkward but would it be possible to change my accommodation?'

'Your accommodation? There is a problem? I apologise. We were assured it was a very good apartment and it's in a very good area.'

'No, no, the … the apartment is fine. It's lovely. It's just that … well, if there was an alternative, I'd be very grateful.'

Jiří's forehead concertinaed in a dozen lines as he looked towards Leo. 'You both want to move?'

'No, just me.' Anna winced, hoping she didn't sound like a spoilt diva.

'Is it because the apartment is unfurnished? I am sure we can help with that.'

'No, nothing like that.' Anna hated to sound so ungrateful or even difficult.

The other man's mouth firmed, unhappiness shadowing his pale face. 'I will speak to the office manager but it might be difficult.'

'I'd be really grateful if you would ask.'

Worry lines deepened on Jiří's forehead. 'You know, this apartment in Košíře is very convenient for the tram to the brewery where you will be working. And it is a very green neighbourhood.'

'It is but it's for … personal reasons,' she said with quiet emphasis.

Jiří stared at her with incomprehension for a moment and then shrugged rather fatalistically. 'I will see what I can do but it might…' He spread his hands out without finishing the sentence.

While they'd been at the counter a few other people had arrived, gathering in small groups around the table and making inroads into the pastries. Leo, Anna noticed, was of course chatting away to a very pretty blonde woman.

Jiří rushed over to an imposing-looking man. From his sudden deferential demeanour, Anna guessed this must be his boss. Then, like a persistent sheepdog, the young man began rounding everyone up.

'Welcome to Prague and to the *Sdílená Kultura* cultural exchange. I am Jaroslav, the Head of the Cultural Office for

Europe here in Prague. It is our wish to extend the hand of friendship through one of our biggest exports to our fellow Europeans. We are very happy that you have come here to learn how to make what we all know is the best beer in the world.'

Everyone laughed at that, although Anna wondered at the pomp, given there appeared to be only two of them on the scheme.

'As you are aware we are delighted to be able to invite our British friends to spend some time in two of our very fine breweries so that they can share the wonder of Czech beer among their compatriots. I'd like to thank the Šilhov and Crystal breweries for their generous sponsorship of the scheme and for offering each of them a placement. Thank you also to the trade attaché at the British Embassy, the Czech Beer and Malt association and The Brewers of Europe, who will be judging the final presentations of our two young brewers, Anna Love and Leo Knight, to decide which of them will win our grand prize, kindly sponsored by Heinmann Brew Tech, who will be supplying the brewing equipment for the winner. In addition, the winning beer will be presented at a new Czech Christmas Beer festival, which will take place in the Malé náměstí.'

There was a polite round of applause. Anna looked over at Leo and he glanced back at her, raising his eyebrows. They hadn't talked about the fact that they both wanted to win. Although the odds were much lower than Anna had first assumed, thinking 'd be far more people on the placement scheme, why did she have to be up against bloody Leo Knight? She really wanted this and she couldn't believe that he was as hungry for it as she was. He had a rich and generous family who would back him.

After a further five minutes, Jaroslav wound up his official spiel and left them 'to talk among themselves and get to know each other a little' – which was rather ironic, given that there were only two of them and they actually knew each other rather well. Anna knew, for example, that Leo was incredibly messy, leaving an untidy trail of possessions in his wake like a tornado ripping through. Although, to be fair, so far she hadn't tripped over any shoes or found abandoned underpants or soggy towels on the floor of the bathroom. She sighed. There was still plenty of time.

The pretty blonde laughed loudly and everyone turned her way as she patted Leo on the arm, leaning into him and smiling up into his face. 'You are so funny.'

Anna felt the familiar curl of resentment. She wasn't jealous – there was nothing to be jealous about. It was more disappointment that he was still the same.

'Anna, this is Jakub.' Jiří interrupted her thoughts. 'He runs the Šilhov brewery here in Prague. He is going to be your host.'

'Hello, it is a pleasure to meet you. I'm very honoured that you have travelled all this way to come and learn about Czech beer.' Jakub's face creased into a well-worn wrinkled smile. 'What do you think of Prague?'

Anna swallowed and smiled into his homely face with its very whiskery sideburns. 'I haven't had much chance to explore yet, but I hope to very soon.'

'And try lots of our very fine beer.'

'Of course,' she said, warming to him.

She sneaked a quick look Leo's way and noticed that he'd been joined by a young man wearing trendy dark-framed glasses and sporting a very sharp haircut.

'That's Karel from the Crystal brewery,' said Jakub with a stony expression, noticing her quick interest. He shook his head, his mouth turning down at each corner. 'Too consumed by new ideas. Everything has to be different, novel, innovative. Whereas some of us prefer to build on the base of history and custom. Beer has been brewed for hundreds of years; I think some of us know what we're doing.' He pursed his lips. 'You will learn how real beer is brewed. Why make changes when the product is already perfect?'

'Your English is very good,' said Anna.

'My grandfather was a pilot for the RAF in the war and he married an English woman, my grandmother. After the war he came back to run the brewery. Then the communists came. I was lucky to work there but we were no longer allowed to own it.' Jakub's lips twisted. 'Luckily when it was handed back I had the proof to make a claim that it was my family's. I have preserved many of the traditions that have been in place for hundreds of years. Of course there have been some changes but I don't throw the baby out with the bathwater. I think you know this saying?'

'I do,' said Anna, smiling, charmed by his obvious passion.

Across the room she saw the blonde girl hand her phone to Leo. She almost laughed out loud. Three days in Prague and he was already collecting phone numbers.

'Of course, there is so much more to the city than beer. We have much art and culture, and of course the newest installation by the famous Czech artist David Černý, *The Spitfire Butterflies*.' Jakub pulled a comical face. 'They are giant butterflies made from Spitfire planes. I'm not sure my father the pilot would have approved, but I'm most intrigued.' He glanced over at the younger brewer. 'I'm not so set in my ways I can't enjoy something new.'

'They sound fascinating.' Anna smiled at him, genuinely intrigued. 'They must be huge.'

'I believe they are.' He looked down at his watch and gave her a shy but mischievous smile. 'If you'd like we could make a detour via the Quadrio shopping centre to see them on our way to the brewery. It's quite a big detour really but we can also see Kafka's rotating head on another installation by Černý.'

Charmed by this unexpected playfulness peeking out from his serious persona, she nodded. 'That sounds like a great idea, I've heard about Kafka's head and seen pictures. I'd love to see that.'

'Excellent. Shall we go?' He gestured for her to lead the way.

Some of the stress that was holding her stomach in its tight grip eased. Jakub was a sweetie and she had a feeling they were going to get along just fine. In fact she felt that of the two placements, she'd definitely got the better end of the deal.

Chapter Four

'Night, Leo.' Veronika waved at him from behind her desk as he left after his third day at the Crystal brewery. She was the assistant here, although he'd say she took her duties rather lightly; her mobile phone and her social life seemed to take up most of her attention. He didn't mind as she'd been very generous offering to take him out.

'Bye,' he replied.

'And thank you again for last night,' she said, lowering her voice, peering up at him from beneath her eyelashes. He grinned at her. They'd had fun. She'd flirted, he'd flirted, but nothing more.

'Thanks for showing me round,' he said. 'That was a nice bar. And I loved the beer.'

'We should do it again. I know lots of great places to drink in Prague.' She flashed him a bright, hopeful smile. 'How about tomorrow after work?'

'Can't do tomorrow but maybe next week.' Natálie, the girl he'd met at the induction day, had sent him a text offering to take him to Loď Pivovar, a floating brewery on the Vltava, the following evening, and he'd already accepted.

'Leo!' Karel shouted from the mezzanine floor above. 'Wait up, I'll walk out with you.'

Leo watched as Karel ran lightly down the metal steps. His desk on the mezzanine was surrounded by the stainless-steel pipes and tanks of the brewery. His new boss ran a mile a minute, incapable of sitting still or being quiet. Karel had a habit of propelling himself across the floor between his desk and the large touch screen that managed the computerised production process. He was very proud of the fact that he could operate elements of the production from his mobile phone.

As they walked down the cobbled streets, Karel apologised for not spending much time with Leo so far. 'Sorry it's a bit crazy at the moment. I'm sales manager and marketing director, as well as head brewer. I hope the guys have been looking after you.'

'Yes,' said Leo. 'I'm enjoying getting my hands dirty.' That morning, he'd been loading the mash ton with malted barley grains, inhaling the familiar scent before the mashing began.

'That's good, although I do want you to do more. We need to discuss some ideas for the beer you're going to make. When you win it's going to give us a lot of publicity. This is the first year of the placement scheme, so lots of people are interested.'

'Don't you mean *if* we win?' Leo laughed at Karel's overconfidence. 'It's a competition, remember.'

Karel made a rude hand gesture and grinned back at him. 'It's Jakub Šilhov. There's nothing to worry about with that old man. He wouldn't know how to come up with a new recipe for beer if someone threatened to take his dumplings away. He only knows one way to make beer. Here we can do anything we want. Push boundaries. Experiment. Life does not stand still and neither should beer.

We can buy in some different hop varieties. Jakub insists on using the original Saaz hops and a triple decoction. I mean, what a performance. I'm more inclined to infusion but you can play around..'

'Thanks,' said Leo. He had no strong views either way, but decoction, where a portion of the mash was separated and heated, was time-consuming and affected the length of production. An infusion was much simpler.

'And a lot of it is down to marketing. It's all very well saying you've been making the same beer for two hundred years but … tastes change. People get bored of the same old, same old.'

Leo nodded. 'I can't wait to get started.'

'Nor me, man.' Karel grinned at him. 'Brewing is in my blood, even if it was taken away from me.'

'Taken away?'

'Yeah.' Karel's mouth twisted. 'My family's brewery was taken into state ownership during communism. When the communists were ousted, my father couldn't prove ownership, but his brother could and kept the whole lot.'

'That's tough.'

'Yeah, tell me about it,' said Karel, his eyes narrowing.

'My father had lots of innovative ideas. It's taken me ten years to get Crystal up and running, and now we've got distribution through the Czech Republic and I've recently done deals with Germany, Poland and Lithuania. One day I'll reclaim my heritage, and then we'll see who makes the best beer.'

From the vehemence in his voice, Leo had no doubt he would.

They parted at the tram stop as Karel was catching the metro home.

When Leo walked into the flat he was greeted by the sound of music coming from upstairs and the smell of something delicious. His stomach growled. Lunch had been a disaster. Whatever he'd picked had not been what he thought it was and tasted predominantly of pickled cabbage, which he hated. He had yet to find the local supermarket and had been existing on very nice bread from the bakery and a hunk of cheese he'd bought in the convenience store on the way home.

He walked into the kitchen to find Anna dancing to Dua Lipa's *Dance the Night*. Grinning to himself he leaned against the door frame and watched for a moment as she shimmied while stirring something in the pan on the stove.

'Leo!' She jumped when she turned. 'When did you get back?'

'Long enough to see you strutting your stuff. Nice moves, by the way.'

It took a second for her to turn starchy and shoot him a disapproving look.

'I wasn't expecting you.'

'I live here.'

'How could I forget? But you haven't been around until later most evenings. I'll be out of your way in fifteen minutes.'

He frowned. 'You don't have to get out of my way.'

She shrugged and busied herself filling the kettle.

'Something smells good.' He sniffed and walked over to poke the wooden spoon she was using into a saucepan of what looked and smelled like bolognese sauce.

She ignored him as she got out a large saucepan and reached for a packet of dried spaghetti from the cupboard.

'You always did make the best spag bol,' he said, dipping the spoon in and holding up a dollop to his mouth and blowing on it before taking a mouthful. 'Mmm, that's good.'

'Leo!' She dropped the spaghetti and scowled at him, her eyes squinty and cross.

He winked at her, laughing at her outrage. She wasn't really cross, just surprised. He'd always liked keeping her on her toes. She was far too serious most of the time. 'You still got it.'

She folded her arms. 'Help yourself, why don't you?' Her sarcasm bounced off him as he smiled at her.

'I already did. But I'll try it again, to double-check.' He dipped the spoon back into the sauce knowing it would irritate the hell out of her.

'Leo! That's … that's disgusting! I can't believe you put that spoon back in.'

'It's no worse than kissing,' he said with a dismissive lift of his shoulders. He saw her swallow and some small, petty part of him was pleased to see that it had provoked a reaction. 'I haven't got any communicable diseases. Not that I know of.'

Anna's mouth pursed mutinously and then a devilish light glimmered in her eyes. 'Yeah, but what about mine?'

He laughed and pointed the spoon at her. 'Nice one, Anna. Very cute.'

She sighed and rolled her eyes at him. 'Seriously.' The kettle reached boiling point and clicked off beside her and she picked it up and poured it into the pan.

'Looks like there's plenty there,' he said, looking at her, wide-eyed and hopeful.

She ignored him and salted the water, turning her back on him. 'I'm immune to the puppy-dog eyes, Leo.' Her dry voice made him smirk.

He glanced at her back, stiff and straight, a little sad that she seemed to have lost her sense of fun.

'Food tastes better when it's shared,' he volunteered.

Still she didn't turn but he noticed that when she picked up the pasta packet she shook out an additional portion. A sly smile touched his lips.

'Would you like me to lay the table outside? It's a nice evening.'

He saw her shoulders rise and fall and heard her exhale an exasperated breath.

'You never give up, do you?' she said, easing the pasta into the boiling water.

'Not if something's worth sticking around for, like your very excellent spaghetti bolognese. Can I get you a beer?'

She croaked out a laugh. 'Go on then. And yes, you can

lay the table. And you can grate some parmesan. You might as well make yourself useful.'

'I'm always useful,' he said shooting her a quick grin. 'Adorable, too.'

'I wouldn't get carried away, now.' She pursed her mouth. 'Be grateful I've agreed to share dinner with you. I won't be making a habit of it.'

'Understood.' He nodded solemnly but couldn't help spoiling it by saluting her.

'Parmesan, Leo,' she said, pointing to the fridge. 'Grater in there.' She pulled open a drawer and then moved out of the way to let him remove a bowl from the cupboard by her knees. As soon as he was out of the way she ducked down to grab two plates from the same cupboard and swung around to pop them in the oven. Their syncopated moves could have been choreographed – or maybe, he wondered, it was muscle memory.

Ten minutes later they were sitting outside in the last of the sunshine. The sun was starting to dip below the horizon.

'Cheers,' said Leo.

'Cheers,' said Anna.

'And thank you. I knew you wanted to eat dinner together, really.'

'No, Leo, I really didn't. Don't waste your time trying to charm me. I'm immune. Save it for your new Czech lady friends. I'm sure they'll appreciate it.'

'I'm making friends, meeting new people. I went out with someone from work for a drink,' he protested. 'She was showing me around.'

'You can't help yourself, can you?' she said bitterly.

He held up both hands. 'I'm a free agent. I've got nothing to apologise for.' He was done with justifying himself to her all the time. She'd never listened then, when she had every reason to, so she certainly wouldn't start now.

She raised one sceptical eyebrow.

'Bloody hell, Anna,' he exclaimed. 'Why do you always have to think the worst?'

'Perhaps it's something to do with being proved right most of the time.'

'No, you were always wrong.' Leo threw down his fork, his appetite evaporating. 'Thanks a lot for dinner but I'm not hungry anymore.' He knew it was childish to storm off but he didn't deserve this. He liked women, they liked him, but he'd never lied to anyone, and despite what she thought, he never cheated and never led anyone on.

Chapter Five

Anna's phone rang as she boarded the tram on her way home at the end of her first week. The days had flown by, there was so much to learn and it was all so interesting, but the evenings, on her own in her bedroom watching Netflix, had dragged. She and Leo had avoided each other since dinner on Wednesday.

Finding a seat quickly, she answered to hear Jiří's voice.

'Anna, I have some good news. We have found you a new apartment.'

'Oh, that's wonderful.' Anna sat a little straighter in her seat.

'It's in Praha 14.' His tone didn't sound celebratory in any way. She heard him suck in a breath and knew he was about to deliver less welcome news.

'And is that bad? I'm guessing it will be much further out.'

'It's not bad, you would have a flat to yourself, but, yes, it would be further to travel every day, but it is on the metro. I must be honest with you. It has been empty for a while and I haven't been able to view it. I can't guarantee what it will be like.'

Given she'd already turned down one very nice flat, she was hardly in a position to complain.

'I'm sure it will be fine.'

'We have a limited budget,' he said with a note of apology. 'So we have to...' He trailed off.

'No, no I completely understand.' Anna felt bad enough that she was being difficult. If Jiří and his colleagues knew the cosmic sod's-lawness of the situation, they would realise that she wasn't being awkward. 'That is great news. It's very good of you to find me somewhere new and I really appreciate it. Thank you. When can I move in?'

'Soon,' said Jiří, his voice bright as if he knew this might be a problem but wasn't going to acknowledge it.

'When?' she asked. 'Soon' was far too vague. She couldn't keep hiding from Leo in the flat.

'I'm not sure yet. As soon as I can get the keys – but I'm not sure when that will be.'

Anna wrinkled her nose, knowing she ought to be grateful. It wasn't Jiří's fault she was in this situation and she didn't want anyone at the *Sdílená Kultura* to know what had caused this desperation to move. It would look so unprofessional. She was banking on what she learned on this placement to persuade her uncle to let her brew her own beer, and if she could win the equipment, that would be the icing on the cake. That was the main prize for her, although showcasing her beer in Prague would be a coup. After that, how could her uncle say no?

After finishing the call with Jiří, she immediately texted Steve to let him know.

Good news. The organisers have found me a new apartment, so I don't have to share.

Gr8. Didn't like that Lennard bloke at all.

Fingers crossed it's soon. She thought it best to temper expectations otherwise he might keep asking and it didn't sound like Jiří was that confident about the timeframe.

Give me a call tonight, after rugby training.

She sent him a thumbs-up and a kiss, wondering if he missed her. There'd been so much to think about here, she hadn't really given him much thought, but they were grown-ups in a mature relationship. At least she could guarantee that after a couple of pints in the pub he'd leave alone, unlike her uncle, who needed female attention as much as he needed oxygen.

She let out a breath that whistled through her teeth. Now was not the time to dwell on her aunt and uncle's battlefield of a marriage. It only made her wish she'd known her own parents better.

Steve didn't respond to that, so she put her phone away and leaned back in her seat, feeling the pleasant buzz of exhaustion. It might have been a long day but she'd relished every moment of it. Despite her tiredness, excitement predominated as well as a thrill at how much she was learning from Jakub and his very small team. It really was a huge honour to be working in the Šilhov brewery with someone like him, who lived and breathed beer. He'd never married and the brewery and his employees were his family.

She half laughed to herself. It was all so different from the Talbot family brewery, now run by her uncle and her male cousins. They had no passion for brewing and left everything to managers and a series of head brewers, which she'd always found difficult to understand. When her father had been the head brewer, things had been very different. After he died, his assistant, grumpy, surly Ronnie, who had had a streak of loyalty to her dad a mile wide, had taken over. During the summer holidays, although she was a girl, he had taken her under his wing, and before he retired, he had taught her as much as he could, believing that one day she'd be involved. After him there been several head brewers, none of whom had been invested in the business, using it instead as a stepping stone to other things. Uncle Henry couldn't see that that was part of the problem. They brewed mediocre beer because no one cared anymore. And that was why she was here: to learn even more so that she could make her mark. Unfortunately, with only seven per cent of the company shares, she didn't hold any power.

Relaxing, she watched the city slide by through the window, admiring the view of the stately buildings lining the riverside as they crossed over the Vltava, and comparing her journey favourably with the tedious bus journeys home in London in rush-hour traffic.

It seemed that her journey was to be book-ended by phone calls, because her phone rang as she was disembarking the tram,.

She was pleased to see it was Rebecca, her cousin, calling. They were close in age, and as the females in the family, had banded together, even though Becs, like the rest of the family, was sports mad. For Anna she was almost like a sister.

'Hey, Anna.'

'Hi, Becs.'

'How are you doing? Steve was useless when I asked what your place is like.'

'It's really nice. Lots of wood and sloping ceilings. Plenty of character.'

'And you've got a dodgy flatmate, apparently.'

'He's all right,' said Anna, careful with her words.

'Steve says he's a cocky git who thinks he's God's gift to the ladies. Don't tell me he's another one like my dad,' she said with a groan. 'I think it's a bit of a cheek, putting you with a complete stranger. He could be a serial killer for all you know.' While it was tempting to giggle at that one, Anna held her breath, praying that Steve hadn't said anything specific. Leo was not that uncommon a name, but the mere mention of it might trigger an unwelcome tirade. She wondered how happy her family would be to hear that Leo was not at all a complete stranger.

'Don't put up with any crap, will you? Although you know Steve will sort him out for you, if you need him to.'

'Actually I've asked the organisers for a place of my own.'

'Oh, that's good,' said Becs. 'So what's Prague like?'

'Do you know, I haven't had chance to see much of it,' she said before adding with a quick laugh, 'apart from *The Spitfire Butterflies*.'

'The what?'

Anna explained about the bright-purple and blue-metal

art with the body of a Spitfire plane and moving butterfly wings.

'Quirky. Anything else?' asked Becs.

'Not yet,' she replied with a touch of regret, her attention caught by a row of beautiful nineteenth-century buildings with ornate stone scrolling around the windows. 'What I have seen is beautiful, but I'm waiting 'til Steve comes out and then I thought we'd do some touristy things together. I'm going to book a boat tour and some other stuff.'

'Lovely. I know he's really missing you.'

'Is he?' asked Anna deliberately injecting her voice with a laugh.

'Well, the rugby season is about to start, so at least you know he's occupied. But the reason I rang you, as well as to find out how you're getting on, is to let you know the good news. The company dividends were decided at the board meeting and we're getting one this year! You'll be getting a payout very soon, nice enough. Although there'll be a bit of a delay because Peter Jones dropped down dead.'

'No!' Anna clutched the phone. The poor man had only been in his fifties.

'Yes, it's very sad. We've had to get new accountants, which Dad is in a right old tizz about. Honestly, he's biting everyone's head off every five minutes. He's a nightmare.'

Anna raised her eyebrows but refrained from saying anything. Her uncle was probably more bothered about not receiving personal attention from Peter's very attractive assistant, Annabel, with whom he lunched rather frequently.

'Thanks for letting me know.' This year's meagre

payment would be tucked away ready for when she broached setting up her own brewery line within the Talbot brewery to make a Czech-style craft beer.

'Mum sends her love.'

'How is she?'

Becs gave an audible sigh down the line. 'Not happy. Dad's got himself a new *friend*.'

'Oh, I'm sorry.'

'Don't be. I don't know why she puts up with it.'

'Hopefully it won't last long.'

'They never do,' said Becs, resignation strong in her voice.

'Give her my love. And to you.'

'Will do. Thanks, Anna.'

'You know where I am if you need to talk.'

Becs snorted with a mirthless laugh. 'Thanks, honey. I think we've said it all a million times, but I appreciate it. I'd better go. Take care, speak soon.'

Anna put her phone away, wishing there was more she could do for her cousin. Her aunt and uncle's marriage was a complete mystery, revolving around the constant cycle of Uncle Henry developing a flirtation with some woman, Aunt Hazel getting wind and furiously seeking the other woman out, putting the fear of God into her and seeing her off.

Anna thought of her own parents, who'd been the opposite and – what she now realised must be very rare – tactile with each other, communicative and open in their expressions of love. They'd been good friends, a team, whereas she thought of her aunt and uncle as individual members of the family team, often in competition with each other.

Anna saw that her stop was coming up and left the tram to walk to the apartment in the dying warmth of the day. As she mounted the first flight of steps in the apartment block, Michaela poked her head out of her front door.

'Hi, Anna. How was your first week?' Michaela's genuine interest perked her up, and, thinking of Jakub at the brewery and how he reminded her of Ronnie, she immediately smiled. 'It was good. Really good.'

'That's great. Would you like to come to the pub with us? We can celebrate the end of the week with beer and food. We have big news, too.' Her elfin face glowed as if she wanted to burst with it.

Anna had spent the last couple of nights in her room and she really rather liked Michaela, so she nodded enthusiastically. 'That would be lovely, thank you.'

'Great. Come down at seven.'

With that she withdrew behind the door and Anna heard her gaily telling Jan something in rapid Czech before it shut. Anna paused for a moment, reflecting that Prague must be rubbing off on her; it was rare for her to accept a spontaneous invitation like that. Or maybe it was that she was sick of her bedroom walls and keeping out of Leo's way. That frisson over the spaghetti bolognese had unsettled her.

When Leo bounced into the apartment half an hour later clutching a couple of bottles of pale golden beer, she'd showered and changed and was sitting on the roof terrace with her phone, having finished a FaceTime call with Steve, who was looking forward to the river tour she'd promised to book.

'Look what they gave me,' he crowed through the open doorway. 'Homework.' He held up a couple of bottles of beer in one hand. 'Want to try some?'

Anna, with plans for the evening, felt more relaxed, and she laughed at his gleeful expression, even though she didn't want to. It was impossible to be around Leo and not succumb to his joie de vivre.

'Why not?' she replied with a tentative smile, not sure how to act around him. He seemed to have forgotten their last argument. And, after all, this was why she was in the Czech Republic, to learn as much as she could about Czech beer. She'd tell him later that Jiří had found her a new place.

'I'll get some glasses,' he called, having already disappeared from view, and a minute later he stepped out onto the roof, beaming.

'Isn't this great?' he said. 'What a view to come home to with a beer. Life's good. How was your day?' He slid the bottle-opener keyring from his pocket. 'I had an amazing week but tell me about yours. What did you do? Was it awesome? Are you loving it?' Leo's questions spilled out like champagne overflowing from a flute.

She stared at him for a minute, wondering if he was taking the piss. They hadn't spoken a word for two days. A little bud of warmth lit up inside her. Typical Leo. Slow to

57

anger, quick and generous to forgive. It would be churlish in the extreme to be rude to him, let alone resist this effervescent enthusiasm.

'Yes, it was awesome, and yes, I'm going to love it,' she said with a laugh. His interest, in comparison to her cousin Becs's utter disinterest, was a boost and, like a flower warmed by the sun, she couldn't help but open up.

'Let's try these bad boys,' said Leo, flipping off the tops. 'And then you can tell me all about it. The Crystal brewery is so cool. And Karel has some great ideas. He's really experimental and not afraid of trying anything new.'

Anna laughed again. 'Possibly the opposite of my day then. Jakub is a third-generation beer maker and he likes – no, loves – the tradition of it all.'

Leo, who'd poured the beers, lifted his glass. She took hers and chinked it against his.

'Cheers.'

'*Na zdraví*,' said Anna.

'Ah, yes, well done. When in Prague. *Na zdraví*.'

For the next half-hour, they chatted with relative ease about their day, Anna telling Leo all about the old cellars and the huge wooden mash tuns housed in the old stone building of Šilhov brewery, while Leo told her about the high-tech computerised pipework and stainless-steel finish of the Crystal brewery. Before long they were asking each other questions, fully immersed in the subject of beer, and suddenly it was seven o'clock.

Leo jumped to his feet, almost knocking his chair over. 'I need to put on a clean T-shirt. Don't want to go out stinking of beer before I even get to the pub.'

'Another date?' Anna tried to sound non-judgemental.

'Not tonight.' He smiled at her. 'Michaela and Jan invited me to the pub. I thought you were coming, too?'

'Yeah, right. Of course,' said Anna. Why hadn't it occurred to her that Leo would be included in the invitation? They'd probably invited him first. Everyone always wanted Leo's company.

Still moving, he unselfconsciously stripped off his T-shirt, giving her another flash of that lean, muscular body and bringing with it a flush of awareness. Her whole body felt on edge, unsatisfied. What was wrong with her? The sooner she got out of here the better, even though it was such a lovely flat.

When they knocked on Michaela and Jan's door, five minutes later, the couple were ready and waiting and the four of them descended the stairs in high spirits to walk to the pub, which was only a couple of streets away.

The lively pub was in a cellar, with lots of posters on the walls, and long trestle tables. Michaela and Jan, clearly a popular pair, waved to several people before heading to a table in the corner. No sooner had the four of them sat down than a waiter was at the table ready to take their order.

'Georg, this is Leo and Anna, they've just moved in. They're English.'

'*Ahoj*,' said Georg. 'What would you like to drink?'

'Beer,' said Leo and Anna in unison, catching each other's eyes and grinning.

'In Czech Republic, you have to drink beer,' said Jan. 'We are the biggest consumers of beer in the world. We drink one-hundred and eighty litres per capita, although according to other reports its only one-hundred and twenty-eight litres. I'm not sure which is right but it is a lot.'

'We know,' said Anna. 'I told you we're on a placement scheme but the ultimate prize is brewery equipment.'

'Which I'm going to win,' said Leo, winking at Anna. 'And have my beer at the Christmas Beer Festival.'

'You think so, do you?' said Anna, lifting her chin, not sure if he was teasing or being over-confident. The competitive Talbot side of her was suddenly fired up, perhaps fuelled by the fact that she really needed to win that equipment. Why *did* Leo want it?

'You probably know more about beer than I do,' said Michaela, unknowingly defusing things. 'But we can teach you how to order in Czech.'

'That would be great,' said Leo. 'So far everyone has spoken really good English but I think it's rude if you don't at least try.'

'It's okay. It's a very difficult language to learn.'

'How do you ask for two beers, please?'

'*Dvě piva prosím*,' said Michaela.

Leo dutifully repeated it and Michaela corrected his pronunciation. Anna, who had a good ear, was able to repeat it perfectly, much to the other woman's delight.

When the beer arrived, Jan lifted his glass and grinned at Michaela. 'To the *chata*.'

'To the *chata*,' she replied and then turned to Leo and Anna. 'Jan's uncle has gifted us his *chata*.'

'To the thingy,' said Leo, lifting his glass and taking a sip.

'What's a *chata*?' asked Anna.

'No idea,' said Leo with one of his quick wide smiles, 'but it sounds like it's worth drinking to.'

She tried to give him a repressive look but it was impossible when he was grinning like a monkey.

'It's a small, country home,' explained Jan. 'But not like a house. Ours has water and solar power. But some are huts with nothing. There we have a little plot of land—'

'We're going to grow vegetables,' Michaela interrupted. 'And strawberries and raspberries.'

'It's near the lake, so we can swim,' added Jan, beaming.

'And there's no internet or computers or mobile signal.'

'And we have a big fireplace and a firepit.' Jan nudged her, obvious excitement on his face.

'And you can have an axe to chop wood,' said Michaela teasing him.

'Yes,' said Jan in a gruff voice showing off his muscles in what Anna imagined must be a lumberjack imitation.

'And we're going to renovate the inside and make it ours.' Michaela clapped her hands. 'I can't wait.'

It was lovely to see their bubbling enthusiasm and Anna exchanged a quick look of amusement with Leo.

Michaela caught them and laughed. 'Sorry. We sound crazy. It's just that we've been wanting a *chata* of our own for a long time. My family has one but it belongs to my grandparents, it is full of their old, old things – I mean, I love my *babička* but –' she wrinkled her nose '– not her taste. There are so many of us and not much space. It will be nice for me and Jan to have our own with space for our friends.'

She paused suddenly and said, 'You must come. It is very typical Czech. Different from living in the city.'

'Sounds cool, I'd love to,' said Leo.

It did sound wonderful. Anna had a sudden longing for the countryside. Although Prague seemed to be very green, she'd lived in the country for so long, she missed being outdoors, going on hikes and walking much more.

'You have to work for your supper,' said Jan with one of his dry smiles. 'There will be lots to do. The garden is very overgrown and like Michaela said, inside the house, we have plenty of work to make it more comfortable.'

A touch of envy nudged Anna. How wonderful to put your own stamp on your own home.

As an Instagram home-makeovers addict, she constantly pored over reels, finding new ideas and learning about DIY. She'd done as much as she could in her rented flat but the landlord wasn't keen on any permanent changes, although she'd managed to put up some shelves, decorate the lounge and, her *pièce de résistance*, build a window seat in the bay of her bedroom, which the landlord had yet to find out about. Somehow, her attempts to create a cosy home made her feel more connected with her mum, who'd always been painting and renovating furniture, sewing cushions and curtains, reusing old china and filling it with wax and wicks to make candles and picking flowers from the garden to fill vases in the kitchen. Anna felt a touch of sadness as she recalled how happy it made her mother to take time and care to put together their home. According to her aunt, she'd been 'quite the homemaker,' although the disparaging way it was said never made it sound like a compliment.

'What about you, Anna?' asked Michaela. 'Would you like to come to the *chata*?'

'Erm … that would be nice but I'm not going to be around for much longer.'

Across the table Leo raised one eyebrow, his face suddenly impassive. He didn't say anything.

'You're leaving!' Michaela gasped. 'But you've only just arrived. What is wrong?'

'I'm not leaving Prague but I'm moving to another apartment.'

'When?'

'Soon.'

'Soon?' barked Leo. 'And when were you going to mention it to me?' His stony expression, so at odds with the bright smile seconds before, immediately brought a flood of guilt.

'But why?' asked Michaela, looking from Anna to Leo. 'And you?' she asked him.

'Just me,' said Anna, trying to sound nonchalant.

'But why?' asked Michaela again. 'Your apartment is the best in the block.'

Anna looked at Leo, who once again raised that taunting eyebrow. He had no intention of making this easier for her, even though he knew full well it was the right thing to do. One of them had to go. In fact, if he'd been any sort of gentleman he would have offered. She glared at him.

As if he read her mind, he held up his hands. 'Your choice.'

'Hardly,' she snapped.

'What, I'm holding a gun to your head? I haven't asked you to leave. There's no reason you have to.'

'For God's sake, Leo. Stop being so obtuse. Of course I can't stay.'

Leo shrugged while Michaela looked on, fascinated. Jan, whom she liked the most at that moment, studied the top of his beer.

'What is the problem?' asked Michaela, innocently enough. Anna suspected that she hadn't meant to sound so direct.

Leo leaned back and folded his arms, leaving her to answer.

A burst of rage flashed through her and she wanted to slap the complacent smirk from his bloody face. Under the table, her hands clenched into irate fists to stop her giving in to the urge.

Leo continued to look at her and the gap in conversation stretched as he took a leisurely sip of beer.

Frustrated beyond all bearing, Anna snapped, 'Because we used to be married.'

Chapter Six

Leo's beer went down the wrong way and he found himself coughing and choking as Michaela, like a Wimbledon spectator, kept moving her wide-eyed gaze back and forth between them.

He could tell from Jan's odd, stiff jerks that he was kicking his girlfriend under the table but, to be fair to her, she seemed too dumbstruck to say anything.

'Nice one, Anna,' he'd said, annoyed as much at himself and his own contrariness. He'd pushed her into saying something and now he realised that it brought the awkwardness between them into the public domain and created a drama in which he didn't want to be a player. He'd spent the last six years sublimating his feelings and consigning all thoughts of her into a very large mental dustbin.

'Well, you weren't helping, sitting there being all condescending. As if this situation is all my fault.'

'It's no one's fault but some of us are trying to be grown-up about things.' How he managed to sound so reasonable when he wanted to strangle her, he'd never know. 'You're the one that's made a big thing of it.'

'No, I haven't,' Anna snapped, with that tell-tale flush of anger.

'Yes, you have. Why did you pretend you didn't know me?'

Michaela's eyes looked as if they might burst out of her head but Jan hung onto her arm as if physically holding back her lively curiosity.

'I didn't…'

He saw her swallow.

'Didn't what?'

'I didn't mean to. I was shocked. At first, I wasn't even sure it was you – because you were the last person I expected to see – and the sun was behind you.'

'I bet it was one hell of a shock – given you walked out without a word to me, six years ago.'

Her mouth tightened but, damn it, he'd deserved an explanation back then, still did, although he no longer cared. It was her problem. He'd been done with her a long time ago.

'Don't play the innocent,' she said furiously. 'You know why I left.'

'No, Anna. I don't,' he replied, with icy bitterness, and even now the sense of hurt flooded back, momentarily paralysing him. He could still remember coming back to the flat they shared and the stomach-wrenching, sick feeling when he realised it was empty – she'd gone.

'I left,' she bit out the words, enunciating carefully 'because you were all over Savannah Aitken.'

'For crying out loud, Anna. I told you over and over. She was a friend. She didn't know anyone. I was being *nice* to her.' Beautiful, lost Savannah had been one of those people who was all front on the outside and desperately insecure on the inside. She'd needed a friend, hadn't she? But Anna had always questioned her motives, insisting that she wanted Leo.

'You were encouraging her. She wasn't going to take no for an answer.'

Leo pursed his lips. If Anna couldn't trust him, that had been her problem. She should have trusted him. He'd married her. The biggest commitment and promise he could make. He swallowed. He'd loved her; the vows he'd made had been for ever. He wouldn't ever have been unfaithful. Savannah had been a friend. Anna should have trusted him.

Anna stood up. 'Sorry to drag you into this, Michaela and Jan. If you don't mind, I'm going to head back.'

Michaela rose, too, distress crumpling her pretty face. 'I'll come with you.'

'No, it's fine,' insisted Anna. 'I don't want to spoil your Friday night.'

Leo rubbed his hand over his forehead. Nothing between him and Anna had changed. He'd been a fool to believe they could put the past behind them and be friends. That was never going to happen.

He watched the two women leave.

'Another beer, my friend?' asked Jan with a sympathetic smile.

'Yeah, why not?' He gave him a limp smile in return.

Maybe Anna moving out was for the best... But why did he feel more than little sick about it?

———————

When he returned to the flat, her door was shut, not that he'd expected her to wait up for him. The next day she stayed in her room virtually all day, only coming out when he went into his own room. On the Sunday morning, while he enjoyed his tea and toast on the roof terrace, he started to wonder if he should go and knock on her door. Was she okay? He wandered back into the kitchen listening hard. No sound of her. Maybe he should make her a cup of tea and leave it outside her door. Or maybe it would be easier all round if he went out for the day, then she could have the run of the flat. That would be fairer.

He scrolled through his phone and pressed call.

'Hey, Natálie. It's Leo.'

'Leo! How great to hear from you.'

'You said you'd show me the best places to drink beer.' She'd been so welcoming at the initial induction meeting, and earlier in the week, she and her boyfriend and their friends had made the offer when he'd met them at the floating bar.

'Sure,' she said, obviously pleased to hear from him. 'We're all meeting for lunch today. Want to join us?'

'That would be great. What time?'

They fixed a time and when he put down his phone, Leo turned to find Anna hovering in the doorway.

'Morning,' he said, determined not to fall out again.

'Morning,' she said with a nod.

'I'm going out—' but before he could say, 'to give you some space', she interrupted.

'I gathered. With Natálie.'

Leo's heart sank like concrete boots in a river. What was the point of even trying to tell her that Natálie was a friend? And, the smaller, meaner part of him that didn't come out very often said, why should he? Why bother to prove her wrong?

'Have a nice day,' he said. 'I don't know when I'll be back.' Hopefully she'd enjoy having the place to herself and he could quash the lingering guilt about making her feel uncomfortable in her own home.

But the petty boy inside who was still pissed off that she hadn't trusted him had to have the last word. 'Don't wait up.'

Anna had no intention of waiting up. She was going to enjoy the freedom of having the apartment to herself – at least, that's what she told herself. By mid-afternoon she'd cleaned the kitchen, the bathroom and her bedroom, swept the roof terrace, tried to read a book and started watching a film on her laptop. It was official, she'd had enough of her own company. She picked up her phone. Steve would almost certainly be at the rugby club. Instead she FaceTimed Becs.

'Hey, Cuz. How's it going?' Becs beamed at her down the line.

'Good. How are things at home?'

'Mum's moved through the plate-smashing phase.'

'Ouch.' Anna winced.

'She's worked out who Dad is spending his evenings with, so no doubt Operation See Her Off will commence. Dad's such an idiot. I bet you count your blessings you've got someone like Steve. He'd never do anything like that to you.'

'No,' said Anna. 'He's one of the good ones. I haven't caught up with him for a few days. There's a lot to take on board at the brewery. It's fascinating. The building is so old—'

'Oh, God, you're turning into old Ronnie. What else have you been doing?'

'I've been quite busy, you know, settling in.'

'Anna! Have you done any sightseeing?'

'Not yet. But I will.'

When she put the phone down a few minutes later, she looked around the apartment again and decided that it was too late to go into the city centre, but she should at least explore the local area.

An hour and half's wandering confirmed that it was a lovely area to be in. The nearby park was absolutely stunning with its riverside walk and its interesting pavilions, wells and observation deck, and she felt much better when she returned to the apartment. For the rest of the evening she watched a film and cooked herself dinner, trying hard not to keep half an ear out for the front door.

However, Leo had been true to his word about not waiting up. The next morning it appeared he hadn't come home. Anna ignored his open bedroom door and marched into the bathroom. No doubt tucked up with Nátalie. And it was nothing to do with her. Just Leo being his usual self. She was here to learn about beer and win those tanks, that was the most important thing. She would ring Jiří and ask if there was any update on the new flat.

'I have good news, Anna,' said Jiří as soon as he picked up the phone as she was arriving at the road to the brewery. 'I will send the keys this week and you can move in on Saturday.'

'Oh, that's wonderful. Thank you so much.'

After a brief conversation, in which she learned she'd be on the twelfth floor but the view would be good, she arrived at the doors of the brewery considerably heartened by having a moving date. That would make life so much easier. All she had to do was survive the next five evenings, which, given Leo seemed to have found a new lady friend, wouldn't be that difficult.

Heading into the building, she was immediately comforted by the familiar smell of the mash fermenting in the open tanks. This was why she was here.

All the tension of the weekend melted away, leaving her shoulders feeling easy again. It was still a miracle to her that something as complex as beer was made from the simple ingredients of grain and water. Of course there was a lot more to it than that. The ability to manipulate ingredients and processes to create such different flavours was where the magic lay, and she was excited to learn more. The Czech brewing process was *the* gold standard and had been copied the world over ... but to her mind, never equalled.

This week she was going to be shadowing Jakub, learning all aspects of the brewery processes, and then she would be working alongside the assistant brewer for the next few months, starting work on the small batch special brews in preparation for creating her own brew to present to the judging panel, along with her marketing and sales strategy. For a moment she stared at the thick stone walls, which had been here for hundreds of years and had seen generations of brewers pass through the building. There was such a lot to learn.

'Good morning, Anna.' Jakub's bellow made her jump but his wide smile immediately reassured her. She couldn't help but learn; his passion, enthusiasm and energy were inspirational and he never seemed to mind her asking stupid questions.

He'd set up a second desk in his office for her to use as a base, although he'd explained that the work would be very hands-on and she'd get involved in everything from tasting the beer through to ordering the grain supplies, and lots of technical testing and checking.

She'd already learned that he lived on his own and she suspected from his thin frame and the long hours he spent at the brewery that he didn't look after himself. He reminded her so much of Ronnie, who'd often been so absorbed in the brewery that he forgot to eat.

'Morning, Jakub,' she said. 'Here.' She handed him the cup of coffee that she'd picked up for him en route from the tram stop, along with one of the *koláče* she'd brought in for him.

'For me?' he asked surprised.

'Yes. I bought some at the bakery this morning and I thought you might like one. And I bought myself coffee, so it seemed rude not to bring one for you, too.'

'That's very kind of you. I missed breakfast this morning.' He wolfed the pastry down in such quick hungry bites, Anna wondered if he'd had dinner the previous night.

Within an hour she was absorbed in the work and all thoughts of her difficult weekend and where Leo had got to last night had been swept away. For the time being. Thank goodness she only had five more sleeps at the apartment before she could move out.

Chapter Seven

'**D**amn!'

Leo heard the expletive from the other side of his bedroom door and immediately poked his head out. For the last twenty minutes he'd been trying to ignore the obvious sounds of Anna moving out but his conscience was pricking him. He ought to offer to help.

She'd left him a note in the kitchen on Monday, telling him she'd be moving out this weekend, which had eased the pressure on him. He'd stayed out as much as possible this week so she could have the flat to herself, but drinking on your own, pretending to watch football and scrolling through your phone soon got tedious. Also, he was knackered. Roll on this evening when he could actually enjoy a quiet night in.

A more strident swear word came from her bedroom, bringing him back to the present.

'You okay?' he asked, stepping into the hallway to find

Anna hopping about on one foot, her arms bearing a pile of wooden posts, clearly trying to carry too much. The sunshine coming through the skylight caught the coppery lights in her hair, reminding him of the first time he'd seen her, slightly hesitant, in the doorway of the bar where they'd first worked. She'd been like a shy doe emerging from the forest.

'Dropped the bedhead on my foot,' she ground out.

'Is the taxi here?'

'Yes.'

'Why didn't you ask him to help?'

'His English isn't that good.'

'Would you like a hand?'

'No, I've got this.'

Pointing out that she clearly hadn't would only put her back up but, damn it, why couldn't she accept some help for once? 'Don't be daft, Anna. I really don't mind helping you.'

She sighed as if his reasonableness was a pain in the neck. He almost smiled at her resigned expression when she grudgingly said, 'Thanks. There's not too much. Mainly the bed ,which I've dismantled.'

'I'd have helped you with that.' He bit back his exasperation. She'd always been so independent and determined to do everything without leaning on anyone else.

'I'm perfectly capable of wielding a screwdriver,' she said, arching an eyebrow, a quick dart of amusement flashing in her eyes. It was as if now she was leaving, she could afford to be herself again instead of holding herself so stiffly apart.

'You don't need to remind me,' he said with a quick laugh. 'You're never going to let me live that shelf down, are you?'

'That was a shelf?' she asked, her eyes widening in amusement.

They both burst out laughing.

'It wasn't that bad,' he said.

She sniggered. 'Leo, it was the most temporary shelf in the history of shelves. It didn't even last twenty-four hours.'

The bedroom shelf he'd put up while she was out one morning had been his attempt to impress her, because she was so very capable at everything around the house. Admittedly there was a slight slant to it but, pleased with his work, he'd placed a vase on it containing a pink rose, to welcome her home. Unfortunately, in the middle of the night, the whole thing had collapsed with an almighty crash which had jerked them both awake, hearts racing with fright. After that, they'd rolled about laughing before falling into each other's arms, their bodies softening into each other.

For a moment they looked at each other as the memory, like the tumblers of a safe, clicked into place. Leo's lips quirked. It had been an unhurried, gentle interlude, if he remembered rightly, her warm body welcoming his in the dark, cocooned beneath the covers. For a moment he could almost feel that warmth, the slow slide… His pulse tripped a little and then that familiar sensation of panic placed its cold fingers on his heart.

'If you're going to help, you can start by bringing that.' Pursing her lips, she pointed to the roll of bed slats and a bag of pillows and bedding in the centre of her bedroom.

'No problem,' he said, trying not to let his sudden fear show. He couldn't go back there. Those memories were too painful.

'Thanks,' she said and walked out of the room.

'My pleasure,' he replied in a deliberately calm tone.

She gave him a sharp look over her shoulder, clearly unsure whether he was taking the piss. With laden arms, he followed her down the two flights of stairs.

The taxi driver was on his phone and having a cigarette, leaning against the driver's-side door, and didn't so much as look up when Anna put the first load in the boot of the car.

By the time she'd finished loading up, most of the back seat was full. She slammed the door and made her way round to the passenger seat at the front.

'Right,' she said, her body suddenly stiff with awkwardness.

Leo swallowed hard, regret twisting his gut. It was what she wanted and he had to respect her for that – but when would he see her again?

'Are you going to be all right at the other end?' he asked, looking at the packed car.

'Yes,' said Anna but he saw the quick flash of uncertainty in her eyes.

He knew that slightly shifty look. Narrowing his eyes, he studied her. 'You're on the top floor.'

Her mouth dropped open. 'How did you know? Not the top but the twelfth.'

'Good guess.'

She opened her mouth and he held up a hand to stop her, fuelled by determination. 'I know you're quite capable. But at least admit we can be friends and friends help each other.'

He could see the hesitation wavering in her face before she turned and looked at the back seat of the taxi. 'There's no room.'

'Yeah, there is. Room for a little one. Come on, I'll go in the back.'

———

From his squashed position in the back of the car, Leo surveyed the tall blocks of flats as they wound their way through the huge residential estate. It was very different from where they'd come from. Admittedly everything looked very clean and tidy but the uniform, functional square buildings felt a little austere and soulless. There were attractive green spaces and walkways but it felt to him like a university campus. They pulled up outside one of the more faded blocks. The taxi driver was keen to be off and this time willingly helped them unload, dumping everything on the pavement outside the front door. As soon as the last bag was out of the car, he jumped back in and drove off, leaving Anna surrounded by her belongings, and making Leo very glad he'd come.

'Want me to wait here while you go and investigate?' he asked.

'Thanks,' she said with a nod and went into the building.

A minute later she returned, her mouth turned down in the picture of disillusionment. 'Guess what? The lift is out of action.'

'Ouch,' said Leo, wincing. That was a lot of stairs to climb.

'Well done,' she said with a touch of sarcasm.

Leo gave her a wary glance, instinctively knowing he was in trouble but not why. 'What?'

'For not saying, "I told you so."'

'I know.' He beamed at her. 'I'm rather proud of that.'

She rolled her eyes but he could see the slight curve of her lips.

'Come on, let's get this stuff off the pavement and inside. Then, Sherpa Tensing, we can make the first assault on our ascent.'

'And how come you're Sir Edmund Hillary.'

He grinned. 'I just am.'

Her fledgling smile bloomed and, as if the starch had been removed, she softened and put out a hand to touch his arm. 'Trust you to find the lighter side. Thanks, Leo.'

He looked upwards through the angles and planes of the stairwell. 'Let's do this.' He slapped his legs. 'May my thighs forgive me.'

Twelve stories was twenty-four flights of stairs. By the time they reached Flat 56, there was a faint sheen of sweat across his forehead and he was desperate to remove his sweatshirt. They were both a little out of breath.

'Bloody hell,' he said dropping the bag he carried by the door.

Anna nodded, clearly incapable of speech. They'd both overloaded themselves, trying to carry as much as possible in one trip. She slotted the key into the lock. Neither of them commented on the grimy window next to the battered front door.

As soon as the door opened they were assailed by a musty cabbage-soup smell.

'They said it might need cleaning,' said Anna.

'Mm,' said Leo, looking down at the dated flooring with its slight greasy sheen.

Inside the hallway it was dark and, when Anna flipped the light switch, a single bare bulb cast ominous shadows in the tiny space like some Cold War interrogation room. Several doors led off the hallway, which made Leo think of some macabre fairy tale and wonder what was behind each one. Anna had always said he was too fanciful.

'Take your pick,' he said, trying to sound cheerful. The dingy hallway was not filling him with confidence.

Anna opened the door straight ahead, which led into a large empty room. The walls were painted an industrial green that toned perfectly with the green scuffed flooring. Opposite, wide windows led outside to a high-sided concrete balcony. Another bare bulb hung above them. The chill in the air held a touch of damp and Leo could see suspicious darker patches in the corners of the room.

Anna walked over to the door to the balcony. 'It's spacious,' she said, turning round. 'And there's a view.'

'Anna, it's a dump,' said Leo flatly. 'And depressing as hell.'

'It needs a good clean. Besides, the other rooms might be okay,' she said, but even he could see that she didn't hold out much hope. Giving the room one last look, Anna strode back to the hallway and the blank doors.

As if she were confronting the enemy she grasped one of the door handles. The door opened onto a bathroom. It was tiny with a stained bath and a poorly mounted tap that sat like a wobbly tooth on the grimy ceramic sink. Leo gave it an experimental push and, as expected, it swayed on the spot. Anna shot him an impatient glance and he turned his attention to the walls. They sported the only colour in the room, the pinkish hue of the mouldy grout that outlined many of the white square tiles covering every surface, bar the ceiling.

Leo saw Anna's chin lift as she stepped backwards out of the room – she wasn't going to admit defeat. He admired her for it, but he was also exasperated. He watched as she opened the door to a double bedroom. Again, it was a good size but the dull magnolia walls were splotched with tiny black spores of mould that coated the seam between ceiling and wall around the window.

'This is the flat that the seventies forgot,' said Leo, nodding towards the old-fashioned built-in wardrobes, which sagged in the middle.

'It just needs some work. A good clean, a few coats of paint.'

'It's more than that. It needs gutting and starting again.'

Anna didn't say anything. Instead she turned and crossed the hallway to the kitchen, a narrow galley with a mix of mismatched cabinets, and doors, where they were still intact, in varying shades of grey. For some reason the ancient electric cooker, which squatted in the centre of the room, pulled away from the wall, leaving a square patch in the faded brown lino, encircled with a lifetime of crumbs and grease.

Anna surveyed each room in complete silence, her shoulders hunching higher and higher with every minute.

Leo stayed in the kitchen looking out of the window, his fists clenched impotently as she opened the final door to what was likely a second bedroom. The more he said, the more her stubbornness would set in. In the silence of the apartment, he heard the quick intake of breath of a suppressed sob and immediately strode after her. He couldn't do it. There was no way he was going to let her stay here. Not just because it was Anna. He'd have insisted with anyone. He wouldn't leave his worst enemy here.

She stood with her back to the door and he could see the tension in her shoulders. She turned and he saw the sheen of tears in her eyes. Unable to help himself he drew her into his arms, her forehead resting on his chest. 'There's no way on earth I'm leaving you here.'

For a moment she was stiff and then he heard her suck in a long, slow breath. 'I'm not even going to pretend I can do something with this place. It's like it's had the very soul of it sucked out.'

Leo was slightly surprised by her choice of words as her

body softened into his embrace. Normally Anna was the pragmatic one.

'Anna, you can't stay here,' he said gently. 'You know you can't. Come back to the apartment. We can work things out.'

As he gave in to the indulgence of holding her, something shifted inside him, triggered by the familiar scent of her and the comfortable way she fitted against him. Muscle memory, he told himself, that's all. When she lifted her head and looked up at him, her lips slightly parted, he felt his pulse quicken and he had to fight the urge to lower his mouth to hers.

'Come on, let's get out of here,' he said abruptly, deliberately shifting his gaze to the tattered curtains on either side of the grimy windows.

'What am I going to say to Jiří?' Her teeth caught her lip.

'I'd have a lot to say to him. First of all, how dare he send you to a complete and utter shithole like this.' Leo gritted his teeth as a wave of anger on Anna's behalf swept over him.

Anna touched one of his clenched fists, a quick, reassuring, I'm-okay gesture.

'To be fair to him, he came up with this very quickly. He did tell me it had been empty and he hadn't been able to view it himself.'

'Well, he can shove it equally quickly.' Leo paused and looked down into her soft brown eyes. 'Seriously, Anna. We can share the apartment. We're both grown-ups, we can make it work. We can draw up rotas so we can minimise contact if that helps – agree to stay out of each other's way at certain times. I don't know ... Saturdays, Mondays, Wednesdays and Fridays, you have the lounge, I stay in my room. Something like that, if that works. Right now, you're going to order another Uber and we'll start our descent.'

'Thanks, Leo,' said Anna, opening her phone app.

'And you can take me out for a large beer later today.'

'Deal.'

Chapter Eight

'I've got a suggestion to make,' announced Leo the next morning, as he bounded into the kitchen looking as fresh and bright as a buttercup in the dawn. She looked up from the text she was sending Steve. Illuminated by a shaft of sunlight from the overhead Velux window, his hair almost looked like a halo, and with that handsome face and, in repose, the slightly sulky (and very sexy) mouth, he could have been a fallen angel. Transfixed, she stared at him, not knowing what to say, while her pulse stuttered a little. For some reason her gaze focused on his lips, always so quick to smile. With his slight tan, that mop of blond hair and the well-washed jeans and soft T-shirt, he looked like a surfer dude. Knowing Leo, he'd probably spent the whole summer on the beach.

She ducked her head and focused on finishing her text, adding a 'missing you' that she hadn't intended as well as a couple of extra kisses.

Having pressed send, she eyed Leo warily, trying not to

reflect once again on how flipping good-looking he was. That spontaneous hug yesterday in the middle of the other apartment had unsettled her and she'd spent the whole evening in her room unpacking and rearranging things. Anything to stay out of his way. He'd been so kind to her. She didn't want him to be kind. She didn't want to remember the good things about him. Having lost her heart to him once, she couldn't bear the agony again. She needed to reinforce herself against his kindness and that wonderful irrepressible energy. Leo was the sunshine that attracted everyone. Someone like her would never be enough to hold onto to someone like him – not for ever. It wasn't that she had a huge inferiority complex – well, maybe a slight one – but she'd witnessed her aunt's constant vigilance, always looking for the next clue to her uncle's latest 'friendship'. Which was why Anna had walked away last time. Before Leo could. There would always be someone waiting to step into her shoes.

She realised Leo was still waiting for an answer to his question.

'And what's that?' she finally asked, all too aware of how the snug T-shirt fitted him a little too well and, despite her self-pep-talk mere seconds before, caused an unwelcome pang of longing. Not going there. She did not fancy Leo, not any more. Muscle memory, that was all, a vestige of how she'd felt a long, long time ago.

'Want a coffee?' she asked, feeling it would be churlish not to offer when she'd made a whole pot. She'd nipped out earlier to the bakery down the street to buy fresh bread and had come back with a bag of fresh pastries.

'Yes, please.'

'And one of these? A thank you for rescuing me from District Thirteen.' She pushed the paper bag towards him. 'They're still warm.' The little pastries looked rather like overgrown jam tarts with dough shells and filled with a rich, dark plum jam.

'Yum. What are they?'

'*Koláče*, apparently. They just came out of the oven and smelt so delicious I couldn't resist.'

'So,' said Leo with a playful twinkle in his eye, 'I have a proposition for you. You can't spend all your time avoiding me in the flat. It's not healthy and I don't want to make you feel you have to. I know I've been out a lot but … I can't keep eating out every night. So how about we pretend we've never met before. We don't talk about the past, don't make any assumptions or presumptions about each other and don't bring up old grievances. A completely fresh start.'

The words sounded rehearsed, confirming that they had indeed been considered, but Anna was impressed for all that. They showed a maturity and thoughtfulness that the madcap, impetuous Leo of old wouldn't have been capable of. Although she wasn't supposed to be thinking like that. 'And I'd like to cook dinner for you this evening. It's daft us eating separately. We might as well take it in turns.' He held up his hands. 'I'll do some shopping.'

'Okay,' she said, still wary, wondering how this was going to work.

'Great.' He held out his hand. 'I'm Leo Knight. I'm twenty-eight. I live in Richmond in London and I want to open a craft brewery. I'm here because I'm passionate about beer and the Czechs make the best beer in the world.'

She took his hand and shook it, playing along, trying not to remember the first time he'd held her hand.

'Anna Love. Also twenty-eight. I'm an orphan and grew up with my aunt and uncle and three older cousins, Becs, James and Tim. I live in a small village outside Milton Keynes and … I want to be head brewer of my family's brewery one day.'

'Seems like we have something in common,' said Leo taking a seat and biting into his pastry. 'Mmm, this is good, thank you.'

'You're welcome.'

'I'm going to play tourist today,' said Leo with his irrepressible grin. 'I'm going to drink Pilsen and eat dumplings.'

Dumplings and beer sounded really good. A tug of longing pulled at her even as she nodded politely at him. Leo had always been able to make life more fun, wherever he was and whatever he was doing.

'We could join forces, you know,' said Leo. 'As part of our truce. And you can pretend, just for one day, that you don't hate me.'

Startled, she turned to face him. 'I don't hate you.'

'Whatever,' replied Leo. 'But we could play at tourists and have some fun.'

It was that irrepressible quirk to his mouth that did it. The one that made him look like a naughty toddler about to admit to his latest misdemeanour with great glee.

Why the hell not? Leo's company was better than being

on her own all day and she'd barely seen the city because she'd been waiting for Steve to visit. And exploring with someone else was always more fun.

'Okay, if we can see the Charles Bridge and the Castle.' She felt guilty that she'd not yet seen either, especially as wherever you went there was nearly always a view of the castle overlooking the city.

'Excellent. See, that wasn't so bad, was it?' said Leo. 'Leave in ten?'

When they boarded the tram fifteen minutes later, Anna hadn't planned not to talk to Leo, but she was quite happy to take in the unfamiliar streets as they trundled through. He seemed happy with her silence, too, but then Leo's basic disposition was to be happy. Nothing ever fazed him.

It didn't take long to reach Anděl metro station, where they disembarked from the tram along with a flow of people all headed the same way.

'We need to buy tickets,' Leo announced as they approached the entrance.

'Really?' drawled Anna, giving in to a sudden urge to tease him. 'I had no idea.'

'Very funny.' He nudged her with his elbow and, just like that, being with him felt familiar and easy again. 'I was talking out loud. Lead on. Since you're such a smartarse, you can buy the tickets.'

He gestured towards the unmissable bright yellow machines. Anna straightened and headed towards them. It was only when she was halfway across the forecourt that it occurred to her: she'd taken the lead. She automatically took a back seat these days because Steve always led the way, sorting out tickets and bookings. Somehow, without thinking about it, she'd relinquished that sort of responsibility and relied on him. After always being the outsider at home, running to keep up and to fit in with her adopted family, it had been a relief to find someone who focused on her, looked out for her and loved her as she was. Now she realised that maybe she leaned on Steve too much and had given him the wrong impression. She'd been lazy in putting forward her opinions and wants, too grateful for his attention. In truth, she wasn't really a dutiful follower.

Thankfully, the ticket machines offered an English option, so she was able to buy the tickets with relative ease.

'Here you go.' With a touch of pride, she handed over his ticket before adding, 'Make sure you don't lose it.'

Leo laughed. 'That was six years ago. Are you ever going to let me forget it?'

'What?' She frowned.

Now it was his turn to frown.

'You remember. When I left the train tickets on the table in the carriage of the first train from London when we changed trains. That time we went to the Edinburgh Festival.'

She snorted a laugh as it all came back. 'I do now.' Sobering slightly, she also remembered how, in inimitable Leo style, he'd charmed the female train manager into not throwing them off the train at the next stop. Women always loved Leo.

Just like they loved Uncle Henry. Anna winced, remembering the slow deflation of her aunt's confidence over the years. How she was always looking over her shoulder. Anna wasn't going to be that woman.

Quashing the memory, she headed for the escalator, pleased to see that the metro was very easy to navigate, and Leo fell into step beside her.

'This is very grand,' he said as they walked through a cavernous hallway with large marble tiles on the curved pillars.

'It was built during the communist regime,' Anna told him, remembering what she'd read in her guidebook earlier that morning. 'Dedicated to the Czechoslovak-Soviet friendship and built in the Soviet style. Originally there were lots of propaganda reliefs and this station was called *Moskevská*, named after the city of Moscow. As part of the "cultural exchange" –' Anna's fingers made quotation marks '– there was a metro station built in Moscow named after Prague.'

'Still like to do lots of research, then,' teased Leo.

Anna nodded. 'It was a long drive here and it's amazing what you look up on your phone.'

'Have you looked up somewhere for brunch? I'm starving.'

She allowed herself to look smug. 'Of course.'

'Excellent.'

The metro train arrived and a few stops later they disembarked at Můstek, where the green and yellow metro lines intersected. Using her phone Anna directed them down a wide cobbled pedestrianised street, full of shops featuring familiar European brands: Desigual, Zara, Douglas, Nike, Swarovski and Mango. Further down the road, their route followed a one-way street before they came to an old Gothic gate next to a gorgeous Art Deco building.

'The café's in there,' said Anna, pointing to the cream building with its huge arched windows on the first floor and dramatic square ones at ground level. The entrance in the middle was even more striking, with a huge cupola over it featuring an ornate mosaic above a semi-circular balcony with intricate ironwork railings. Inside the airy entrance hall, decorated with stained-glass windows, were a café and a restaurant. They turned left across the mosaic-tiled floor into the beautifully appointed Art Deco room.

'This is some place,' said Leo, looking up at the magnificent glass chandeliers and the ceiling's simple but elegant pale blue and white plasterwork. 'Is that a fountain?' He pointed to the water feature at the other end of the room as they took their seats and ordered coffee. Anna chose a delicious-sounding basket of pastries while Leo selected eggs Benedict with Prague ham that he wanted to try.

'Well, this is one way to spend a Sunday morning,' he said , glancing around the busy room.

'Yes,' said Anna, guiltily thinking of Steve out on the rugby pitch.

'So how's the family?' asked Leo suddenly. 'Still excelling at everything? I'm assuming the boyfriend is one of James's rugby mates.'

Anna stared at him, unnerved by the accurate guess.

'Why would you assume that?' she asked, her spine as stiff and straight at a broomstick.

'Is he?' Leo cocked an eyebrow, barely restraining the ghost of a smirk.

'He might be,' she conceded.

'That's a yes, then.'

'And your point is?' She tried to keep her voice light.

'No point at all. And what about your aunt and uncle?' He stuck to the bargain but she could almost hear the unspoken question: 'still married?'

'They're fine.' Anna studied his blank face.

'And where do you live now?'

'I still live in the village. I've got a flat above the pet shop.'

'Not too far from the family, then.' Leo scowled but before he could say anything more, Anna said, 'No' firmly, her tone ending any further discussion of her adoptive family.

'How about your family?' she asked, her stomach cramping a little at the thought of Aurelia, Leo's mother, possibly one of the kindest people she'd ever met. Losing contact with her had been a big regret but it had been the right thing to do.

'She's great,' said Leo, his eyes brightening. 'She and Ernesto are as much in love as ever. He's pretty cool for a stepdad. She's getting all excited, hoping that Raph is going to marry his girlfriend Lia.' His expression changed and he gave her a cool stare. 'She's hoping that one of her boys will be happily married soon.'

Anna refused to rise to the bait. 'That's nice,' she said equably, but learning that there was no unmentioned fiancée in the wings brought more relief than it should have done.

'Giulia's eight now. She was a toddler when you last saw her. She's quite a pickle, that one. Baby of the family but she twists Ernesto around her little finger.'

Again Anna's heart blanched at the memory of the little dark-haired girl who'd loved to sit on her knee and listen to bedtime stories when she and Leo babysat. Rather than say anything, she took a large bite of croissant.

'So do you and what's-his-name live together?'

'Steve,' she said, narrowing her eyes, irritated at Leo pretending not to know his name. 'And no, we don't. I'm sharing a flat with an old schoolfriend, but Steve and I are looking to buy somewhere together next year.'

Leo nodded.

'What about you? Do you have a significant other?'

Leo laughed. 'You know me. Life's too short to restrict myself. Still playing the field.'

'No surprise there,' said Anna.

'You asked,' said Leo and then he leaned back in his chair. 'Look, we can carry on bitching at each other or enjoy the day. My fault – we agreed we wouldn't talk about the past.'

Anna stared at him for a moment.

'Yeah, yeah,' said Leo. 'I'm all growed up.'

'I didn't say anything.'

'You didn't need to. I'll be nice to you.'

Anna glared at him. Why had he said that? Again, it was as if he were the wronged one. She'd done the leaving, but only because she knew he would never change, and she'd come to the conclusion that she might have repeated a pattern and married the equivalent of her uncle. With an inward sigh, she decided, in the spirit of their truce, to say, 'Thank you,' and move on.

They meandered through the streets, weaving through fellow tourists and eventually arriving at the town square with the old town hall. Anna glanced at her watch.

'If we wait a few minutes we can watch the astronomical clock strike the hour and see the twelve apostles.'

'Have you swallowed that guidebook again?' asked Leo, back to his usual cheerful self. That was one thing about him, he didn't bear a grudge. Not that he was entitled to.

'No. I like to read up on things before I go and see them. Then I get to actually look at them instead of peering at my phone all the time googling everything.'

'Good point. Okay. I'm happy to wait for lift-off.'

A crowd of tourists had already gathered in front of the famous clock tower, peering upwards at its colourful face, adorned on either side with small figures including a macabre skeleton. As the bells began to chime the hour, the skeleton began to ring the bell in its hand and two wooden windows above the clock opened to reveal the procession of twelve apostles.

The whole performance lasted twenty-seven seconds, one of the guides informed her group in heavily accented English. Anna listened in to other facts that were being relayed, rather charmed by the whole experience. It fascinated her to know that the clock had been here for so long and was the oldest astrological clock in the world. There was something about history that put your own life into perspective. People had lived, loved and laughed for hundreds of years before her and sometimes it was good to remember that.

They spent some time in the square, looking up at the historic buildings, stepping along the cobbles and absorbing the atmosphere. Anna smiled and Leo caught her.

'Penny for them.'

'I was thinking how lovely the city is. I'd never really thought what it might be like. There's so much history here, it permeates the fabric of the buildings and layers the streets.'

'I know what you mean,' said Leo. 'It makes me feel quite inadequate.'

'You!' Anna couldn't hide her surprise. Leo was the golden one, rich, handsome. Everything came easily to him.

'There's so much culture here. Art, architecture, theatres – people have created things. What's my legacy going to be? It makes you aware of your own mortality and how small we are in the grand scheme of things.'

'I was thinking along similar lines, although funnily enough I didn't think of inadequacy. I thought more of how minor our problems are when you set them against the shared experience of history. I remember my mum saying we should live our lives to the full because we're here for such a short time.'

Her mum had been a positive force of energy, always ready to see the good in things rather than the negative. Her regular pithy comment, 'Well, we can't change things, we have to work with them,' had steered the family through many a rainy day, cancelled event or disappointment.

'Good philosophy,' he said with a nod, the shadow of sympathy in his eyes.

Anna swallowed her guilt. Poor Mum had no idea that her own life would be cut so short, which made it even worse that Anna had never lived up to that adage. She'd been so desperate to blend into her new life without causing any trouble, in case her aunt and uncle changed their minds about having her, that she'd absorbed their ways and values, never defending their snippy comments about her cheery mother, whom they clearly hadn't approved of.

She decided things were getting a bit too serious. 'Shall we head to the bridge?'

The bridge across the Vltava was much wider than Anna had supposed it might be and was lined with statues, which she immediately wanted to know more about.

'So what can you tell me about the bridge, Tour Guide Barbie?'

'It's old,' said Anna with a giggle. 'I didn't look this one up, I'm afraid. I don't know anything about it.'

'Why don't we walk across? We're going to be here for a while. Veronika has offered to show me around one weekend. It's always better to hear about a place from people who are native, I think.'

Anna wasn't going to ask who Veronika was. In a few weeks' time she'd have Steve here to show around.

'You're right. You get a different perspective.'

'Yes, like the time my great-uncle Pavel tried to push his

wife off the bridge and the truly dreadful occasion when my great-aunt Sophia dropped her handbag over the edge.'

Anna giggled. 'You idiot.' That blithe irreverence had always been able to make her laugh. Already she could feel the lightness of spirit that being around Leo had always given her. Or maybe it was the autumnal sunshine. Either way it felt good.

They walked across the bridge among all the tourists, both of them stopping to take pictures with the leisurely ease of people on holiday. Anna couldn't remember the last time she'd not had to be somewhere by a certain time.

They meandered past shops peering in the windows. Passing the impressive baroque façade of St Nicholas Church, they found themselves walking uphill on a cobbled street just one car wide, lined with cream-and-golden stone buildings and with attractive double-lanterned lampposts which at home Anna would have described as Victorian, although that couldn't be the right word here. The buildings varied in style, some with detailed stone covings, others topped with statues. There were elaborate sculptured porticoes, plaques, decorative window sills. Everywhere, there was something new to see and Leo was as quick as she was to observe a new feature, like a wrought-iron balcony flamboyantly framing a large upper-storey window, or the carved columns of the Romanian Embassy.

They were so busy chatting and pointing things out to each other that all of a sudden they were at the top of the hill and almost upon the castle. Following the cobblestone lane up a sharp right turn, they came upon the perfect viewpoint. Below them, the city opened out on a magnificent vista of spires, turrets, gables and cupolas, grand stone buildings with terracotta tiled roofs, the whole scene dappled by patches of greenery. The straight lines of the buildings guarding the waterfront, with their symmetrical windows. Gothic towers, baroque cupolas, white gables.

After admiring the view in comfortable silence for a good ten minutes. Leo turned to her.

'It must be time for a beer. This place needs more time and we can come back another day,' he said with an enthusiastic grin, without even looking at his watch. 'I know just the place.'

'It's not even eleven o'clock.' Anna shook her head.

'It will be by the time we get there. It's about a fifteen-minute walk.' He turned the screen of his phone towards her, showing a line of little blue dots on a map.

Anna smiled. 'So you haven't looked up anything about the sights of Prague, but you have researched the best places to drink beer. Why aren't I surprised?'

'You wouldn't want to miss out, would you?'

Retracing their steps, they walked back down the hill and took a few turns not far from the bridge before arriving at *Lokál*, a building on a corner. Inside, Leo led the way past busy tables, all of them full, down a set of stairs to a stone-vaulted cellar, the scarred tiled flooring proof of the pub's popularity. Anna marvelled again at Leo's confidence. It was as if he knew where he was going. Simple, well-worn dark wooden tables filled the room, while the bar itself was all modern technology with a stainless-steel counter over a glass cabinet containing stainless-steel tanks and the pump equipment to ensure quick delivery from tank to glass.

'Wow,' she said, the hairs standing up on the back of her arms. Okay, so she was a beer nerd. 'That's some bit of kit.'

'I know,' said Leo, throwing her a delighted smile. 'Natálie said I had to visit this place. What are you going to have?'

'I'll have a Pilsner Urquell,' said Anna. How many new friends had he made since he'd been here?

'And how do you want it poured?'

Anna cocked her head slightly. Was this a trick question? 'In a glass?'

'Lesson number one in Czech beer coming up,' replied Leo, without a hint of condescension as they chose a table and each picked up a menu. 'There are several pour options. Pilsner insist that their beer is only poured by a trained tapster. There are three options: *hladinka*, a standard pour; *šynt*, which is two fingers of beer, three fingers of foam and a finger of empty glass, or *mlíko*, which is nearly all foam apart from a sliver at the bottom.'

'You know your stuff,' said Anna, scanning the menu, a little embarrassed that she didn't know this.

'That's the bit I've been swotting up on. We make the perfect team, you with your touristy knowledge and me on the food and drink. We could eat here too, if you fancy it.'

The place felt very authentic but also pleasantly touristy and she was keen to try the beer.

'What are you having?'

'I'm going to try a *mlíko* as it's not lunchtime yet,' he teased. 'Less beer but plenty of flavour. So I've been told.'

A waiter appeared to take their order. Anna was about to play it safe and order a standard beer but at the last minute she ordered the same as Leo because she was intrigued. That was his effect: he'd often persuaded her to do uncharacteristic things. She could imagine Steve's response. He didn't hold with fizzy lager, no matter how often she'd tried to explain that real pilsner was nothing like the gassy lager so freely available in English pubs. He'd run screaming from a glass full of foam.

When the beer arrived they took simultaneous sips, Anna ending up with foam on the tip of her nose, which Leo immediately swiped away for her. A frisson ran through her at his casual touch, igniting nerve endings that she'd hoped were impervious to him. Although she froze, she carefully maintained an impassive expression. It probably hadn't been so much as a blip on his radar, while for her it had been a quick electrical surge of bitter awareness. Leo had always been able to affect her without even trying; that had been a big part of the problem. It was far too easy to love Leo. From the day she'd met him, she'd fallen hard, even though she'd known he was way out of her orbit. It had been the biggest surprise of her life, the first time he'd kissed her.

She took a gulp of the foamy beer, rolling the texture around her mouth, savouring the sweet, creamy flavour.

'That's delicious,' she said, perhaps a touch over-enthusiastically, determined not to let Leo know that his touch had affected her in any way.

'It is,' said Leo, perusing the menu. She took advantage of his concentration to watch him as those deep brown eyes, still the colour of whisky, flecked with gold, narrowed as he pondered his choices. No one would ever have said Leo's face was one for playing poker, every emotion flashed across those mobile features.

He was totally absorbed in the menu and clearly not the least bit aware of the battle going on in her body as her hormones clamoured for his touch. God, she'd been in his company less than a day and already, she was reverting to the same old pattern. It was just physical attraction, she told herself sternly. It didn't mean anything – any more than it would mean anything to him. Their short marriage had been a colossal mistake. Leo thrived on novelty and jumping into things without thinking. She'd fallen for him so hard that it had blinded her to reality. So she'd been equally spontaneous and married him – and her one and only flirtation with spontaneity had ended in heartbreak.

At that moment, Leo looked up and smiled at her, that sweet, guileless smile that had reeled her in, the very first time she'd laid eyes on him.

'I'm spoilt for choice. I can't decide between the Prague ham and whipped horseradish or the Frankfurters and whipped mustard and horseradish. '

He gave her one of his endearing grins.

She rolled her eyes, determined to harden herself against his charm. 'Yes, I'll share with you.'

'I hoped you'd say that.'

'You knew I would.'

'Because I know you love your sausage.' He paused and pressed his lips together as if that might recall the inadvertent double entendre. 'What I … I … um … meant

... is that I know you really like ...like ham. Meat. So I kind of figured...'

'I'm happy to share, Leo,' she said. Amused by him tripping over his words but keen not to be a complete pushover, she added, 'But I do want to try a dumpling so why don't we order a main course, Czech Goulash, dumpling and dill sauce.'

'Done,' said Leo. 'I'm starving.'

'You're always starving,' said Anna, once again without even thinking.

'I know.' Leo grinned, his eyes meeting hers in that shiny joyful way that made her heart speed up. Being around him was always fun but she had to remember that that was all it was. You could never take Leo too seriously. She'd made that mistake before.

Chapter Nine

'Leo! Leo! I need your help.'

At the sound of Anna's shout, his heart lurched and he jumped off the kitchen bar stool, turned the pan on the cooker off and ran to the top of the stairs. Over the last two weeks, they'd fallen into an easy routine of travelling to work together very early and returning separately at around four o'clock. Nice and natural. Today he'd beaten Anna home and had decided to cook a pasta dish for dinner.

'What's the matter? Are you okay?' At the foot of the stairs, Anna stood panting, looking dishevelled and red-faced. Despite that, something caught at his heart. He'd always thought she was beautiful, with her fine-boned features and that delicate chin, which gave her a touch of the fey.

'F-fine. I need your help. Come on, hurry. I don't want to miss them. Put some shoes on.'

She nodded towards his bare feet as he came skittering

down the stairs. Before he could ask any more, she'd turned and was running back down the flight of stairs to the hall. Reassured that she wasn't hurt or in any real distress, he stood for a moment to catch his breath and let his heart subside into its rightful place. Even so. as he yanked on a pair of trainers to follow her, he wondered what had got her in such a tizz.

'Come on,' she yelled as he approached the front door downstairs and then, like a puppy playing a game of catch, she dashed away down the street. Intrigued, he could do nothing but go after her as quickly as he could. He caught up with her as she turned the corner and came to a halt in front of a large skip.

'Look what I've found.' Like a monkey she was already mountaineering her way up the side of the skip. She scrambled into it and with her arms held out for balance stood on top of a pile of discarded furniture.

'Junk,' he said.

'Not junk. Furniture. Vintage furniture. A table, four dining chairs, a stool and two armchairs. Perfect for the apartment.'

Leo squinted at the motley assortment of furniture. 'They're knackered. Which is why someone's throwing them away.'

Anna held up one of the dining chairs. He winced. Not only was it falling apart, it was also bloody ugly. 'That is hideous.'

Anna put a protective arm around the chair back, cuddling it, and gave him an earnest look. 'Shh, you'll hurt its feelings.'

Something inside Leo lit up at that moment and he remembered exactly why he'd fallen in love with Anna Love. That hidden whimsy that every now and then surfaced, pushing aside the too serious, conventional approach to life. It had been that side of her that had enchanted him. The side of her that was sublimated most of the time.

'I don't think it's the sort of chair that has feelings,' he said smiling up at her, amused to see the old Anna back in force.

'You don't know.' An impish smile filled her face as she handed the chair down to him. 'Besides, when it's been done it up, it will look completely different. With a bit of sanding, a coat of paint, some glue and TLC, you'll change your tune.'

Leo wrinkled his nose, taking the chair from her and looking more closely at the scarred wooden legs and the stained upholstery. 'Anna, it's going to take more than TLC to make this look anything other than a reject from the big furniture sale in the sky.'

'Want to bet?' she said standing above him. With the sun behind her catching the red lights in her hair and her fists planted on her hips in that take-no-prisoners stance, she looked like Wonder Woman on a mission. 'Here.' She handed him a second chair. 'You can take them to the flat. I'll keep guard so that no one else takes the rest of the stuff.'

'No one else is going to want it,' he said.

'It's free furniture. And we don't have any furniture.'

'If it looks like this we don't want any furniture.'

'When did you get so negative?' she asked, clearly forgetting their ground rules.

He rolled his eyes. 'Getting that table up the stairs could be fun.'

Forty-five minutes later, he found himself opposite Anna trying to manoeuvre the table around the return on the first floor.

'It's stuck,' he said, unable to lift it over the railing as Anna pushed from the other end.

'Where there's a will there's a way,' she muttered, trying to raise her end. 'We need to lift it a bit higher and then—'

'No shit, Sherlock. Why didn't I think of that?' groused Leo, still unable to believe that Anna had persuaded him to do this.

'If you push it that way,' she suggested.

'No, it needs to go higher.'

'I'm not—'

'Do you need some help?' asked a dry, amused voice and Leo glanced down through the railings to see Jan.

'Yes, please. We appear to be stuck.'

Jan came closer to investigate. 'And you didn't think that perhaps the legs could be removed?' he asked, studying the underside of the table.

'Outside my area of expertise?' said Leo, frustration edging his words at the obvious solution.

Anna slapped her forehead. 'Of course. I'm so stupid.' She lowered her end. 'I don't suppose you've got a screwdriver we could borrow, have you?'

'You're talking to a Czech man,' said Michaela with a bright laugh as she appeared from behind Jan. 'He has *zlaté české ručičky* – golden, little hands. We Czechs are very resourceful and inventive.'

'Great. Sooner rather than later would be good,' said Leo. Being wedged against the wall with a table top digging into his shoulder wasn't the most comfortable position he'd ever found himself in.

'Sorry. I'll go now.'

As Jan disappeared into the other apartment, Michaela peered at the table. 'Where did you get it?'

'From a skip on the street,' said Anna. 'I think I can do something with it. And if it goes wrong, it was free.'

Leo appraised Anna from behind the table. 'I didn't know you were a D.I.Y. buff.'

'There's a lot you don't know about me,' she said with an arch expression, one that he did know well, and it reminded him of all the things he did know about her, like the sounds she made in her sleep, her habit of burrowing into the duvet as soon as she woke up and how she'd slept, curled up and tucked in next to him, her knees nudging his bottom. The memory of her soft body next to him sent a quick surge of awareness through him and he had to hurriedly think of cold showers, porridge and slugs to divert the blood flow that had decided to head south. In his awkward position it was almost impossible to adjust his jeans.

'Yes. I've seen loads of reels on Instagram where people upcycle things. I've been really inspired and I've tried a few things at home. Look,' Anna said showing Michaela her phone Jan set to work taking the legs off the table. 'This one is one of my favourites. Look how they make this old cabinet look so much better. Watch. I reckon I could do that.'

Together they watched the reel and Michaela beamed at her. 'I have an old bureau of my aunt's at the *chata*. It's useful but not pretty but I can see how I could make it look so much better. What are you doing this weekend?' she asked suddenly.

'We're going on a food tour of the city, "The Best of Prague",' volunteered Leo. 'It's been organised by *Sdílená Kultura* for us.'

'Oh!' Michaela's eyes widened with quick envy. 'I did that tour last year. Even though we live in Prague we still learned so much. It's amazing. You'll have so much fun but don't eat before you go, whatever you do. And don't plan to eat afterwards. It's a shame, I was going to invite you to come to the *chata*.'

'You know what she really wants,' teased Jan. 'Some extra labour.'

Michaela shot him a quick, naughty grin. 'Maybe you could come with us the next time. It would be so much fun, wouldn't it, Jan?' Michaela clapped her hands.

'Yes.' Jan gave them a cheerful grin. 'Sweeping, cleaning, chopping, sawing. So much fun without all the modern luxuries. You haven't warned them that it's very basic? We have no furniture and the beds are blow-up mattresses. You have to bring your own bedding. And there is very limited hot water.' He beamed before adding, 'I put in a solar water heater for my uncle last summer. Before then there was *no* hot water.'

'You put it in yourself?' said Anna, her eyes lighting up with instant admiration.

'I told you, he has golden hands.'

'I'm not sure you should be telling everyone that,' Leo muttered. 'People might get the wrong idea.'

Michaela frowned, not following.

Anna rolled her eyes. 'He's being rude.'

Jan, who got it, grinned and wiggled his fingers towards his girlfriend. 'I've got golden hands.'

She laughed and ducked out of his range. 'Use them on the legs,' she said pointing to the table.

'Always happy to use them on the legs,' said Jan, his wink making both women laugh even more.

With a bit of twisting and lifting, once Jan removed the last of the table legs, he and Leo were able to get it up the stairs.

'Would you like a drink?' asked Anna. 'We can sit on the roof terrace while the men sort the table out.'

'I deserve one,' said Jan, a cheeky grin lighting up his face, 'but Michaela doesn't, she hasn't done any work.'

Michaela gave an outraged gasp.

'I think you're dicing with danger there, mate,' said Leo.

'I would love a drink. Do you have any wine?' asked Michaela

Anna pulled a face which made Leo want to reassure her. He could have predicted that she'd apologise. 'Sorry, no. I haven't bought any because I don't know anything about the local wine.'

'Then I shall go and get a bottle of Moravian wine for

you to try and some of Jan's favourite beer and we shall educate you.'

'I'm always happy to be educated,' chipped in Leo, relieved that he'd had help to carry the table up the last flight of stairs. It wasn't heavy but it was awkward.

'No beer until the legs are back on,' said Michaela, with a teasing tap on Jan's nose. 'I'll go down and get some wine and beer. I'll be back in a minute.'

'Why don't you stay for dinner? I've made my mama's Amatriciana sauce, it's a special recipe. It's very good,' said Leo.

'Modest much?' said Anna.

Leo raised an eyebrow and she wrinkled her nose. 'Okay, okay. It's delicious.' She turned to Michaela. 'He's a really good cook.'

Jan and Michaela exchanged one of those couples looks – the sort where they manage to have a discussion without words – before Michaela said, 'That would be great. I don't have to cook tonight. We take it in turns.'

'Why don't I go and put the pasta on,' said Anna, squeezing past them and going on ahead, before Leo could answer.

'You two been together long?' asked Leo as he grasped the flat, table top and went up the stairs backwards.

'Four years. We met at Masaryk University in Brno and we knew each other when we were there but then we met again at a friend's birthday. We moved in here two years ago. It's very expensive to rent in Prague but we both work here and we both earn a good salary. Michaela works in publishing and I work for an engineering company.'

'Ah, hence the golden hands.'

Jan gave a modest shrug. They managed to get the table around the corner and into the living room where the rest of the rescued furniture was gathered in a sorry little circle.

'*No ne!*' exclaimed Jan.

'I know,' said Leo, assuming that Jan was as appalled by the junk as he was. 'Bloody hideous, isn't it. But when Anna gets the bit between her teeth, there's no stopping her. She's a stubborn as a donkey.'

'Donkey?'

Leo did a quick heehaw which didn't remove Jan's puzzled expression. He dug out his phone and quickly used the translate app. '*Osel.*'

'We say a fluffy lamb can grow up to be a big fat ram. But, no, Michaela will be very envious. This is original TON furniture.' His eyes widened. 'Table, chairs and armchairs. You did well. This is vintage. A real find.'

'Really?' Now that he looked more closely, beyond the battered and badly painted wood, Leo could see the craftsmanship in the slender bending of the wood used on the chair backs and the gentle curves of the table. It appeared Anna had a good eye, but the pieces needed some serious work and he didn't have a clue where one would start.

'Yes. This is iconic Czech design and it's still made today.' Jan ran a hand over the bentwood curve of one of the armchairs. 'With some love these will be beautiful. I'm so happy that you are making them good again. The TON factory for bentwood furniture, *Továrna ohýbaného nábytku,* that's the direct translation, was started in Bystříce pod Hostýnem in the nineteenth century and it's still there today. One of the oldest original factories in the world. Michael Thonet, the founder, was a great designer and his family ran the company until the Fifties, when it was nationalised and became TON. Their stuff has always been really well made.'

Anna came in as he was talking and beamed. 'See, told you. I could see the potential as soon as I saw it.'

Leo raised a sceptical eye. 'I thought you said it was free furniture.'

'That as well,' agreed Anna.

'I have wine,' called Michaela bursting into the room holding a bottle aloft. She stopped dead when she saw the accumulated furniture. 'You got all of this from a dumpster?

Jan grinned at Leo. 'What did I say?'

'Isn't it lovely?' said Anna. 'Or rather it's going to be.'

'What will you do?'

'Er ... um.'

'Good question,' said Leo, grinning at Anna.

'Take off all the mouldings, sand it down and paint it. Put some new legs and different seat covers on them and they'll look like new,' she said.

Michaela jumped in. 'Or you could wax it and keep the natural colour and buy some fabric to reupholster the chairs. I've got a staple gun you can borrow.'

Anna gave the other woman a winning smile. 'Thank you.'

'Small point,' said Leo, already envisioning the living

room turning into a workshop, not that he minded. Anna's enthusiasm for her project was rubbing off on him and sparked a desire to learn as well. There'd been few opportunities to get involved in any DIY growing up as his stepfather was hopelessly impractical and always booked tradespeople to complete that sort of job around the home. 'What about tools? And supplies? Buying those won't be easy. You're going to need a translator.'

'Jan has lots of tools and I work with fabric and I've refurbished a few items. Nothing on this scale, but I have a good eye,' said Michaela.

'Perfect, because I think I might have the practical skills but I'm not always good with colour and decorative detail,' said Anna.

'Michaela is very artistic,' said Jan. 'She knits, she sews, she paints, draws. And offers my tools.'

At Anna's stricken face, he smiled and patted her arm. 'It is okay, you can borrow my tools. I can tell you will look after them.'

'Are you sure? That's really kind of you.'

'Of course. I know where you live, I can find them when I need them.'

'If you don't mind, that would be really helpful. I'm not even sure what I might need.'

'Jan has everything,' said Michaela. 'We rented our apartment because it has a garage to keep his collection. He bought a cement mixer in Lidl last month.' She rolled her eyes. 'Because everyone needs one. He was like a boy at Christmas.'

'I'll show you later, if you'd like,' said Jan.

'The workmen need refreshment,' announced Leo as he straightened up, having replaced the last dining table leg.

'You can open the wine,' said Michaela, handing over a tall slim bottle. 'This is from Mikulov in South Moravia, near our *chata*.' Her eyes crinkled in delight. 'I love saying that. It's so exciting. But yes, the wines from this region are excellent. They're a well-kept secret. We like to keep them to ourselves. They're so good.'

Anna invited them all out onto the roof terrace, directing Leo to grab the corkscrew as she already had glasses.

Michaela sat at the little bistro table. 'I am very jealous of this.' She waved her hand at the view. 'It's very special.'

'We won't be able to use it for much longer. It's getting colder every day.'

'Yes, it's mild for Prague at the moment.'

Leo, charged with opening the bottle, filled the glasses with the pale straw-coloured wine.

'*Na zdraví*,' he said, pleased he'd remembered.

The others chorused it and all took sips from their glasses.

Leo who'd drunk a lot of good wine, thanks to eating in some of the best restaurants in the world and his mother's knowledge of fine Italian wine, was surprised by how good it was. He took a second enthusiastic sip. 'This is lovely.'

'I told you,' said Michaela, both smug and proud at the same time. 'Wines from South Moravia are excellent. This is Vinselekt Michlovský. You can buy it in the supermarket and it's a good one.'

'I don't know much about Czech wine or food, really,' said Anna.

'Except that you love a dumpling,' teased Leo, reminding her of their day in Prague.

'I do love a dumpling,' she admitted. 'We had them at Lokal for the first time, they were delicious. Dense and fluffy at the same time, if that makes sense.'

'It does. You must come to dinner this weekend. We were going to go to the *chata* but we decided to stay here. Now we have friends coming on Saturday and I am making potato dumplings. Come in the afternoon and I will teach you.'

Anna considered for a moment. 'I'd love to but my boyfriend is coming over for that weekend.'

'That's a shame but there will be another time.'

'But I'm going to need some help in the DIY store. Would you mind helping me? And where is the nearest store?'

'No problem. It's Jan's second home but I will come take you because you'll need a translator,' said Michaela. 'What are you doing after work next Wednesday?'

'Meeting you at the DIY store?'

'Yes.' Michaela gave her an approving grin. 'We have a date.'

'Not without me,' said Jan, shaking his head. 'You can't go to the store without me. And you have to go to U Rotta.'

Michaela patted him on the arm. 'It's his favourite.'

'Well, I'm coming too, then,' declared Leo. 'You're not leaving me out. I might miss something.'

Anna laughed. Having Leo along would make the visit

more entertaining; he always brought the fun. Steve wouldn't have been quite so keen on a visit to a DIY store, which immediately brought a stab of guilt because today was the first time in days she'd thought about his forthcoming visit. Did that make her a bad girlfriend or just busy and happy?

Chapter Ten

A nna's phone rang as she peeled off her white wellies, having spent the morning in the mash room. She glanced at the screen, not intending to answer, but was surprised to see Steve's name flash up. They usually spoke in the evenings after work. Guiltily she wondered if she was even thinking about him at the moment. Coming to Prague had given her the space to realise that a lot of what they shared was routine and regularity. There was nothing wrong between them but then again, it wasn't … right? Perfect? Fun? She was loath to define her disquiet and stared down at her phone.

'Steve?' she answered.

'Hi, Anna. I needed to call you. I've got good news and bad news.'

'Aha.' It wasn't the first time he'd prefaced a call this way.

'I've been selected for the Village Sevens.'

'Congratulations, that's brilliant,' she said automatically, mentally thumbing through her memory bank to work out which tournament he was referring too.

'Yeah! I'm so chuffed.' His voice vibrated with delight.

Silence ensued as she realised that he was expecting her to join the missing dots. It took her a minute to pick out one of the files in said memory bank. Village Sevens. It was a local pub's all-day rugby tournament that involved as much drinking as rugby playing, and she wasn't sure 'selected' was quite the word.

'It's this weekend,' he said in a sudden rush as if he were pulling a tooth out and the word dump would make the news less painful.

'This weekend?'

'Yeah, I know I was supposed to be coming over to see you but … of course, if you really want me to come, I will.'

If Steve didn't come, she could go to Michaela and Jan's and eat dumplings, was her first thought. Immediately, she felt disloyal, but then it did sound as if he really wanted to play, and, after all, she wouldn't be pining at home for him.

She found herself telling him it was fine and that there'd be plenty of other weekends.

She slid her phone into her pocket and went to find Jakub. They had a meeting to discuss the beer that she was going to make for her presentation and she wanted to pick his brains about the malting process. Unlike many brewers that bought in malted grains, here at Šilhov they malted their own barley. She wanted to propose using a low percentage of lighter caramel malt in her beer to give it a mild sweetness, a bready flavour and a light golden colour that she felt would have universal appeal. Here in the Czech Republic women often drank beer, but she wanted to create one that would appeal to women back in the UK.

'Anna. Take a seat,' said Jakub inviting her into his office, which she still found fascinating with its huge wooden desk tucked under the very low sloping beamed ceiling. A big old-fashioned heater, tiled in green majolica, filled much of the opposite wall. She guessed it was needed in the winter, given the thickness of the stone walls of the old monastery building.

It took her quite a while to persuade Jakub of her ideas but once she'd promised him that she would maintain the same production standards, including the brewery's triple decoction, he agreed to let her experiment with some batch brewing. Over the next few weeks, she would make a start. That was the easy bit. What was going to be harder was coming up with a concept to sell the beer. She needed a name, packaging design and marketing ideas that would stand out in a crowded market – and that was where she was completely stumped.

Despite those concerns she was bubbling with excitement about her beer ideas when she arrived to meet Michaela and the others at the DIY store.

'You look happy,' said Michaela, greeting her with a quick hug. 'You have had a good day.'

'Yeah. I've got the go-ahead from my boss to make my beer.' She glanced over her friend's shoulder, spotting Leo heading their way. 'But I can't talk about it in front of Leo. We're in competition. I don't want him to know the details.' She didn't think he'd copy them or anything but she was wary of exposing her ideas to daylight. They were like her babies and she wanted to hug them to her a while longer.

'Ah, okay. So let's go choose some paint.'

'I've made a list of what I think I need.' She'd spent the last couple of nights poring over Instagram and YouTube videos.

'You'll find everything here, I guarantee it,' said Jan from behind her before he swept his girlfriend into an enthusiastic hug as if he hadn't seen her for weeks. She giggled and smiled up at him as she kissed him on the mouth. Anna swallowed and sneaked a glance at Leo. He used to greet her like that. To her embarrassment, he caught her and gave her a tight smile. The sight of that small, hurt smile elicited a stab of guilt. For the first time, she asked herself if maybe she'd misjudged him. When he was with her, he'd always made her feel like she was bathed in the glow of his sunshine and the focus of his light.

Then she ducked her head, telling herself she was being foolish. Leo was charm personified; he could make anyone feel like that. It was his superpower. But he would have moved on if she hadn't left him first. Savannah Aitken had been more than ready to step into Anna's shoes, even if Leo refused to admit it. Steve had his faults, and he might not be as charming and exciting, but she always knew exactly where she was with him. She could guarantee he wouldn't look at another woman. She ignored the voice that suggested her only real rival was a rugby ball.

Anna could have happily spent the whole evening prowling the aisles of the hardware store. She realised she had a kindred spirit in Jan. As they browsed, he translated and together they exclaimed over products, drooled over tools, and she told him what she wanted to achieve with the furniture. She needn't have bothered with her research, because Jan was far more knowledgeable and made lots of helpful suggestions and recommendations. After half an hour, she realised Leo had wandered off. When she spotted him chatting away to one of the female shop assistants she felt a familiar flare of irritation.

'He's a friendly guy,' said Jan, observing the direction of her gaze.

'Too friendly,' she said.

'I think it's his way.'

Anna, determined not to discuss it, pointed to a tin of matt paint that had caught her eye and they talked about its suitability before calling Michaela over for her opinion on colours for the bureau. Her eyes sparkled before she pronounced it dull. 'Some colour would be nice. Have you thought about painting the walls of the lounge? It's lovely and light and you could get away with colour. In the winter it's going to look very stark but if you painted the cabinet a warm colour and the walls a dark contrasting colour, it would make it cosy, especially with the open fire. Ludmila has a spare sofa in storage, I'm sure you could borrow that, and we could find some nice throws and cushions. You could make the apartment look so homely.'

'But we're only here for six months,' protested Anna, very half-heartedly. Suddenly she could see the apartment in the coming dark nights and had a vision of amber and dark teal.

'Six months is still time to make a home,' said Michaela.

Anna tilted her head, considering. It could look wonderful and suddenly she was consumed with an urge to make it happen. 'But would Ludmila let us?'

'Ludmila won't mind.' Michaela laughed. 'She loves colour. You should see her apartment. It is full of bright, beautiful things, a treasure chest.'

'I'll think about it but in the meantime…' Anna added a tin of wood paint to the basket along with sandpaper, sanding blocks, replacement sheets for Jan's sanding machine, brushes and masking tape.

Once everything had been paid for, Michaela and Leo began lobbying for a trip to the pub.

'Before we go we must take you around the corner to see the original U Rotta building,' insisted Michaela. After barely a minute's walk they rounded a corner and Anna smiled at the fresco-painted frontage of the elegant structure, which now housed a Hard Rock Café. It was decorated with elaborate leafy motifs as well as several large images of workers using the tools that would have been sold by the original incarnation of the store. The soft yellow paint made it look as if the sun perpetually shone on the building … which of course made her think of Leo.

'We need to get a photo,' said Leo, already taking out his phone and walking to the other side of the square so that he could also capture the extravagant tracery of the ironwork around the fountain in front of the building. 'I can airdrop it to you, Anna.'

When he was satisfied with his pictures, Michaela linked her arm through Anna's. 'Now we can go for a drink. We'll go to the Prague Beer Museum,' she said with a decisive nod.

Jan pulled a face. 'We should go to the Pivnice u Zlatého tygra, Golden Tiger, it's more authentic.'

'Yes but the Beer Museum does flights of beer. They can try more.'

Jan shrugged.

'Sounds good to me,' said Leo, amenable as usual.

As it was only across the street, it seemed an excellent idea, although Anna was worried it sounded a bit touristy. She was relieved to find that it was the sort of unpretentious pub she appreciated, where the focus was on the beer.

With over thirty beers on tap, it took a considerable amount of time and discussion before Anna and Leo opted to share a flight of five beers (rather than the ten that Leo had toyed with) so as to 'maximise the taste opportunities', as he put it.

'I'm going to have the Lucky Bastard, from Brno, Moravia,' said Michaela, 'because it's romantic. It's run by a young married couple and she says the name comes because he has her.'

'Nice,' said Leo.

'I'm going to have the Bernard, which comes from Bohemia,' announced Jan after his careful perusal of the menu.

'You know we're going to want to have a taste of both,' said Leo with one of his cheeky smiles.

Anna sighed and gave Michaela a consoling look. 'Sorry, he's right.'

'We know you now. We wouldn't expect anything else,' teased Michaela, giving her a quick hug.

When the beer arrived, the four of them spent several minutes trying each other's, discussing the merits, laughing and joking.

'It's so nice to have people that appreciate our culture,' said Michaela.

'I could happily live in Prague,' said Leo. 'It's a great city.'

Anna stared at him. Of course, he'd lived in the States and in Italy as well as in London. He was used to travelling and moving around. It had never occurred to her that she could live in another country. For the first time she realised that she felt at home in the city. At home with the people. Despite only being at the brewery for a short time, she'd become fond of the slightly taciturn Jakub and the other workers there, who were all always very keen to help her and educate her. Michaela and Jan had been so welcoming, and, for a change, she felt she belonged. As for Leo...well, having him around was much more of a blessing than she'd ever have thought. At home she'd often been lonely, even in the middle of the pub surrounded by her cousins, Steve and their friends. She was always the outlier, the one that didn't quite fit. Leo, she thought with sudden insight, never allowed her not to fit; he had the ability to scoop her up into the conversation and make sure that she was included. If she was quiet he would check in with a look, a nod and, in the old days, a quick touch of her hand or a gentle nudge, always aware of her. The recollection touched her and she had to fight the urge to lean over and squeeze his hand to say thank you for all the times that he'd done that for her.

'The city is great but you must see some of the countryside while you are here,' said Michaela. 'And some of the other cities. It is the most beautiful country in the world.'

'I think you might be biased,' said Jan, toying with her hair.

'I don't think so. You have to come to the *chata*, don't they, Jan?'

He nodded. 'We're going down in a few weeks. There won't be many more times before the winter but there is work we want to do before the spring. Anna definitely should come. I think she could be very useful.' He winked at her.

Leo pretended to look outraged. 'I could be very useful, too.'

'He could,' said Anna with a straight face, before she added with a teasing smile, 'as long as you don't ask him to put a shelf up or drill a hole in a straight line.'

'She's right,' said Leo with a doleful sniff. 'But –' his irrepressible smile reappeared '– I'm very good at supporting the workers with endless cups of tea and coffee and biscuits. And I'm excellent at sweeping, hoovering and team-building.'

'To be fair,' Anna said, 'he is.'

'In that case you can be on my team,' said Michaela. 'We'll leave Anna and Jan to do the DIY things and we will be the support crew.' She sat up straighter, clearly enthused by the idea. 'Maybe we should cancel our guests and go to the *chata* after all.'

'But then Anna wouldn't be able to come,' Leo pointed out. 'When does the boyfriend arrive?'

Anna's jaw tightened. 'He's not coming now.'

'Oh, no,' said Michaela. 'I'm sorry. Is there a problem?'

'No,' said Anna, trying to sound airy and unaffected, but in the face of the couple's obvious affection for each other, tears pricked her eyes and she felt a little sorry for herself. 'Something came up, so he's had to cancel.'

She deliberately avoided Leo's piercing gaze. She didn't want or need any sympathy. It was fine. Everything was fine.

'Well, I'm sorry for you that he's not coming,' said Michaela, 'but it does mean you can come to dinner on Saturday and meet some people and help me make dumplings.'

'Be careful, Anna,' warned Jan, giving his girlfriend a squeeze. 'It'll be more than dumplings. She'll make you work.'

'I won't…' Michaela pouted a little before saying with a twinkle in her eyes '…maybe I will.'

'I don't mind.' Anna liked being busy and useful and it would stop her worrying about the fact that she wasn't as disappointed as she should be about Steve not coming. They'd been together a while. They were well over the honeymoon period. But it still was a little bit of a kick to her ego that he'd rather play rugby than come and see her. She needed to remind herself that what they had was solid. She never needed to worry that he might look elsewhere. He adored her … and okay, so perhaps he was a bit selfish sometimes but that didn't mean he didn't care about her.

Next to them a group of rowdy lads burst into song, reminding them that it was getting late and they all had work the next day, plus all the DIY purchases to carry home.

As they walked to the metro, Leo fell into step with Anna.

'You okay?' he asked.

'Yes,' she said, not wanting to talk about it.

'I'm sorry about Steve, not coming, I mean. Sorry that I … I was a bit crass.'

'It's fine.'

He nudged her. 'I know you, Anna Love. You always say it's fine when it isn't.'

'Okay, it's not fine but there's nothing I can do about it now.' Her throat was tight but something in Leo's quiet support made her blurt it out. 'He'd rather play rugby than come and see me.'

'Bastard,' said Leo so equably that she burst out laughing.

'I know. I'm being a princess, aren't I?'

'God, no, Anna. Not at all. I was trying to slag him off … but in a nice way because … well, he is your boyfriend.'

With a sigh, Anna turned to him. 'At this moment, feel free. I'm pissed off … more that I'm such a bloody pushover. And this is the beer talking, so don't read too much into it. He's normally very reliable. '

Was it wrong to be talking to Leo like this? Disloyal? She wasn't sure, but he was very good at listening and making her feel that perhaps she deserved a little better.

Chapter Eleven

'I think we should stop now,' he said, putting down the sandpaper, 'before my nails are wrecked. My fingers are worn to the bone. I think we need beer.'

'Leo,' said Anna with a laugh, which is what he'd been aiming for, 'it's half past three in the afternoon and we'll be going to Jan and Michaela's in a few hours.'

He smiled, unabashed. 'But it's five o'clock somewhere.'

'I've only just got started,' she said, gesturing to the wide expanse of table top that she was halfway through rubbing down.

'We started at ten.'

'And stopped for a two-hour lunch, when you dragged me to the coffee bar and a walk in the park.' Both of which he'd done deliberately to stop her brooding. He could tell she was, because of the little furrowed line that kept appearing on her forehead, and it was back again. She'd barely said a word in the last hour. Shame Anna couldn't see what a knobhead her boyfriend was. Fancy cancelling a trip two days before.

'And now it's beer o'clock.' He grinned at her.

'It's not beer o'clock,' she said shaking her head, laughing at him all the same.

'All this sanding is making me thirsty.' He turned pleading eyes on her. 'And we need a new playlist.'

She laughed. 'Don't let me stop you. And it's my turn to choose the music.'

He stuck his bottom lip out and battered his eyelashes at her. 'It's no fun drinking on my own.'

'You're bored, aren't you?' she asked.

'Who, me?' He clutched his dusty shirt.

'I promise you the table is going to look fantastic when it's done.' She turned and surveyed the room. 'This place could look really amazing. Tell you what, I'll let you pick the next playlist.'

'Deal,' said Leo who was done with sanding for the day. He didn't mind hard work but this was beyond tedious and they did need something more comfortable to sit on. It was starting to get too cold to sit outside, and the bistro chairs, which they'd now brought inside to sit on, really weren't that comfortable, not even with the cushions they borrowed from Michaela.

He scrolled through Spotify and with a quick smile selected a dance anthems playlist. As the beat of 'It's My Life' began to pump out through the Bluetooth speaker he'd set up, Anna's head shot up.

'Not fair!' she said, her head already nodding to the beat.

He turned up the volume and watched as her body began to move in rhythmic little bounces.

'Dance with me,' he said, stepping into the empty space of the lounge floor.

'Leo!' she chided but her eyes sparkled, like he knew they would. Anna loved her dance music and she had quite a voice. 'I want to get this done.'

'Don't be boring,' he said. In their flat she'd happily sung along to anthemic choruses in perfect tune, while dancing with unselfconscious musicality.

'I'm not boring.' She glared at him.

'Yes, you are,' he said, knowing he'd found the touchpaper to her fuse. She never turned down a challenge.

She threw down her sandpaper, gave him the side eye and took the hand he held out.

He notched up the volume, the bass thumped out and there she was, instantly appearing in front of him. Anna Love, waving her arms above her head, her hips swinging, her eyes closed as she sang along.

He slipped out to the kitchen to grab two bottles of beer and handed her one. She took a sip before using it as a microphone, bellowing out the lines, her eyes laughing at him as she moved around. Every now and then she'd clink her bottle against his as she spun around, shaking her hair.

'No Limit' came on and she grinned at him, picking up the beat, whirling gracefully like wind through a wheatfield. They danced to another three songs before they both collapsed breathless on the floor.

'God, that was fun,' said Anna laughing up at him,

lifting her bottle to her lips, her eyes dancing with energy and mischief.

It hit him like a lightning bolt and almost felled him on the spot. Anna Love, the woman he'd once loved. There she was again. Shining and happy. It was as if she'd stepped out of a shadow and was suddenly in full colour again, like she'd been six years ago. Inside he felt a quick clutch of fear.

'I'd forgotten,' she said, her eyes turning sad. 'Forgotten what fun … what dancing…' She swallowed and picked at the beer label. He caught the sheen of tears for an instant before she blinked. 'And now you've successfully distracted me. I reckon I can get the rest of this done –' she gestured to the table top '– before we go down to Michaela and Jan's. Damn, I was going to nip and out get something to take.'

'Why don't I nip out now and get some flowers and a case of beer and you can carry on.' He shot her a wink, as much to keep things matey as to hide the nip of alarm. He wasn't going to fall for her again. He couldn't. He might not survive a second time. 'And I'll leave the music on for you.'

As he left the room, he nodded to himself. She was still smiling and singing along as she wielded her sandpaper and block – that line between her eyebrows banished.

A couple of hours later, they stood on their neighbours' doorstep, him clutching a crate of beer while Anna held the bunch of flowers he'd picked up from the little corner shop.

'*Ahoj*,' Jan greeted them and invited them in. There was

already a hubbub of noise coming from the inside of the flat.

'Oh, wow,' said Anna. 'This is lovely.'

'Thanks,' said Jan. 'It's mainly Michaela's work, although I did the floor.'

'It's gorgeous,' she said and immediately bent down to smooth her hand over the wide, oak boards lining the floor. 'And the skirtings.' Leo glanced at them, not really sure what she was talking about. All he noticed was the nice cosy glow created by the soft lighting and the group of people crowded together in the living room.

'Everyone, this is Leo and Anna. They're the Brits upstairs.' Jan pressed a beer into his hand and quickly introduced them to Petra and Andrej, Tereza and Marek, Zdeňka and Lubica. Leo blinked and grinned. 'Nice to meet you all. I'll try and remember all your names.'

'Hello,' said Anna, a little shyly, almost tucking herself behind him.

'Don't worry,' said Zdeňka, smiling back at him from soft brown eyes. He couldn't miss the spark of appreciation there. 'There are only two of you. We will remember your names.'

'Leo,' Michaela greeted him. 'Anna. I'm so happy that you are here.'

'Thank you. These are for you.' Anna handed her the flowers.

'Thank you. Come, take a seat.' She guided Leo to a chair next to the small armchair in which Zdeňka sat with Lubica on her other side. 'Anna, come with me. You wanted to see how dumplings are made.' She led Anna away while

Leo sat down. The two women immediately engaged him in conversation asking him what he thought about Prague, where he lived in England and how long he was staying.

He surveyed the décor and commented on the fine fashion drawings on the walls. 'That's Michaela,' said Zdeňka. 'She's very talented. She makes her own clothes and has an online shop with Lubica.'

Lubica leaned over. 'We make all sorts of things to sell – felt hats, scarves, socks – and Ondřej built the website for us. And Zdeňka looks after our social media. She's an influencer. We were all at school together.'

'Part-time influencer,' Zdeňka added. 'The rest of the time I'm the marketing manager for a commercial property company. It's very dull. I post lots of pictures of offices and empty spaces. It's much more fun doing clothes and accessories. Are you on Instagram?' she asked. 'You could be a model.' She gave the buttons on his shirt a thorough examination as if contemplating undoing them there and then to check out the goods.

'I'm on Instagram,' said Leo. 'Not tried my hand at modelling.' Not his thing at all, even though he'd had quite a few offers over the years, most of which were probably because his stepfather was an Italian movie star, although this summer he'd been approached by a model-agency scout on the beach in Italy.

'You should give it a try. I'd love to feature you on my Insta account. I've got some men's shirts that came in last week.' She eyed him with a predatory gleam in her eye. 'We could have some fun doing a shoot.'

'I bet we could,' he replied with a grin, liking her style.

Direct, pretty and confident, Zdeňka was his kind of woman. Someone who knew the score, was looking for a little fun and not out for commitment. Someone who didn't make his stomach contract in alarm.

'Leo's flat has an amazing roof terrace,' said Jan.

'That sounds perfect.' Zdeňka's eyes widened playfully. 'Tell me more.

'What do you want to know?' asked Leo. 'It has a great view, a table and chairs and it's pretty private.'

Zdeňka whipped out her phone. 'What are you doing the weekend after next?'

Leo laughed, again appreciating her direct, no-nonsense, no-beating-about-the-bush approach. She knew what she wanted and she went out to get it.

'I'm not sure I have any plans yet.'

'And your girlfriend?'

Leo smiled at the not so idle question. 'I don't have one. Anna is my roommate.'

'Ah,' she said, her satisfaction obvious.

'Why don't you come round and inspect my roof terrace?' Leo asked.

'I can do that. Why don't you give me your number?' She handed him her phone.

'You work fast,' he said, his mouth twisting in amusement, taking it from her.

'Why not?' She lifted her shoulders in an elegant shrug, raising her dark brows at him. 'Who comes late harms himself.'

'Zdeňka!' Michaela chided her in a teasing tone. 'Leave him alone. You've only met him.' She took the phone from

Leo and handed it back to her.

'But he's so pretty,' she said with a pout, not seeming the least bit put out at Michaela's intervention. Around them everyone laughed.

'Leo, why don't you come and help me and Anna in the kitchen.' He couldn't help noticing the severe reprimanding glare she sent at Zdeňka as she tugged him away.

The tiny kitchen looked like the aftermath of a party rather than the prelude. There were utensils covering every surface, empty cartons and packets strewn amongst them along with bags of flour and discarded potato skins. In the midst of it all Anna stood over a bowl, using a fork to bind together a mixture of egg, potato and flour. He noticed the counter space immediately around her was clear and chuckled to himself. He could bet she'd been trying to impose some sort of order.

He came to stand behind her, poking his head over her shoulder at the ingredients in the bowl.

'Trust you to turn up when the work's been done,' said Anna with a dramatic heavy sigh, wrinkling her nose. 'She made me grate the potatoes.'

'Of course,' said Michaela, with a gay laugh.

'So what's in them?' Leo nodded down at the bowl.

'Pre-cooked potato, peeled and then grated, then you add flour, egg and some salt.'

Michaela inspected Anna's work.

'That's about done. Now you need to take it and roll it into a cylinder that will fit in this pan.' She pointed to a pan of water heating on the hob.

'Okay,' said Anna.

Leo leaned back against the cabinets, watching her work. As always when she was carrying out a task, she was completely absorbed, her head down and her lips pinched together.

'You can help,' said Michaela, throwing him a tea towel.

'No problem,' he said, crossing to the sink and the haphazard pile of utensils on the drying rack. At any moment the whole lot could come crashing down like Jenga. He gingerly eased one of the larger pans from the top and began to dry it.

'So what's on the menu?'

'We're having traditional roasted duck, with braised red cabbage and potato dumplings.'

'Smells amazing,' said Anna. 'I love red cabbage.'

'So does Jan,' said Michaela as her boyfriend appeared behind her and laid his hands on her shoulders. With four of them in the kitchen it felt very crowded.

'I do.' He squeezed her shoulders and dropped a kiss on the top of her head.

She ignored him and said with a huff, 'But we have to use his mother's recipe because he says it is better than my mother's.'

Jan nodded with a teasing smile on his face.

'And don't get me started about the potato-salad recipe.' She threw her hands up in the air, dislodging his. 'Every family has their own special, potato-salad recipe – it is always different and at every family party we find ourselves with three or four different potato salads because everyone insists on bringing theirs because it is the best. It's crazy.'

Jan pulled back her into his arms and kissed the side of her face. 'It's family,' he said. 'Who needs another drink?'

Leo volunteered to help him serve more drinks, leaving Anna and Michaela to put the dumpling into a pan of boiling water.

'Dinner will be ready in twenty minutes,' advised Michaela as they left the kitchen.

When they were all seated, rather snugly, round a table for six which had been extended with an additional, round bistro table at one end, Leo found himself squeezed in next to Zdeňka. It was quite a crush but everyone seemed in high spirits. Clearly there were some deep-rooted friendships here, judging by the good-natured teasing and banter going on and the obvious affection between them all. He fought the threatening pang of envy and wondered if perhaps his strategy over the last couple of years hadn't been the right one. He'd amassed plenty of casual acquaintances and social friends who kept loneliness at bay, and he had his family, but there was no one who was his alone, and that was how he intended to keep things. Love had not been kind to him and he wasn't about to give it another chance.

He turned back to Zdeňka as she poured him a glass of wine and focused on flirting with her as Michaela and Jan brought out several laden plates which they placed on the already crowded table.

'Please help yourself, Leo,' said Michaela. 'This is a typical Czech meal.'

Leo didn't know that much about Czech food and asked

what was typical. Over the next ten minutes he was bombarded with suggestions of what he should try.

'You should try Baramboky – that is a good restaurant,' said Tereza on his left.

'Or Cestr.'

'If you like desserts, try Eska,' came another suggestion.

'And their burnt potatoes in ash.'

'There are so many great places to eat, and not just in Prague,' said Petra. 'You should try visiting South Moravia or the Bohemian countryside.'

'And Slovakia,' said Lubica. Everyone laughed.

'Explain to me. You were Czechoslovakia. When you split in two, was there bad feeling between the two?' Leo was intrigued by this.

Again everyone laughed. 'No, we're sisters,' explained Lubica.

'Best friends,' said Jan.

With everyone smiling and tucking into their food, Leo decided the question had been answered, so he asked another that had been plaguing him. 'I've seen a few Vietnamese places, which seems odd because we're a pretty long way from Vietnam and I've not seen much evidence of other ethnic cultures.'

Petra smiled. 'It comes from the communist times. Vietnam was also a communist country, so we had good relations with the state. A lot of Vietnamese people came here as guest workers and when communism fell, they stayed. There is actually a huge Vietnamese market in Prague. It's called SAPA or Little Hanoi and if you like Vietnamese food, it's definitely worth a visit.'

'I had no idea. You learn something new every day. Which is why it's great to be here for a while, to learn more about the country. I've lived in the States, Italy and the UK.'

'That's very lucky. Imagine our grandparents, they weren't able to travel during the communist regime. That's why our *chatas* are so popular. It was a place to escape to in the country. We're all excited to visit Michaela and Jan's country house when it's ready. Knowing Michaela and Jan, it will be amazing.'

'They've definitely got an eye,' said Leo, glancing around the room. The layout was very different from the flat upstairs and although it didn't have as much character, Michaela and Jan had made the most of it. A cosy, wood burner sat in a corner of the room against a sage-green wall. Black floating shelves contained ornaments, vases and lamps and the wall was decorated with black-framed pictures. The remaining walls were cream, and one of them had been left unornamented so as to set off a large palm plant. The big L-shaped sofa covered in terracotta linen was dotted with cushions and throws in various shades of dark green and umber. It gave the room a warm, earthy feel which made it easy to relax. It was stylish without being pretentious, comfortable without being cluttered.

He could see Anna looking around. Did it remind her, like him, that their apartment, even with the addition of her soon-to-be-refurbished furniture, was rather sparse? But it was starting to feel like home, especially this last week and today. He'd got used to her being around, got used to cooking for two, got used to chatting over his day with her, arguing about what music they should play, her bossing him about the bits he'd missed when sanding the chairs. He'd got used to her quick smile when he teased her, the pensive look on her face when she was lost in thought and the sight of her legs and the scent of her hair when she was fresh out of the shower in her cotton robe – the one that he could see her nipples through, although he hadn't pointed that out to her.

'Leo?' Zdeňka's voice interrupted his thoughts.

'Sorry, I was miles away,' he apologised.

'Somewhere nice, I think,' she said in a throaty murmur.

Leo took a hasty gulp of wine, willing the image of Anna's smooth skin and small, pert breasts out of his head. That way lay madness – plus, she had a boyfriend. He was much better off focusing on the here and now, rather than the past. Zdeňka was gorgeous and available and also secure enough in herself to trust him.

'How long have you been an influencer and how does it work?' he asked, regaining his equilibrium and resorting to tried and tested small talk. Thankfully it was a subject that Zdeňka was only too happy to expand upon and he was able to listen and nod, while corralling his wayward brain away from the sort of thoughts that could only lead him into trouble.

Chapter Twelve

I t would have been impossible to miss the woman with bright blue hair and an equally bright smile who was standing waiting at 38 Dlouhá, the meeting point for the Best of Prague food tour.

The morning air was chillier than of late but that was only to be expected now they were moving into early October. Leo had bought firewood so he could light the wood burner in the lounge, an idea that had definite appeal. Although Leo, being Leo, hadn't actually got round to buying the kindling or firelighters, so they'd yet to enjoy its cosy warmth.

'Hi, I'm Agáta,' said the woman with the blue hair, looking up from her clipboard. 'And you are?'

'I'm Anna and—'

He, of course, stepped forward to say, 'Leo. Nice to meet you. I'm really looking forward to this tour. Although four hours of eating is going some.'

Agáta laughed and responded to his open, friendly smile – just like everyone did, Anna thought.

'Ah, you're from *Sdílená Kultura* . Very nice to meet you. Jiří says I have to look after you well.' She grinned, her bright red lipstick widening her smile. 'It will be my pleasure. And it is not all eating, there is quite a lot of walking, too.'

She could almost see the sparks of energy radiating from the woman. For a moment she wished she had that kind of presence that made people notice you straight away. Anna tended to fade into the background and people didn't see her. Sometimes she felt invisible, especially next to her loud and overachieving second family, who were all brilliant at sport and outdoor things.

The wonderful thing about Leo was that he *had* seen her. Made her feel beautiful, special and a person in her own right. But then again, she'd learned over the months they were married that he had that magical gift of making *everyone* he spoke to feel that they were important. If he was charismatic, she was the opposite – was there even a word for it? Uncharismatic?

'We're waiting for some other British tourists and then we can go.'

Anna nodded and gazed around her, looking at the worn cobbles lining the narrow street, filled with quiet, solid buildings which looked as if they'd been sheltering their residents for hundreds of years. Everywhere she looked, the city was layered with history that gave it an atmosphere all of its own. She didn't think she'd been to another European city quite like it.

'Amazing, isn't it,' Leo said and she glanced round to find that he'd gravitated to her side rather than Agáta's. 'The city. I think you could stay here for a year and still find something new to see. I love exploring new places, don't you?'

Anna hadn't ever really thought about it, and now it was like the sun coming out inside her as the realisation dawned: yes, she did like exploring new places. Her second family tended to prefer the gravitational pull of their own home and village, and none of them had moved away, so she'd tended to frame her life in their terms. This sudden observation made her realise she had set quite a lot of limits upon her habits and routines.

'Do you know what?' she said with sudden vigour that clearly took Leo aback, because his eyes widened. 'I do. It's not something I've done enough of. I'm going to pick a new place to visit every weekend while I'm here.' Steve had now booked flights for the following weekend but she felt she'd wasted time already waiting for him before exploring.

'That's a great idea,' said Leo. 'We should make a list. And top of it has to be Prague Castle because we still haven't done that.'

Anna's heart jumped a little at his use of 'we' but if she was honest she rather liked the idea of having someone else to explore with, other than Steve. Someone to get lost with, someone to share the highs and the lows with. 'There's a bar that overlooks the Old Town square that's a must do. That's going on the list.'

She pulled out the paper diary that she still carried and

opened it at a notes page where she began to scribble a couple of ideas.

'You do know you could use the notes app on your phone.' Leo nudged her, bringing her back to the present.

Agáta gathered everyone round and gave them a brief introduction to the tour. 'Prague is a food hotspot. Czechs have been rediscovering a taste for food which has exploded within the last ten years. You may know that until 1989, we were under communist rule. During that time all the restaurants had to have the same menu with the same food and the same prices.'

'No!' breathed Anna and Leo in unison and caught each other's eyes.

'God, that sounds miserable,' said Leo, as Agáta handed out some black-and-white photographs that captured examples of bygone menus.

'Not so now,' said Agáta enthusiastically. 'Now we have artisan food all over the city, all over the country. And I'm going to take you to our most famous product. Anyone guess what that is?'

'Beer,' said Leo and Anna in unison again.

'That's right,' she said as the two of them smiled at each other.

Marshalling them along the pavement and keeping up a steady stream of chat, Agáta steered them into a stone-built pub on the corner of the next street. Although it was only eleven o'clock in the morning, the place was already filling up with early lunchers. She sat them down at a long trestle table that had been reserved for them and explained about the different beer styles, while Leo and Anna exchanged slightly smug grins because they knew this stuff already.

'Wonder if anyone will go for the *mlíko*?' whispered Leo in Anna's ear and she couldn't help but smile back at him as they heard both of the middle-aged Englishmen in the party voice their disgust at the idea of a pint which was predominantly foam. 'If I'm paying for a pint I want a pint,' one of them said, so loudly that his wife gave him an embarrassed poke in the ribs. 'Colin,' she hissed.

'Well, it's just a gimmick.'

Anna knew it was this rudeness and Agáta's forced polite smile that made Leo pipe up, 'Two *mlíkos* here, please, Agáta.'

Anna was a little bit proud of him as Agáta shot him a grateful look.

When the beers arrived, so too did a selection of dishes for everyone to try. Colin eyed Leo and Anna's foam-topped beer with a sneer. 'Looks like you were cheated there.'

'Don't think so,' said Leo with his usual geniality, tapping his glass against Anna's. '*Na zdraví.*'

'Very good,' said Agáta, her words warm with approval.

'Tastes lovely and the great thing is, it doesn't make you feel bloated,' he announced to the table at large, with an irrepressible grin that prevented it sounding as if he were giving a lecture. 'We've got a full day ahead of us. I don't want to peak too early.' He patted his perfectly flat stomach in a comical gesture that had the other woman laughing, although not Colin.

'This is very typical Czech food,' explained Agáta,

indicating the plates in the centre of the table. She waved a hand in the direction of each, 'Pork Schnitzel with potato salad, a selection of sausages with mustard, marinated Hermelín cheese, fried cheese with tartare sauce, and this, my friends, is marinated carp with onions, which is a very traditional Czech dish. It's normally served as a main dish but I wanted you to try it.'

'Carp,' hissed Colin to his wife and friends. 'I'm not trying that. It's a bottom feeder, disgusting. Any fisherman knows that.'

'Shh,' whispered his wife.

Agáta smiled gamely. 'The carp is kept in fresh water for a few days, which cleans out the mud from the veins. Try it, it's delicious.'

'I notice you're not eating anything,' said Colin. Anna couldn't believe his rudeness.

With another of her gracious smiles Agáta said, 'If I ate with every tour I would be as big as the castle. Have you been there yet?'

Colin's grunt was audible enough that Leo leaned over the man, took a piece of the fish and onion, put it on his side plate and then forked some up and tasted it. In the spirit of solidarity, though she wasn't particularly a fish lover, Anna followed suit.

'Wow, that is really good,' she said with genuine surprise. 'I'm not great on fish but that is lovely.' She smiled at Colin's wife. 'You should try it.'

The woman leaned over her husband and took a piece, while he muttered under his breath.

'Anna, you've got to try this cheese,' said Leo,

immediately handing the marinated cheese dish to her, his face lit up with his usual enthusiasm. Being with him made her so much braver and bolder and without a qualm she took a piece of the cheese. She'd barely swallowed the first mouthful before he was asking what she thought. 'Do you like it?'

'Yes, it's really good.'

Agáta chipped in, explaining how the cheese was produced, her eyes lighting up with passion for her subject. Anna envied her that unselfconscious ability to be herself. She was exactly the sort of person Leo was always drawn to. They were like two sides of the same coin. Bright, bubbly and super-confident.

As they sampled their way through the dishes, Leo's infectious interest spread around the table and soon everyone in their separate groups began to loosen up and share notes and opinions on the different foods. The atmosphere was warmed by good company and beer. Leo handed the plate of carp across the table.

'Go on, Colin,' he said, 'Give it a try. You wouldn't want to upset our lovely hostess, would you?' Once again, as Colin's wife clapped a hand over her mouth, hiding her amusement, Anna reflected on how her ex-husband was such a charmer.

Colin, shaking his head, took the plate, saying, 'You're a one and that's a fact, lad.' To his credit he took a mouthful and chomped away as everyone watched him.

'That wasn't bad at all,' he announced to a quick round of applause. He took a quick bow. 'Not sure I'd choose it again, mind.'

From there they moved on down the street to Nase Maso, a very smart butcher's shop where Agáta explained how the owners worked with specific farmers in the Czech Republic to ensure the best quality meat. 'They make their own sausages and smoked meats from traditional recipes. We are here to try their famous meatloaf, which is very popular.'

There was no doubting the popularity of the shop as there was a constant queue crowding into the spotless space, with its white-tiled walls and floors and huge, glass cabinets displaying an array of products. Anna had never thought that a butcher's shop could be so trendy but they'd definitely nailed it here. As she was examining one of the fridges containing a plethora of interesting-looking sauces and broths that made her mouth water and want to cook, Leo leaned down next to her and said, almost as if he'd read her mind, 'I could buy some of that beef and some of the *Lokal* sauce. We could have it for our dinner.'

'Sounds like a plan,' she said, unconsciously echoing him.

'Love it when a plan comes together.'

As Leo was buying the food, one of the women sighed. 'This meat looks amazing. We're staying in a hotel. Are you in an Airbnb?'

Anna explained – and got quite a kick out of it – that she and Leo were living here for several months.

'Oh, how wonderful. And together.' She leaned in with a smile. 'The two of you do make a lovely couple.'

Anna stared at her for a second. The woman looked sincere. It gave Anna an unexpected jolt. She always assumed that everyone wondered how on earth she'd managed to snag Leo, who was so obviously out of her league.

'Make the most of it. I wish I'd done something like that at your age. How wonderful to be able to immerse yourself in the city. This is my fourth visit and I love it. Can I give you a tip? The Wallenstein Gardens. They're not far from the Charles Bridge on the other side and on a busy day there are never that many tourists. It's a really lovely place to sit and be quiet right in the middle of the city.'

'I'll add it to my list,' said Anna, taking out her phone and opening up the notes app.

'I'm guessing that could be a very long list,' the other woman teased. 'You should go to one of the theatres. You're spoilt for choice here. Opera, ballet, plays and black-light theatre – you don't need to speak the language. There's mime, puppets and quite a few English-speaking productions.'

After another snack, of *chlebíček*, open sandwiches, which they ate in a little covered arcade between the butcher's and a charming bistro called Sisters, Agáta rounded them up and like obedient sheep they trotted after her. Leo fell into step with Anna still munching on one of the sandwiches.

'Who knew egg and sundried tomato would be such a tasty combination?' he said as they walked along.

'I don't know where you put it.' Anna's waistband already felt a little snug and they were headed to a restaurant for lunch where no doubt there'd be more treats in store. Thankfully it was a half-hour walk to their destination, which she hoped would help build her appetite.

Leo gave her his usual disarming smile. 'High metabolism, Love.'

The word gave her a start and she wondered if he'd even noticed that he'd used it. She remembered the first time he'd said it to her. They were going out for dinner and, emboldened by his admiration, she'd opted for a slightly more daring dress than she'd normally wear, which was daring in itself because she hardly ever wore dresses. It showed what little cleavage she had and clung to her hips. Leo's dumbstruck look when she'd walked in the room in the bright red dress amazed her and all her self-consciousness had faded away the minute he said, 'Looooove,' and walked up to her and kissed her soundly on the lips. She wondered if he still fancied her or was indifferent to her now. Her heart lurched in her chest, as if shying away from the thought that he might be indifferent. It shouldn't hurt because she shouldn't care, but she did, a little bit.

The restaurant contrasted dramatically with the pub they'd started in. A wall of glass windows formed a backdrop for a long table where they seated themselves, with smart waiting staff in black and white hovering attentively.

'Reminds me of our first date in London,' murmured Leo in her ear, as, with those impeccable manners of his, he pulled out one of the bentwood chairs for her.

Anna's mouth quirked at the memory. The date had been a disaster, the restaurant too formal and the hushed silence inhibiting. It was only when they'd stepped outside into the dark rainy night and he'd hurriedly confessed with boyish earnestness that he was trying to impress her that she'd realised he was serious about her. Leo Knight was interested in Anna Love. It had been one of those magical earth-tilting moments. It would be so easy to fall back under Leo's sunbeam-fuelled spell, to enjoy the sunshine of life with him and a carefree existence … though one she knew was without substance. And she couldn't do that. He treated everyone with the same easy charm. With a fixed smile she turned to her neighbour on the other side, the nice American woman, Louella.

'What do you think of the tour?' she asked, almost wincing at the trite small-talk opening.

'It's a gem,' said Louella. 'It was recommended by some friends who were here last fall. It's quite a marathon but that girl's so knowledgeable and it's like she really wants us to find the best food in Prague. I love that she's so enthusiastic. Almost evangelical. It makes a nice change, you know, when someone's really proud of their country. It's only a little place but they punch above their weight. Have you been to any of the towns outside of Prague? Just gorgeous.'

'I've got some on the list.'

'Well, you make sure you visit them, honey. Life is too short not to do as much as you can while you're on this earth. My Walt died last year and we didn't travel because there was always a reason we shouldn't. I really regret that. Make the most of every moment.' Her eyes shone with tears and she put a hand on Anna's wrist. 'Don't ever think there's always tomorrow. Do things now because you can, don't put them off.'

The insistence in her quiet voice as her eyes held Anna's made her remember her mother and her positive attitude. When she answered, 'I will,' she felt like she was making a promise to her mother.

'Make sure you do,' Louella said, patting Anna's hand. 'You make sure you do.' And with a complete about-turn as if the moment between them hadn't happened, she said, 'What do you think of this wine. Rather lovely, isn't it?'

Anna agreed as she took a sip of the pale golden wine. This one was a *tramín* from Znojmo in South Moravia and was characterised by its hints of roses, or so Agáta told them. Anna knew she liked the delicate floral flavour of the dry wine.

The group worked their way through another succession of delicious dishes, including an amazing piece of beef with a rich root-vegetable sauce, which Anna decided was her absolute favourite. The beef was melt-in-the-mouth and the thick accompanying sauce was sweet and creamy. She was also taken with the bread dumplings, which were light and fluffy, like no other dumplings she'd ever tried, as well as the *Přeštice* pork sausages and the grilled asparagus in hollandaise sauce. Everything was perfectly cooked and it was difficult not to eat too much because it was all so wonderful.

The next call was Eska, a buzzy, busy bakery with a trendy vibe within that Agáta explained was an old fabric factory. With clever styling, the interior retained its open airiness but also managed to be welcoming, bright and chic.

Initially they were served the house speciality: burnt potatoes with ash and cream espuma, a foamy concoction that set the subtle potato flavour off to perfection. Anna really didn't think she could eat anything else but then the pastries appeared, modern takes on traditional Czech desserts, so she had to try a tiny bit of each. Once again Leo was sitting next to her.

'Do you think we could take some home?' she whispered to him. 'I don't want to waste them but I can't eat any more. This *větrník* is divine. I love the caramel icing *and* the cream filling *and* the choux pastry.'

'I'll eat yours,' said Leo, a hopeful gleam in his eye as he looked at her plate.

'Leo, you can't possibly eat any more,' she squealed with mock outrage.

'Try me.'

'You can't.' She laughed as he pouted.

He pretended to think about it for a moment before giving her a rueful smile. 'No, don't think I can. God, we've been spoiled today. I'm definitely going to ask for a doggy bag – and take these home. We can have them for breakfast tomorrow. My treat,' he said with a mischievous wink.

'Your treat, you cheeky beggar. Don't think I've forgotten you helping yourself to my bolognese sauce.'

'Yes, you have,' he chided with a teasing smirk. 'You know you have.'

'You're so cocky, you know that.'

'Yup but you love it.'

His confident throwaway response hit her unexpectedly hard. She had loved that about him, loved and feared it –

and for a static-filled minute, despite being surrounded by other people, she stared at him and he stared back.

'Mmm,' she said, not knowing what to say. She picked up her fork and shoved a mouthful of the pastry into her mouth. He did the same.

'Good, eh?' said Agáta, oblivious to the tension between them.

'Very good,' said Leo through a mouthful of cream and choux. 'A bit too good. I was discussing with Anna whether we could take a doggy bag home.'

'It is a frequent question,' replied Agáta with another of her boisterous laughs. 'They have little boxes for this very reason. Next we will go for a cocktail made with traditional Czech Becherovka which was created for stomach problems, so it is an excellent digestif.'

After leaving the bakery, armed with boxes and bags as the café sold their own coffee, which Leo insisted on buying, as well as a cellophane-wrapped packet of gingerbread, they walked the short distance to Liquid Office, another well-designed modern space with a central bar lined with bar stools where they finished off the day with their signature Becherovka sour, made with gin, yuzu, bergamot and basil. Anna decided it was like an early taste of Christmas and immediately wondered what the festive season would bring. She hadn't booked her flight home for Christmas, hadn't given it that much thought. A very small part of her rather liked the idea of staying holed up in the apartment on her own with a pile of good books, the wood burner – she'd need to learn how to light the thing – and a cosy blanket. Christmas at her aunt and uncle's was always so bloody competitive and active with games, pub quizzes, football and rugby. It was exhausting and the New Year's Eve party at the rugby club had been the same for the last five years: very loud, with the same old faces, same conversations.

Doing something different for a change was very appealing, although she doubted very much she could persuade Steve to come over and spend Christmas here. He'd want to spend the festive season with her family, heading off for the annual Boxing Day football match. He fitted in perfectly with them; better than her, in fact. What would Leo be doing for Christmas? Would he stay here or head off somewhere exotic and glamorous with his family? She couldn't imagine he'd want to stay here with her.

Chapter Thirteen

Anna closed the door of the apartment and skipped down the stairs on her way to the airport. She was looking forward to seeing Steve. Looking forward to being special to someone. Seeing the way Jan and Michaela were with each other made her long for that feeling of being one of two.

'Someone is in a hurry.' Ludmila appeared in her doorway looking trim and immaculate in what Anna thought might be a Chanel suit.

'I'm going to the airport to pick up my boyfriend.'

'I hope he's as handsome as the young man you're living with. Now he is something. A good, kind, decent man. Always has a smile for me. Carried my shopping home for me the other day.'

'Sounds like Leo,' said Anna, with a bland smile. She really did not want to be talking about him.

'Michaela tells me you used to be married.'

Thanks, Michaela. Anna stared at the older woman, a

little nonplussed by the segue. 'Yes, but it was a long time ago. We were very young. We've both changed since then.' She definitely had. No longer young and idealistic about relationships.

Ludmila gave her a long, direct stare before she said, 'People do change but their basic essence never does. He has good values. A kind heart. And joie de vivre, a zest for life.'

Anna nodded. She really didn't want to discuss Leo's virtues. She was well acquainted with them. That was why she'd married him in the first place. These days she set much greater store on steadiness and reliability. Joie de vivre was all very well but it didn't provide much stability. In her view, you never quite knew where you were with it.

Annoyingly these thoughts continued to plague her all the way to the airport. It seemed she was never going to get Leo out of her head.

The smell of roses wafted under Anna's nose from a gorgeous bouquet held by the man standing on her left, as they waited for people to come through the arrivals hall. It immediately reminded her of Leo. It was exactly the sort of thing he might do. When she glanced at the man and caught his eye, he flashed her a sheepish smile. She smiled back at him. Romance wasn't dead. Anna wondered how long it had been since this man had seen the person he was waiting for. It made her heart warm a little as she watched him shift from foot to foot, unable to keep still. Pent-up excitement and anticipation were bursting out of him. For a moment she felt a touch of envy. This man must still be in the early throes of the relationship, when everything was bright and shiny. Then she told herself off. She was looking forward to seeing Steve and they'd have a nice weekend together. But it was true that theirs was a grown-up, mature relationship that had flattened out into a steady ship that weathered the ups and downs of life with calm continuity. Still, it was a good way to be.

The man suddenly tensed, his gaze fixed on a woman walking through the glass double doors, and she could almost feel the emotion fizzing out of him. It reminded her of how things had been with Leo when she'd first met him. He was like a firework bursting into her life and she'd been dazzled. Though look where that had got her. She'd been constantly uncertain, never sure if those feelings were genuine. Flashy acts of generosity or romance did not equate to solid dependability. Life with Steve was less blinding but she preferred the feeling of knowing exactly where she was with him. He loved her and if it was a quiet, undemonstrative love, it was no less worthwhile than that of someone who made extravagant gestures.

When she looked up, breaking away from her thoughts, there was Steve ambling forward towards her.

'Hey,' she said with a bright smile, pleased to see him at last.

'Hey yourself.' He wrapped an arm around her and kissed her briefly on the mouth. 'Good to see you. Missed you. Bet you missed me, haven't you?' He winked at her and his hand dropped to squeeze her bottom.

'Mmm,' she said, smartly moving his hand to her waist. 'What are you like?'

He nuzzled her ear. 'You know what absence makes?'

She smiled at him just as he said, 'Very blue balls. Can't wait for a little me and you time.'

'Is that all you think about?' she teased.

'Mostly,' he said with a naughty smirk.

'Come on.' She led him towards the front of the airport building where they joined the queue at the taxi rank, which moved very quickly.

'How was your flight?' she asked as they slid into the back seat of the taxi.

'The flight was okay. It was getting up at four with a hangover that was a killer, especially when we didn't get in until after one.'

'Poor you,' said Anna with an unsympathetic grin. 'That's what you get for going to the rugby club on a Friday evening.'

'It was a good night, though.' He put his arm around her shoulders and drew her closer to him. 'James, Tim and your Uncle Henry were on top form. Right laugh. Then after, we ended up the Punjab curry house and –' he winced '– to be honest, it turned into a bit of a sesh.'

'I can tell.' Anna wrinkled her nose at the slight scent of spices on his breath.

'You don't mind,' he said in the comfortable tone of someone who'd got away with it every previous time. Anna squelched the thought that perhaps for once he might have forgone the Friday night piss-up when he was travelling to see her the next morning.

'I've got some great news, though. Did you know the Czech Republic are playing England tonight in a friendly?' His face lit up in a lopsided grin.

'No,' said Anna with a smile before adding, dryly. 'I hope you're not going to suggest we watch it in a pub somewhere.'

He shook his head, his eyes alight with excitement. 'Even better than that.'

She gave him a quizzical look.

'I've managed to snag us tickets for the Letná Stadium.' With the flourish of a magician producing a rabbit out of a hat he pulled his phone out of his pocket and waved it, looking delighted with himself. 'Stroke of luck I got them. Literally just before the cabin crew made us switch off WiFi. I couldn't believe it!'

'But … I've booked a boat tour. Dinner.'

'Yeah, but this is England. What are the chances? While you're here?' He beamed at her and then his face fell. 'But of course we don't have to go. Not if you really don't want to.'

Anna swallowed, hating being a pushover. Steve did love his sport.

'What time's the game?'

'Kick-off is at six-thirty.' He beamed again, assuming her acceptance. 'I promise you it will be great. You'll love it.'

Loath to fall out when he'd just arrived, she simply nodded. What else could she do?

When they arrived at the flat. Leo looked up from where he was working on one of the chairs in the living room. 'Hey Steve, how you doing?'

Steve stiffened. He'd been dismayed when Anna had explained why she hadn't been able to move out of the flat, and now she was immediately reminded of a dog warily sussing out its territory. She felt guilty that she'd lied, saying she and Leo barely saw each her. She could tell that he wasn't comfortable with Leo's easy familiarity and didn't like being the outsider. It was going to be very tedious if the two of them were going to play pissing contests all weekend. Anna couldn't imagine what it would be like if Steve had any inkling that she and Leo had known each other, let alone been married. A little ball of fear nestled in her stomach like a spiky burr making itself felt.

'We can't,' said Anna, as Steve's hand burrowed into her bra.

'I haven't seen you for weeks,' he said, kissing her again, his hand unbuttoning her shirt.

They were sitting on her bed, the beers abandoned on the side table and Steve's overnight bag dumped by the door. He'd started making amorous overtures the minute it had closed.

'Leo's in,' hissed Anna. 'He'll know.'

'He'll know what?'

Anna blushed. 'That we're having sex.'

Steve's head lifted and he looked at her with a sly smile. 'And what's wrong with that?'

Was he doing this on purpose to make a point?

He pushed her back on the bed, kissing her more deeply. 'God I've missed you.'

His low groan stirred something in her and she began to reciprocate although she was horribly conscious that Leo was about. Thankfully Steve was too busy with his hands skimming over her body to expect any response. Although she was enjoying his touch, she hadn't been yearning for it and the sex was how it always was – nice and straightforward.

He came with a noisy shout and Anna, beneath him, winced, hoping that Leo hadn't heard.

'Sorry, babe, I know you didn't get there,' he said collapsing on top of her.

She simply stroked his back. There was nothing to say. It was nothing new. They'd been together for two years and of course the excitement and passion had died down, although occasionally she wished he would slow down and focus on her but Steve didn't like talking about sex. Actually that wasn't fair, he wasn't capable of talking about it. Whenever she tried to broach what she might like in bed he reverted to schoolboy humour and became silly and childish. He was a terrible prude.

She sighed. He rolled off her and, misinterpreting her sigh, said, 'Glad it was good for you. God, I'm knackered. You've worn me out.'

Within minutes he was snoring softly.

Anna lay there for a quarter of an hour listening to him, conscious of time ticking away, before she finally poked him. It was after twelve and they still had the afternoon, although she'd have to cancel the planned boat trip. Despite her prod in his ribs, he didn't wake.

'Steve.' She shook him but he shrugged her off.

'Let me sleep,' he said and turned over to burrow deeper into bed. Irritated with him, she decided to leave him be. No point in starting an argument. Instead she decided to take a quick shower and slipped out of the bedroom and across the hall, praying that Leo wouldn't come downstairs. From above she could hear the sound of the music playing on his Spotify account. She smiled, thinking of their gentle bickering as they'd put their combined playlist together. A wave of sadness washed over her and she couldn't think where it had come from.

Steve was still dead to the world when Anna came back to the bedroom to dress. She glared at his sleeping form, wrinkling her nose at the pungent fart that he'd let out. She vented her fury on the bedroom door as she slammed it behind her and went upstairs to the lounge. This was nothing new. Why the hell did she put up with it? When had she started allowing this sort of behaviour? Was it because going out with Steve had made her approval ratings within her family soar and she was loath to rock the boat?

Leo looked up as she marched in. 'Don't say a word,' she growled.

His mouth closed with a snap and, focusing on the sandpaper block in his hand as if it was the most important thing in the world, he went back to rubbing down one of the chairs she'd rescued from the skip.

Anna stormed into the kitchen, grabbed another beer and, passing Leo again, strode out onto the roof terrace. Leaning against the rail she stared over the rooftops. In a short while she'd come to love the area; it was so green, quiet and restful. Living with Leo was actually a lot of fun and not what she had been expecting – had she imagined how messy he used to be? She shuddered and let out a quick laugh. No, there was no way anyone could forget how untidy he was. When had that changed?

'You okay?' Leo's voice came from the open door.

She turned and nodded.

'Mind if I join you?' Typical Leo that he'd ask – and she knew if she said yes, he would retreat without taking offence.

'No.' She managed to dredge up a smile for him, suddenly appreciating his quiet presence.

'I take it back about the furniture,' he said, his back to the rail, tilting his head back and lifting a bottle of beer to his lips. In that moment, doused in sunlight, he looked strong and handsome. She watched him swallow, stifling an urge to run a hand down the strong column of his throat.

He flashed her a smile. 'It's looking good.'

So was he. And what was wrong with her? She'd just got out of bed with another man. A man she loved. Didn't she?

Flustered by the unwelcome thoughts, she answered quickly, 'It is, isn't it?' She filled the quick pause. 'When did you have your Damascene conversion to tidiness?'

'What conversion?'

'A biblical reference. It means a complete about-face. You're not messy anymore.'

Leo laughed. 'You noticed.'

'Couldn't fail to miss it. Back then it was like living with a human tornado. What happened?' With a teasing smile, she prodded his arm. 'Is this the same Leo, or a Dr Who regeneration?'

'I'm pretty sure Dr Who was the same but looked

165

different,' said Leo, his brow puckering as if giving the matter serious consideration.

'You know what I mean.'

'Maybe I grew up,' said Leo with a quick shrug that immediately made Anna think he was hiding something.

'Lover boy sleeping off his hangover?' asked Leo, his face suddenly lighting up with a grin.

She pursed her lips. 'Unfortunately.'

'I'm about to make some lunch. Fancy a bite? You can wake him when it's ready.'

'Huh! He can bloody go without,' said Anna, grateful that their conversation had definitely moved on.

When Steve woke up, she was going to make it very clear to him that she was less than impressed.

Chapter Fourteen

'Seven, eight. This is it,' announced Anna, coming to a halt in front of a statue on the Charles Bridge. It was obvious that this was the correct one from the bright patches on the plaque beneath the statue of St John of Nepomuk.

'And why do we have to touch it?' asked Steve, looking up from his phone.

'Because,' Anna said impatiently, having told him this five minutes ago, 'it's supposed to bring good luck and ensure you come back to Prague.'

'And who is this geezer?' Steve stepped back and craned his neck to study the robed figure with a halo of stars around his head.

'He was priest to the Queen,' she told him, hoping no one had heard him being so disrespectful. 'But when he refused to tell her husband, King Wenceslas—'

'Wenceslas! That's not a real king ... is it?'

'Yes, King Wenceslas IV, to be precise.'

'I thought he was some chap in a Christmas carol.'

Anna heaved out a sigh of exasperation but bit back her instinctive retort that he was being a dick. They'd already had a row when she complained about him being hungover and not making an effort for their first weekend together in weeks. 'He was a real king who had the priest thrown into the river when he refused to reveal the content of the Queen's confession. The priest drowned.'

'Not so lucky for him then,' said Steve, peering over the parapet of the bridge as if he expected to see the priest floating by. They watched one of the boats come out from under the bridge. 'It's quite a river. Wide. I wouldn't mind going out on a boat next time.'

'If you hadn't booked tickets for the football, we would have done.'

'Anna, give it a rest. Admit it, the football was worth coming to Prague for.'

'What, and I wasn't?'

He slid an arm around her. 'Of course you were. The game was an added bonus.'

Anna forced a smile. The game had been a very long ninety minutes in which they'd had to keep very quiet when England scored because they were seated at the wrong end. Dinner had been a snatched doner kebab from outside the tram stop. The evening had fallen a long way short of the romantic date night she'd planned.

While Steve was squinting back down at his phone, Anna's attention was caught by a couple further along the bridge by another statue. Her interest piqued no end when he dropped to one knee. The woman's face was a picture of bright shock and happiness that brought an instant smile to Anna's face. She watched them, her own heart expanding for them, as he rose to his feet and she threw her arms around him. They embraced, talking excitedly to one another, their bubbling enthusiasm almost palpable. Anna's smile widened and the man glanced over and caught her eye. She grinned at him, responding to the delight glowing from his face, and put her thumbs up before nudging Steve in the ribs. Glued to his phone, he was oblivious and grunted, 'What?'

The newly engaged man held up his phone and gestured to Anna. 'Would you mind taking a picture of us?'

She smiled at his strong accent and, delighted to be asked, walked quickly towards them to take the proffered mobile.

'I'd love to and many congratulations. You from Ireland?' She squinted at his face, recognition glimmering.

'Yes, from Kerry.'

Then it clicked. 'You're Connor Byrne, the chef?'

'I used to be,' he said with a grin. 'I'm plain aul' Connor Byrne these days and this is my beautiful bride-to-be, Hannah.' He beamed proudly at Anna while Hannah rolled her eyes with a good-natured but nonetheless sparkly grin. 'He's the romantic.' Despite her words, she shot him a look full of love that made Anna's heart ache just a little.

Steve, who'd followed her blindly, still engrossed in the screen of his phone, barely glanced up.

'That's lovely. I hope you'll be very happy,' said Anna, feeling oddly tearful on their behalf. They did indeed both look happy. Like a sunbeam slicing through dark clouds, a memory lit up in her head – of her and Leo standing on the steps of Chelsea Register office, bursting with bright hope for everything in front of them, and feeling then that it was all within their grasp. Something squeezed in her chest like an accordion and she wished she could turn the clock back to that time, when there were still so many possibilities, when the future was the sunrise of a new day. When she'd been crazy in love with Leo.

Sharp pain gripped her heart, binding it tight with regret and sorrow. She sucked in a quick breath.

That had been the problem – she'd been so in love with him it had scared her. Once they were married, the fear that she couldn't hold on to him had grown week by week. Especially when Savannah Aitken, with her perfect figure, girlish laugh and long-hair-tossing charm, came along. Losing him like she'd lost her parents would be terrible. And yet she'd lost him, anyway. Because she'd tried to insure herself against the loss before it even happened.

She had been the one that had given up and walked away because she knew he would fall out of love with her. Because, according to everything she'd ever been told, love like that didn't really exist. Her aunt always spoke of her parents in a slightly syrupy tone, sympathetic while intimating that their 'sweet' relationship would never have survived long-term.

'Do you fancy a beer?' Steve's voice intruded her thoughts.

Anna stared at him. She'd been so lost in her memories she'd almost forgotten he was there.

'What?' she asked, a little bemused. She knew she

shouldn't but she studied him, comparing him to Leo. Steve was sturdy, dependable, a palette of taupes, beiges and mushrooms. Leo was a sunburst, bringing light into the darkest corners. Something uncomfortable settled in the pit of her stomach, heavy with the weight of disquiet.

'Beer? Lunch? There's an Irish bar near the square.' He was already tugging at her to turn her around and head back towards the Old Town.

'We can't drink Guinness in Prague,' said Anna with mock horror. 'It's sacrilege.' Though she was only half joking.

'It's a sports bar, we can catch the second half of the Liverpool game.' Steve shot her a winning smile.

'Or we could walk up to the castle and have a beer up there,' replied Anna. 'There's a fantastic view over the city.'

Steve pulled a face. 'Do we have to? I'd really like to see the Liverpool game.'

'And I'd really like to eat at Kuchyň,' said Anna, the forced smile in her eyes hiding her irritation.

She saw the set of his jaw and lifted her chin.

'Or we could go and watch the game.'

Anna shook her head. 'You can watch the game anytime.'

'Come on, it's Liverpool. We can go to your restaurant next time I come over.'

Suddenly Anna couldn't be bothered to argue the toss. It was a watershed moment. She really didn't care where they went because either way it was suddenly very obvious to her that both of them wanted very different things.

When the final whistle of the game blew and the pub erupted with a cheer, Steve was immediately embroiled in the post-match breakdown with his immediate neighbours, two brothers from the Wirral, and Anna had made up her mind. She surreptitiously checked her watch. Before he left for his flight, there would be a brief window of time when they were back at the apartment and she could sit down and talk to him. All she had to do was work out the phrasing in her head for the 'it's not you, it's me' conversation they were going to have to have.

As they opened the front door of the apartment a gale of laughter came from upstairs.

'Looks like someone's entertaining,' muttered Steve. 'You still need to think about moving out, you know. I've never liked the idea of you sharing the place with that guy. He's a bit of a tosser.'

Surprised by his belligerence, she should have pointed out that in fact it was the first time Leo had invited anyone over. Instead she asked, 'What makes you say that?' She genuinely wanted to know. Leo had never fitted in with her family nor, it appeared, with Steve. Why was that?

'You know,' said Steve with a vague flutter of his hands as they went into her bedroom.

'No, I don't.' She put down her handbag on the bed and turned to face Steve who'd stuck his chin out in a familiar truculent stance.

'He's the sort that thinks he's better than anyone else.'

'Again,' said Anna with a smile on her face, trying to

defuse his unwarranted antagonism, 'what makes you say that? Come on, what's he done to you? He's harmless.'

Steve shook his head. 'I dunno. I don't like him. And he's too familiar with you, as if he knows you. I don't like it.'

'You're being silly. He's just a friendly guy.' Even to her own ears, Anna's words sounded false and over-bright as her heart did a funny pitter-patter. Leo and she had fallen into easy familiarity. Cooking and eating together. Chatting in the doorway of the bathroom while she waited for him to clean his teeth. Walking to the tram stop together every morning.

'There's something about him, like he knows something the rest of us don't. When he smiles, I can see it. Like there's a secret joke going on.'

Anna turned away, feeling hot all of a sudden and dreading the conversation that they were about to have. She had a feeling Steve was going to get nasty and bring Leo into it.

'And he swaggers around this place as if he owns it.'

She tried a small laugh, still with her back to him, going through her handbag as if she were looking for something. 'He does lives here.'

'It's like he thinks he's God's gift. Like he expects everyone to be pleased to see him. Like he's something special. I dunno.' Steve lifted his shoulders in an aggrieved shrug.

'He's not one of the lads,' she said, feeling the need to defend Leo out of a sense of fairness. Leo didn't fit Steve's conservative, traditional worldview of how a man should be. The worldview held by her adopted family. They'd always found Leo's differences objectionable and she'd undeniably let that influence her. She'd grown up with the same narrow, risk-averse, conservative values and had remoulded herself to fit in with the family.

'Actually Steve…' Before she could finish, he spoke over her.

'I fancy a cup of tea. Last chance to get a decent one before I get home. And I'll stick this in the fridge, you can never be too careful with sandwiches.' He was already heading for the stairs carrying the bag of supplies he'd bought on the way back because, as he'd said a dozen times, 'They always charge a ridiculous amount for food at the airport and on the plane.'

Coward that she was, Anna nodded and followed him up the stairs. Another five minutes wasn't going to make that much difference to what she had to say.

Chapter Fifteen

'Just look at me over your shoulder, Leo.' Zdeňka grinned at him from the other side of the roof terrace. 'With the view behind you, it's going to look great.'

'What, like this?' he asked with an exaggerated pout, putting his hands on his hips and thrusting out his hips, channelling Harry Styles.

She giggled. 'That's absolutely perfect. Leave it unbuttoned. It's sexy. I'll take a few pictures and then you can try the other shirt on.'

He posed as she took pictures and she laughed as he played up to the camera, not taking it the least bit seriously.

'Now try this one,' she said, putting her phone down and pulling a bright yellow shirt from its hanger. Draping it over one of the bistro chairs, she stepped in front of him, sliding her warm hands under the shoulders of the shirt he was wearing to ease it down his arms, her eyes dancing with flirty promise as they held his. Just as the shirt slid down his arms, he heard footsteps behind him and

Zdeňka's expression brightened with sudden mischief. Leo turned to see Anna and Steve walk out onto the roof terrace carrying a couple of shopping bags. Anna's eyes immediately shot to his and for a second there was a flash of acute awareness between them, which paradoxically made him ache and feel guilty at the same time. She gave so much away with her beautiful clear grey eyes; they spoke a whole language and Leo had always felt he was the only one that could interpret it.

Despite the feeling of disquiet, he beamed at her and Steve. 'Hey, guys. This is Zdeňka. Anna, you met her before at Jan and Michaela's.'

'Hi,' said Zdeňka, in a low sultry voice which appeared to have dropped an octave. She draped an arm round Leo's shoulder, her bright pink lips curving into a pussycat grin. Anna adopted her classic poker face, giving nothing away, which used to drive him mad. That along with her habit of always saying she was fine when she clearly wasn't. He'd always had to coax her feelings out of her, treating them with infinite patience, like shy hedgehog babies.

'And this is Anna's boyfriend, Steve.'

Zdeňka turned her flirtatious smile up a dozen watts and shot Anna a knowing look and then glanced back at Leo. 'Ah, yes, Michaela told me all about –' she paused '– the two of you.' There was no mistaking the throaty emphasis on the words.

Leo's stomach clenched. Had Michaela mentioned that he and Anna used to be married? That would amuse someone as mischievous as Zdeňka no end.

Anna gave him a fierce glare as the hands at her sides knotted into tight, white-knuckled fists.

'It must be fun sharing a flat with Leo,' said the other woman with a naughty smirk.

Anna gave her a polite smile. 'He's house-trained.'

'I'm sure he's a lot of other things too,' she murmured. 'What is it they say in England? Good husband material.'

Leo's audible intake of breath caught Zdeňka's attention and she gave him a wide-eyed look of innocence. 'Just an observation, *zlatíčko*.'

Anna shot him a horrified glance followed by a more surreptitious one at Steve, who was clearly oblivious to the messy undercurrents of breath-caught-in-the-lungs tension swimming between them.

Thankfully Zdeňka turned her attention elsewhere. She could have had quite a career pulling the wings off butterflies.

'And have you done any modelling, Steve?'

Leo almost laughed out loud at Steve's horrified expression when he dropped his bag of shopping on the floor.

'No,' said Steve turning red as he bent to pick up the cans of Coke and packs of sandwiches and crisps that had spilled out of the bag.

'Shame. Leo's a natural.' Zdeňka hand ran across his chest with predatory familiarity that he knew was generated by the appearance of an audience. It was obvious that she had bags of confidence and wasn't above amusing herself at someone else's expense. Since she'd arrived an hour before with a pile of shirts, a flirty smile and wandering hands, she'd made it quite clear she'd be happy to go to bed once they'd got the job done.

'Would you like to try on a shirt for me?' asked Zdeňka, walking up to Steve with a wink. She knew she was making him uncomfortable but clearly didn't care.

'Er … um…' Steve looked at Anna, pleading for help. Anna shot Leo a filthy look as if the situation was all his fault. Something soured in the pit of his stomach.

'Leave him alone, Zdeňka,' said Leo. 'Which shirt do you want me to try on next?'

'This one.' She picked up the yellow shirt that she'd put down earlier. 'Makes me think of you as a lion,' she purred up at him, easily distracted from teasing Steve.

When Leo looked back, to his very great relief, Anna and Steve were already moving back through the French windows. Great. Anna seemed very uptight. Was she pissed off with him? They'd been in a really good place this last few weeks and he'd been enjoying her company.

'Your flatmate is very pretty,' said Zdeňka, her eyes beadily watching his like a blackbird spotting a worm.

Leo gave a non-committal smile.

'It must be hard living with her.'

'Not really,' said Leo, his heart sinking as he saw Steve returning to the roof terrace and realised that he was coming to retrieve a stray can of Coke. He'd just picked it up as Zdeňka said, 'I don't believe you. There's still chemistry there. Michaela told me that you and Anna used to be married.'

Steve dropped the can of Coke and it exploded on the stone tiles, spinning round, spraying fizzy soda everywhere. Leo swallowed and closed his eyes, unable to believe that the words had been released, like the proverbial genie.

Steve looked at him, his face turning puce, his shoulders hunching up around his ears, reminding Leo of an angry wrestler.

'What the—? You and Anna? You're fucking kidding me.'

He marched over and took a swing at Leo, who tried to move but was caught squarely on the chin. Steve packed a bit of power and Leo lurched backwards, landing on the table, which promptly collapsed under him with a crash.

Zdeňka stepped back out of the way, her hand over her mouth.

'Steve! What are you doing?' Anna came rushing out, her appalled gaze zipping between Leo on the floor and Steve nursing his knuckles. She stood between the two of them. Leo wanted to close his eyes, to avoid the coming car crash. Anna's face was lined with confusion and anxiety.

'Is it true?' Steve demanded, his head lifted like a pugnacious boxer ready to take another swing.

'Is what true?' Anna's voice quavered.

'Him and you.' Steve's finger pointed at Leo and then at Anna, contempt scoring angry lines into his face.

Anna's eyes shifted to Leo, a guarded expression settling in her eyes. He saw her swallow.

'You were married to him?' Steve spat the question as if the words were pure poison.

She met his eyes and nodded. Leo admired her for not flinching and not trying to make any excuses.

Steve looked as if he might be sick as he repeated. 'You were married to *him*.'

Anna nodded again.

For a moment, despite his aching jaw, Leo actually felt sorry for him. There was so much pain in his face.

'For how long?'

She blinked and opened her mouth but nothing came out.

'Six months,' said Leo.

'I wasn't talking to you, you bastard,' snapped Steve, glaring at him before he whipped his head back to face Anna. 'You were married to him. And you didn't think to mention it.'

Anna blushed vivid scarlet.

'And I guess the two of you have been getting to know each other again, have you?'

'No!' cried Anna. 'Not like that. I didn't know how to tell you.'

'Didn't know how to tell me that you're shacked up with your ex-husband? I'm not bloody surprised. Especially as you hadn't ever mentioned being married. You must think I'm a right schmuck. Did it amuse the pair of you – your little secret? Except it appears the whole neighbourhood knows, everyone apart from me.'

'Nothing's happened,' said Anna, a desperate pitch to her voice.

'Nothing's happened!' he echoed. 'Apart from the fact you've lied to me and made me look a right berk.' Steve jerked a thumb towards Leo, shooting him a bitter look. 'He must have been laughing his socks off. I need to get out of here.' He pushed past Anna but she grabbed his arm.

'Steve, wait. Let me explain.'

'Explain the fuck what?' He shoved her away from him so violently she stumbled forward, almost losing her footing.

Pushing himself upright, fighting the head-spinning sensation, Leo took a step forward and caught her by the arms to stop her fall. Steve grabbed him and wrenched him out of the way, stepping up to stare Anna in the face.

'You're a lying bitch. I bet you've been sleeping with him. No wonder you were always so quick to defend him. I'm done.' He turned and strode back towards the apartment.

'No!' she shouted. 'I haven't done anything wrong. How dare you speak to me like that. It shows how little you really think of me, which is why I was planning to end things with you before you caught the plane.'

'What? You were going to finish with me?' Disbelief echoed in every word.

She lifted her chin. 'Yes. I'm sorry but it's not working anymore.'

'Funny that.' He jerked his head towards Leo.

'It's nothing to do with Leo. We've both stopped making an effort. I don't think either of us loves each other anymore. I'm being honest.'

'Honest? That's fucking ironic given you've been shacked up with your ex-husband for weeks. You wouldn't know honesty if it bit you on the bum. We're done.' With that he stomped down the stairs.

'God, I'm so sorry, Anna,' said Leo, worried by the shocked pallor of her cheeks.

She looked up at him and all he saw was confusion, as if she hadn't quite processed what had happened. Without thinking and completely ignoring Zdeňka, he folded her into his arms to comfort her. At first Anna's body was stiff and angular and then, like a rag doll, she sagged against him, her head buried in his chest.

Chapter Sixteen

For the next few days, Anna kept herself to herself, actively avoiding Leo, which was surprisingly easy, although perhaps he was giving her some space. She ignored the messages mounting up on her voicemail. Sadness warred with relief. Steve had been a big part of her life and she'd clung to the familiarity of the relationship because it was easy but it hadn't been right for a while and she'd avoided doing anything about it.

Her cousin Rebecca had phoned first and Anna made the mistake of answering, sure that she was going to get a bollocking but equally sure she was going to tell her cousin she deserved better. No surprise, then, that Becs opened her conversation with 'What the hell are you playing at?'

Before Anna could say anything, Becs said, 'You've really cocked things up this time. Steve is livid. How could you do this to him? And with that Leo, of all people. Did you know he was going to be out there?'

'No! Of course not,' said Anna, stung by the accusation. 'It was a complete shock – which is why I didn't say anything.'

'Well, the cat's well and truly out of the bag now. James told me Steve was planning to ask you to marry him, next year. You can kiss goodbye to that one, now.'

'Or I can realise that I've had a lucky escape.'

'What do you mean?'

'I mean I put up with his crappy behaviour for too long. We both settled into a rut. Habit. Security. It had run its course.'

'Are you saying that to save face?'

'No. This weekend, even before he found out about Leo, I realised that it wasn't right anymore.'

'Are you sure? I mean … he's not the most exciting man on the planet but he's steady and he'd never let you down.' Her voice trailed off.

'You mean like Uncle Henry.'

There was no answer. Anna knew Rebecca meant exactly that.

'I feel a bit sorry for Steve. He's very upset, thinking that you've been lying to him and laughing at him behind his back.'

'I never laughed at him,' said Anna. Guilt spilling up like bile. 'And I didn't lie to him.' Although lying by omission was pretty much the same thing. 'But I do admit I should have told him about knowing Leo.'

'He didn't even know you'd been married before, Anna.'

Anna winced. That *had* been deliberate omission on her part. For the first year she'd separated from Leo, whenever his name came within the family, her terrible and ridiculous mistake was raked over like they were mining for diamonds among the ashes. Then they stopped mentioning him, and it had never come up in front of Steve.

'Have you've done the right thing? You've not gone and fallen for Leo again, have you? This isn't a reverse rebound thing?'

'I'm not sure reverse rebound is a thing. It's nothing to do with Leo. I found I didn't actually miss Steve that much and then when he came this week…' She paused. 'I realised he was a selfish prat. And I didn't want to be with him anymore.'

'Harsh but honest, I guess. You know Mum thinks you're mad. And James is furious. There's a lot to be said for someone as reliable and dependable as Steve.'

'I know. You might have mentioned it. But it's not enough. I want more.'

'Don't we all,' said Rebecca with a wistful note in her voice.

Anna hung up thoughtfully. She had done the right thing, even if it did leave her as the odd one out in the family again. They'd all loved Steve – although it sounded as if Rebecca understood. Whatever – dependability wasn't a good enough reason to stay with someone.

A noise caught her attention and she sat up, watching as a white sheet of paper appeared under the door along with an empty Lindt chocolate cardboard sleeve. Intrigued, she rose to her feet and picked up the paper. Leo had drawn a little cartoon – she'd forgotten how good he was at drawing – depicting a stick woman with a sad face and a plate of chocolate. Underneath he'd written, 'Sorry the chocolate won't fit under the door but I'm looking after it for you 😊'

Beneath it there was a second drawing of a stick man, his mouth covered in chocolate, an innocent look on his face, with the caption 'I tried'.

An involuntary smile touched her mouth. Leo at his sweetest. It brought a flood of memories. When they'd been married he'd often left her little drawings and messages pinned up in various places: the bathroom mirror when he left the house before her, on the fridge when he was coming home late, stuck on the television when he was out watching football. This wasn't his fault at all. She was the one who had blurted out the truth to Michaela and Jan. He hadn't done anything wrong and he certainly hadn't done anything to deserve the big bruise he was currently sporting along the right side of his jaw. That was partly why she was avoiding him, because she felt so bad that Steve had thumped him and that he'd still come to her defence when Steve had pushed her. The dark purple shadow exacerbated her guilt. She had made a mess of things but none of it was Leo's fault.

Five minutes later after, she made her way up the stairs to find him.

'Don't suppose you saved me some chocolate?'

Leo, who was lying on the floor absorbed in a book with music pumping from his phone, started and then gave her a sheepish grin.

'Good job I bought two bars,' he said, wriggling to a sitting position and looking up at her. 'Would you like a cup of tea? And look, I bought kindling and firelighters. I was waiting for you before I lit the fire for the first time.'

'You don't need to make it for me,' she said but he was already on his feet and leading the way into the kitchen. She followed and took up residence on one of the bar stools as Leo opened a cupboard.

'Here you go – your favourite, I seem to recall.' He handed the bar over to her and she traced the familiar gold name on the front of the packet.

'Still my favourite,' she said with a sad smile, as her heart pinched at his thoughtfulness.

'Mine, too.' His cheerful grin warmed her. Leo had always been so open and easy. 'Of course it tastes so much better if you share it.'

'It does?' She quirked an eyebrow.

'Absolutely,' he replied, his eyes twinkling.

Her heart did another one of those funny little hitches. She had chocolate and suddenly things didn't seem so bad.

Leo settled down beside her, handing her a mug of tea, and she carefully unwrapped the foil on the chocolate and offered him a piece.

They sat side by side munching without saying anything.

'So how are *you* feeling?'

She turned to look at him and for the first time checked over her emotions, in the same way she might pat her body down for injuries. Leo's emphasis on the word 'you' made her realise that she'd spent the week thinking more about how she'd disappointed everyone else and let down the family, and the storm she'd created.

Now she took stock of her own emotions. How *did* she feel?

Relieved.

It was relief. As if tight bandages had been wrapped around her ribs, constricting her, and they'd been loosened. She could breathe more deeply and easily, she could move more freely. It was the weirdest sensation – weird because it was unfamiliar.

She stared at Leo as she absorbed the implications.

'Anna?'

She smiled at him. 'I feel better.'

'Better. Because of the chocolate?'

'No, better because I feel ... lighter, looser, easier.'

Leo's eyes widened. 'Really?'

'Really.' Her face lit up and she raised her arms. 'I feel released. Is that awful?'

'No. I'm surprised. I thought you'd be upset.'

'So did I.' She laughed and, giving in to the feeling, hopped off the stool and did a little spin. 'But I realised Steve was a selfish prat and he didn't deserve me.'

'Wow. And you only discovered that now?'

She nudged him with her elbow. 'Tell me I'm an idiot, why don't you. I kept telling myself that's the way he is and I didn't mind it ... until I did, if you know what I mean.' She caught her lower lip between her teeth as the implication sank in. She hadn't minded until she'd compared the way he treated her to the way Leo treated her. Steve had wooed her and made her feel important. It was only over the last year he'd started taking her for granted and making less effort – but then, couldn't the same be said of her?

'When we first got together, he was wonderful.'

'And then he was a selfish prat,' insisted Leo with one of his naughty grins.

A smile curved her lips. Irrepressible as ever.

'Got any plans for the weekend?'

And that was Leo all over, moving on to the next thing without pushing to win the point.

'No. Except I'm only going to do things that I want to do.' She jutted out her chin. 'I'm done with trying to fit in with everyone else.'

Leo pretended to cower. 'Scary. I was going to ask if you fancied going to the castle and doing a proper tour.'

Anna gave it a couple of seconds' thought, that's all it took. 'Yes. That is something I'd like to do. I can't believe I've been here all this time and haven't been there properly yet.'

'Leave in ten?'

'What, now?' She laughed again, reassured by how well she knew him. Typical Leonardo Knight. Always ready to dive straight into something.

'Why not?'

'Half an hour.' She needed to shower and make herself look respectable.

'Twenty minutes,' said Leo with a teasing grin. She definitely felt lighter, especially when he added, simply, 'Go for it,' and poured himself another cup of coffee.

Today they approached the castle from a different side, walking up several flights of stairs and steep slopes. Anna started to puff as she tried to keep pace with Leo's longer strides but, without her saying anything, he adjusted his pace to a more leisurely stroll. Another one of his qualities: he looked after those around him.

'How was your week at work, darling?' asked Leo with a teasing lift of his eyebrows.

'Good,' she replied. 'Actually, really good. For the first time this week, I felt like I knew what I was doing. You know those first few weeks or so when you don't know where anything is kept or how anything works. This week I actually felt a help instead of hindrance. Jakub is so patient but exacting so it's a relief to be useful at last.'

'I know that feeling. I thought the first two weeks I'd bitten off a bit more than I could chew. But I'm finding it really inspiring. Karel has loads of ideas and I love his approach. Always prepared to consider something new.'

Anna laughed. 'Unlike Jakub who doesn't like anything to be done differently. He thrives on tradition.' She paused and imitated his accent. 'Why change perfection?'

'Did you know Karel is his nephew?'

'What! No! I had no idea.' Anna mused on the surprising news for a moment. 'Although come to think of it, he does mention him quite a lot, although with considerable disdain and disapproval. I thought it was because he's such a traditionalist.'

'They don't speak anymore, apparently.'

'That's a bit sad. They both want the same thing but are so divided on how to achieve it.'

'Bitter rivalry. Makes a good story and Karel isn't above using it for marketing purposes.'

'It's a shame because Jakub has no other family. I think he's wedded to the brewery because he's lonely.'

'It is sad. And what about you? Are you still lonely?'

Anna blinked, surprised by the unexpected turn of the conversation. 'Who says I'm lonely?'

'You've always been lonely.'

'No, I haven't,' blustered Anna, suddenly realising that Leo was right. She *had* always been lonely. Ever since her parents died. Hard as she'd tried, she'd never fitted in with the Talbot family and this week had confirmed it once again. Steve had been a crutch, helping her to belong, but she never had, even with him at her side. If anything, this week had emphasised how much of an outlier she was. They all supported him rather than her. He was more family to them than she was.

Leo simply folded his arms and looked at her.

Anna glared at him. How come he always knew her better than she knew herself.

'Have you heard from him?'

She shook her head. 'No, but I have heard from Becs. She's not impressed. She thinks I should go back home and give up my place on the scheme. She reckons if I do that and apologise properly to him, he'll forgive me.'

'And what do you want to do?' asked Leo.

Anna glanced down at her phone and his gaze followed hers. The red dots were on her WhatsApp, her voicemail and her message app symbols.

'Let me guess, they're not messages of support.'

She shook her head and met his grave expression with one of her own. 'No. I stopped listening to them. I kept hoping Becs might be on my side.'

'What do you want to do?' he asked gently.

She wrinkled her nose but pressed ahead because with Leo she had always been able to be honest. 'I want to stay put. I've lived my life trying to live the Talbot family way. I'm never going to get it right because I'm not one of them.' Her voice broke, defeat flooding in. She had tried. She really had.

'No, you're not one of them. You're you.' As always Leo homed in on the issue and as always he was on her side. 'You're Anna Love and you should be who you want to be.'

'Easier said than done, when you owe everything to other people. If it wasn't for them I'd be in an orphanage or foster home.'

'They might have taken you in as an orphan – but you are still family. Just because they brought you up, you shouldn't feel beholden to them for the rest of your life. In most families, parents accept that their children become their own people. and let them go their own way. Parents love their children but that love shouldn't be conditional or a burden.'

Anna thought of all the messages sitting on her phone. 'I've been avoiding their calls,' she admitted.

'I'm not bloody surprised. You should delete them.'

She stared at him. 'I can't.'

'Yes, you can. Do you think you've done anything wrong?'

She gave a half shrug. 'Not precisely. I should have told

Steve but I lied by omission and yes, it was cowardly – to avoid explaining things. But funnily enough they've all forgotten that *they've* never mentioned that I was once married. It's almost as if they thought I was soiled goods and it might damage my prospects with Steve. So they're just as bad.'

Part II

Chapter Seventeen

On Saturday morning Leo bounded into the kitchen clutching a carton of milk and a bag of pastries. Anna still in her dressing gown because it was only seven in the morning, looked up from her phone where she was perusing the headlines on the BBC news website, deliberately avoiding the sports news because she no longer felt she had to keep up with rugby and football scores – which, she decided, was actually quite liberating.

'How do you fancy going mushroom foraging?' he said. 'I've bumped into Michaela downstairs and she and Jan are going to Křívokslátsko, a national park. They've invited us to join them. It's a bit of a drive but apparently the conditions are perfect after yesterday's rain. And it would be nice to get out of the city.'

Anna's initial instinct was to say no but Leo forestalled her.

'What else were you going to do? I've never been mushroom picking.'

She considered for a moment and looked out of the window at the crisp autumn sky, blue, dotted with the odd wispy cloud, lit with low golden sunshine. The truth was, aside from washing and changing the sheets on her bed, she had no real plans.

'I don't know anything about mushrooms,' she said.

'You don't need to worry about that. Apparently Michaela's an expert. We can learn from her.'

Half an hour later, Leo was waiting by the front door, looking like a poster boy for the rugged outdoor life in blue cargo pants, a pale blue Henley stretched across his chest – had it always been that broad? – and a navy beanie hat crammed onto his blonde curls, which made them fan out around his face like a naughty cherub. He was talking to Ludmila, who as always looked immaculate. Today she wore an elegant full-length cashmere coat in a rich burgundy that matched her lipstick.

Anna touched her own hair self-consciously. She rather liked its slightly longer length now, and feeling feminine for a change. A memory trickled into her brain of being taken to the hairdresser by her aunt. 'She needs to have it cut short,' she'd told the hairdresser. 'I can't be doing with the tangles. And I don't do braids.' Anna had cried when she'd seen her hair on the floor. 'Don't be silly, Anna, darling,' her aunt had said. 'Short hair is much more practical.' But to Anna it was a symbol of all she'd lost. Her mother had brushed it for her, plaiting it into an elaborate fishtail each morning when she was at primary school.

Tears pricked at her eyes at the recollection.

'I love your hair slightly longer,' said Leo with that unerring ability of his to read her mind.

'Thanks.' The word rasped hoarsely from her constricted throat.

'You okay?' asked Leo, and it struck her yet again how he easily he was able to tune in to her emotions.

'Mmm,' she murmured, repressing her feelings. Being practical. 'Fine.'

Of course, he shot her a sceptical glance and, of course, he didn't say anything as he ushered her out of the door. That was Leo all over, always empathetic – but was that to her or everyone?

'I hear you are going to pick mushrooms,' said Ludmila. 'I hope your trip will be fruitful.' She looked at Anna. 'You look lighter, my dear.'

'Lighter?' Anna stared at her.

Ludmila gave her an enigmatic smile. 'Lighter in spirit. When I saw you last, I felt you were weighed down.'

Anna blinked at her, wondering what Michaela had been telling her. Lighter? How was one lighter?'

'You've lost some of the load you were carrying. It suits you.'

Leo raised an eyebrow at Anna and Ludmila turned to him. 'And you, perhaps you should think about picking up a load now and then. You can be too light. Sometimes you need to take things seriously.'

With that she left, her beautiful wool coat flaring behind her as she disappeared through the doors.

Jan, jangling his car keys, passed her in the doorway. He caught Leo's eye. 'She's very wise, that one.'

Anna and Leo exchanged a dubious glance. Anna was left feeling a little unsettled by Ludmila's words.

'Perfect conditions for *houbař*,' said Michaela, who was clutching a wicker basket as she almost bounced out of the car into the chilly morning air. 'That's Czech for mushroom picking.' Despite the walking trousers, she wore what looked like a dozen colourful scarfs and a big stylish jumper with a woolly knitted hat that almost tamed her flyway blond hair. Even dressed for a day outdoors, she looked stylish and feminine. Anna studied her and resolved to buy herself a nice scarf and cuter headgear. The bobble on Michaela's woolly hat bobbed about with her excitement, her face bright and intent. Even the normally imperturbable Jan seemed up for an adventure.

Their enthusiasm was infectious, especially after the hour-long journey to get there, and Anna felt a little frisson of anticipation. Initially, she'd said yes to the trip because it was something to do and she didn't want to be left out, but now she was here, her interest was piqued. The back-to-nature vibe of the morning appealed to her, as did the thought of foraging for their own food. It wasn't something she'd ever done or even considered before.

From the bottom of her basket Michaela produced

several small pocket knives. 'We need these because it's best to cut the mushroom stem low to the ground.'

They left the car park and began to walk along a trail straight into the forest, their feet making papery rustles through the ankle-deep golden leaves. Autumn was making its mark, coating the forest floor with a russet spectrum of yellow, oranges and browns. Impulsive puffs of wind whipped the leaves into the occasional flurry, like wild animals startled into flight. Anna found herself glancing over her shoulder as if she might catch sight of something flitting from the shadow of one tree to another, dancing on the very periphery of her vision.

Shaking off the fanciful thought, she focused on the task in hand. Already Michaela and Jan, their heads bent, were scanning the ground. Anna searched for the telltale white mushroom caps. That was, she assumed, what they were looking for, although it was a bit like looking for a needle in a haystack.

Leo fell into step beside her and the two of them followed the Czech couple as weak sunshine filtered through the branches overhead, creating pockets of dappled light.

He had his hands shoved in his pockets and strolled along with nonchalant ease, as if he had no expectation of finding anything. Anna suspected he was as clueless as she was.

'Hele!' called Michaela and turned to beckon to them. 'Look.' She pointed down at a mustard-brown mushroom with a creamy bulbous stem, so well camouflaged among the leaves that Anna wondered how she'd seen it. 'It's a porcini and a good size.' Carefully Michaela cleared the leaves around the satsuma-sized mushroom and dug along the stem before cutting it off close to the ground, leaving some behind. With a triumphant grin she held it up. 'Here.' She handed it to them to take a closer inspection. 'See the spongy underside. These mushrooms don't have gills. This is a good size. If they're very small then leave them. This type of mushroom can grow quite big.' After taking a sniff, with a blissed-out expression on her face, she popped it into her basket. 'Now we look around because they often grown near to one another.' She crouched and her hand scrabbled through the leaves, gently brushing them back.

'And more,' called Jan from less than a metre away, and scuffed back the undergrowth to reveal two more mushrooms.

Now that she knew what she was looking for, Anna's confidence grew and she diligently scanned the ground, suddenly determined to find something, driven by the competitive spirit that had been drilled into her. With her cousins, everything was always a contest, the fastest, the fittest, the strongest, the loudest. And Anna the slowest, the weakest and the quietest. She never quite made the grade.

Unfortunately, the harder she looked, the more elusive the mushrooms seemed to be, and she began to feel frustrated, especially now that Michaela and Jan seemed to be on a roll, bending to scoop up their finds with increasingly regularity.

After half an hour, her neck aching a little, she stopped and huffed out a breath. This was hopeless – she was never going to find anything. The familiar sensation of inadequacy began to envelop her, pressing down on her shoulders, as she slumped under the weight of failure. With a sigh, and as much to stretch the muscles at the back of her head, she looked up, and watched a solitary leaf quiver at the very end of a branch before losing its tenuous hold and, with a dying breath, flutter down to the forest floor.

When she looked up she found Jan watching her.

'Do you think that leaf was worried it was one of the last to fall?' he asked with a whimsical smile.

With a shrug, she lifted her shoulders, staring at him uncertainly, not sure whether he was making a point or not. 'I've no idea. Do leaves have feelings?'

'Lots of folklore features forest spirits – the Leshy, Dryads, Nymphs, the Ents. Why not?'

He looked so earnest, Anna had to smile, and rather than tease him, she gave into her own musings. 'Actually, do you ever get the sense that there are things here, just out of sight, and when we turn to catch them, they hide?'

'Always,' said Jan, his eyes widening a little. 'Throughout Europe there are lots of fairy-tales set in the woods. *Hansel and Gretel, Goldilocks and the Three Bears, Little Red Riding Hood … Beauty and the Beast.* The location is always outside the safety of the village. They represent the unknown, beyond the boundaries.' His eyes twinkled. 'Don't worry, I'll protect you.'

Anna shook her head. 'I don't need protecting. And I don't believe in fairies and witches.'

Leo, appearing at Jan's side, shook his head. 'No, you've never needed protecting. But everyone needs a little looking after now and then.'

Anna didn't like the direction the conversation had taken and deliberately wandered away to the right, her eyes studying a patch of ground by a fallen log.

'Aha!' said Leo and she turned to find him dancing on the spot, his hips wiggling triumphantly. He looked ridiculously pleased with himself. 'I found one. I found one.' He held up his knife as if he were about to perform a ceremonial sacrifice and knelt down. 'Come to Papa, little one,' he crooned as he carefully cleared the leaves around it and gently sliced through the stem. Cradling it gently in his hands he studied it. 'My first ever mushroom.' He grinned.

Anna's first instinct was to say, 'I hope it's not a poisonous one,' but at the sight of his broad beam, the words shrivelled on her tongue and she was once again reminded of his capacity to find joy and happiness in the simplest of things.

Instead she smiled back at him. 'Congratulations. Would you like me to take a picture of you with your mushroom?'

Leo's grin widened. 'Yes, please,' he said and immediately struck a pose, pretending to kiss his mushroom as if he were a chef.

As she took the picture on her phone of Leo standing in one of the shafts of sunshine slanting through the trees, the light glinting on his blonde hair and his eyes shining with happiness, she felt a little zing in her heart. A burst of warmth blooming as she acknowledged that he was gorgeous, both inside and out. What you saw was exactly what you got. There was no side, no hidden agenda with Leo. A pure spirit. For a moment, she wondered if she'd ever truly appreciated that before. He certainly wasn't the least bit competitive.

What was wrong with her? Clearly, the forest spirits were messing with her, making her soft. She chased away the fanciful thoughts and turned her attention back to the task in hand. If it was the last thing she did today, she was going to find a bloody mushroom.

'Anna, Leo. Come see this.' Michaela called from the other side of a small glade and they hurried over. She pointed to a taller, pale mushroom and then, keeping it at arm's length, gently tapped it. A tiny puff of green genie smoke billowed out of a small hole in the top of the cap.

Anna stepped back. 'What's that? Is it poisonous?'

'It's a miracle of nature,' said Michaela. 'It's a stump puffball. It's not poisonous when it's young but this one is too mature, so it wouldn't taste so good. This is how it spreads its spores. Mushrooms are fascinating.'

'Don't get her started,' said Jan, taking her elbow and helping her rise to her feet.

They wandered on with the sun heating the day. The concentration was starting to give Anna a headache when suddenly she spotted something. She frowned and quickly glanced sideways to make sure Leo hadn't seen it. Stealthily, as if it might make a getaway, she approached the large brown lump. It was huge, the size of two fists, but it had the same colouring and texture as the mushrooms Michaela had been collecting. Anna felt a burst of excitement.

'Look,' she called. 'I found one. Is this one edible?'

Michaela came over to check. 'Oh my, Anna. That is one

big porcini,' she said throwing her arms around her with a big hug. 'The biggest I've ever seen.'

'Go Anna, go Anna,' called Leo, punching her arm and doing another one of his daft dances.

With a blush of pleasure, she knelt down and carefully sliced through the slightly spongy stem.

'That is a good one,' said Michaela with a sigh. 'Very good. You win the prize for the best mushroom of the day.'

Leo hugged her. 'You're the mushroom queen.'

She giggled because it was silly and it was only a mushroom, but they were both so pleased for her. If it had been Steve or her cousins, they would have doubled down and hunted even harder to try and beat the find. This was so much more fun. She felt their joy in her triumph more than her own.

It seemed that now she'd found one, her eye was trained, and as she looked more closely she began to see a few more, but that first one had been enough. She smiled to herself and paused for a moment, struck by a clear, piping chorus of birdsong echoing from high above them. When she looked up she caught fleeting glimpses of a tiny dunnock darting from tree to tree, while a nosy chaffinch hopped up and down, peering at them from a branch. There was a sense that the forest was alive around them, although starting to shut down for winter, and as she looked, really looked for a change, she noticed how the vivid green moss carpeted the base of trees, while paler lichens dotted their bark, and how the leaves had drifted to echo the contours of the ground. She took in a deep breath and smelt the musty, earthy aroma. Her feet sank into the soft mulch. Her senses woke up one by one, absorbing the sensations of the forest, and a deep sense of contentment settled upon her, one she hadn't felt in ... she couldn't remember how long.

'Here, Anna,' called Leo, beckoning her over. There were several porcini on the ground and she crouched next to him, helping to clear the leaves from around his finds, as he sliced through a stem and moved on to the next. Suddenly their heads were almost touching and they both looked up at the same moment. His eyes locked on hers and his gaze was unusually solemn as it searched her face, as if looking for something. It unsettled her, making her feel a little lost, and when he gave her a gentle smile and looked away, it was as if she'd missed something.

To break the moment, she reached for another mushroom – of course, at the same moment as he did – and their fingers brushed. She almost started at the little electrical tingle that tickled her nerve endings but she didn't pull her hand away. Suddenly she wanted his touch, wanted to feel his hand on hers, wanted that connection even though it unnerved her.

Leo pulled his hand away first. 'You can have this one,' he said, with one of his warm smiles, generous as always. It pierced her heart. He was a good man. Always had been.

'We're going to have a fine dinner,' said Jan, coming up behind them, carrying Michaela's basket.

Leo rose and handed over his mushrooms, which he'd been collecting in his beanie hat. Anna stood up and also held out her latest finds.

'Only if you're cooking,' said Leo. 'My expertise with

these fun guys – fungis, geddit? –' he nudged Anna '– runs to mushroom omelette.'

'Michaela will make her famous mushroom goulash. As you have collected the food, you have to eat it too. This evening. Come have dinner.'

'That would be great,' said Leo, running a hand through his hair. Why did Anna have to notice the sun catching its golden highlights? Or how well he fit the autumn scene? Why was she so aware of him? 'We'll bring the beer.'

Amused rather than irritated that he hadn't consulted her, Anna rolled her eyes at Michaela, but at the same time she remembered how Steve had often accepted things on her behalf because it was something he wanted to do and assumed that she would go along with it. In contrast, Leo's response was spontaneous, of the moment, rather than thoughtless or selfish.

Chapter Eighteen

'Michaela didn't mention this hill,' said Anna, slowing down as she puffed breaths into the chilly morning air. She was reasonably fit, but her calf muscles were complaining about the workout on the steep incline. During the most delicious dinner of mushroom goulash the previous evening, their neighbour had insisted they should visit Petřín Hill. 'We should have taken the funicular.'

With his usual bouncy puppy-dog enthusiasm Leo had convinced her that it would be far more fun to walk up through the park and 'experience' it rather than sit with other tourists.

'The clue was in the word "hill",' said Leo and with a good-natured grin grabbed her hand to pull her along.

'Very cute,' she said, although she was laughing.

'You know you're having a good time, really.' Leo threaded his arm through hers.

Rather than admit it, she rolled her eyes at him, although in fact she was enjoying herself enormously. She wondered if he was ever unhappy or sad or took anything seriously. Even his proposal had been a bit of a lark.

'Let's get married,' he'd said, as they stood at the top of Primrose Hill admiring the skyline view of the City, on a walk not dissimilar to this one. And because she'd loved him, and was young and stupid, and there was romance in the moment, she'd said yes.

Swept along on the high of love, they'd decided to marry on her parents' wedding anniversary, six weeks later, at the Kensington and Chelsea Register Office. It had been a conscious decision not to involve their respective families, Leo's because Ernesto was away on location and hers because she knew her aunt and uncle would think it was all too rushed.

At the time it had seemed symbolic. Making a deliberate decision to follow in her parents' footsteps rather than fall into line with her adopted family's approach.

Of course, when she and Leo split up, her aunt and uncle were the first to say they knew it was a mistake. Why, she wondered, did people take such great delight in 'I told you so'?

'I suppose you're going to want to go up to the Observation Deck,' she said, tilting her head right back to gaze up at the steel girders of the Petřín tower, which bore a strong resemblance to its inspiration, the Eiffel Tower.

'Of course. You're not scared of heights. And the exercise will do us good.'

'"The exercise will do us good!"' Her outraged echo made him laugh. 'You've just made me climb up a mountain.'

'Come on,' he said, disengaging his arm and taking her hand and dragging her towards the entrance. 'I'll pay. And we can take the steps slowly, old lady.'

'Who are you calling old lady?'

'Only two hundred and ninety-nine steps,' he commented as they began the ascent.

With a half-hearted groan, she shut up and focused on putting one foot in front of the other and breathing. The staircase wound round the outside of the tower and, despite the strenuous workout, she was distracted from her aching thighs by the view. Through the metal latticework, she caught tantalising glimpses of the city, and with each flight of stairs the view altered slightly.

Hauling in a big lungful of air when she reached the top, she had to admit, as they stepped out onto the octagonal platform surrounding the steel structure, that the climb had been worth it. The panoramic view was one that you could look at a dozen times and each time find something new to see. With a happy sigh she scanned the skyline. She could see exactly why Prague was so often referred to as the City of a Hundred Spires.

Along the valley, the castle dominated the view, standing guard over the city, keeping a watchful eye on the buildings below with their distinctive cream walls, topped with bright terracotta tiles. The jumble of roofs was interrupted by the soaring, verdigris-topped spires punctuating the skyline, all kept in check by the boundaries of the Vltava, where riverboats, long and sleek, puttered between the bridges. Spread below them, the trees on the slope were burnished in flaming autumn finery.

'I feel like I'm starting to know my way around,' Anna said as they stood studying the different landmarks. 'That's St Nicholas Church, the Charles Bridge, the Old Town Square.'

'You can't miss the Church of our Lady before Týn,' Leo responded, his arm brushing hers as he pointed. 'When you see the city like this, you realise there's so much more to explore. So many wonderful buildings … and breweries.'

'And also, how lucky we are that we have all this time,' said Anna. Exploring on her own wouldn't be nearly as much fun as with someone else, and with Leo … well, you never quite knew what fun you'd have.

'We ought to make the most of it, you know. We should choose a new place to visit every weekend. We could make a list and then pick one at random each week.'

And there he went again, full of bright ideas.

'For a moment there I thought that sounded very organised for you, but then you had to throw the random element in,' teased Anna.

'What can I say, I have a talent for spontaneity.' He grinned at her. 'And most of the time it pays off. When did I ever make you do anything you didn't want to?'

'There was that time at the Bar Flamenco when you had me dancing on the table and I almost broke my leg.'

'Nuh-huh,' said Leo, shaking his head. '*You* decided it would be a good idea to do a little stamping with attitude on the table. Not me.'

'It was flamenco,' she protested, laughing, and wrinkled her nose at him. He had a point, although he was the one that had helped her up onto the table top and whooped and cheered when she did so. 'And you didn't stop me.'

'Why would I? You were having a good time.'

It was easy to have a good time with Leo.

'We're definitely going to have to come here again,' said Leo as they descended the last of the steps. 'There's still much more to see, but I'm ready for some lunch and a beer.'

'You're always ready for a beer,' teased Anna.

'When in Prague,' he replied with an insouciant smile. 'Lead me to the monastery.'

They left the park and walked along a pretty tree-lined lane with the creamy stone walls of the park on one side.

'You could almost believe we're in the middle of the country rather than in a city,' commented Anna. This really was such a fascinating and beautiful city, and she loved that there was so much greenery about.

Their walk to the Strahov Monastery took little more than ten minutes and they found the brewery easily. Inside, the cool white interior with its sinuous, curved bar and polished copper trim immediately appealed to Anna.

'This is lovely,' she said, glancing round at the clean, light, bright space with its whitewashed walls, which set off the rather austere dark wooden benches and tables. It was easy to imagine generation upon generation of monks sitting here over the ages.

'Beer,' said Leo, immediately heading towards the row of taps mounted on a big copper stand. She followed in his enthusiastic wake as he grabbed a menu from by the door and immediately shared it with her. 'What do you fancy?'

They scanned the selection, Anna noting the hops and the ABVs as well as the names and descriptions.

'It's got to be St Norbert's,' she said with a smile, remembering the couple on the bridge.

'Oh, good. I couldn't decide between that and the Amber Lager. I can try yours.'

They exchanged another in-tune smile, making Anna reflect upon how good it was to be with someone who spoke the same language.

Within minutes they each had two glasses, each with an inch of a different beer. The friendly barman, Ivan, happily talked them through the different flavours. 'This is our autumn special,' he said as Anna took a sip of the seasonal pale ale.

'Oooh, I like. Here, Leo.' She handed her glass to him without a second thought.

He took a sip. 'Nice. Try mine.' He pushed his glass towards her.

For the next fifteen minutes they tasted, sipped and compared before settling on their final choices. Of course, by then Leo was Ivan's new best friend.

'Cheers, mate,' Leo said as they took their drinks, leaving Ivan to serve another customer.

'How do you do that?' asked Anna, taking a sip through the foamy head of the lager.

'Do what?'

'Make everyone fall in love with you,' she said a touch irritably, waving one hand at him.

'I'm being friendly.'

'Hmm. I was friendly first.'

He lifted his shoulders. 'I like people. I guess I'm predisposed to think well of them. My brother was the opposite. He had a tough time when we were growing up. It's not every day your mum marries a movie star. It plunged us into a whole new world but it was easier for me because I was younger, so I didn't have as much to compare it with. Raph got burned by people using him. It made him very cynical, whereas for me it opened up a whole new world. I guess I'm more like my mum than him. She likes to embrace new things and she loves people. Although everyone assumes because Raph is the suspicious, careful one that he's much more sensible than me.' Leo's mouth twisted and Anna saw an unfamiliar scowl on his face. 'He's the reliable one that everyone can trust. I'm the flaky one.'

Anna stared at him. She'd only met Raph a handful of times and yes, he was the dark to Leo's light, with an air of calm authority about him. She could see why people would automatically defer to him rather than to Leo. But Leo was implicitly honest.

'You're not flaky,' she told him.

'Aren't I?'

'No, not at all.' She realised it was true. 'You are reliable. You're a good friend to people. You care about them and you don't let them down. I suppose some people might … well, be suspicious that you make friends so easily. Are you really sincere?'

'If you show people you like them, in general they like

you back. If you're suspicious then they they're going to be wary.'

'Yes, but not everyone has the confidence to bound in like a puppy, expecting everyone to like them.'

'Yes, but why assume people won't like you? And if they do, don't worry about it. That's their problem. You could spend all your life trying to please other people. Just be yourself.'

Anna swallowed. Maybe her tongue was loosened by the beer but she was surprised when the words slipped out. She asked in a very quiet voice, 'What if you don't know who yourself is?'

Leo leaned over to take her hand. 'That's the saddest thing you've ever said. You're Anna Love. You're a good person, who looks after others. Kind and decent.'

'But nothing special. And now I sound whiny.'

'You've never been whiny in your life, Anna. And you are special. Super special. I don't think you've ever given yourself enough credit for the duff hand you were dealt. You lost both your parents at a young age, but you were old enough to remember them and be shaped by them. Then you moved into a completely alien environment.'

Anna started. '"Alien environment"! That's a bit dramatic, isn't it? My aunt and uncle gave me a home. They gave me everything. They treated me the same as their own children. They're my family.'

'I know they looked after you and gave you a home but... I feel sometimes that they squashed you. Made a square-shaped Anna when you should have been an oval-shaped Anna. You had to fit, rather than be you.' Leo looked a little diffident, fiddling with his beer glass, as if maybe he'd said more than he meant to.

Anna shook her head. 'You're wrong, Leo. They didn't have to take me in. I needed to adapt. I was the one that came into their home. I was the cuckoo in the nest.'

'Rubbish. You still should have been allowed to be who you are.'

She scowled. He had no idea. But for a fleeting moment, she wondered what oval-shaped Anna would have been like.

Chapter Nineteen

'This is going to be so much fun,' said Michaela as they walked down the stairs, each clutching an overnight bag and a pile of bedding. Leo agreed. He'd been looking forward to this weekend and escaping the city, even though today's sky of unbroken cloud was flat and grey. Winter was creeping towards them and the temperature had dipped by several degrees in the last couple of weeks.

'You do know she's going to put you to work,' said Jan, with a wink at him and Anna.

'We don't mind,' she said.

'Speak for yourself.' Leo laughed before adding, 'Although I'm not sure how much use I'll be.'

'Yes, don't let him near any power tools,' teased Anna.

'Hey. Whose side are you on? I'm very good at cleaning up,' he protested, playfully poking Anna in the side. 'I can be your assistant. Hand you the screws and whatnots.'

Anna winced. 'Whatnots? Oh, Leo, Leo. What are we

going to do with you?' she asked with a mournful sigh, although those lovely expressive eyes glinted with laughter.

'Well, work or not, it feels like we're going on holiday, especially when we get to play hooky,' declared Leo, as he wedged his and Anna's overnight bags into the back of Jan's Volkswagen Passat. The roomy boot was already packed to the gunnels with Jan's tools, bedding, food, beer and several boxes of tiles that were for the kitchen. It resembled an elaborate Jenga puzzle. Take the wrong thing out and everything would come tumbling out.

Jan shook his head, giving Leo a pitying look. 'Don't let Michaela hear you say that. She's delighted to have two extra pairs of hands. You'll have to work for your dinner.'

'In England, we say, "Sing for your supper". That's your department, Anna.'

Puzzlement creased Jan's face until Leo explained. 'Anna's a brilliant singer. She's got a gorgeous voice.' Inside, a little voice of his own reminded him that she had a gorgeous face, a gorgeous soul and a gorgeous body, not that she'd ever believed him when he told her so. Despite her willowy build, there was a softness about her that had drawn him from the first time he saw her. She'd brought out his protective instincts, even though she'd always made it clear she didn't need looking after.

'So has Jan. You can sing together this evening,' said Michaela, with the blithe assurance of someone who had no idea how harmonies worked.

'I can hold a tune,' said Anna, blushing. 'Leo's exaggerating,'

He wasn't, but he wouldn't embarrass her any more,

219

although he found the blush endearing. She'd always downplayed her abilities, perhaps because they hadn't been valued by her adopted family. He had to stifle the urge to give her a hug and tell her she was brilliant because no one else ever had. She'd overcome a tragedy and had never felt sorry for herself. She made the most of every situation and just got on with things.

With everything loaded, the four of them piled into Jan's ageing estate car, Michaela in the front with Jan, Leo and Anna in the back.

'How long will it take us to get there?' Anna asked as she struggled to plug in her seatbelt. When Leo leaned over to help, his hand brushing hers, her familiar scent teased him and he felt an unexpected longing for how things had once been.

'About three hours if the traffic is good,' said Jan. 'Most people's *chatas* are only forty-five minutes or an hour away. Driving this far for a weekend is unusual but it's because it is where my family originally came from.'

The initial part of the journey through Prague was slow going until they reached the motorway.

'Sorry, it's not a very interesting journey at first,' Jan apologised. 'But the fastest way is to take the toll road to Brno and then drop down towards the Austrian border. But I promise when we get nearer, it will be better.'

'So where are we going?' asked Anna, opening up her phone. 'I know it's Southern Moravia but that doesn't mean much to me.'

Leo nudged her with his elbow. 'And you do like to know where you're going.'

'We're going to near the Austrian border. The nearest town is Pavlov, but we are right by the Věstonice reservoir, which is a big nature park.'

'Can you spell that?' asked Anna, as she brought up the Google maps app.

'Anna is the go-to navigator,' said Leo, as he watched her input the journey. 'Whereas I have absolutely no sense of direction.'

'It's true. He's useless.' Anna looked up from her phone and then quickly glanced back again.

Leo smiled to himself. An old in-joke. He had no sense of direction, unless it was in the bedroom, where he knew due south.

'I have my moments,' he murmured, and was gratified when Anna made a stalwart attempt to move the conversation on, her cheeks reddening. He leaned back in his seat and folded his arms with an ever so slightly smug grin on his face. He really shouldn't take pleasure in Anna's discomfort, but sometimes it was gratifying to know she wasn't immune to him. He knew women liked him but Anna had always held back. It was that cool reserve that had first attracted him.

Anna stared out of the window at the rolling green countryside, which offered occasional glimpses of orchards and vineyards dotted with traditional white buildings and the now familiar terracotta-tiled roofs. Michaela had told her this was South Moravia and this particular area was known for growing almonds and grapes. She was grateful that they were at last coming off the slip road of the motorway into somewhere called Hustopeče. Acutely aware of Leo beside her, she'd been tracking their journey on her phone as a distraction, although her left foot had developed a constant jitter which was nothing to do with being cooped up in a car.

'We should take a quick detour to show you the town square and the church, shouldn't we, Jan?' said Michaela, suddenly warming to her role of tour guide. 'St Wenceslas and St Agnes is very modern, built in a circle. I think it's beautiful. Jan isn't so keen, it's too modern for him.'

Jan grunted from the driver's seat but obligingly turned off the main road down a side street. They emerged in a large, cobbled square with an extraordinarily contemporary church on the right. With its tall tower and the curved walls that swept down into a graceful curve of white stone it made a striking contrast to the rest of the buildings.

'Now that is beautiful,' said Jan pointing the stone-and-white rendered building opposite. It was five storeys high, with arched windows, an oriel window, a gable and a square tower with a clock and a turret. It might have been an architectural extravaganza with all those features but, when viewed as a whole, it was a quiet, calm building, elegant in its simplicity.

'I agree,' said Anna, looking round the square. 'Everything is so clean and tidy,' she marvelled, taking in the litter-free pavements and the hanging baskets on every lamppost.

'Now the road crosses the reservoir,' announced

Michaela, pointing to the bridge spanning the centre of the body of water. 'Imagine, before this you would have had to drive all the way around.'

Jan laughed. 'It wasn't that far, only ten or so kilometres.'

Once they'd crossed the reservoir, the roads became progressively smaller until they finally turned onto a dirt track, along which the car bumped for a few minutes before the path petered out in what seemed like the middle of nowhere.

'Here we are,' said Michaela, jumping out of the car before Jan had even switched off the engine. 'Our *chata* on the lake. Come see.'

By the time Leo and Anna had unfolded themselves from the back of the car, she was scrambling up a small grassy bank on their right. At the top she stopped and turned. 'Come on,' she called.

Leo paused. 'Do you want a hand?' he asked Jan.

The other man shook his head. 'In a minute. Go take a look. I've seen it before.' His indulgent smile as he watched Michaela disappear gave Anna a small pang of envy. 'This really is her favourite place. We're so excited that it's ours.' Although his words were quietly spoken, Anna knew they expressed the couple's deep feelings for the place.

'Come on, then,' said Leo, reaching for Anna's hand to help her up the bank. When they crested the small slope, the land flattened out, leading down to the lake.

'Oh,' said Anna.

'Wow. What a spot.'

The pretty wooden cabin sat a few metres from the

water's edge, the tall apex of its roof against the backdrop of brilliant blue sky reflected in the flat sheen of the water. Apart from the birdsong, the distant splashes of ducks in the reeds and the breeze whispering through the leaves in the trees around them, there wasn't a sound.

Michaela simply sighed and clasped her hands to her chest, looking up at the house. 'And it's all ours.' Her eyes brimmed with tears and Jan, who'd caught up with them, put an arm around her shoulders to give her a hug.

'It's all good.' She brushed at her eyes. 'They are happy tears. I'm so glad to be here and to be able to share it with friends.'

The house had two storeys and was much larger than Anna had expected. Hadn't Michaela said Jan's uncle's family had built it themselves? The lower walls were built of rough-hewn stones, the upper walls clad in wood. As she came closer she could see that some things needed a bit of TLC. Despite this, the house was a great design. What caught Anna's attention most was the upper-floor window nestled in the high inverted V of the roof, with its large balcony and what she could bet was a prime view over the water.

'It's gorgeous,' Anna told Michaela, who beamed with quiet pride, her eyes still glistening with tears.

'Yes, there is a lot to do but the structure is good. Come inside and see.'

She skipped up the steps, unlocked the door and threw it open with an excited giggle. Anna followed more slowly, taking in her surroundings. Through the trees she could make out a couple of neighbouring structures but at a far enough distance to offer privacy.

The front door opened into a narrow corridor with three doors off to the left and three to the right. At the end of the corridor was a ladder that went up through a large square hatch.

Michaela opened the first door on the left and Anna stepped in. It reminded her of an old people's home with its row of high-backed armchairs facing the grime-streaked windows. Despite the big windows it felt dark and cramped and not particularly inviting.

'We spend most of our time outside in the summer,' explained Michaela as if reading her mind, and walked on to the next room. 'This is the kitchen,' she said, pulling a face, and Anna could see why.

The dark area beyond was tiny with a set of very dated marbled Formica-fronted units taking up a small portion of the back wall, two up and two down, sandwiching a tiny metal sink and a rust-spotted stove hooked up to a large gas cylinder. A rack holding several plates clung to the ugly cement block wall. It sagged in the middle, a couple of its spindles missing, like gapped teeth, and looked in danger of imminent collapse onto the square wood-veneered table beneath it. A thin, weak stream of daylight struggled through a tiny, dusty window, on the opposite wall, that looked out on the trees at the side of the house.

'I know. It's very ugly. It's going to be a lot of work to make it beautiful,' said Michaela with a forlorn sigh. 'So many weekends.'

Anna studied the sad little kitchen, her eyes zeroing in on the rotting floor and noting the old-fashioned wood panelling on the walls. Despite the dated fittings and decaying fabric, her brain ticked away, already thinking of fixes that she'd seen thanks to her obsession with Instagram home improvements.

'What would you do?' asked Michaela.

'Me?'

'Yes. If this was yours, what would you do?'

Anna took a considering breath. There was so much potential here.

'I'd take up the floor.' With one foot she tapped the boards, which had wide drafty gaps. 'Put new boards down. Sand and polish them.'

Michaela clasped her hands together. 'That sounds good.'

'And I'd remove that wall and knock through to the front room with the view. Make it a kitchen you live in.'

'Yes!'

'And I'd put bi-fold doors where the windows are. Scrap the units at the back and replace them with a single run, and then put in an island area with seating in the middle. And I'd do something with that old dresser. You could upcycle it to tie in with whatever colour scheme and units you decide on.'

'I was going to get rid of it, although it is very useful. We keep all the china in there. But you're right, I can do something with it. I'm going to keep it. Now come see the bedrooms.'

Michaela pushed open the first door on the right in the corridor to reveal a big empty room with dusty floorboards which creaked as she stepped on them. 'It's very cosy when we light the fires.' She pointed to a large stone chimney breast on the far wall and the open fireplace with a pot-bellied wood burner. 'Or it will be when we have a bed in here. There used to be bunk beds in here for all the children – it would sleep six – but we took them out.' She shot Anna an impish grin. 'For now. One day we will buy a big bed for me and Jan but until then we have air beds.'

She guided Anna to the next room. 'This will be your room. I hope you don't mind sharing. But there is an air bed each and it is a big room.'

Although a substantial size it was still smaller than the room next door and, like the other room, had a fireplace, though smaller, with another wood burner, and wooden clad walls Two small windows looked out onto the woods at the back of the house.

'And here is the bathroom with Jan's famous shower.'

The bathroom was basic and consisted of an old tin bath with a shower head mounted above it and around it a plastic curtain covered in pink fish.

'And the toilet?' asked Anna.

Michaela wrinkled her nose. 'Not so good. There is a shed outside. There is no proper plumbing here. The water comes to the house in a pipe from down the road but there is no waste. But I promise you, having hot water in the shower is a luxury. It used to be cold only.'

Anna laughed. 'This is luxury. I'm used to camping, and my cousins like wild camping, so this is fine.'

'And now the best bit.' Michaela moved to the end of the corridor to climb the rickety ladder. 'Watch your step.'

Anna followed her up, taking each tread gingerly. At the top she stepped gratefully from the ladder into a living room under the sloping eaves. Light poured in from the big triangular windows at the front of the house. How on earth had they got them up here? The walls were clad in honeyed wood from the floor to the very apex of the roof. On the wall at the back of the room was a huge stone hearth, around which large floor cushions were arranged so that guests could take in the view from around the fire.

Michaela crossed to the balcony doors, opened them and stepped out into the early evening sunshine. She rested both hands on the wooden balustrade, her face tilted up to the sun.

'This,' she said simply, waving one hand towards the still, shimmering water.

'Yes,' said Anna, understanding immediately. It was all about the view and the sense of being at the heart of nature. Trees in an arc of vivid green tumbled down to the water's edge, some clinging to the sandy banks, their trunks twisted to maintain stability. Directly in front of the *chata* a grassy field sloped down to the reservoir. An old tree trunk lying on the ground had had one side removed to turn it into a seat with a perfect vantage point. Birds wheeled in the sky, and away in the distance on the far side of the water rose purple-shadowed hills .

'There are actually three reservoirs here,' explained Michaela. 'When they were created they flooded the forests and a village, Mušov. You can still see the church, which is on a tiny island all by itself.

'That's sad but it is very beautiful.' Anna thought of the

people who'd once lived in the village and wondered out loud what had happened to them.

'Jan's grandparents were from Mušov. They moved to Brno, and Jan's uncle came back to build his *chata*. He never had children and his health is not so good. Jan's father has his own house further down the reservoir which we have used before. Jan's uncle doesn't want to manage the *chata* anymore, which is why he's given it to us.' Michaela clasped her hands over her heart and did a little skip of excitement.

In the meantime, they could hear the sound of the men below who had obviously begun to unload the car.

'I guess we ought to help,' said Michaela, with a mischievous smile. As soon as she descended the ladder she began directing Jan.

'You can show Leo your room,' said Michaela, with an airy wave of her hand as she took the box of food supplies from Jan and went into the kitchen.

'This is us,' said Anna, as Leo dropped the two air mattresses on the floor.

'Cool,' he said giving the room a cursory look and immediately crossing to the log burner, kneeling on the floor and opening the iron door.

'Men and fire,' said Anna. The wood burner in the apartment was definitely Leo's domain.

'Always.' Leo grinned up at her from where he crouched. Her mouth went dry as she took in his delightfully dishevelled appearance – rolled-up shirt sleeves and untucked shirt.

'Mmm,' she said, her vocal cords feeling a little tight.

Tonight she'd be sharing this room with him, and all she could think was: where was she going to change?

'Who's ready for a drink?' called Jan from the kitchen.

'I reckon we deserve one,' said Leo.

'Yes,' said Anna, her voice squeaky.

'You all right?' asked Leo.

'Just the dust,' she lied. 'I need a drink.'

And that wasn't all she needed. A cold dip in the lake might be called for.

Chapter Twenty

Leo lounged on the picnic blanket, near the firepit that Jan had lit using kindling from fallen branches and the logs stacked outside the *chata*. He listened to the two women chatting about ideas and improvements to the building as Jan went down to the water's edge to pluck several more bottles of beer from the crate he'd lodged in the reservoir to keep it cold. This was definitely Leo's idea of a good weekend, being outdoors in the fresh air, albeit with a good thick jumper on, with nothing to do but kick back and enjoy the fresh air and the company.

'Here you go,' said Jan, deliberately dripping cold water on Leo's face. Anna and Michaela, who had swapped to white wine, both laughed as Leo shot up in shock and yelled his surprise. Jan simply grinned, flipped the crown caps of the bottles and handed him one. '*Na zdraví*,' he said, tapping his bottle against Leo's.

'Want to help me with the grill? We have *klobása* and chicken and some vegetables to cook.'

'Sure,' said Leo. 'If you tell me what *klobása* is... It's not sheep's intestines or anything?' He pulled a childish face.

'You're thinking of haggis,' said Anna, rolling her eyes toward Michaela.

'It's a pork sausage made with paprika, herbs and garlic.'

'Ah, count me in, then,' said Leo.

'Can I do anything to help?' asked Anna.

'Yes, come slice up the vegetables while Jan gets the barbecue lit.' She lowered her voice but still spoke loudly enough for both men to hear. 'We have to let them play with the fire.'

Jan lunged towards Michaela in retaliation, making her giggle, and the two of them wrestled until it ended in a kiss. Leo felt a sharp pang, decided it was uncharitable envy and deliberately avoided looking at Anna. Did she remember them being playful together like this? It felt like such a loss. Pain twisted in his heart, sharp and fast like a dagger thrust.

'Get a room, you guys,' he said.

'Cooking time,' said Michaela and dragged Anna off to the kitchen, while Jan took him to the shed, where they unearthed an ancient grill and a sack of charcoal.

They ate the marinated chicken thighs and spicy *koblása*, with slices of grilled courgette, red peppers, onions and plump juicy tomatoes, and hunks of fresh bread that were invaluable for soaking up the juices, as they sat around the dancing flames of the firepit with a bottle of south Moravian wine, which Leo had to admit was pretty damn good.

By the time the light was long gone, warm lethargy had

invaded his limbs, and when Michaela suggested they all turn in, the thought of bed was more than inviting.

He'd already spotted Anna's stricken expression earlier in the day when they'd inspected where they were sleeping and he knew she was worrying about the logistics. It was such an Anna thing to worry about.

'Why don't you go in first,' he suggested. 'Get ready.'

'Thanks,' she said with a grateful smile, the little worry lines around her mouth receding immediately.

When he came into the room, a solitary candle stood on top of the wood burner and Anna was tucked into her bed, motionless as a corpse on the opposite side of the room. Although it was tempting to wish her a cheery goodnight while she played dead, he thought better of it, blew out the candle and undressed quickly, leaving his boxers on. It didn't take him long to settle his body into a comfortable position but his brain lit up like fireflies in the dark with thoughts of Anna. The memory of when he'd first got to know her decided to repeat on loop and he snorted quietly to himself, remembering how, while working behind the bar, he'd had to coax her out of her shell like a suspicious tortoise. From day one, her no-nonsense, don't-take-any-crap demeanour had fascinated and intrigued him. So different from other women he'd met. Despite, in his opinion, being a stunner, Anna was not only uninterested in her looks but dismissed any comments about them. Compliments were treated with scepticism, flattering remarks with a flat refusal to listen, let alone accept them.

His eyes grew accustomed to the gloom and through the window he could see the shapes of the trees against the sky, which was alive with tiny pinpricks of light. Gradually his eyes began to droop and he felt himself sliding into sleep.

He surfaced from the dream trying to hang onto the wisps of its cosy warmth – sunshine, a beach, kissing, kissing Anna. Yeah, kissing Anna, holding her soft body – which had poofed away leaving disappointment and the remnants of a hard-on that was unlikely to get release any time soon. As he lay there he heard a soft sigh and the whisper of bedclothes and realised that Anna was awake. She turned again and this time uttered a huff of annoyance. Closing his eyes, he tried to go back to sleep, but his whole body, still humming from the kiss in his dreams, was acutely aware of Anna on the other side of the room. There it was again. Another sigh, this time accompanied by a louder huff and then a protracted rearrangement of her feather duvet, which rustled like soft plastic.

It was impossible to ignore, and tension tightened his muscles, making it even harder to ignore her presence on the other side of the room.

'Anna,' he eventually said into the dark. 'What's wrong?'

The lengthy silence irritated him even more and he knew that it was his own frustration that made him terse.

She huffed out another sigh. 'My mattress is deflating.'

'What?'

'It's going down. I think I've got a slow puncture. Do you think Jan has a repair kit?'

Leo burst out laughing. Only Anna would consider repairing a bed in the middle of the night.

'He probably has but I'm not sure he'd be too happy to

be woken in the middle of the night. And repairing a hole by candlelight could be quite a challenge.'

'Not helping, Leo,' she said, tossing again.

'Sorry.'

Her response was yet another huff.

After a minute's silence, he said, aware of his heart banging in his chest, 'Do you want to come in here?'

It took her a moment to reply. 'No, I'm fine. I've arranged my duvet so I can lie on some of it.'

There was more rustling as she tried to get comfortable. He turned over, sleep not so much evading him as getting up and leaving the country. His inward curses each time she tossed and turned brought him to a fever pitch of irritation, as much with himself as with her. After ten interminable minutes, he spoke through gritted teeth.

'Just get in here, for God's sake.'

'I'm fine.'

'You're not fine and you're keeping me awake.'

'Well, I'm sorry about that.' Her sarcastic voice rang out. 'I do apologise for disturbing your beauty sleep but I'm basically sleeping on a wooden floor, your highness.'

'For fuck's sake, Anna. We've shared a bed before. One more time is not going to kill you. You can thank me in the morning when you're feeling rested.'

'Hmph,' said Anna ungraciously but he heard her kicking off her covers. He moved to the far side of the mattress and turned down the duvet to accommodate her. 'You need to talk to me, I can't see.'

Suddenly there was a whompf as Anna tripped on the

edge of the mattress and fell on top of him, her head narrowly missing his crown jewels.

'Steady on,' he grunted, startled by the narrow miss. She lay there with her head burrowed between his legs, her soft breath whistling along the hairs on his thighs. Suddenly he wasn't feeling quite so alarmed, something altogether different.

'Er, Anna. Do you think you could er … erm, move.'

She lifted her head, her hair brushing his skin. He had to clench his fists to stop himself reaching to stroke her head.

'Yes. Sorry.' She moved again, trying to gain purchase on the mattress, and one hand grazed his stomach. He sucked in a quick breath.

'Anna get into bed, will you.'

'Sorry, did I hurt you?'

'No,' he said tersely, horribly conscious of the sudden rush of blood down below.

'I didn't mean to headbutt your nuts. Are you okay?'

'I'm fine,' he said through gritted teeth. Surely she must know what she was doing to him. 'You missed.'

'Phew. I wouldn't want to be responsible for damaging your manhood and depriving the world of future Knight babies.'

'For which I'm very grateful.' Every part of him was now on high alert. Shit, this had been a very bad idea. 'Now get in and go to sleep.' He hoped she would put the snap in his tone down to disturbed sleep and not to the chaos triggered in him by her closeness and the familiarity of her warm body.

Anna edged her way under the duvet and settled in on

the far side of the mattress. The fire had died down and was nothing more than a dull glow in the stove. Cold air seeped in where the duvet stretched across the divide between them. He lay on his back, staring out of the curtainless window at the myriad stars spread like fine lace across the sky, millions of incalculably huge numbers of years away, but much as he focused on them, he was horribly aware of Anna. His mind crackled with memories: her skin, the scent of her hair, the way she slept, one leg crooked, the little noises she made in her sleep.

She fidgeted on her side of the bed, almost falling out, in what he assumed was her earnest desire to keep as much distance as possible between them. Every time she moved, it was a reminder of how close and yet how far from him she was. This was next to torture. He reached out and put a hand on her waist to roll her over. 'Anna, you're not going to spontaneously combust if we accidentally touch.'

'I didn't want to disturb you.'

'You're disturbing me more by treating me like I'm a wet squid that got in the bath with you.' Exasperated, he slid an arm beneath her shoulder and pulled her to him, so her head rested on his shoulder. 'Now go to sleep. It can't get any worse than this, can it?'

She let out a snuffly laugh, her breath tickling his skin. 'That's your solution?'

'Yes. It's the worst that can happen and now it has.'

'Not the worst,' countered Anna.

'The worst of your imaginings. Now we've got that out the way, we can go to sleep.'

She was still a little stiff but he could feel her gradually relaxing against him.

'Better?' he asked.

'Yes,' she said. 'It's more comfortable. Don't get any ideas.'

'Wouldn't dream of it.' He breathed deeply, inhaling the scent of her, her hair soft beneath his chin. He could do this. Remain immune. They were friends. They'd reached a good place. They could share a bed and it could be platonic.

With a small smile he dropped a silent kiss on her hair and her hand tightened on his waist.

'Thank you, Leo.'

'For what?' he asked, his body starting to soften with sleep.

'For being you.'

In the dark he smiled. It feel good to be valued for himself and not compared to anyone else, like his brother for instance. Now that she was nestled next to him, the warmth of her body relaxing against him, all was good. He closed his eyes. Anna. Here. All was good. As the fuzziness of sleep enfolded him, he was vaguely aware that perhaps this *wasn't* such a good idea … but it felt so good.

Chapter Twenty-One

G od, the birds were loud. It was her first conscious thought. The second was that Leo had quite an erection going on, which was currently poking into her hip. Keeping the rest of her as still as possible, she turned her head from where she was sprawled face-down next to him, one leg hooked over his. A sleepy snuffle suggested he wasn't yet awake and she took the chance to study him. If it weren't for that sexy, sulky mouth in repose, his blonde hair haloed in the bright morning sunshine pouring through the window would have made him look far too much like an angel for comfort.

The light planed the lines of his jaw, catching the golden, sugary bristles on his chin, bringing back a memory of the light sandpaper rasp of his skin over hers, and early-morning kisses. Her mouth dried and sadness filled up inside her. Her fingers itched to touch his face.

'I know you're watching me,' murmured Leo, his voice husky with sleep. 'Stop it. It's creepy.'

'It's not creepy if you know,' retorted Anna.

'Mmm.' Leo wrapped an arm around her waist and pulled her top half closer to him, burrowing his face into her neck. 'You're so lovely and warm.' His body softened ... well, most of it ... beneath her. She was still very aware of his morning stand-to-attention and held her breath, waiting for him to realise and perhaps pull back. She didn't want to embarrass him but he was clearly still half asleep. She ought to pull away herself but the soft sleepiness in his voice caught at something in her and she couldn't bring herself to. Instead she smiled and allowed herself to savour the moment, his warm body, skin on skin, and the soft huffs of his breath against her neck. Her fingers idly traced his spine, her hand splaying over the muscles in his back. Six years on, he was even more beautiful. A small bud of desire unfurled a heated sensation between her thighs. She closed her eyes and lay still, her body flooded with contented wellbeing. If she stayed like this, it would be enough.

Leo gave another sleepy sigh. 'I miss you,' he whispered into her neck, his breath sending a flutter across her skin. Her hand on his back tightened, holding him closer, but the lump in her throat stopped her from saying anything. Instead, her heart ached at the words.

His lips grazed her skin, a touch so gentle it was barely there, but it sent flickers of awareness dancing across her body. She held her breath, not wanting him to stop. His hand slid up from her waist and cupped the underside of a breast.

'Leo,' she whispered on a sigh and turned her head. His eyes were open, staring at her with earnest softness.

'Anna,' he whispered back, his gaze never leaving hers, those blue eyes bright, watchful and something else… Wary? Hopeful? Guarded? She wasn't sure which but she hated the vulnerability she could see there. Turning onto her side, she lifted her hand to stroke his chin, her thumb catching his lip. His soft groan ignited a slow heat inside her as his hand slipped over the swell of her breast, caressing and reverent. She sucked in a breath, their eyes still locked. Looking away would have been impossible. It was if they were suspended in the ray of sunshine that bathed their bodies, a world apart from reality at that moment.

He leant forward, his eyes never leaving her face, moving so slowly, giving her the chance to bolt if she wanted to. She didn't. The yearning inside her intensified. Want. Need. Desperation.

She reached up to touch his face, her eyes telling him everything he needed to know.

With a sigh, his lips softened into a wistful smile as his mouth closed in on hers.

That first kiss was like coming home after a long arduous expedition away, sinking back into comfort. Slow, languorous. They took the time to test, tease and explore, their mouths shaping and moving over each other's with the fluid grace of a murmuration. It was an easy slide from uncertainty, that bashful getting to know each other again, testing the waters, through to growing familiarity and then on to the climb of passion. The bright, still morning was punctuated with their fevered breaths, sighs and gasps.

'Anna.' Leo wrenched his mouth from hers and laid his

hot forehead against hers, pulling away from her body, gripping the wrist that was currently slowly stroking him. 'We have to stop.'

'We don't have to,' she said.

'Yes, we do. I can't do this. Not again.'

She stared into his eyes again, trying to get a read on him. It was as if her desire had been buried metres deep under the frozen tundra. No one had ever made her feel quite the way Leo did. This sensation that she might die if she didn't get *there*. She was desperate for his touch. 'I want you. You want me.' In that moment, she realised that there had never been anyone but Leo for her. She loved him. She ran a hand over his chest but he grabbed it, pushing it away.

'Anna, stop.' His mouth crimped into a straight line. 'We're not doing this.'

She flinched, surprised by the sudden bite of his words.

'There's no going back for us.' Leo pulled back, rolled off the mattress and sat up with his back to her.

She had to force her hand not to reach out and touch his smooth back. Hurt wrapped around her like ivy choking a tree. She had to mould her face into a blank mask as she lay there and looked up at the ceiling, holding tightly onto her emotions.

'Yeah, you're probably right,' she managed. 'Just forced proximity playing tricks on us.'

'Yeah,' said Leo, not turning round. 'Probably that.'

He stood up and leaned down to retrieve something from his overnight bag, the sunlight catching on the golden hairs of his muscular thighs. Maybe it was lust, not love.

And maybe there'd be blue pigs flying over a rainbow during a blue moon.

'I'm going for a swim,' he announced. He grabbed a towel and his shoes and strode out of the room. As soon as he'd gone, Anna allowed her face to crumple. She didn't give in to the tears that threatened, but instead berated herself for being such a fool. Of course Leo wasn't interested in her anymore. There would be no second chance for her.

'Morning,' said Michaela, immediately pushing a pot of coffee towards her. 'Did you sleep well?'

Her bright-eyed beam, full of enthusiasm and happiness, made Anna determined not to dwell on this morning. Michaela had been so looking forward to welcoming them to her *chata* that Anna didn't have the heart to spoil this weekend.

'Not bad,' she said. 'These look nice.' She nodded to the basket of pastries. Michaela, with her usual stylish attention to detail, had prettied up the breakfast table and it sported an embroidered tablecloth decorated with daisies, a bright blue pottery vase full of wild flowers, and a stylish glass jug with matching glasses. 'Someone has been busy.'

'Jan has been to the bakery in Pavlov. And I did some fussing.' She smoothed her hand over the cloth. 'This belonged to Jan's grandmother. His mother passed it down to us.' Michaela's smile was full of fondness. 'She has her own grandmother's. I think it's special when you can use things from the family, especially when they're as beautiful as this. It's too nice to live in a drawer and only be brought out for big occasions.'

'It's beautiful,' said Anna, reaching out and touching the heavy linen, tracing one of the flowers, reflecting that it was a lovely sentiment. She had nothing of her mother's or of either of her grandmothers'. Her aunt and uncle prized practicality over aesthetics or sentimentality. No family heirlooms. Tablecloths in their house had always been plastic-covered.

'When you make things look beautiful, it makes a meal an occasion, a moment, don't you think? And it shows people that you care.' Michaela beamed at her. 'We are so happy that you and Leo came here with us. I know we haven't known you very long but I think it is already a good friendship.' She stood up and moved around the table to give Anna a quick hug and as her feminine, floral-patterned dress wafted in the light breeze it triggered a memory.

A woman in a pretty dress, the hem lifting and dancing, leaning down in a garden, picking flowers. Her mother. She'd always worn dresses. And loved flowers. Other memories bloomed like watercolour splodges on paper. Long slender gladioli taken from the garden, bright sunshine-y daffodils and fragrant pink roses, the petals of which Anna had stroked and sniffed, because she could reach them from her mother's lap. Pain whipped through her.

Her khaki cargo pants and black long-sleeved T-shirt felt heavy on her body and constricted her limbs. She looked down at the thick fabric and wished she'd brought something a little prettier to wear, especially after this morning. Her body felt so much easier and all of a sudden she longed for something light and loose.

'I wish I'd bought a dress with me. I feel...' She pulled a face, not wanting to put into words the lumpen, unfeminine way she felt.

'I have one you can borrow. We're about the same size, except you're taller than me.' Michaela jumped up and disappeared, then returned with a pretty, floral cotton dress with puffed sleeves and a shirred bodice. 'Here, you can wear this.'

'Thank you. It's lovely.' Anna could already imagine wearing it, the fabric flowing around her knees. 'When we get back to Prague, could you recommend somewhere to get my hair cut and maybe come with me to translate? I've left it for so long, it needs ... something.'

'Makeover?' said Michaela with a sudden gleam in her eye.

'No, just ...well, maybe it's time for a change.' Anna suddenly felt ridiculous. This wasn't about proving anything to herself or Leo. She didn't need his approval. His reference to 'oval-shaped Anna' had been sitting fermenting in her brain, like grain in a mash tun, for the last week. That was all it was.

'Where's Leo?' asked Michaela. 'Still in bed?'

'No, he went for a swim.' She pointed towards the water and sure enough there was Leo emerging from it, walking towards them in his black jersey boxers, sweeping his wet hair back. Something twisted low in her stomach at the sight of him.

'Whoa!' Michaela fanned herself. 'He's one fine man.' She shot Anna a mischievous look. 'That must be hard to resist.'

Anna's skin heated with a rapid blush as she was reminded of the humiliation of his rejection.

'It's really not that difficult,' she said, attempting to sound insouciant rather than bitter.

'Morning,' said Michaela. 'How was the water?'

'The water was great.'

He plonked a wet kiss on Michaela's cheek.

'Eew, you're wet,' she squealed, pushing him away.

'But adorable,' he teased, winking at her.

Anna rolled her eyes. She seemed to do a lot of that when he was around. 'Go and get dressed, Leo, and stop flaunting your abs. No one's impressed.'

He raised an eyebrow as if to point out that her hands hadn't been complaining not so long ago, but with his usual grace he simply patted his stomach. 'All bought and paid for.'

'Very nice,' said Michaela with a cheery grin.

He saluted and sauntered off towards the house.

Leo was Leo. Always had been, always would be.

'He's very cute,' said Michaela.

Anna shrugged. 'Yes, and everyone thinks so.'

'Even you.' Michaela gave her an encouraging smile.

'That ship has sailed,' said Anna.

'Are you sure? Sometimes he looks at you and he looks sad.'

Anna's heart pinched, false hope jumping in where it had no place to be. She shook her head. 'You've got it wrong. He's far too busy having fun. I think Zdeňka's very keen.'

'Oh, they're two of a kind.' Michaela gave a dismissive wave. 'They like to flirt. There's nothing there. There are some that use their charm to get what they want and hurt people by being careless. I don't think Leo is like that. He likes you. A lot.'

'No,' said Anna, quickly ignoring her final statement. 'He isn't like that.' He was warm, funny, generous and kind. She'd ignored so many of the good things about him, focusing too much on the fear of what it would be like to lose him. Look where that had got her and now she was in love with him all over again and he clearly didn't feel the same anymore. Not that she could blame him. She was the one that had walked out on him and now she was realising she'd might have made a terrible mistake.

Chapter Twenty-Two

'This is really lovely,' said Anna as they drove through beautiful green, rolling countryside, the hills topped with smatterings of rocks.

'This is the Palava Protected Landscape Area. There are lots of trails and walks. You can walk from Pavlov to Mikulov, it's not too difficult and takes about two hours.'

The town of Mikulov was an absolute delight, Anna decided, with its old stone buildings perched on the hillside, glowing in the early evening golden sunshine and topped by the distinctive Lock building, which Jan explained was a castle built in the 1200s. It had been burned to the ground in 1945 but restored in the '50s and was a hodge-podge of cream buildings topped by terracotta roofs, with a verdigris onion-topped spire. Opposite was another striking rounded hill. 'That's Holy Hill,' said Michaela. 'Another good walk. It's protected landscape with lots of wildlife and wildflowers and people make a pilgrimage to the church, St Sebastian. It is one of the oldest Ways of the Cross in the Czech Republic and people have been coming here for hundreds of years.'

When they reached the town centre, Anna's attention was captured by a striking building.

'I love that, what is it?' she asked, pointing to the distinctive black-and-white decoration on an elegant house on one side of the town square. White figures dressed in mediaeval costumes covered the walls in little vignettes, boxed in with elaborate floral motifs.

'That is sgraffito and dates back to the Renaissance.'

'It's beautiful. I think I saw something similar at Prague Castle but I didn't know what it was.'

'You mean the Schwarzenberg Palace. That is a very good example.'

'Can we take a closer look?' asked Anna.

'Yes. I thought we could have a local beer here in the square. It is good for people-watching,' said Jan.

'Always need to try the local beer,' said Leo, sitting up straighter in the back of the car. 'Good for our beer education.'

'Do you need any more beer education?' Anna teased, determined that there wouldn't be an atmosphere between them. Michaela and Jan were such good hosts, she didn't want them to feel uncomfortable.

'Always,' said Leo.

Jan and Michaela laughed. 'It would be rude for us not to help,' said Jan.

As they were walking along the street, Michaela stopped and tugged at Anna's arm. 'This is where I bought the glasses and jug.' She dragged Anna into the shop, leaving the men to continue along the road.

Inside were tasteful displays of stylish stationery, fragrant artisan soaps, pretty tablecloths, napkins, glasses – and the most adorable candle holder, which Anna immediately decided to buy. Just as they were about to leave Michaela pointed to a pretty red dress.

'That would look lovely on you.'

Anna wrinkled her nose. 'I'm not sure about red.'

'Oh, but it would be perfect with your colouring,' insisted Michaela, taking it down from the display, holding it up against Anna and guiding her to a nearby mirror.

Fifteen minutes later, Anna found herself emerging from the shop with the dress and a bag full of items that would make the apartment much more homely.

'I'm not sure shopping with you is such a good idea,' teased Anna.

'Oh, it is. I know all the best places. And the dress you've bought is lovely.'

'Thank you. It's funny because I'm not really a dress person,' said Anna. 'But I love this one you've lent me and the one I've bought.'

'Why not?' demanded Michaela. 'They suit you. You have an elegant shape.'

Anna laughed and fanned the fabric of Michaela's dress around her legs, relishing the feel of the material wafting around her. No one had ever described her like that before. 'Thank you.'

Michaela pressed her again. 'Why don't you wear dresses?'

Anna thought about it. 'I don't know. It was never a thing at home. My aunt always wears skirts and blouses and I don't want to look like her, and my cousin Rebecca is either in jeans or sportswear. I guess I never think of buying one.' Her mother had worn dresses, soft cotton summer dresses in the garden and smart shift dresses for special occasions.

They joined the men outside the Hotel Galant. Anna was not surprised to find that it had its own brewery on site and brewed four varieties of beer. Of course it did.

She and Leo pondered the choices for a little while at the bar, before Leo opted for the Galant 11, a dark lager, while Anna chose the much lighter, gold coloured Galant 10. They took their drinks to the garden, which had a view of Holy Hill.

They sat and chatted in the sunshine, talking mainly about Michaela and Jan's plans for the *chata*, including Jan's vision of a vegetable patch at the side of the house and Michaela's ideas for the kitchen, including how they might revamp the old-fashioned dresser.

'If you take off all the mouldings, sand it and paint it a dark blue, you could add light wood handles which would really stand out against the blue – and put a matching wooden top on it. Or you could put on trendy copper or brass handles. You can get these really cool satin copper ones, which would look lovely against the blue.' Anna did a quick search on her phone and brought up the picture of the handles she'd been hankering after ever since she'd seen them.

'I like that idea,' said Michaela. 'And we could paint the

cabinets in the kitchen the same colour and it would all blend.'

'Where will you get the cabinets?'

'Jan is going to build them.'

Anna felt a tinge of envy that they had a project.

'I could get used to this,' said Leo, wiping the foam from his upper lip. 'This place is idyllic.'

'You should see it during the wine festival. It gets very busy with tourists from all over Europe. You must come and stay in September.'

Anna and Leo exchanged glances and it was Anna who spoke first. 'We won't be here.'

'Ah, yes. The beer competition.' Jan cocked an eyebrow. 'How is it coming along?'

Anna nodded. 'I think I'm nearly there but I need a name for my beer, which is the difficult part. The brewery is so old, it's hard to find something traditional. And then we have to present our beer and our marketing and sales plan to a panel at the British Embassy in the next three weeks. And they'll choose which one will be presented at the Christmas Beer Festival.'

'Whereas the name is the easy part for me, but I don't have the beer yet,' mourned Leo. 'And as for a presentation…' He shuddered.

'I thought you'd enjoy being the showman.'

'That bit's fine. It's the computer bit, putting together slides and things. I don't have the patience. But I don't need to worry until I have a beer I'm happy with.'

'Why haven't you made the beer yet?' asked Jan.

'Because Karel is happy to let me play. And there are a

thousand options. There's no pressure because he likes to flit about from idea to idea.' Leo's mouth turned down. 'There's always the possibility of something better.'

'Jakub has been quite strict. There is no deviation from the process, which was frustrating at first but has been good discipline. He has steered my direction but listened to my ideas.' Anna didn't want to rub it in but she was very happy with what was in the tank and she was looking forward to trying it in the next week or so.

'But how can you have a name, if you don't know the taste of the beer?' she suddenly asked.

Leo wrinkled his nose at her. 'Who says the name has to reflect the taste? It's about marketing. A good name and branding sells. You've got the perfect one.'

'I have?'

'Yes. *Láska*. Love, in Czech. Your surname.'

'I don't think so.' She laughed. 'Not all of us have egos as big as yours.'

Leo clutched his heart. 'You wound me.'

'And now,' said Michaela rising to her feet, 'We'll take you to dinner at one of our favourite restaurants, to say thank you for all the help.'

'Surely we should be paying for dinner to say thank you for the accommodation,' protested Anna as Michaela walked on a few paces ahead of them.

'Next time,' insisted Jan.

'If you're sure,' said Anna.

'Anna, be honest,' teased Leo. 'Wild woman-eating lions aren't going to stop you coming back. You're desperate to help Jan build that kitchen.'

'Does it show that much?' she asked with a laugh.

'Yes. I had no idea you were so into this DIY stuff. You never used to be.'

'I learned a lot in the last few years. People change.'

'They do,' said Leo, his eyes meeting hers with a steady look.

Anna experienced a tiny frisson of unease. 'I don't think you've changed a bit.' Even as the words left her mouth, she knew they were untrue. Leo was even more lovable than he had been before but she couldn't tell him that. Especially not when he clearly didn't feel the same way anymore.

'And that's where you're wrong. You've got no idea.' She was shocked by the stricken look on his face and the bite of bitterness in his voice. 'I've definitely changed, although some might say not for the better.' He turned away from her and strode off to catch up with Michaela.

When they sat down at the restaurant, Leo kept quiet for the first few minutes, studying his menu, even though it was in Czech and only a few words were recognisable. He needed a moment to swallow his irritation.

'Does anyone want an appetiser?' asked Jan.

Leo shook his head. His appetite had seeped away.

Yes, he had changed and no, it wasn't for the better. And he didn't like himself for it. Once he'd been a one-man woman. Since their divorce, he'd jumped from bed to bed, determined not to get involved with anyone. In his defence, he'd always made his intent clear. No false promises. No commitment. No long-term plans.

He wasn't the man he used to be or the man he was brought up to be. He knew his mother worried about him.

And the irony was that that Anna, with her latent mistrust, had been the one person who had had the best of him. He'd committed to her. He'd married her … for keeps.

'I love this place,' said Michaela, looking around the modern styling of the restaurant, at the contemporary bare bulbs suspended from the ceiling complemented by the greenery that trailed down the white walls. It was simple and sophisticated without being overly fussy.

'They produce their own wine at the Silova Winery. The wines are excellent. We should have a bottle of Rivaner 2023, it's a nice dry wine.'

'Leo?'

He tuned back into the conversation, realising that the three of them were staring at him.

'Sorry, miles away.' He dredged up a smile.

'Jan's translating the menu. What do you fancy?' explained Anna.

Leo really wasn't that hungry but he listened to the choices, all of which sounded good.

'Have you decided what you're having?' asked Anna, doing her best to look innocent.

'What? So you can plan your choice around mine?' Despite everything they knew each other so well. Where food was concerned, as in so many things, they shared similar tastes, and often chose things so that they could try what they both liked.

It reminded him that her throwaway comment hadn't been meant to hurt him. He needed to keep his stupid heart under lock and key while she was around. She was never going to trust him and he couldn't afford to fall for her again.

She gave him a winsome smile. 'I can't help it if I have food envy anxiety. I was thinking about the dumpling filled with pulled pork and kohlrabi or the venison or the rolled chicken with pumpkin mash and vegetables.'

'And you'd like me to have one of them, so you can have a taste?'

The last remnants of his bad mood evaporated at her gleeful response. 'That would be awesome.'

Now it was his turn to roll his eyes and grin back at her.

Jan persuaded Leo to order a beef broth while he had a creamy cauliflower soup. The smell when both arrived had Leo salivating. They were beautifully presented with herb trimmings and lacy crispy onion garnishes. When he took the first mouthful, he closed his eyes as the rich savoury taste, with a slight undertone of sweetness, streamed across his tongue. The flavour. It was extraordinary. He groaned and, when he opened his eyes, Anna was watching him with a thoughtful half-smile on her face.

'Want to try some?' he offered and dipped his spoon into the bowl and offered her a mouthful.

She gently held his wrist to keep it steady and all he could focus on was her mouth and throat as she swallowed. 'Mmm,' she said, her eyes on his, the husky appreciation in her voice reinforcing a sense of intimacy. A tingle shivered down his spine, lighting up desire. Judging from the way she was looking hungrily at his lips, he guessed he wasn't the only one feeling it. Luckily Michaela and Jan were too absorbed in conversation to notice the silent communication between the two of them.

'Good?' he asked, his voice vibrating a little with the feelings rushing through him. What the hell? Why was he fighting this so hard? They were only going to be in Prague until the end of the year. Maybe he should prove Anna was right all along and suggest a no-strings thing.

'Very good,' she said, her eyes still locked on his.

'You want more?' he asked, deliberately lowering his voice so she had to lean forward to hear him. Her lips parted and all he could think about was kissing them. The urge was almost painful.

Her eyes widened at the question and the not so subtle subtext. Her gaze never wavered as she gave a slight nod and said, 'Yes.'

His heart lurched. Warning bells ringing. The danger wasn't that he would hurt Anna, but that she would irrevocably hurt him. She'd broken his heart once; there couldn't be a second time.

Turning his gaze from hers, he picked up his wine and raised it in a toast. 'To Michaela and Jan. Thank you for inviting us to your lovely *chata*.'

His main course was an absolute triumph of light fluffy dumpling and perfectly cooked sweet, savoury and salty pulled pork with a light rich jus. Anna's venison was fall-apart tender in the mouth. Although the food was divine, he couldn't wait for the meal to be over. Sitting opposite her was turning into torture.

Chapter Twenty-Three

Within a few days of returning from the *chata*, the imminent date for the presentation took up all of Anna and Leo's thoughts, which was probably as well, she reflected. The easiness between them had gone and there was a carefulness to their interactions that hadn't been there before. Leo had lost some of his jokey liveliness and grown much quieter.

Whenever he was in the apartment, her heart bounced in her chest at knowing he was there. In the bathroom she could smell his shampoo, teasing her with the cedarwood scent that was so much a part of him. In the kitchen when he was making coffee, she'd covertly study him, the tiny hairs on the back of his neck, the pinpricks of bristles shadowing his face and the naked feet beneath his jeans, which shouldn't have been sexy but were. When he was in his bedroom, like now when she was trying to concentrate while working on her laptop in her room, she could hear him moving about, always making her aware he was only the other side of the wall.

Anna shook her head and focused back on the computer screen, desperately trying to push images of Leo out of her head. Even though it was only half six in the morning, she browsed through another tranche of beer adverts from all over the world looking for inspiration. Pinterest, Instagram and Google had become her best friends during the last few days.

Time was running out and she was trying to work every second she could. And she was absolutely paranoid that she might lose the presentation. Normally she autosaved everything to her One Drive but the WiFi in the apartment had a habit of dropping out and yesterday she'd lost a chunk of work.

The presentation was in less than two weeks and she still had to come up with a name, branding and marketing strategy for her beer. She wanted to appeal to women without excluding a male target audience, but without a name, all of that was irrelevant.

She gave it an hour before she dressed and got ready for work. Jakub was still keen to push a traditional style of packaging and for her to choose a generic name, and at this point she was almost ready to give in, except her beer was perfect. At the official final taste test, she'd been thrilled with its lovely light golden colour and effervescent flavour, which was exactly what she'd been hoping to achieve. Her mouth twisted. Maybe she should call it Leo. What would he make of that? He'd probably love it; after all he was the one that had suggested she called her beer after herself.

With that thought foremost in her mind, she hurried off to work and, an hour later, bounced into the brewery, excited as always by the familiar slightly musty smell of the hops, which were piled in sacks in the half-lit store room. She carried the now institutional two cups of coffee and had had her usual exchange with the cheerful man in the bakery who urged her to try new pastries today.

Jakub looked up as she entered his office and passed the coffee across the desk towards him.

'No pastries?' His eyes twinkled behind the lenses of his glasses.

'You'll get fat,' said Anna, giving his spare frame a laughing glance before she produced a paper bag from her rucksack.

He ignored her words and took the scissors from his pen pot and cut neat precise cross on the top side of the bag and lifted out his pastry.

'I thought they looked nice for a change,' said Anna.

'*Kohoutí hřebeny*,' said Jakub, nibbling at the icing-sugar-dusted puff pastry, a drip of plum jam oozing onto his chin, which he swiped away. 'Rooster combs, like the birds have on their heads.'

'Ah, yes, I see that,' said Anna, studying the curved pastry.

'Come, sit, drink your coffee and then we will go down to the mash room. I have brought some bottles for you to look at and then we need to brief the designer. Have you decided on a name?'

Anna blushed a little. ' Not yet. There is…' She hesitated.

The more she'd thought about it on the way here, the more she thought it might work. Jakub would probably hate it. 'There is one idea…' No, she liked it, she needed to sell it. It would work. She lifted her chin and met Jakub's gaze with calm confidence.

'I think it should be called Love Beer. *Láska Pivo*.'

'Love Beer.'

Jakub tilted his head this way and that way, as if he were tasting the words, letting them slide across his brain from one side to the other. The seconds ticked by and her palms turned a little clammy. Now she'd spoken the name out loud, she'd given life to it, and now she was absolutely convinced it was the most perfect fit.

Still he didn't say anything and she shifted her bottom in the wooden chair, aware of her seat bones resting on the hard surface.

Then he looked at her, his face scrunched like a wrinkled walnut.

'You don't like it,' said Anna, although hadn't she expected as much?

He stroked his chin for a further minute. Anna, perched on the very edge of her seat, wanted him to get on with it. As the seconds ticked by her conviction grew, and ideas for branding, which had been so elusive, all popped into her head. She'd go for minimal branding on the front of the bottle, a big red heart-shaped label with the word 'love' in block capitals, white out of the red. It would have great shelf appeal. The whole concept clicked into place, clear in her mind.

Jakub propped his chin on his hands, elbows on the

table, as if preparing to make a great pronouncement. Anna clenched her thighs.

'No, I don't like it.' He shook his head. 'Not at all. It is not Šilhov Brewery.' With a sigh, he put down his coffee, picked up a pen and twisted it in his fingers.

Her back teeth locked together in disappointment.

'It is not something old Jakub would sell ... but –' his eyes lit up with a gleeful expression '– sometimes it is good to confound people. This is your beer and you are the next generation. There is tradition but there is also room for innovation. You have embraced the tradition but at the same time you have a vision and I think this will wake people up.'

'Really?' Anna blinked at him. 'Really?' She stared at him. 'We have a name?'

'You have a name. Well done. It is not my taste but I think it is absolutely right. Now we'd better get to work, there is not much time. Shall we call the designer and ask him to come here so you can brief him? Do we need a sexy shaped bottle?'

Anna's eyes widened.

'See I'm not so stuffy after all.'

She laughed and patted the arm of his wool jacket. 'No, you're not. Not at all.'

If she'd bounced into the brewery that morning, when she left she was positively leaping, enthusiasm buzzing through her system like electrical charges.

'You have a visitor,' said Jakub.

'Me?' Anna glanced up from the lab desk, her eyes darting to the clock on the wall. It was five fifteen already. Where had the day gone?

'Your Leo.'

A little skitter ran through her veins at the phrase. Jakub had heard all about her flatmate who worked for the rival brewery but she'd never given any indication that he was anything more than that.

'He's here.' Her eyes widened in surprise.

'Yes.'

'Oh.' For some reason she felt flustered. Leo. Here. They had barely spent any time together since they'd returned from the *chata*. Deliberately, on her part. It was getting harder and harder to be around him. Those early-morning kisses had reignited all her feelings for him.

Maybe he'd forgotten his flat keys. In fact, that had to be it. She frowned. Back in the day he'd always been locking himself out of their flat.

'Would you mind telling him I'll be down in a minute?' She caught her lip between her teeth. 'I need to finish this.' It was going to take her at least ten minutes if not fifteen and she really couldn't leave it, even though her heart danced at the thought of seeing Leo. Bad heart.

Jakub lifted a brow and smiled. 'Don't worry, take your time. I will entertain him. He works with Karel. I might be able to educate him, while he's here.'

Fifteen minutes later, when she went down into the bar area, where visitors finished the official brewery tour with a beer tasting, she found Jakub and Leo deep in conversation over half-drunk glasses of beer.

'Hey, Love.' Leo beamed at her and raised his heavy glass. 'Nice beer.'

Anna looked alarmed for a minute.

Jakub shook his head with an understanding smile. 'It's not yours. It's Šilhov beer. I though the boy should try a quality beer.' Despite his words there was a teasing twinkle in his eyes.

'You should come to dinner, Jakub. Shouldn't he, Anna? We've invited our neighbours, Michaela and Jan and Ludmila.'

'We have?' Anna stared at him, a little bemused. They'd only very briefly talked about cooking dinner when they crossed paths in the kitchen that morning, suggesting it would be a nice way of saying thank you to the couple downstairs for the weekend in South Moravia. At the time the conversation had been a bit of relief because she'd been having a hard time not being distracted by his bare-chested torso. Her libido had been on high alert ever since they'd come back from the *chata*.

'Well, we talked about it and then I saw Jan this morning and Ludmila, so I invited them. Saturday. You didn't have any plans, did you?'

He knew damn well she didn't have any plans. Her social life revolved around him, Michaela and Jan.

'Right,' said Anna, and was even more surprised when Jakub, having ruminated on the invitation for all of a minute, said very slowly, 'I would like that very much. Thank you, young man.'

'Excellent,' said Leo, clearly pleased with himself. 'Right. Are you done?'

'Done?'

'Yes, finished for the day.'

Anna, dying to ask what he was doing here, lifted an eyebrow. What was he doing here?

'Yes. Go home,' said Jakub. 'There is no more you can do today.'

'Excellent, we can start planning the menu.'

Within a few minutes, she was standing on the other side of the big, wooden brewery doors, shivering slightly in the dark.

'What are you doing here, Leo?'

'I was passing and I thought I'd see if you fancied going for a drink and maybe something to eat.'

'You were passing?' Anna didn't believe a word of it.

'Okay. Hear me about. You always talk about how nice Jakub is and that he's a bit lonely. He doesn't have any family. And Karel's the same...' He let the sentence hang but Anna knew.

'You've invited Karel as well, haven't you?'

Leo beamed at her. 'Great idea, yes?'

She let out a peal of laughter at the innocent expression on his face. 'I'm not sure about that – but it's sweet.'

'Sweet!' Leo wrinkled his nose in disgust.

'Yes. Very sweet.'

'I was going to offer to buy you a drink and maybe

dinner...' His attempt at sounding disgruntled made her laugh.

'Dinner sounds good. I'm starving. I didn't stop for lunch today.'

'Excellent. There's a really nice restaurant between the Charles Bridge and the Castle that I've been recommended.'

'Of course you have.' She fell into step beside him. unable to stop a little spring of happiness bubbling up inside her. Everything felt better when Leo was around. Perhaps she could school herself for that to be enough.

Despite it being a chilly October night, Charles Bridge was still alive, buzzing with tourists posing and taking pictures. No surprise, really, because in the dark, with the Castle lit up in the background and the glow of the riverside restaurants reflecting on the water, it was the most picturesque scene. Totally romantic, in fact, and Anna swallowed a pang of envy at the couples sauntering along arm in arm, enjoying the almost festive atmosphere. There was always something special about being on the bridge, no matter what time of day, whether early in the morning when she'd had it to herself aside from the odd runner jogging past and people coming back from the bakery with bags of bread, or at midday when the wide road thronged with tourists, artists and buskers. As she thought about it, her arm brushed Leo's, their hands touching for a brief second. Then, to her surprise, he linked his fingers with hers and gave them a squeeze.

She sneaked a look at his face in profile but he didn't look at her and kept walking as if holding hands was completely natural. Even though her pulse skittered along like a pony at a fast trot, she didn't say anything, just relished the warmth of his hand around hers and the little spark of hope that danced in her breast.

Halfway along the bridge he stopped. 'Selfie? With the castle in the background.'

'Why not?' she said, trying to sound nonchalant.

When he slung his arm around her, pulling her into shot, the moment was pure deja-vu… They'd posed this way a thousand times in dozens of places. The urge to nestle in and kiss his neck like she'd done so many times before overwhelmed her and tears pricked her eyes. She was as love with him as ever. Only now she knew that she'd made a terrible mistake. Leo was reliable and dependable. He'd shown it in so many ways while they'd been in Prague. Gradually she'd become aware of his true character. Back then she'd been too immature and stupid to see the real prize beneath Leo's charming, sunny veneer.

Painful regret kicked through her. She could have had it all and she threw it away.

'Smile, Anna,' urged Leo, holding up his phone.

She dredged up her best cheesy grin, ignoring the hollowed-out sensation in her chest. Leo had made it clear there was no going back and she had to live with it. Could she manage, though, with these crumbs of friendship? The casual touches that came so easily to him? And what would happen when he did find another woman? How would she bear it?

'I'm loving the Czech wines,' said Anna, taking a big sip of the Pinot Noir Novosady from Čejkovice that the waitress had recommended to go with her duck breast with carrot, orange and lavender. It complemented the flavours perfectly, as well as going well with Leo's dish of deer steak with kale, black mushrooms and seaberry, which of course she'd insisted on trying. The venison melted in the mouth, so tender she'd almost moaned out loud, and she'd had to stop herself because she didn't want to make sex noises in front of Leo.

The restaurant with its open kitchen was small but embodied the clean, simple sophisticated style that she'd come to expect in the more expensive restaurants. The service was impeccable, with the knowledgeable owner taking her time to help them with their choices.

'This is a lovely one,' said Leo. 'Maybe when I open my craft beer venue I'll serve Czech wines as well.'

'Great idea. Where will you open this mythical venue?'

'No idea yet. I need to win the equipment first. What about you? What will you do if you win the equipment?'

'That's easy. Well … if I can persuade my uncle, it will be. I want to set up a small line at the Talbot brewery. As long as it doesn't cost him anything, I think I can get to him agree. Although he's still of the view that women don't get involved in brewing. And he's not interested in trying anything new … a bit like Jakub. Although at least Jakub prides himself on the quality of the beer. Uncle Henry churns out the same old.' She sighed. 'Don't get me started.'

'You could stay here.'

'Here?'

'Yeah. In Prague.' He looked a little sheepish for a moment. 'I've fallen in love with the place. I could imagine living here.'

Anna tilted her head. It wasn't something she'd considered … until now.

'I know what you mean. I feel at home here. More than I ever thought I would.' Now the idea had been mooted, it lodged in her head like a small, determined tick. Maybe Jakub would keep her on. Maybe she and Leo could carry on sharing the apartment.

And maybe small pink pigs would go flying across the sky. She was daydreaming. Not like her at all. Leo's influence. He always had made her think bigger.

When they'd finished their meal and said goodbye to the friendly staff, they wound their way through the quiet streets and historic buildings, their breath misting in the crisp night air.

'Want to go up to the Castle?' asked Leo. 'Bet there's a great view.'

She nodded her assent, and they wandered through the cobbled streets up the slope towards the buildings dramatically outlined against the sky by strategically placed lighting, the castle looking as if it had been conjured from a fairytale. For once there wasn't a soul up there. Their feet echoed in the quiet lanes and they chatted in low tones, as if they had agreed not to disturb the sleeping streets. When they came to the viewpoint, they had it to themselves. The city spread out beneath them, glittering with soft lights, casting a magical glow over the river that curved round the buildings.

Together they leaned on the parapet of the wall, in the comfortable silence of good friends. Anna felt her heart tilt with gratitude. She reached out and took Leo's hand.

'Thank you for being my friend,' she said.

Leo paused for a moment before he squeezed her hand and then leaned in to kiss her cheek. 'Being friends with you is easy. I...' She saw him swallow in the half shadow of the buildings and there was the briefest of pauses before he added, 'Thanks for being my friend, too.'

What he had been going to say? Friends was as good as it got and she had to accept that much. She'd opened herself up, that night in the *chata*, and he'd turned her down. He'd drawn the line and she had to stay on the right side of it.

Chapter Twenty-Four

On the morning of the dinner that had gone from a simple supper, a thank you to their neighbours, to a full-on three-course dinner party for nine, Anna returned from the hairdresser, bouncing along on happy feet, thrilled with her new hairstyle. She now had lots of layers and a gently feathered fringe that sat above her eyes, instead of the heavy curtains that skimmed either side of her face.

When she saw herself in the large oval mirror, surrounded by scented lotions and potions that sweetened the air, she looked younger and, oddly enough, happier. It was as if, like a snake, she'd sloughed off an old skin. Slipped out of square-shaped Anna into oval-shaped Anna. She felt so much lighter – as if she'd shed more than her hair.

And though she hadn't done it for anyone but herself, she was looking forward to Leo's reaction when he saw her.

He was in the kitchen when she ran lightly up the stairs, his back to her, peeling carrots.

'Hi, Leo,' she said.

'Hey,' he said without turning round.

'How are you doing?' she asked, standing poised in the doorway.

'Good. Onions chopped. And the beef smells great.' Before she'd gone out she'd left the beef, which she'd scored with shallow cuts and filled with bacon, to marinade in a delicious-smelling blend of melted butter, thyme, garlic and marjoram.

Still he didn't turn around and she waited as he sliced the carrots into small pieces.

'You've been busy,' she said for want of anything to say.

'Yup.' Finally he turned around and she smiled at him, waiting for his response. To her surprise his face tightened – infinitesimally, but it was there – and then, as if nothing had happened, he carried on. 'I've chopped the onions, peeled and chopped the carrots, chopped the celery for the sauce.'

'Great,' she said, swallowing her disappointment. 'I'll get started on the pudding, then.' She had a simple dough, of flour, butter, eggs and sugar, to make the base of the tart, which would then be topped with fresh plums and part-baked before she added a mixture of egg yolks, icing sugar and cream, and baked for a further twenty minutes.

They had decided upon the menu together over the last few nights, finally coming up with marinated cheese to start with, followed by *Svíčková na smetaně* , beef tenderloin with traditional root-vegetable sauce, and bread dumplings, and for dessert a plum tart. They had divided up the list of tasks the night before. It was quite an ambitious menu, given they were cooking Czech food for the first time, but Anna was hoping that although there was a lot to do, it would be quite straightforward.

With an internal sigh, she washed her hands and started assembling the ingredients for her dough.

'Nice hair, by the way,' said Leo, reaching into the cupboard beside her, barely glancing her way.

'Thanks,' she replied, wilting a little inside. Was it her imagination or was his tone begrudging? As if the words had to be forced out. What had she been expecting? It was hardly a Clark Kent to Superman transformation, after all, but it had made her feel special. She thought Leo, with his innate empathy, might have noticed that inner glow and commented. Perhaps he wasn't as in tune with her as she liked to think.

She watched as he melted butter in the frying pan and slid in the onions, her eyes focusing on the flex of his forearms like some sort of lovesick teenager. Her skin itched, she was so aware of him.

Leo glanced up and she looked away quickly, turning to crack eggs into the dry mix for her dough, but fumbled and missed the bowl. An egg fell with a splat on the tiles. They both stared down at it for a moment. Leo grabbed a cloth and knelt to clean it up as she dropped to the floor with a piece of kitchen paper. They ended up on their knees, nose to nose over the broken egg, their eyes meeting for a few long-drawn-out seconds. Neither of them said anything, the sudden tension as thick as fog. Anna stared into Leo's eyes, unable to break her gaze. He stared back, his eyes dropping to her lips. She felt herself sway forward, the magnetic northern pull of his lips towards hers. A dull ache of longing spread through her chest. Then, with a snap, Leo straightened and scrambled to his feet. 'I think you've got this,' he said and busied himself rinsing the unused cloth under the tap.

As the goosebumps subsided on her skin. Anna applied herself to the task with the diligence of a worker bee in a hive.

They carried on their respective tasks in silence for the next few minutes. Anna felt as if the atmosphere between them was stretched taut, like an elastic band close to snapping.

'Want me to chop the bread for the dumplings? asked Leo.

'Thanks.' And then to fill the silence, she added, 'They're in the breadbin.'

He glanced at her. 'I know. I put them there last night.' He turned away again, the quiet between them so charged, the air almost crackled.

As he worked, the rasp and cut of the knife on the stale bread grated on her nerves. His moves quick and sharp. Each chop filled the air, almost as if he was deliberately trying to rub her up the wrong way.

In retaliation she pounded at her dough, working out the frustration chafing her body. He didn't need to make it so obvious that the thought of kissing her was so unwelcome. With the dough mixed, she almost savaged it as she rolled it out to fit in the tart tin.

'Are you trying to kill those plums?' asked Leo, his mild curiosity like flame to the fuse of her irritation. Did he not feel the same pressure? That feeling that she might burst out of her skin any minute?

She looked down at the plums she was ramming into the top of the dough.

'I think they'll be fine, they're about to be incinerated,' she said, shoving the whole thing into the oven.

'Here you go.' Leo pushed the bowl of cubed bread towards her. 'All done. What do you want me to do next?'

Her mouth tightened on the words she couldn't say. Instead she grabbed the bowl and tipped in the eggs.

'You could weigh me some flour,' she said with an edge to her voice. She knew she shouldn't add but she did anyway, 'If it's not too much trouble.' She picked up the open bag of flour to hand to him.

'It's no trouble.' His tone was low and gravelly. 'Nothing's ever too much trouble for you, Love.'

That did it! She tossed the bag towards him, deliberately showering him in flour.

Time slowed as she watched in shocked disbelief at what she'd done.

And then she swallowed as Leo, his face coated in white, stared back at her. Blue eyes in sharp contrast as he blinked furiously at her.

'What was that for?'

'Because you're driving me mad.'

'I'm driving *you* mad.' He glared at her.

She stood her ground, nerves sizzling at the fury burning in his expression.

He took a step towards her, his hands clenched by his sides. She raised her chin, not giving an inch.

'Anna Love,' he ground out, low and dangerous.

She swallowed. Good and mad was the only way to describe him right now. But she wanted him mad. She was fed up with having to keep her emotions in check, from hiding what she felt.

His Adam's apple dipped several times. 'Oh, fuck this,' he said under his breath, and swiped at the flour across his face with his forearm before reaching for her, his hands clamping on her arms, leaning in to kiss her with a fierceness bordering on desperation, as if she were the very last drop of water in a desert.

The spark leapt between them as fast and furious as a crack of lightning, and the kiss went from inflammatory to an inferno within seconds. His mouth scoured hers as if he were seeking redemption from every sin on earth. But she gave back with equal hunger, her heart exploding with a flash of delight and excitement as it thudded like the hooves of a Grand National winner. Reason and coherent thought went out of the window as she pressed closer, enveloped by the scent of him, the warmth of him, the feel of him. Her legs almost buckled as they turned into noodles but Leo was there to hold her up.

He smoothed a floury hand down her hair, his breathing harsh. 'I can't fight this anymore.'

'Good,' she said, lifting a hand to his face, stroking away some of the flour and the slight lines of concern around his eyes.

'I love you. Never stopped. It's been killing me these last few weeks.'

Love surged in her chest, a tsunami of heat and joy. 'I love you.'

They stood looking at each other. Leo's eyes were sombre and serious as he focused on her face. His fingers tracing her lips.

'I've been trying to deny it and then you come in this morning, your hair in that just-out-of-bed mussed-up style, and smile at me, all sexy and serene, like the Mona Lisa, as if you know all the secrets of the world and … I'm gone. Completely and utterly.'

Chapter Twenty-Five

Anna couldn't help herself. 'Then take me to bed.'

'I thought you'd never ask.'

'I'm not asking,' she said feeling a little bit pleased with her assertiveness.

'Anna, love,' Leo's words finished on a heartfelt groan that vibrated through her chest, sparking little fires of want throughout her body.

She found herself pressed up against the worktop, Leo's mouth on hers, her hands tugging at his T-shirt, pulling it out of the way, desperate to touch, while he was clumsily working his way down the buttons on the front of her dress.

With their mouths fused together and the air punctuated with breathless moans, she melted, softening into his touch. 'Oh, Leo.'

She'd missed him. Missed this. His body, harder and firmer, felt so good beneath her roving hands as she explored the muscles and planes of his broad shoulders, the lean waistline and, oh God help her, that delicious bum. He nuzzled her neck, licking and nipping, and she threw her head back, lost to the sensations ripping through her. At this moment she could die a happy woman.

'I like this dress, a lot,' Leo growled pulling back for a second to look down at her breasts. 'God, Anna. Look at you.' His hand slipped inside her bra, sliding across her sensitive nipple. She let out a squeak and he grinned. 'Still works for you.'

'Not fair,' she hissed, her fingers at his belt buckle as his continued to tease, setting off an unbearable ache between her legs.

'Ah, Leo,' she gasped, as he peeled back the lace of her bra and put his mouth on her. She could already feel herself building up to climax. 'Stop! Stop! Ahhh. Don't stop.' His tongue, hot and wet, made her pant and her knees shake, the pressure of desire weighing her down. 'Oh, don't ever stop.' She felt the hot prickle of tears. She'd thrown all this away and it had been her own fault. Her insecurities, her fear.

'Anna?' Leo lifted his head and immediately his hand went to her face, a finger stopping the tear that had escaped. 'Oh God, I'm sorry.'

'No, don't be. It's a happy tear. I missed you.'

'I missed you.

Everything inside her was fizzing, like an unopened Grand Prix podium bottle of champagne threatening to explode at any moment.

'Leo, please,' she said, unable to bear the stroke of his tongue over her sensitive nipple.

'Please what?' He looked up at her, grinning.

She sighed. The picture of him with his hand cupping her breast and his wicked smile was melting her heart. If he didn't take her to bed right now, she might have to kill him.

They half ran, half stumbled down the stairs and then had a push-me pull-you tussle as they tried to guide each other into their respective bedrooms.

Leo, ever the gentleman, finally let Anna tug him into hers. She paused to close the door behind them and then they stood and faced each other. His eyes were bright and his bare chest heaved as he stared into her eyes. She swallowed. She wanted to press her lips against the tanned skin, across his pecs and the light dusting of blond hair.

'Are you sure?' Leo asked, his voice tight and scratchy.

She nodded.

'There's no going back after this,' he said and his eyes held a fierce expression that turned her heart inside out.

'I know,' she said. She peeled her dress down her body and stepped out of the light folds of fabric that fell to the floor.

His breath hitched. She heard it, a tiny half-swallowed gasp. His hand reached for her and then stopped in mid-air, his eyes softening and his gaze skimming over her body, as if he could scarcely believe his luck. 'Anna, love.' His lips curved in an almost disbelieving smile. Then he reverently touched her shoulder, one finger slipping under her bra strap and sliding it down, his hands on her arm sending tiny shivers racing across her skin. A hand captured one of her wrists, then the other hand repeated the movement on the other side. Anchoring her hands at her sides, he leaned forward and nuzzled at her bra, his lips tracing the edges of the lacy fabric, sending flares of excitement racing along her nerve endings.

Mesmerised by his gentle care, she watched him as, still holding her wrists, he took his time, tasting and touching her breasts, her nipples, her neck before he knelt and pressed soft kisses across her belly. She could have pulled her hands away but she found his hold exciting. He was in control but she could break it at any time. It made her feel cherished, the sole focus of his attention.

When he nuzzled at her beneath the scrap of lace that covered her, she let out a breathless murmur, as tiny pulses of white heat fizzed and burst through her like lightning flashes. 'Leo.'

She swayed a little, determined not to break his hold. To show him that she was all in. That she was his for the taking. Last time he'd been the one to pull back. It had to be his choice this time. She needed that reassurance that he wanted her as much as she wanted him.

His kisses slid back up her body and then he was on his feet again, facing her. His eyes on hers.

She lifted her chin and raised her hands, still manacled by his. 'My turn.'

He smiled, let go of her hands, put his fingers to her waist, slid down her lace knickers and waited for her to step out of them. With fumbling fingers, she unhooked his belt buckle, then, holding his gaze, undid the button and the zip of his jeans. He blinked and she saw his jaw clench. She smiled and pushed his jeans down his hips, one hand tracing the length of him through the fabric of his underwear. The sibilant hiss of his in-drawn breath made her smile with satisfaction. He stood perfectly still as she ran her fingers up and down before releasing him from the confines of his jersey boxers, feeling the smooth silk of the skin that covered the rock-hard flesh. Soft and strong. She eased out a breath, her legs a little shaky as she stroked him a couple of times. He groaned her name, low and throaty. 'Anna.'

Then he slid a hand around her waist and pulled her against him, his hand cupping her head, his mouth capturing hers with hungry need. She answered kiss for kiss, straining against him, wanting and needing more.

Somehow they made it to the bed, backing up kiss by kiss. She fell back and he shoved down his jeans the rest of the way, took something from his wallet and lay down beside her, taking her into his arms, the kiss gentling as his tongue traced the outline of her lips. She closed her eyes, her heart pounding hard and that demanding insistent throb between her legs growing stronger with every beat.

He moved over her and she took his face in his hands. 'Yes, Leo. Yes.'

Pleasure exploded as with a long slow slide he filled her, his face taut with tension.

'Anna,' he sighed.

'More,' she gasped and clutched his back, pulling him towards her, wrapping her legs around him. 'More.'

With a lunge, he pushed deeper and set a driving pace which she met, hip thrust to hip thrust, glorying in the sensations flooding her, the rasp of the hairs on his chest on hers, the chafe of his legs against hers, the breathless gasps that came from both of them as the pleasure rose and peaked.

Lost to everything but sensation, they matched each other. Their sighs and moans, a language of their own, urging and straining, pushing each other on, closer and closer to the elusive finishing line that felt forever just beyond them.

Anna felt Leo tense and tighten, felt him try to hold back. 'Leo!' she ground out. 'Don't stop.' She pulled him close and then felt the hot fierce flood of her own release as he drove into her one last time, calling her name with a long low cry.

They lay sprawled together, his hand stroking her cheek, her fingers on the small of his back, until their breathing finally settled and conscious thought returned.

Leo turned and kissed her along her jaw. 'I don't suppose there's any chance we can cancel dinner tonight.'

'No,' groaned Anna.

'It's going to be interminable.'

'It is,' she agreed.

'Whose bright idea was it to invite everyone?'

'Yours,' she said with a laugh as he burrowed into her neck, his head shaking with laughter.

'How quickly do you think we can get rid of everyone?'

'Leo! It will be fun. And it was your idea.'

'Yes, but this is more fun.

'This is going to have to wait. We need to get ready.'

'Getting ready involves shower time,' said Leo, immediately perking up and giving her a quick grin.

Anna laughed. She might have known he'd still find a silver lining.

———————

Anna felt so lit up that she was pretty sure she glittered like a *Twilight* vampire. It was ridiculously fanciful, but in this moment it was if the sunshine had come out inside her, shedding light into every corner, igniting little pockets of joy, suffusing her with happiness.

Definitely the Leo effect, she decided, as she heard him greeting someone downstairs.

'We're pretty much there,' she said to herself. Everything was under control. All the dishes were prepared and the table laid.

She went through into the living room and surveyed the table.

'False alarm,' called Leo, tripping up the stairs with a case of beer and a bottle of wine. 'Jan wanted to drop these off early so we could get them in the fridge.'

She laughed. 'I hope you didn't tell him his timing sucked.'

Leo grinned. 'Not in so many words, although Michaela will probably guess. She's been desperate for us to get back together. It wouldn't surprise me if she hadn't deliberately put a hole in that mattress.'

'Leo! She wouldn't.' Anna shook her head and fussed with one of the napkins.

'Don't worry. Michaela will approve,' said Leo, touching

the pretty yellow linen tablecloth, his hand grazing hers, sending a fresh tingle up her arm. 'Of the table settings, I mean.'

'It's not for Michaela,' said Anna. 'It's for me. Just looking at the table makes me happy. I hope it makes all the guests feel happy and see that we've made an effort for them.'

'Just need some flowers,' said Leo. He leant down and from one of the chairs tucked beneath the table produced a bunch of orange and yellow roses. 'These are for you madam. I got them earlier when you were out having your hair done but they were forgotten in the heat of the moment.'

Anna blushed. 'They're lovely.'

'So are you.' Leo brushed the back of his hand across her cheek. Anna's heart, already a dangerously mushy mess, melted some more.

'They're perfect.' She held them against the tablecloth. 'That's so thoughtful, thank you.'

'I have my moments.' Leo bent at the waist in a little bow.

'You do. Thank you.' She'd planned to kiss him briefly to show her thanks but when he looked at her like that, smiling, happy and just such a ray of sunshine, she forgot herself, wrapped her arms around him in a spontaneous hug and kissed him right on the mouth.

She felt his smile as her lips pressed against his and his hands moved around her body to cup her bottom, pulling her tighter against him. The kiss deepened and turned into something entirely different but Anna cast all care aside, enjoying each touch, her senses tuned into the moment. Warm hands, the scent of roses, a softness inside, nerve endings dancing and Leo's mouth roving over hers. His breath mixing with hers.

She pulled back and looked at Leo, the steady blue eyes unwavering as he stared back at her. Her heart tripped and she felt the fall. She was in love with him and this time it was something very different. She'd changed. Now, she was her own person. Someone who wasn't going to worry about anyone else's views or opinions, someone who didn't need to fit the family mould. She was whatever-shaped Anna she wanted to be and she could do whatever she wanted.

'Shall I light the fire?' he asked and then grinned at the unintended double entendre.

'I think that horse has well and truly bolted,' said Anna, laughing back at him as he struck a match and set light to the pile of kindling and firelighters he'd laid in the grate earlier.

The buzz of the intercom interrupted them once again, and this time Anna went to the front door to find Zdeňka and her friend Lubica on the doorstep.

'Hello,' said Anna, who had quite forgotten that the two women had been invited. Bathed in the golden glow of Leo's attention, she beamed at the other woman. 'Come in. Let me take your coats.' Zdeňka blinked, clearly surprised by her effusive welcome.

'Thank you for having us,' said Lubica, presenting Anna with a beautiful box of Steiner & Kovarik praline chocolates.

'Yes,' said Zdeňka, brushing an imaginary piece of lint from her striking fuchsia dress. For once Anna didn't feel dazzled by her vibrant attractiveness, she felt her equal. Smiling to herself at this revelation, she led the other woman up the stairs.

'Leo.' Zdeňka greeted him as if she hadn't seen him for years and kissed him on each cheek. 'Lovely to see you.' Then she lowered her voice but not enough that Anna couldn't hear. 'You got my text?'

'Yes,' muttered Leo, again as if he didn't want to be heard. 'Sounds perfect.'

'I'll text you the address and see you there.' The she raised her voice, 'And thank you so much for inviting me. It's such a treat.' She eyed him flirtatiously.

Anna ignored the brief conversation between them. Clearly they hadn't wanted anyone else to know but she had to wonder what this arrangement was and when it had been made. It must have been before she and Leo had slept together?

Zdeňka was touching his forearm and she said in that low breathy sex-siren voice, 'I hope you can cook.'

'Me and Anna are kitchen demons,' said Leo, smooth as ever, seemingly oblivious to her hungry gaze, and escorted her and Lubica to the sofa, around which Anna had arranged a few of the dining chairs so that they could have drinks around the fire before dinner. 'Have a seat, ladies. Can I get you a drink?'

Anna told herself off for the brief flare of jealousy. Zdeňka was a friend to Leo, and perhaps wanted more, but he wasn't interested.

Michaela, Jan and Ludmila arrived shortly afterwards, bringing with them a couple of extra chairs.

'I'll pick them up again tomorrow, if that's okay,' said Jan. 'Because we've got family coming for lunch.'

'No problem,' said Anna, as she turned to greet Ludmila, elegant as ever in a powder-blue dress and a matching walking stick.

Michaela caught her by the arm. 'You look … different.'

Anna blushed. 'You saw my hair this morning,' she said. 'Come in and have a drink. Zdeňka and Lubica have arrived. I hope you're going to like the food. Leo and I have been cooking all day. I made dumplings. Like yours.'

Michaela narrowed her eyes thoughtfully but didn't say anything, although a small, very slightly smug smile played around her lips.

They joined Zdeňka and Lubica as Leo played drinks monitor, and the conversation flowed with remarkable ease. Although with Zdeňka, Michaela and Ludmila aboard the entertainment ship, there was never any question of uncomfortable silences.

After twenty minutes, Anna anxiously glanced at the clock. Where was Jakub? Had he chickened out of coming? And where was Karel? Had they each decided not to come because the other was coming? As Leo passed her, going back to the kitchen to top up the drinks, his hand brushed hers.

'Don't worry, they'll be here. They won't let us down. In the meantime, let's sit everyone at the table.'

Luckily the minute everyone sat down around the dining table, just as she began serving the marinated cheese starter, Karel rang the intercom and Anna, opening the front door, was relieved to see that Jakub had arrived at the same time.

'Look who I met in the corridor,' said Karel, handing over a box of different beers. 'Thought you'd like to try some different local specialities.'

Anna glanced at Jakub, whose expression was unreadable. 'I brought these, but of course you are familiar with them.' He'd brought a case of the brewery's beer.

'Thank you,' said Anna, her bright smile a touch anxious. Had this been a terrible idea? 'Come on through and meet everyone.' She led the way up the stairs to a burst of laughter which gave her some relief. At least everyone else was getting on.

She introduced the two men, ushering Jakub to the seat next to Ludmila as they were the closest in age. She needn't have worried. Ludmila with her innate grace immediately engaged Jakub in conversation. Karel sat next to Leo and the two of them were soon laughing and joking with Michaela, Zdeňka and Lubica.

Anna sat near Jakub and Ludmila, initially to help keep things flowing, but it was soon apparent that Ludmila didn't need any help, so she went out to the kitchen to slip the plates for the next course into the oven to heat.

Leo came up behind her and even before he brushed her hair aside to kiss the back of her neck, goosebumps rose on her skin.

'How much longer until we can throw everyone out?' he murmured, his breath fanning across the sensitive skin.

'Everything will be ready in ten,' said Anna, trying not to let herself be distracted.

'You're no fun,' he whispered, his lips trailing across the curve of her jaw.

'Leo,' she whispered, her nerves hyped up and jangling in response.

'Yes, Love.'

She turned and leaned into him, kissing him. 'You need to behave.'

'Why?' He ran a finger down the front of her neck to the hint of cleavage exposed. She sucked in a quick breath, quite forgetting why.

A burst of laughter from the other room reminded her that they had seven guests waiting to be fed.

'You need to start slicing the roast beef,' she said faintly.

'Mmm,' said Leo circling her waist and pressing her to him.

'Leo. The beef.'

He pulled his head back, a pout on his lips. 'How can I be expected to think about boring things like beef, when all I want to do is to take you to bed? I'm dying here.'

She laughed. 'Well, die more quietly, please.'

He groaned and buried his face in her neck. Unable to help herself, she put her arms around his neck and closed her eyes, savouring the feel of his body against hers. She could stay here for ever.

Another burst of laughter forced her into action and she pushed him firmly away. 'There. Stand there. Just while I get my breath back.'

Leo, being Leo, looked delighted with himself. She narrowed her eyes at him. 'Don't let it go to your head.'

'Wouldn't dream of it.' Despite her making him stand apart from her, she could feel his gaze on her the whole time. Trying to distract herself again, she leaned into the dish and sniffed. 'It smells good. I hope everyone likes it. I'm starting to think that maybe we shouldn't have attempted Czech food and given them a curry or something.'

'It's all going well. Don't worry. And Jakub turned up.'

'He did and he hasn't been rude to Karel yet. Although there's still time.'

'It's not your problem. We've done a nice thing, inviting Jakub to dinner because he's lonely and doesn't eat properly.' He rested his hands on her shoulders, grounding her. 'It's not your problem. Enjoy yourself. We've been looking forward to this and the food is going to be amazing.'

'Though you say so yourself.'

'Come on. We're a dream team, this food is going to be a triumph.' He touched his mouth in a chef's kiss. 'Let's get everyone seated.'

Before he went back to the other room, he gave her bottom a quick caress, leaving her flustered again.

Anna began to transfer the food into piping hot bowls. When she carried the beef through, the rich creamy scent of the *svíčková* sauce filling the air, everyone stopped talking.

'That smells amazing,' said Michaela.

'I hope it tastes as good,' said Anna, putting the serving dish on one of the table mats, noticing with a sinking heart that Karel and Jakub were staring in stony silence at each other. She shot Leo an anguished look, and he followed her back into the kitchen.

'Do you want me to remove the knives?' he asked before adding, 'Don't worry. They'll be fine.'

'God, I hope so,' said Anna.

Leo helped her carry out the accompanying dishes of dumplings, cranberries and whipped cream.

'Do you think we've got enough?' she asked in a whisper.

'Anna, I promise you, we're going to be giving Jakub and Ludmila doggy bags and still be eating beef for a week.'

She stifled a laugh. He was probably right.

Everyone sighed with appreciation as Anna and Leo sat down. 'A toast to our hosts. Thank you very much for inviting us into your home. It is very good to be here. And to meet new friends. *Na zdraví*,' said Jan raising his drink.

Glasses were tapped and Anna looked around, the candlelight casting a golden glow on everyone's smiling faces. She felt a bud of heat flower inside her and exchanged a quick look with Leo at the opposite end of the table. He lifted his glass and gave her a luminous smile, the blue of his eyes glowing in the ambient light. Despite all the people around them, he still managed to make her feel the centre of his focus. She could have been the only person in the room. She exchanged a faint smile with him before turning to Karel on her right, who had asked her a question.

'Sorry,' she asked, having missed it.

'I said, how is it working in the Šilhov brewery with

Jakub here?' He jerked a thumb towards the older man, with an open, engaging grin.

Before Anna could answer, Jakub interrupted. 'At least she is learning how to make beer properly. The way it should be made.'

Oh no, here we go.

'The proper way?' asked Karel.

'Yes,' said Jakub. 'You think it's old-fashioned but these methods have been used for hundreds of years. Why change them?'

'Because people want new and different flavours,' said Karel, jutting out his chin. 'And the new methods are more cost-effective, more rational, more optimal.'

'And you would throw away hundreds of years of heritage for novelty,' said Jakub.

'No, we're building on hundreds of years and improving on them.

'They don't need improving. They have stood the test of time.'

'Gentlemen, you're both right,' interrupted Ludmila, forceful despite her quiet words. Anna could see the steel in her, which must have stood her in good stead in her ballet career. 'And you're both wrong.'

They stared at her like a pair of children pulled up by their mother and far too polite to embroil her in their argument.

'What is the most important thing when you are making beer?' Ludmila threw the question out to the whole table. 'Michaela?'

'The taste.'

'Jan?'

He nodded. 'The taste.'

As she went around each person, everyone agreed, and when she reached Karel and Jakub, she simply tilted her head.

They both responded like a pair of sulky schoolboys. 'The taste.'

Ludmila, holding court rather beautifully, then turned to Leo at the head of the table. 'And what is the best-tasting curry, Leo? I know they eat a lot of it in England.'

He shrugged his shoulders, giving her his sweet smile. 'I don't know. There are so may. It depends what you like, whether you like a creamy korma, a semi-sweet, spicy Goan curry or the clean fragrant flavours of a Thai curry.'

'Michaela, which wine is best?'

Michaela turned her mouth down. 'Again, I couldn't pick one.'

'Jan, which Czech beer is best?'

Jan laughed. 'There is no right answer.'

'Exactly,' said Ludmila and then turned back to the two men. 'If you care so much about the beer, all you should care about is pleasing your customers. Giving them what they want and not arguing about silly things like whether the way it is made is better. Everyone likes different things. If everyone liked the same books, we'd all be reading the Bible.' She smiled. 'There is a wonderful phrase. I don't know who said it first. Before you judge a person, walk a mile in their shoes. I think you should both go to each other's breweries and spend some time there.'

'Yes,' piped up Michaela. 'Perhaps you could learn from each other.'

Surprisingly, it was Jakub who spoke first. 'I think … Anna has shown me that you can change things without losing everything. I think we should do this.'

Leo and Anna exchanged amazed looks. Karel blinked several times and then nodded. 'I think I would be interested in coming to Šilhov. Do you really think that a triple decoction is necessary? What about a double?'

And suddenly the two of them were off, talking with passion about beer.

Ludmila winked at Leo and Anna.

'Would anyone like some more food?' asked Anna, standing up.

'Yes, can I get anyone another drink?' Leo rose to his feet as well.

'I would like the recipe for the beef,' said Zdeňka as Karel held out a hand to Jakub, saying, 'I will call you on Monday and we can make the arrangements.'

'Excellent,' said Jakub, extending his own hand to shake Karel's.

It appeared a *détente cordiale* had been achieved.

Karel turned to Anna. 'I would love some more of your very good beef. I like it very much.'

'I too like it,' said Jakub.

Normal service resumed as Anna dished out seconds before taking the casserole dish into the kitchen to refill. Leo joined her and wiped his forehead.

'Phew. I can't believe it,' he said.

'Amazing what good food and company can achieve,' replied Anna.

'Whose bright idea was it to invite everyone round for dinner again?' he asked with a cocky smile.

Her hands slid up his arms and gave him a squeeze. 'All yours, of course.' She leaned forward and gave him a kiss on the lips. 'Do I have to tell you how brilliant you are?'

He straightened up and grinned at her. 'No, but you can show me.' He glanced at his watch. 'How soon can we get rid of everyone?'

Chapter Twenty-Six

He stretched, his body languorous and soft, and smiled, sated with the high of good sex and a feeling of blissed-out contentment. All he needed now was coffee and his life would be complete.

Next to him, a warm body nestled into him, soft legs entangled with his, and he slowly opened his eyes for the second time that morning.

He smiled as the memories and emotions from last night flooded into his brain.

'You're looking very pleased with yourself,' she murmured, her nose nuzzled into his neck.

'I don't recall there being any complaints,' he said, leaning in to kiss her.

'None here,' she said, her eyes softening. 'Although I do need to get up.'

'What for? It's Sunday. We could stay in bed all day.' He wrapped his arms around her waist, wondering whether he should mention where he was going with Zdeňka later that afternoon. Should he take Anna with him?

'It's half-past eleven.'

'You're no fun,' he grumbled, smoothing a hand over her hair.

She giggled. 'We've already had seconds this morning.'

'And what's wrong with thirds?'

'I'll go and put some coffee on.' She gave him a quick smirk, knowing that she could always bribe him with a caffeine fix.

He managed to steal one last kiss before she slipped out of bed, grabbed her robe and left the room. With a contented sigh, he flopped back into the pillows, hands behind his head, and gave in to another luxuriating stretch before swinging his legs over the side of the bed. Clothes were strewn across the floor on his side of the bed. His eyes fell on the square bottle of Jo Malone Blackberry & Bay body lotion Anna had always used on her soft silky skin before she slid into bed beside him. He lifted the bottle, squirted a tiny bit on the back of his hand and brought it up to his nose. The familiar scent almost floored him, and he had to take a moment to steady himself against the kaleidoscope whirl of memories that hurled themselves at him. He put a hand out to hold onto the shelf beside the bed.

For a moment he stood calming himself, taking long slow breaths in and careful breaths out. This time would be different. He would take things steadily, show Anna that he was reliable and that they had a future together. Maybe they'd married too quickly. He'd seized the moment, perhaps been too impulsive, and Anna, rather than believe that it was because he loved her so much he couldn't help himself, had thought it quixotic. Much as his family had. When their marriage broke up, his brother Raph, the sensible one, had told him he'd been 'rash and foolhardy'.

Second time around he was going to be much better prepared. There'd be no surprises. No one could accuse him of not thinking things through properly. He frowned. He'd been thinking of taking Anna with him this afternoon but maybe it was better if he didn't. Perhaps he should wait. He wanted to have a conversation with Raph, to prove that he'd thought this through properly and to ask for his support and advice.

This was the first place he was going to look at. He didn't want to be accused of being 'rash and foolhardy' again. It would be better to talk to his brother and see if the place had potential before he said anything to Anna.

———

'I was going to suggest going out for a walk,' said Anna, pulling up her jeans, 'but it looks cold out.' She gestured at the low grey clouds filling the sky and the lingering fingers of frost around the edge of the window frame. 'Maybe a day for a fire and film.' She gave him a smile, conjuring up memories of Sundays after late shifts, when they hadn't bothered dressing and had watched *Avengers* films together. 'I haven't seen *Thor* for a while.' Now her smile was teasing.

'What is it with Chris Hemsworth?' Leo grinned at her

as he sat in his towel on the end of her bed. 'He's really nothing special, you know.'

Anna laughed. 'And you are?' It was a conversation they'd had a time or two before.

'I'm here, that's the difference.'

'You are.' She leaned over and kissed him. 'I guess I can make do.'

He kissed her back. 'Unfortunately, I have an appointment this afternoon.' Even as he said the words, he regretted them. They didn't sound like him and even though it was the truth, it sounded like an evasion.

'Oh, right,' said Anna. 'Not to worry. Looks like I'll have Chris all to myself.'

'I arranged it the other day. I'm meeting someone.' Now it sounded defensive or as if he was making excuses.

'Leo. I know we live together but that's by accident rather than design. You still have your own life. Us sleeping together doesn't change that.' She flicked a glance towards the open door of her bedroom, then towards his.

That little sliver of panic sliced into him. 'Sleeping together?' He couldn't keep the sharpness out of the question.

Anna caught her lip between her teeth and lifted her shoulders. He noticed that she deliberately didn't say anything.

He held out a hand and took hers in his, linking his fingers through hers. 'It's more than that. A lot more.'

'A lot more,' she said, nodding in agreement with a gentle smile, and wrapped her arms around his neck and kissed him. Relief shimmered through him.

'I was thinking about moving some clothes into a drawer here.' He needed to make it clear that there was some permanence to this. For him this was the future.

'Good idea. Then you don't sit there naked while I'm dressing.' She nodded at the towel around his waist.

'Oh, I like watching you get dressed.'

'Creep,' she teased. 'And we don't live in each other's pockets. I'm going to curl up and watch a film, although I might get you to light the stove and then you can go out and face the cold while I stay here nice and toasty.'

While part of Leo wanted to explain where he was going, the other half wanted to keep things under wraps for the time being. He didn't want to say anything until he had some firm plans.

'Perhaps when I get back, we could open a bottle of wine, get out the cards, play strip poker and see where the night goes.'

Anna laughed. 'Probably the same way as it always went. You were always terrible at strip poker.'

He grinned at her. 'I seem to recall it never really mattered because it ended the same way.'

'You cheated.'

'Of course I did. I wanted to get you naked.' He raised his eyebrows at her and she giggled.

An hour later, Anna had cleared some space and he'd moved some underwear into her chest of drawers. It felt like a tentative but significant step forward. There was plenty of time to talk about their future together, but at the moment he was going to enjoy making Anna smile and watch her blush a million times a day.

As he was cleaning out the wood burner, the intercom buzzed. Damn. She was ten minutes early. He'd planned to meet Zdeňka outside. Not that he didn't want Anna to know who he was meeting but it was easier not to have to explain anything.

Anna, who was downstairs cleaning the bathroom, beat him to the intercom phone.

'Hello.'

As he descended the stairs he heard Zdeňka's bubbly voice.

'Ah Anna, can you tell Leo I am here.'

'Sure. Are you coming up?'

'Tell her I'm on my way,' interrupted Leo.

Anna looked up to where he was standing on the middle step.

'Leo says he's on his way down.'

'Okay,' said Zdeňka.

Leo took the rest of the steps quickly. 'I'm going out with her to meet a friend of hers. I … I said I'd help him with something.' That was almost the truth. If he took the lease he would be helping Zdeňka's boss with something.

Anna gave him an understanding smile. 'It's fine. Like I said, we don't have to live in each other's pockets.'

'I won't be that long. I'll be back with you and Chris before you know it.'

The long low, white building on the end of the tiny cobbled street in Vyšehrad was nothing special but Leo knew, the minute he saw it, that once the walls had been painted they'd look clean and bright. This was the first place he'd looked at and he was telling himself not to get too excited but he couldn't quell the low-level buzzing in his belly. The location was perfect and the rent within his budget, although it would be better if he could persuade his brother to invest. Of course, if he won the competition and the equipment, that could be the clincher. And if his beer was on show at the Beer Festival that would be great publicity. Then again if Anna won it … it would be equally good for both of them.

Leo's eyes roved around the outside of the building, noting the good-sized, although very overgrown, garden with its little weed-infested cobbled path winding through the heavy shrubbery to a solid, if cobweb-encrusted, wooden door.

'And here you have good access for deliveries, with parking,' said, Tomáš, Zdeňka's boss, pointing to the rutted lane at the side of the building.

Leo nodded as Tomáš took a bunch of keys out of his messenger bag and invited Leo and Zdeňka to follow him. In his pocket in his heavy down jacket Leo crossed his fingers. The outside needed a lot of work but it was just work. Labour rather than rebuilding. He had to hope that the building was structurally sound. He could bet Jan would help, and Michaela. It could be their winter project and he would reciprocate at the *chata* in the summer.

Although he was getting ahead of himself. The inside could be a disaster.

Inside, the first big room, empty of any furniture, was echoey and very chilly but not, to his relief, damp. The vaulted ceiling needed painting and sported a fiesta of cobweb bunting. The terracotta floor was sound, although in need of a good clean. What made Leo smile was the size. It would make the perfect taproom. It didn't take much to picture where he would put the bar and the taps, or where the tanks could go. Now he wished he had brought Anna, to share with her the ideas that were bubbling up and to listen to the suggestions she was bound to make. Damn, he should have brought her. She would love it.

'And here are the cellars,' said Tomáš, leading them into a second room. 'It was a small winery many years ago but the owner died and his children are not interested in starting again.'

Leo nodded.

Zdeňka pushed her hands deeper into her coat pockets. 'It's a lot of work. Very old-fashioned. I would want something more contemporary. Easier to start a business, not having to worry about making the building right.'

Leo nodded. He didn't want to seem too keen, not in front of her boss. Most people took him at face value, but he did share some of his brother Raph's business acumen. He would definitely negotiate on the rent. He was going to make an offer on this place. It felt right … although he had to check a few other things first. They spent another twenty minutes walking around the building, with Leo praying that Anna was wrong about his poker face. He really wanted this place. She would love it, too. He played it very cool, agreeing with Zdeňka every time she drew his attention to a fault or a flaw. Tomáš didn't seem to mind this at all. Either his English wasn't very good or he had a soft spot for Zdeňka, because he met each of her comments with an indulgent smile. In fact, Leo realised it was definitely the latter, when Tomáš's gaze lingered on Zdeňka's face when she wasn't looking. Poor guy had it bad, but then Leo ought to empathise: he had it bad for Anna. And he wasn't going to mess it up this time. He was going to prove to everyone, not just her, that he had staying power and that he could be relied upon. This place was going to be the start of something. Something he and Anna could build together.

Chapter Twenty-Seven

'Leo!' Anna ran up the stairs, dying to tell him about her day.

He had his back to her and his mobile to his ear when she went rushing into the kitchen. He waved and carried on talking, an unfamiliar grave expression on his face.

She studied him. He'd seemed a little preoccupied his week – or at least preoccupied by Leo standards. Occasionally his face suggested he was thinking deeply about something.

'Thanks, Raph. Appreciate it. Speak later.'

He ended the call. 'Hey Anna, love.' He wrapped his arms around her and kissed her on the mouth, just like he did every time she arrived home from work.

'Hey, Leo Knight. Everything okay with the family?' Leo had spoken with his brother nearly every day in the last week, with Raph ringing him several times. Did they know about Anna and Leo getting back together? Leo hadn't said anything. Maybe they didn't approve.

'All fine,' said Leo. 'How did it go? No one killed each other?'

'It was amazing! Honestly, Jakub was like a dog with two tails and Karel lapped it up.' Today, Karel had come to the Šilhov brewery to spend the day with Jakub. As the day had progressed, Anna had repeatedly noticed the family resemblance between them, especially when they took a sip of beer and savoured the flavour, their identically shaped eyes half closed in reflection and contemplation.

'That's great. A good way to round off the week.'

'Yes. They left the brewery together and were going to dinner with Karel and his sister. I'm so pleased for Jakub, it would be wonderful if they could be a family again.' For a moment her smile slipped. Her family had been very quiet. Since she'd made it clear she and Steve were done, there'd been very little communication. In fact she couldn't remember the last time she'd heard from her aunt or Rebecca. The former didn't matter but she and Becs had always supported each other, especially when they were younger when things had been tense at home.

'Talking of which, our adopted family, Jan and Michaela, said to knock for them at seven.'

'Great. Are we going to tell them about us?' Anna smiled at the thought, remembering Michaela's avid curiosity. She'd dropped by twice this week on made-up pretexts.

'Not straight away. Let's tease Michaela a bit longer.'

'I think she might have guessed on Saturday night.'

'Yeah, the "can I borrow some milk?" ploy was rather obvious on Monday evening. Shall we play it cool and then

I'll kiss you when the beer arrives. That'll surprise Little Miss Matchmaker.'

'I think I'll go have a shower.'

'Okay. I've got a couple of calls to make.'

Anna went downstairs wondering about the many calls he'd been making all week.

'Hey, Zdeňka,' she heard him say. 'Yeah, what time? I can make it a bit later. I need to make sure Anna is…'

She'd moved out of range and couldn't hear the rest. She gritted her teeth, dying to know what was going on, but she refused to ask. It would look as if she didn't trust him. And that's where everything had gone wrong last time.

A quick shower revived her and she decided that, so long as she wore plenty of layers, she was all set for a Friday night out with Jan and Michaela. They had booked a table at a rooftop bar in the Old Town Square, promising that they wouldn't be cold.

Leo was equally bundled up, his blonde curls peeping from beneath his black beanie. He kissed her thoroughly at the front door before they set off. Anna clutched the lapels of his coat to steady herself. 'Maybe we should stay home,' she said, with a breathless laugh. Kissing Leo would never get old.

'That was to tide us over until the big reveal.' He gave her one last kiss and then they closed the front door and took the stairs down to Michaela and Jan's apartment.

Although the air was crisp, the location was spectacular and well worth the expensive menu. Anna had been amused by the laborious journey to the rooftop floor, which had involved several staircases and a lift. Despite the chilly weather, which had everyone huddling under blankets with heaters blasting out above them, the terrace was busy. It was definitely a tourist hot-spot and Anna appreciated Jan and Michaela bringing them there. The panoramic view took in the nearby square tower of the astronomical clock and, beyond, the twin Gothic towers of the church of Our Lady before Tyn – as well as a bird's eye view of the terracotta-tiled roofs stretching away on all four sides.

'This is fab,' said Leo, his head turning this way and that like a curious owl. 'You can see everything.'

'Not quite everything,' said Jan, with an amused smile. 'But it is good to come once. It is very touristy.'

'Are we still tourists?' asked Anna.

'No,' said Michaela. 'You're family. Our family.'

'That's a lovely thing to say,' said Anna, exchanging a quick glance with Leo, who grinned back at her.

A waitress appeared, ready to take their orders.

'I'm going to play tourist and have an Aperol Spritz,' said Leo. 'Pretend it's a gorgeous sunny day.'

'I'm sticking with beer,' said Jan with a shudder, giving Leo a reproving shake of his head.

Leo simply shrugged. 'I like an Aperol now and then. It's my Italian blood.'

Anna who had planned to go for wine, decided that actually it would be fun to try a cocktail and opted for a Kir Royale. Michaela, to Jan's disgust, followed suit.

When the drinks arrived, they lifted their glasses. '*Na zdraví*,' said Jan.

'To us,' said Leo and leaned over to give Anna a kiss full on the mouth.

Michaela clapped her hands together. 'I knew it,' she crowed and lifted her glass. 'I told you, Jan. You owe me three-hundred *koruna*.'

'You said it would happen at the *chata*.'

'No, I only said it might, but I knew it would definitely happen some time.'

He shook his head.

Anna and Leo linked hands and laughed at the pair of them.

'Sorry, mate,' said Leo. 'You have to accept it, she's right. Women are always right.'

'You know she gave you an air bed with a hole in it,' said Jan, smirking at Michaela, who straightened and waved her hand as if to brush her misdemeanour aside.

'I … I…' She blushed bright red. 'I said it might.'

'It did,' said Anna dryly. 'I mended it the second night with a few plasters and some duct tape.'

Michaela tried to keep her mouth still but it crumpled in amusement. 'But you are together now?'

'Yes,' said Leo, putting his arm across, Anna's shoulder. 'We are.'

A happy glow, as bright as the patio heater above them, lit up in her heart.

The next morning, Anna lay next to Leo, propped up on her side, watching him with a gentle smile on her face. A week in, and she still loved watching him. In sleep he was the essence of himself, lying on his back, one arm thrown above his head, his blond curls spread like a halo on the white pillow, totally at ease and comfortable in his skin. Anna had always envied him his happy-go-lucky confidence and that blithe assurance of knowing where he fitted in the world, but now she felt she knew herself. Oval-shaped Anna had emerged since she'd come to Prague, and boy, did it feel good.

Leo's eyelids flickered, the sandy lashes fluttering, centipedes against his skin. A deep breath, a snuffle and then his eyes opened. He woke, she thought, with a soft sleepy glow that ignited ... and then he was dancing, limbs twitching, and straight into action, sweeping her into his arms the minute he spotted her. Immediate delight spread across his face, as if she was the best sight in the world. So very Leo.

'Morning, gorgeous!' He beamed at her and gave her a kiss on the mouth, pulling her on top of him.

'Morning,' she said with the self-same involuntary smile she found herself giving whenever he was around.

'Shower?'

'Mmm,' she groaned. Mr Sunshine to her Miss Slow-To-Get-Started in the mornings. He threw back the covers and bounced out of bed like Tigger's soulmate. 'I need coffee.'

She couldn't help giggle at his unabashed stretch, everything on display, his arms reaching upwards and his chest expanding as he stood in the cold light of the Velux window. Rain spattered in windy gusts on the glass, reminding her that winter seemed to have slid its way in without either of them really noticing.

'God, it's hideous out there.' He glanced up at the skylight. 'A day for staying in bed, except...' He paused and took her hand. 'There's something I want to show you. This afternoon.'

Anna raised an eyebrow. 'Haven't I seen everything already?' she teased.

'I need to be somewhere at two. I want you to come with me.'

'Okay. Are you going to give me any clues?' It was unlike Leo to be this serious.

'No,' he said and then light danced in his eyes and she felt a little easier. 'It's a surprise.'

'Because I love surprises,' she said dryly.

'I'm really hoping you'll like this one.' His eyes held hers, and for a moment she wondered if he was planning something crazy, like getting married again. Fireworks raced through her veins. Or proposing? Although two o'clock sounded very specific. Was she getting ahead of herself? Excitement filled her, like a rush of butterflies swarming in her stomach, their wings beating furiously. She would happily marry Leo a thousand times over.

'I'm sure I will,' she said, laying a gentle kiss on his cheek. This time she knew she could trust him. While he was the same sunshine personality that had brought love and light into her life, he'd also changed. There was more depth to him. He was more thoughtful, more measured, not quite so impulsive. 'In the meantime, I need coffee.'

'Are you sure?' he asked, sliding back into bed and pulling her towards him. All thoughts of a shower were quickly dispelled.

When she finally managed to extricate herself, albeit reluctantly, a good half-hour later, she snagged one of his shirts from the end of the bed and left him propped up on the pillows looking very pleased with himself, while she headed upstairs to make a fresh pot of coffee.

With two mugs of coffee in her hands and heading back to the bedroom, she was passing the front door when there was a soft knock. Putting the cups down and buttoning up Leo's shirt, she opened the door and peered round the frame, expecting to see Jan coming to collect the chairs.

'Hello, Anna.'

Anna's eyes almost burst out of their sockets with exaggerated cartoon-character shock, and despite the very obvious response, it took a good ten seconds for her brain to locate the words. 'Becs! What are you doing here?'

'Surprise,' said Rebecca, with an ironic half-smile. 'Aren't you going to invite me in?'

Anna stared at her cousin for a moment, taking in the long legs and sheepskin pilot's jacket. 'Er, yeah.'

'It's flipping freezing out there.' Becs blew on her hands and stepped over the threshold ... and of course, by the law that anything that can go wrong will go wrong, Leo, asking, 'What's happened to my coffee, Anna, love?', came strolling out of the bedroom ... naked.

There was a ridiculous frozen-comedy moment when Leo looked at Becs, Becs looked at him and then they both looked at Anna.

With considerable aplomb, Leo waved at Becs. 'Hi, there. Long time no see. Just popping to the bathroom.'

With that he sauntered off, quite unperturbed that he was naked, although Anna couldn't help thinking that with that bottom, he carried it off extremely well.

'Well,' said Becs, looking down at Anna's bare legs.

Anna sighed. 'Why don't you take this?' She handed her cousin her coffee. 'Go upstairs. I'll get dressed and see you in a minute.'

Becs raised an eyebrow. 'Looks like you've got some 'splaining to do.' Anna wasn't sure if Becs using their childhood term for explaining was a good thing or a bad thing.

She hurried into the bathroom to find Leo stepping into the shower.

'Coming to join me?'

'Maybe not politic right now.'

'What, now the cavalry has arrived?' Despite the lopsided smile accompanying his words, Anna heard the slight disquiet in his voice.

'It doesn't change anything,' she said, going up to him and pressing a gentle reassuring kiss on his mouth.

He didn't respond and she wrapped her arms around him, heedless of the water spraying over her. In response he gave her a quick squeeze.

'Best get this shirt off,' he muttered. 'Before it gets soaked.'

She stripped off and stepped in with him. Under the stream of water, she kissed his mouth, holding him tight.

They stood together in silence and Anna could feel the stiffness and tension where his muscles bunched.

'What are you worried about?' she asked softly, running her hands over his shoulders.

'Nothing,' he said. 'Nothing at all.' And he kissed her on the mouth, his hands sliding down to her bottom giving it a quick squeeze. 'You'd better get a wiggle on. Your cousin's come a long way to have her say.'

'Well, she can say what she likes. It's not going to change anything.'

Her cousin stood beside the French doors looking out at the view, sipping at her coffee.

Anna detoured to the kitchen to pour herself a fresh coffee and came to stand next to her.

Becs handed Anna her mug and wriggled out of her coat. 'I didn't realise it would be so cold here.'

'It's winter in Central Europe, what did you expect?'

'Go you on being a welcoming host.' Becs draped her coat over one of the dining chairs. 'Nice place.' She took in Anna's little improvements. 'Very nice. I detect the Anna touch.' She felt the tablecloth Anna had bought in Mikulov. 'This is pretty and the furniture is all very stylish.'

'Amazing what you can find in a skip.'

'No! Really?'

'Yes, we renovated it all.'

Becs raised her eyebrows. 'How did you get such a flair

for decorating, given we grew up in the House of Magnolia?'

Anna laughed at that, relaxing a little. 'Thank you. So come on then, spit it out, what are you doing here?' Like Anna needed to ask.

'Don't suppose I can convince you I fancied a weekend away?' she asked with a wry smile.

Her honesty made Anna smile, too. 'No, cuz, you couldn't. Deliver your lecture, get it over with, and then you can enjoy a weekend away.'

'Look at you being all assertive.' Becs gave her an approving nod and a wider smile this time. 'It's good to see you,' she said, taking a seat at the table. 'You look well.' There was a pause before she said more emphatically, 'Really well. You look different. I like the hair.' She kept studying Anna's face as if trying to identify the changes.

'Thank you.' Anna came to sit down with her, deciding that it would be easier to rip the plaster off and get on with the inevitable. 'You didn't think to let me know you were coming. What if I hadn't been here?'

Becs's expression suggested that the possibility was highly unlikely, which was kind of insulting but also accurate about the old Anna. Old Anna. The thought flashed in her head as bright and bold as a lighthouse beam. Old Anna didn't go for weekends at *chatas* with new friends. Old Anna didn't *make* new friends, certainly not easily. Old Anna didn't have longer hair, wear dresses or remodel furniture. Old Anna kept herself to herself and behaved the way the family expected her to.

'The other weekend I was out all Saturday, mushroom picking.'

'Rather you than me.'

'I promise you it was really fun. But we're getting away from the elephant on the table right in front of us.'

Becs's mouth twisted. 'If you'd known I was coming, you'd have made an excuse. Been unavailable. You've not exactly been responding to any communication of late. The family felt drastic action was required.'

'And you drew the short straw?' Anna's mirthless laugh brought a blush to Becs's cheeks.

'Everyone thought I would—'

'You were bullied into it,' said Anna, with sudden insight. She could picture exactly what would have happened.

'I wasn't bullied into it. They knew I was worried about you.' Rebecca's annoyed glare told Anna all she needed to know. Becs was no pushover, so they must have really been relentless.

'Well, you can stop worrying.'

'Can I?' Her face softened. 'What's going on, Anna? This isn't like you.'

Leo, his hair still damp, walked into the room.

'Anyone want a late breakfast? Brunch really?' he asked. 'Toast? Eggs?'

Becs looked… Anna reevaluated. No, it wasn't annoyance on her face, it was more a touch of peevishness, as if she was a little put out. 'If you don't mind, I'd like to talk to my cousin in private.'

He shrugged. 'I don't mind at all and I'm happy to go,

but it's not up to you. Do you want me to leave, Anna, love?'

Anna looked at him, surprised by the uncertainty that tightened the fine lines around his eyes. Although his face remained impassive, that tiny clue made her heart clench.

'No,' she said, lifting her chin, her eyes softening, trying to tell him there was nothing to worry about. 'I'd *like* you to stay.'

Only the tiniest change in the shape of his mouth indicated his relief. If she'd not been watching him closely, she would have missed it.

'Seriously, Anna?' Becs sounded as if what she had to say was completely acceptable and sensible and only an idiot wouldn't want to hear it.

'Seriously, Becs,' snapped Anna, already having decided she was not playing this game. She was a lot older this time round, and distance from the family had provided her with new insight. Leo was right: she'd spent a large part of her life fitting in rather than expanding and finding her own-shaped world. She was done with Old Anna. She was Czech Anna now and she much preferred this version of herself.

'Everyone's worried about you. And Steve is devastated. He realised he was too hasty and should have trusted you. Although –' she nodded towards Leo '– this complicates things.'

Anna raised an eyebrow.

'He wants you to come home.'

Anna sighed. 'It's over, Becs. He might have pulled the plug and stormed off but I planned to finish things with him that weekend. It hasn't been right for a long time, but neither of us wanted to admit it.'

'That's not what Steve says. He loves you. He wants you back, if you … give him some sort of sign.'

Anna laughed. 'He doesn't know you're here, does he? What was the plan? I'm supposed to go back with my tail between my legs and apologise to him and he'll take me back?'

Becs had the grace to look a little ashamed.

'No, he doesn't.' She paused and then launched in. 'But Anna, he's one of the good guys.' Her tone gentled. 'He's the faithful sort.' Completely ignoring Leo's presence, Rebecca gave her a look of entreaty They had both been scarred by her father's wandering eye and roving hands. 'You know that he'd never look at another woman. It's not too late. If you come home, I know the two of you can sort everything out.'

She continued, carefully, patiently. 'Steve cares. He wants you back. I think you're being very hard on him. Life isn't all sunshine and roses. Or high drama. With Steve you'd always know where you are.' She shot Leo a look. 'Although I'm not sure if he knew about this he'd be so forgiving. Sorry, but not sorry, Leo. You wanted to stay.'

Anna lifted her chin. 'I don't need forgiving.' She held up her hand before Becs could say anything. 'Steve and I had run out of steam, we were going through the motions and I think both of us were hanging on because it was safe.'

'Are you sure, Anna?' Rebecca flicked a glance towards Leo. 'No disrespect, but have you considered this might be … well, I mean, Steve might not be as glamorous and exciting – we all know Leo is very pretty – but Steve's solid, you know where you are with him. There's a lot to be said for that.'

'Rebecca!' Anna was indignant on behalf of Leo. 'That was rude.'

Leo shrugged. 'She's just saying what she thinks.' His tone was impassive. Anna wondered what he was really thinking.

'I'm talking about living with the reality of things,' snapped Becs.

Anna smiled sadly at her cousin. They both knew she was talking about her father.

'Look, Anna. I'm thinking about you. The best thing for you,' she said, so gently that Anna almost felt sorry for her. 'As we're talking frankly.' She directed an insincere smile at Leo. 'Steve won't hurt you. He'll never be unfaithful.' Leo folded his arms and glared at Becs, who paused only momentarily before sliding the knife in, right on target. 'You'll never have to wonder whenever he befriends another pretty girl.'

Anna held her gaze but the blow reopened old wounds. What Becs meant was: never have to wonder like their aunt did constantly with Uncle Henry. Like she had done with Leo even after they were married. He would always be a magnet for gorgeous women.

Leo's face was expressionless and, more worrying, he wasn't saying anything to defend himself.

Then he stood up. 'I think I'll leave you two to it.' He looked at his watch. 'I need to be somewhere at two.'

Anna suddenly remembered. 'Oh, do you want me to come with you?'

He shook his head. 'No, it doesn't matter. It can wait,' he said with airy nonchalance, although she wasn't convinced by his quick, almost glib response.

'Are you sure?' she pressed.

'No. It's fine. I'm sure Rebecca didn't come all this way to see the inside of our little place in Prague. Why don't you take her to the bridge and the castle?'

'Okay,' said Anna, but lifted her hand to his face and placed it against his cheek, wanting him to know that her cousin's arrival changed nothing. 'If you're sure.'

He turned his head and placed a kiss in her palm. 'I'm sure. Now wrap up warm. It's cold out there. And if you stay until it's dark, Rebecca can see how beautiful the city is at nightfall.'

He turned to Becs. 'Enjoy Prague, it's a gorgeous city.'

'Thank you.'

'See you later.'

Anna watched him leave the room and heard his steps, his tread a little heavier than usual on the stairs. A tiny shiver of misgiving whispered through her.

Chapter Twenty-Eight

Leo was propped up in bed scrolling through his phone when Anna opened the bedroom door. For a moment she stood in the doorway, her mouth turning a little dry as she studied him all his bare-chested, golden glory, the lamplight shining on his blond hair. She sighed a little as something bloomed, warm and strong, in her chest.

'Hey,' he said looking up, his face softening.

He'd returned half an hour before, after she and Rebecca had returned from dinner in the Old Town, after an afternoon spent wandering along the Charles Bridge and up through the Castle.

'Hey,' she said, her heart full to bursting with simple emotion. He was gorgeous inside and out and it seemed mystifying to her that she still felt like this every time she saw him. Did he feel the earth tilt at the sight of her? 'How was your afternoon? Your ... two o'clock thing.'

'Good,' he said, putting his phone down.

She stripped off her clothes and slipped in beside his

warm body and he immediately put an arm around her. She laid her head on his shoulder, her nose in the crook of the soft skin at his neck and breathed in the scent of him: his favourite Polo aftershave, faded now, and minty toothpaste, but also a touch of the cloying scent that Zdeňka used.

'Everything okay with your cousin?' he asked softly.

'Yes. Thank you.' She leaned forward to kiss him, getting another whiff of that sweet floral fragrance.

'And you've no regrets?' he asked. 'About Steve?'

She leaned and kissed him again, surprised by the tiny touch of tension around his eyes.

'None.' Did he have regrets? Was he worried that she'd become too dependent on him? She thought of her foolish imaginings that morning when she'd thought he might be springing an impromptu wedding on her. What had she been thinking of? He'd clearly replaced her this afternoon with Zdeňka. 'You don't need to worry. I'm not looking for a replacement for him. I know that's not you.'

He pulled away and looked down at her. 'What's that supposed to mean?'

Confused, Anna looked back at him. He sounded annoyed when he should be relieved.

'Just that I'm not expecting you ... well, I'm not expecting this to be permanent.'

Leo stayed silent for a moment, his face very still except his eyes, which flashed with what looked like fury, which was ridiculous. She should have known better. Men like him, like her uncle, they constantly needed new interest, new attention. Leo might be kinder in his disposition but his attention would be captured by someone else before long.

'Why not?' he asked, his voice so quiet she could only just hear it.

'Because … you know.'

'No, I don't.' He stiffened and pulled away from her. 'Explain.'

'Leo, be honest, if we weren't living together, on top of each other, do you honestly think we'd have got together?'

'Probably not but we did.'

'It was a happy accident and we've made the most of it but … it's not going anywhere, is it?' Not once had they talked about the future.

He stared at her and she started to feel uncomfortable. 'Leo? Seriously.'

'And if it was? Would you give it a chance?' he asked.

Anna's smile, sad and regretful, haunted her eyes.

'Leo, you're not that guy. One of us will leave and… Be honest. It will be out of sight, out of mind. You'll move on.'

'You're sure of that?' he asked, holding her gaze.

'Yes,' she said, laying a hand on his arm. She wasn't going to hold him to anything. Rebecca's arrival was a timely reminder. She didn't want to end up like her aunt, constantly having to turn a blind eye to flirtations and liaisons that supposedly never meant anything. 'I love you. The way you are. I don't want you to be anything but who you are.'

Leo's mouth twisted and he glared at her before throwing back the bed covers and launching himself to his feet in one quick surge. With his back to her, he snagged his boxers from the nearby chair and pulled them on before turning to face her.

What did he have to be angry about? She was the one trying to be the grown-up, accepting the situation rather than attempting to change him into something he wasn't. She respected him the way he was.

'Is that what you think this is? A good shag?'

She swallowed, hating him diminishing everything between them to one word. There'd been more, certainly on her part.

'What are you so pissed off about? I haven't noticed you complaining about it.'

'Bloody hell, Anna.' He shook his head but she had no idea what she'd done wrong. She was just being honest. 'You don't get it, you really don't get it, do you?' He hauled on his jeans and then a shirt, shoving his bare feet into his boots.

'Get what?' she asked, kneeling up on the bed now.

He glared at her.

'What, Leo?'

He gave a bitter laugh. 'I love you and you can't bloody see it. I'm still the bloke who's having fun. Still the bloke who can charm his way into everyone's knickers. Still the bloke who's incapable of being faithful, even though –' he glared at her as he spat the words '– have I given you a single reason to think that I would cheat?'

She sank back on her heels staring at him.

'And you haven't been with Zdeňka today?'

'Yes, I've been with Zdeňka today. It was purely business, which you'd have known if you'd come with me.'

Anna's lips tightened. She hadn't meant to mention Zdeňka but it had slipped out.

'And there it is. You still don't trust me.' Despair churned in Leo's stomach. 'I can't do this again, Anna.'

'Do what?'

Leo stared at her. Did she really not know? He went silent, a wave of fury pounding over him, so fierce and consuming he had to clamp his hands into fists to stop them reaching out to shake her.

'You almost ended me when you left last time.'

'Me?' The surprised outrage in her voice pushed his control over the edge.

'Yes, you.' The long-held bitterness spilled out and he didn't care. He didn't care that it made him sound like some sad sack, like a loser who felt hard done by – the words took flight on their own.

'Remember you asked me when I had my conversion to tidiness.' His voice clogged, turning a little croaky.

'Yes.'

'I went to live in a camper van for a couple of months – being untidy in that got old pretty quickly.'

'A camper van?'

'Yeah, a friend had it. When you left the flat ... I moved into for a while.'

Yeah, there was a ton of subtext here and she had to ask. 'A while?'

Raw pain and bitterness rocketed through him. 'Thirteen

months, Anna. Thirteen months, driving aimlessly around the UK before I got my shit together again. Not my proudest time but, hey, it made me tidy. So there's a bonus.'

'Where did you go?'

'Everywhere.' He shrugged. 'I travelled all round Europe and the UK.'

'You didn't stay in one place?' It was almost comical the way Anna was gradually processing the information except all he could remember was the blind pain of trying to lose himself.

'That generally is the idea of a camper van. You know, like being a snail, you take everything with you wherever you go,' he said as nonchalantly as possible, as if it were no big deal when actually it had been BFD. At the time he'd craved solitude, and for the first month he drove from one place to the next each day, without even thinking about it.

Anna stared at him. 'I didn't know.'

'Of course you didn't. No one did. I didn't want anyone to find me. I was a mess.'

He swallowed the ugly lump of shame at his weakness and fought back with anger.

'What did I ever do to make you think that what we had didn't mean anything to me? Why are you so convinced that I'm some sort of playboy who doesn't take anything or anyone seriously? Was I ever unfaithful? What was it I did to make you doubt me? Because I promise you, Anna, I have no fucking idea what I did wrong.'

She drew in a sharp breath as if he'd physically struck her.

But now he couldn't stop. He pushed on, though he

was disgusted with himself for dredging it all up. 'Can you even tell me? Do you even know?' He'd told himself being friends would be enough, that he didn't need to know, but he'd been lying to himself. Now he felt a little sick. What had he done? What was the point of bringing up the past?

'Sorry, I shouldn't have said anything.'

Then he felt Anna's hand on his arm. 'I'm sorry,' she said so softly that he almost believed her. He relaxed his jaw a little but couldn't bring himself to say anything.

'I was a coward. I left you before you could leave me.'

He turned taken aback by her admission. 'I was never going to leave you.'

She let out a breath. 'I was too young and stupid to realise that at the time. I convinced myself you would. Especially when that girl came on the scene.'

'But why? What did I do that made you think I'd go?'

Anna laughed without mirth. 'Have you looked in the mirror? Handsome, charming. Every girl looked twice at you. It was only a matter of time before you moved on. And you always defended her, said she was just a friend.'

'She was just a friend.' The dully spoken words stabbed with all the pain of a dull spoon. 'Did you think so little of me?'

'Not of you, of me. I didn't think I was enough to hold on to you.'

'But...' Leo's confusion made him fumble for words. 'But ... we were married. I thought that ... I made vows to you. Promises. I loved you. I love you.'

'But we were too young. We didn't know each other.'

'I knew that I loved you. That you were enough.' He swallowed. 'Maybe I wasn't enough for you.'

'Of course you were. You were too much for me. Everyone loved you. You made friends easily. Everything came easily and I thought when it didn't, you would go.'

'But you weren't prepared to wait and find out. You bailed … on me. On you.'

'Yeah,' she said in a sad voice. 'I did. But it would have happened in the end.'

'So you're fully qualified with a crystal ball, are you?'

'Leo, I saved us some time. It would have happened eventually.'

'And it never occurred to you to share your concerns.'

'I did…' Her voice was barely a whisper. 'With my family.'

He shook his head, unable to say the words. He might love her but she was never going to love him, not all in.

'But Leo…'

He shook his head, unable to look her in the face because she might see too much.

'Leave it, Anna.'

Slowly he left the room, conscious of the weight of each of the steps he took and when he closed the door, the thud vibrated through his body, echoing the dull pain running through every vein. He had no idea where he was going. He needed to get away. He scrolled through recent texts. There was one place he'd be welcome. Fuck it. Anna didn't trust him anyway. What did he have to lose? He might as well go to Zdeňka's and prove Anna right. He was only useful for a good time and not much else.

Chapter Twenty-Nine

Light snow had begun to fall and when he stepped out of the apartment, he felt like he was the only person in the world. His footsteps left black out of white patches on the pavement. By the time he'd walked a couple of blocks, his hands were numb and his feet stung from the cold.

When he buzzed the intercom, he almost sagged with relief when the door opened and he was able to step inside out of the biting cold.

'Come in,' said Zdeňka, wearing a welcoming smile and a very sexy dressing gown. He smiled back. He might be pissed off and broken-hearted but he wasn't dead.

'Thanks for having me. I didn't know where else to go.'

'I could choose to be insulted by that.' Zdeňka gave him a teasing smile. 'But instead, I'll focus on the fact that you walked all the way here instead down a flight of stairs.' She brushed at the snow in his hair, dislodging a few flakes.

'I didn't want to disturb Michaela and Jan,' he said

flinching at his own lie. He wanted to punish Anna, punish himself. It was a dick move.

'But you knew I wouldn't mind. Especially not now when you're about to sign a contract and I'll receive the commission.'

He lifted his shoulders in a hopeless shrug.

'Take your coat off. I'll get us a drink.'

Shimmying out of his coat, he noticed he hadn't done the buttons up properly on his shirt and it was skew-whiff. No wonder he was so bloody cold, he hadn't even put a sweater on. He followed her into the living area, with its vibrant red sofa and block coloured rugs on wooden floors. Although everything was tasteful and beautifully placed – that was what jarred, everything felt carefully arranged, too carefully – it didn't have the cosiness of his and Anna's flat.

He took a seat, perching on the edge of the sofa, tiredness rolling in. What was he doing here?

'Here you go.' Zdeňka handed him a beer and sat down next to him. He couldn't help noticing her silk robe was draped artfully to reveal a healthy amount of cleavage. Her skin was smooth with a faint tan and he could see the remnants of summer bikini lines.

He took a morose sip of his beer remembering his uncomplicated summer in Italy, with a stream of bikini-clad babes. 'Thanks.'

'*Na zdraví.*' She lifted her bottle and tapped his, and then leaned back curling one slim leg underneath her and extending the other along the sofa. She looked as comfortable as a cat with a belly full of cream, confidence and self-assurance oozing from her. The type of woman who had no expectations. The type of woman Anna expected him to move on to.

'So Leo, why are you here in the middle of the night?'

He gave her a rueful smile. 'I knew you wouldn't turn me away.'

She tutted. 'You're always welcome in my bed but I don't think that's why you came. You have the look of a man on a mission to blow everything apart. I take it Anna doesn't know you're here.'

'It's got nothing to do with Anna,' he all but snarled.

'Ah trouble in paradise. Poor Leo.' She patted his arm and then leaned towards him, her assets clearly on display and pressed a kiss on his lips.

He stiffened and didn't respond. Temptation didn't even come into it. Beautiful and sexy as she was, he didn't want her. He never had. She was good, straightforward fun and in a previous life he would have taken her to bed without a thought, for a carefree romp that meant nothing to either of them.

She pulled back with a minxy smile on her face.

'Leo, Leo, Leo. You came to press the self-destruct button and now you can't do it.'

He sighed and ran his hands through his damp hair. 'I don't know what I'm doing.'

She relaxed back into the sofa, studying him, amusement ticking up the corners of her mouth, making him feel utterly stupid.

'You're trying to prove that Anna is right and you're no good. Sorry, but the only thing you're no good at is being bad.'

Leo grunted, knowing she was right. He'd stormed out, furious – as much with himself as with Anna – wanting to pay her back for her lack of trust.

'She's blind,' said Zdeňka. 'But why?'

Leo lifted his shoulders.

'Leo, think. What is she afraid of?'

Leo was surprised. Zdeňka was shrewd but he hadn't thought she was that perceptive. 'She was the one that left when we were married.'

'Why?'

'I don't know. Everything was fine. I loved her. We were married.'

Zdeňka raised an eyebrow. 'She just left. For no reason.'

He nodded but this time he also remembered that everything hadn't been fine.

'There was … there was a girl. But there was nothing going on. We were friends.'

Savannah Aitken. Now her name popped into his head so inconveniently, so did other memories. Hindsight, that wonderful accessory after the fact, now made him realise that his friendly overtures – and that's all they were – *had* encouraged Savannah, despite his protestations at the time. He'd so wanted Anna to trust him. For her to be the one person that believed in him unconditionally. He assumed that his love was strong enough for both of them and that she would trust him no matter what. Maybe he'd expected too much, especially when it turned out that Savannah had been everything Anna had accused her of. But Anna should have trusted him.

He ducked his head, glancing down at his knees, ashamed. Maybe he had been stubborn.

'She was always afraid I'd leave her.'

'Which –' Zdeňka shook her head '– is exactly what you've done. You're a fool.'

'Thanks. Tell me something I didn't know.'

'You love her.'

'Yeah, I do but it's no good. It's not enough. It'll never be enough.'

'Poor boy. Michaela said you had it bad.' She laughed. 'Michaela told me to behave and leave you alone. She's a soft-hearted romantic, which is why we all love her and do as she tells us.'

'Yes, she does tend to get her own way but in a very nice way.'

'She's the mother of the group, always looking out for everyone, and she took you and Anna into her family.'

'True, she's been good to us.'

'But also naughty.' Zdeňka smirked. 'I hear there was a mishap with a mattress. Jan was a little cross with her when he found out, but she said it worked out for the best.'

Leo shook his head with reluctant admiration. 'And she always looks as if butter wouldn't melt.'

'Sorry?'

'It's an English saying. She's looks very sweet and innocent.'

'She is, truly she is … but she wanted a love story for you and Anna. She says Anna loves you, so I ask again. What is she afraid of? Why does she think you'll leave her?'

Leo lowered his head into his hands, his elbows propped on his knees, his brain too muzzy to think straight.

'Time for bed, I think,' said Zdeňka. 'You can share mine or I can get you a blanket and you can sleep here.' She rose from the sofa and lifted one shoulder in an elegant shrug, revealing more of her smooth skin. 'Your choice.'

'Thanks, Zdeňka, but I think I'd best stay put.' His tired smile made her tighten her lips in rueful resignation.

'Probably a good decision. I hope you won't regret it. It's a one-time offer.' Her eyes narrowed into a sultry cat-like gleam, as she stood with her hand on her hip in a pose that highlighted all of her best features.

'You're very generous. Thanks for letting me stay here.'

'It's no problem, Leo.' She disappeared to return with a big navy blue blanket and a couple of pillows. 'Make yourself comfortable and help yourself to whatever you need. Mine's a black coffee if you're up first and fancy bringing me breakfast in bed.' Again her eyebrows winged up, in suggestion.

He laughed in spite of himself. 'Sleep well.'

'I intend to. You on the other hand probably need to spend a few hours working out how you're going to win Anna over and explain where you spent the night.' With that she departed, waving a hand over her head in farewell.

Leo plumped up the pillows, kicked off his shoes and lay down, pulling the blanket over him. He'd really thought that things had changed but nothing had. Anna had always had one foot out the door, ready to bolt. Nothing had changed. She would never trust him. He'd worked so hard on his plan to prove that he could be steady and reliable, like that idiot boyfriend of hers … but obviously it wasn't in his nature and Anna knew that better than he did. He did have the capacity to love and to love wholeheartedly, to love one woman – but it wasn't enough. Not for Anna.

He would never be enough for her.

He woke to Zdeňka's earthy laugh and looked at his watch with surprise, rubbing his blurry eyes until they adjusted enough to see the time. It was after nine. He cradled his forehead in one hand and sighed.

It sounded as if Zdeňka was on the phone, and very chipper she was too, whilst he felt he'd been flattened by a tank. Throwing off the blanket he hauled himself to his feet and wandered through to the kitchen. Zdeňka stood with her back to him, on her mobile, looking out of the window. Outside, a blanket of snow trimmed the rooftops like icing on gingerbread houses. Zdeňka must have seen his reflection because she turned and broke off. 'Morning, Leo.' Then she said to the person on the phone, 'I have to go. I will make the arrangements.'

She ended the call.

'Michaela says hi, although I don't think she's very pleased with you.'

He groaned inwardly. He gave a weak smile and followed his nose to the pot of coffee on the side, pouring himself a cup. It disappeared in a couple of swallows.

'So what are you going to do?' asked Zdeňka.

'I'm going to check into a hotel.'

'Giving up so easily.'

'Zdeňka, I'm not giving up. I'm facing reality. Anna and I were never meant to be and she's always known it. Just a shame it took me so long to catch up.'

'In that case you can come and look at another property with me today.'

'I don't feel like it.'

She gave him a twisted smile. 'You owe me. Besides, what else are you going to do today?'

Leo shrugged. It was something to do although all his enthusiasm for the project had died. Opening a brewery and pub in Prague wouldn't be the same without Anna.

Chapter Thirty

'Where's Leo?'

'I don't know.' Anna pushed a plate of pastries towards Becs. She'd woken early and, finding that Leo was still absent, had been unable to go back to sleep, so she'd popped out to the bakery, half hoping she might see him on the way, out on the street somewhere.

Groggy with tiredness, she took a big gulp of coffee. Sleep had been impossible after he'd left last night. She kept listening, hoping to hear him come back. When she'd finally drifted off, she had a horrible anxious dream where she couldn't find Leo's number on her phone and every time she did a search, she kept hitting the wrong buttons and misspelling his name.

Becs picked up a pastry and took a big bite, issuing a satisfied sigh as she chewed. 'Fresh. You've been out already?'

'Mmm,' Anna nodded. 'I think me and Leo broke up last night.'

'W-what?' Becs spluttered, having trouble swallowing her coffee.

'He went out. Didn't come back.'

'What do you mean, he went out?'

'Last night. We had…' She paused. 'It wasn't even a row. A discussion. Talk.' She huffed out a lengthy sigh.

'What about?'

Anna screwed up her face. 'I was trying to be honest with him. Not make him feel trapped.'

'What the bogging hell are you talking about?'

'He was worried that I might regret finishing with Steve, so I wanted to reassure him that I'm not expecting anything permanent. I thought he'd be pleased.'

'Run that by me again.' Becs placed her coffee cup down in front of her.

'That's what men like Leo want, isn't it? Not to be tied down. I was trying not to be needy.'

Anna felt like an insect under a microscope under her cousin's stern gaze and began to squirm in her seat when her cousin didn't say anything.

Eventually Becs leaned forward. If she'd been wearing glasses, she would have been peering at Anna over the top of them. 'You pillock,' she said.

'What?'

'He's in love with you and you're in love with him. It's so frigging obvious.'

'That doesn't mean it's going to work out.'

'It doesn't mean it won't.' Becs shook her head, her eyes signalling utter disbelief at what she clearly considered Anna's utter reprehensibility. 'Not all men are philanderers.'

'I know that.' Anna pinched her mouth closed in mutinous defence. But did she?

'I should have said, not all charming men are philanderers.'

Anna's stomach clenched. 'Leo could have any woman he wants.'

With a roll of her eyes, Becs shook her head vehemently as if Anna was the stupidest person on the planet. 'He wants you.'

'Yes, but not enough.' And that was the crux of it. There was always a chance he would walk away, get bored with her, find someone more dazzling, someone like him.

'What are you talking about?' Exasperation and impatience vibrated through her cousin's voice.

Closing her eyes, Anna tried to push away the shame and the pain.

'It was my fault we split up when we were married. I panicked and walked out, thinking I was brave doing it to him before he did it to me.' She cringed at the memory. She'd been such a child. 'I left him a note, telling him how I felt. That I didn't think was enough for him, that I was setting him free.' She turned to her cousin, all the embarrassment at her poor behaviour rushing up in a tide of heat on her face. 'God, I was such an insecure brat. I *wanted* him to come running after me and tell me I was wrong. I was desperate for him to do that. I'd seen Uncle Henry growing up, I knew that's what handsome, charming men were like.'

'Because Dad's a dick,' suggested Becs. 'But he's my dick, unfortunately. Mum knows he'll never change but for the most part he does keep it in his pants. There were a couple of times he's gone too far but both times he's come straight home and told her he made a mistake. I know it's not perfect – but it works for them. They're happy most of the time. He's a flirt ... but I think she secretly quite likes the fact that other women fancy him, but it's her who owns him. He won't ever leave.'

Rebecca's face closed down, bitterness etched into the lines around her mouth. 'And I hate him for that. For setting such a shit example and for her never calling him out on it.' She tapped her fingers on the coffee mug in front of her. 'I need to move away. Like you did. It's not a healthy relationship. But surely you see Leo's not like that. There's a huge difference between him and Dad. Leo doesn't go out with the intention of flirting and feeding off female adulation. He's a friendly guy who can't help himself, lighting up when other people are around, men and women. He doesn't suck people in and make it about him.' Rebecca gave her a stern, direct stare. 'When it comes to you, he looks after you, he puts you first and he does nice things for you. He's a world apart from Dad.'

Anna considered her words, they flashed about for a moment, random jigsaw pieces, and as she tried to make sense of them they began to arrange themselves into a clear picture. But Becs hadn't finished.

'And you, you light up when he's around. I knew as soon as I arrived that something was different. You *never* looked happy with Steve. You were like a sad puppy in tow behind him all the time. Now, it's obvious you're having fun. Doing new things. Leo's good for you. Don't let him walk away.'

Anna covered her face, eyes closed. Leo was Leo, a bright star bursting across the sky, nothing like her uncle. She'd been too blind and prejudiced to see it … and also too scared.

'Too late, he already has.'

'It's not too late. Go after him.'

Anna swallowed, her stomach hollow and empty at the memory of how stupid she'd been. 'When I left him, he didn't come after me. I wasn't that important to him. In a childish way, I was testing him and he failed.'

To her surprise, Becs looked stricken. 'Leo did come,' she whispered, her eyes widening.

'What?'

'Leo came to the house.'

'When?' She felt as if she were in a tennis match, having to return yet another volley.

'The day after you came home.' Becs caught her lower lip between her teeth and Anna was worried she might draw blood. 'He came. Mum told him you weren't there.'

'Leo came to the house?' Cold spread across Anna's skin, as chilling as if she were standing in a draft with wet skin. 'Why didn't anyone tell me?'

With a wince, Becs clamped her lips again. Then she spoke. 'Because we thought it was for the best.'

Anna thought she would choke on the saliva that pooled in her mouth.

Her cousin reached over and put her hand on Anna's forearm. 'You were still so young and … Mum didn't want you to go through what she'd been through with Dad. She honestly thought she was doing the right thing. Dad's calmed down, but apparently before we were born he was pretty bad. Mum was going to leave him but then she discovered she was pregnant with Tim and it was too late. She didn't want you repeating her mistakes. In fact, she blamed herself for setting a bad example and worried that she'd normalised Dad's behaviour. Another reason she … we all supported Steve so much. He might be a boring bastard but he's a steady one.'

For some reason Anna could only see the funny side of that and started to giggle.

'Hello! Anyone home?'

'Up here, Michaela,' Anna called back. 'Our neighbour,' she explained.

For once Michaela's light tread was sedate and her face sombre when she came into the kitchen.

'Do you know where Leo is!' It wasn't so much a question as an accusation.

Anna shook her head.

'He's with Zdeňka.' Michaela folded her arms, her eyes flashing with fury. 'In her flat. What do you think of that?'

Anna thought that she knew exactly what it was like to receive a kick in the stomach. She crossed her arms over her middle as if to protect herself from more physical pain. Leo had gone there. Why?

'Hi, I'm Rebecca. Anna's cousin.' Becs gave Michaela a sarcastic wave. 'Do you think that's helpful?' She turned to Anna. 'And who's Zdeňka?'

'She's a friend of Michaela and Jan's.'

'And Leo's,' Michaela butted in, not so helpfully. 'You need to do something.'

'I need to do something,' Anna echoed, her voice rising in bewilderment.

'Yes. Zdeňka's my friend but I know what's she's like. You have a saying in England. She'll eat him for breakfast.'

Suddenly Anna began to laugh, properly this time, tears running down her face. Leo couldn't have picked anyone more obvious. He might as well have shouted from a megaphone, 'I'm going to prove you right.'

It took her a couple of minutes to get herself back under control, especially with the giddiness rushing through her, like air escaping from a balloon.

'It's my test,' she said, blinking back a tear. A happy tear, because she'd been so blind and stupid up until now.

'What?' Becs and Michaela stared at her as if she'd lost her marbles, and then some.

'Leo's testing me. Pushing back, trying to prove me right, except I know he wouldn't sleep with Zdeňka. He wouldn't do that to me. I'm such an idiot. I pushed him away so he went and did exactly what I told him to do.'

'I have absolutely no idea what on earth you are on about, Cuz.'

'I told Leo that I didn't think he would stick around, that he would move on. He tells me he loves me … and then he goes to Zdeňka's. I don't think so.' Anna felt sparkly and lightheaded.

'Er, hang on, you didn't mention the "he loves you" bit before. I think I might have to slap you.'

Anna ignored her cousin's outraged expression. 'Leo is

mad at me because I cast aspersions on his honour. Telling him that he wouldn't stay with me. So he went out to make a point. It's my turn to man up. I have to go and find him.'

Becs and Michaela were still staring at her.

'I tested him once before and he passed the test. He did come and find me, except I didn't know. It's my turn now.'

'Fight for your man,' said Michaela, nodding with sudden enthusiasm before clapping her hands and saying. 'This is so romantic.'

Becs looked from one to the other. 'I'm so confused. You're happy because he went to another woman and spent the night there?'

Anna nodded, grinning. 'Yup.' There wasn't time to explain. She knew what she needed to do. She had to prove to Leo that she trusted him and knew him well enough to recognise the truth. 'Can you give me Zdeňka's number?'

Chapter Thirty-One

Leo paced. Where the hell was Zdeňka? The last thing he felt like doing was going to view another potential property. The plans he'd made were to include Anna. Everything was supposed to be in place yesterday to show her the premises in Vyšehrad and ask her to stay in Prague with him. He would have signed the contract with Tomáš to set up their own bar and brewery.

It was snowing again, much bigger flakes today, whirling and curling down like feathers spilled from a pillow fight. Over the parapet the grey swirling, water below moved sluggishly. He shoved his hands further into his pockets and kept walking, looking for the statues that Zdeňka had picked as a meeting point. They were on the north side and there were three of them. He spotted them ahead and slowed his pace. She'd said she'd gone to the office to get keys and insisted that he should meet her here. Standing in front of the three statues, he looked up. Three saints. Sigismund, Wenceslas and Norbert.

He moved to stand in front of Norbert. He closed his eyes. He was such a fool. Why did Anna still persist in this image of him? What more did he have to do to prove himself? Except he'd blown that one out of the water by running off to another woman last night. Hunching into his coat, wishing he had a hat and gloves, he checked his watch. Zdeňka was late. With one last glance up at St Norbert's stern face towering above him, he turned and scanned the bridge back towards the Old Town. Among the crowds of tourists captivated by the snow despite the temperature – maybe they were dressed for it – he spotted a swirl of bright red skirt. It caught his attention because it moved quickly, weaving in and out of the other people, with a determined trajectory. He sucked in a quick breath, the icy cold hitting his lungs while his stomach went into freefall.

Barely able to believe it, he stared as Anna came striding towards him, her face a curious mix of apprehension and fury. She walked straight up to him and punched him in the chest. His feet skidded slightly in the slushy snow but he managed to hold his ground.

'That's for running away,' she snapped, her eyes flaring. 'You dumb ass.'

'I'll take it,' he said warily.

'And to Zdeňka's of all places.' She rolled her eyes. 'That was a prime dick move.'

'I know,' he admitted, his heart turning over a little at the sight of her, all furious and fabulous, her scarf tossing behind her in the breeze.

'I panicked.'

She studied him, her mouth forming a wry smile, before she said, 'It's all right, I forgive you. I thought I was doing the right thing letting you off the hook. I panicked, too. I thought if I made out I wasn't looking for commitment or anything, I could protect myself from loving you too much. So what I said was a dick move, too. I do want us to be permanent. Always have. Always will. So I forgive you for running away.'

'You do?' Despite the light dancing in her eyes and the way they held his, he had to ask.

'Leo, I trust you.' The gentle expression on her face, filled with warmth and love, made his heart soar. 'Zdeňka can flirt with you all she likes, but I know there's nothing between you. You're not like that. I should have known it when we were married but I was too insecure and I'd been brought up to believe that men cheated. I know you love me, I just—' She huffed out a sigh and looked up at him, her eyes full of apology. He didn't need the words, he could see it on her face. 'I'm sorry, Leo. Forgive me.'

'What?'

'Forgive me for not believing that you could love me.'

He stepped forward and put his hands on her waist, holding her at arm's length. 'I forgave you a long time ago,' he said, lifting one hand to swipe the corner of her eye where a tear threatened to spill out. 'Will you forgive me?'

'I kind of deserved it,' she said with her usual brutal honesty. 'You tell me you love me, and I tell you you don't.'

'And do I?'

'Hell, yes. You must do to put up with me.' She gave him a watery smile.

'You're not that bad,' he said, smiling down at her exasperated, pissed-off-with-herself face. 'The big question is, do you love me?'

Her face filled with mischief. 'I think I probably do.'

He laughed. 'Well, do let me know when you're sure.'

She slipped an arm around his waist. 'Now's probably a good time.' Raising her face to him, she studied his, her eyes softening. 'Mr Sunshine, you light up my life, spreading joy into all the dark corners.'

His heart fluttered, really fluttered in his chest as he stared back at her. 'Positively flowery.'

'I know. Go me. Who knew?' She stood on tiptoes and wrapped her arms around his neck, pulling him in for a kiss. 'I love you, Leo.'

He kissed her back.

'You're bloody freezing,' she complained a second later.

'That's what you get for running off into the night without adequate clothing.'

'In that case, it serves you right.' But in the next second she was pushing one of her gloves into his hand and had taken off her scarf and was carefully wrapping it around his head.

'Come on, let's go home.'

'Ah, about that. Can I show you something?'

Her mouth twitched. 'I thought I'd seen everything.'

'Anna Love, wash your mouth out. There's something I want you to see.' He winced. 'I need to phone Zdeňka. She was supposed to meet me here.'

'Ah, I should have told you. She's been delayed.'

'You knew I'd be here?'

She grinned at him. 'I told her to have you here. I phoned her and asked her for a little help.'

'Even though I stayed at her place.'

'Leo,' she chided. 'Oh, and there she is.'

He looked up to see Zdeňka striding towards them, grinning from ear to ear.

'I'm not staying but I thought you might need these.' She slipped a set of keys into his pocket, gave Anna a cheeky wink and ran off to Tomáš waiting for her on the other side of the bridge.

'Come on,' he said to Anna. 'Let's go home.'

She nodded and turned around.

'No, we're going this way.'

'We are?'

He nodded as he tapped the address into his Uber app.

Five minutes later they were in the warmth of a cab, although Leo was quite happy for Anna to wrap herself around him to heat him up.

'Are you going to tell me where we're going?' she asked for the fourth or fifth time.

He relented. 'We're going to Vyšehrad.'

She pouted. 'That doesn't tell me anything.'

'No,' he said and kissed her, tapping her nose. 'All in good time.'

The taxi pulled up at their destination and they stepped out, their feet crunching into the soft white surface. The snow had blanketed the roof of the little low building, softening the edges and covering the terracotta tiles, transforming the exterior into a cosy cottage.

Leo led the way to the wooden doors, their feet leaving

prints in the virgin snow, which felt like a sign. A fresh start. Clean and new. He opened a door and ushered Anna through.

'What is this place?' she asked.

'I wondered if you'd be interested in staying in Prague with me. Starting our own brewery with a pub. Maybe here, if you liked it.'

'Here?' Her eyes widened. 'With you?'

He nodded, his heart thudding painfully in his chest, as he wrapped his arms around her and pulled her close, so that they were nose to nose.

Tears shimmered in her eyes, as she lifted her face. 'In Prague?'

'Yes.' He kissed her. 'Our own little place in Prague. What do you say?'

'Leo Knight.' The tears spilled over and she gave him a wonky smile that made him feel ever so slightly tearful himself. 'I'd love to live with you in a little place in Prague. In fact I'd go anywhere as long I'm with you.'

Epilogue

'This is quite something,' said Leo as they stood in the
tiny foyer, having walked up the cobbled street to a
pair of imposing double doors and through a smaller door
set within them. From high in the wall a red light blinked at
them and next to Leo was a set of airlock security doors.
After their names had been checked they were invited
through, one at a time. On the opposite side a young
woman in a black suit and low court shoes met them.

'Mr Knight and Miss Love, nice to meet you. I'm Adela,
the private secretary to the ambassador. Welcome to the
British Embassy. We're very happy to be hosting this event.'

'Thank you,' said Leo with one of his charming smiles,
giving Anna's hand a quick squeeze.

'Yes, thank you,' she echoed, nerves rattling through her
as the woman gestured to the staircase, which was
festooned with evergreens and fairy lights. She and Leo had
already decided to stay in Prague for Christmas and tonight
they were meeting Jan and Michaela for their first visit to

the Christmas Market in the Old Town Square, even though there was still a month until Christmas and two weeks until the week of the beer festival.

Leo squeezed her hand again when she hesitated on the first step, as if her courage had stalled.

'We've got this,' he whispered into her ear. 'Remember Love-Knight.' The suggestive tone of his voice made her want to giggle and chased the nerves away. She'd got this. Oval-shaped Anna was in the building.

The walls of the staircase were lined with museum-style paintings in heavy, ornate frames, portraits of severe-looking old men. Anna gave each one a cursory glance as they walked past, while Leo, nudging her, pulled faces imitating their stern expressions. By the time they reached their floor, she was struggling to keep her own face straight.

Jakub and Karel, standing side by side in solidarity, were waiting in a large lounge area dominated by a huge Christmas tree. Anna smiled at the pair, still amazed that they'd overcome their previous difficulties so quickly.

'Morning, Karel; morning, Jakub. Is the beer here?' asked Leo.

'Of course the beer is here,' said Jakub, a little testily. 'It arrived yesterday, so that it was able to settle overnight and be kept at the optimum temperature.'

Anna gave him a reassuring smile.

'The panel are already here,' said Karel. 'It's quite a collective.'

'Members of the Czech Beer and Malt Association,' interjected Jakub. 'As well as the ambassador, the trade attaché and the head of *Sdílená Kultura* .'

'All very influential,' added Karel.

Anna gulped, any confidence she'd had in her presentation quickly evaporating. Why had she thought she could do this? Her slides might be strong but talking in public wasn't her thing at all. Someone had taken up macrame with her intestines, and everything was suddenly very knotted, including her larynx. Would she even be able to speak?

Leo took her hand and squeezed it.

'You've got this, Anna Love. We've got this,' said Leo in a forceful whisper. It was so at odds with his normal happy-go lucky-attitude, it startled her and gave her a much-needed injection of backbone.

At nine o'clock, as announced by the peal of a nearby church bell, a set of double doors opened and the four of them were invited in. The room was double the size of the previous one, with a fine view out over the city. At the front, next to a grand piano, was a table set up with a microphone and two chairs, next to which were the cool boxes containing the beer.

Ranged in front of the table was an audience, predominantly of men, although Anna noted a few women. Leo and Anna were invited to take seats in the front row.

'Ladies and gentleman, I'd like to welcome you all to the British Embassy this morning. Thank you for coming to the inaugural judging of the results of our first industry Cultural Exchange Programme. We have two beers brewed by our contestants Miss Love and Mr Knight and they will each be doing a presentation to help us decide which beer has commercial merit and will be awarded our grand prize.

I'd like to hand over to the Head of the Cultural Office for Europe, Jaroslav Lebeda.'

'Can we all say a big thank you to His Excellency, the Ambassador, for hosting this prestigious event.' Jaroslav waffled on for a good five minutes, interspersed with polite rounds of applause, during which Anna's leg began to jump up and down. *Please get on with it,* she thought. Every word he spoke seemed to ratchet the tension in her neck and shoulders more tightly.

At last he invited 'Miss Anna Love' to the stage. She rose and gave Leo a nervous glance. He nodded and she went up to the table and opened up her laptop.

'Good morning, everyone.' Her voice quavered a little but she forced herself to sweep her gaze across the audience, making brief eye contact with some of them. 'I have been lucky enough to work with Jakub Šilhov, at the Šilhov brewery, which, as you know has a tradition of brewing beer which stretches back several hundred years.' Smiles and nods came from the audience

'My colleague Mr Knight has been making beer with the Crystal brewery, in a more contemporary style, and I'd like to invite him to join me.'

A murmur of curiosity and surprise rippled through the audience as Leo made his way to stand beside her.

'When we first arrived in Prague, it was obvious that we were going to very different breweries. The old and the new. What we've learned is that there is no wrong or right way to make beer. It is down to individual taste and it's wrong to say one is better than another. They're different.' Leo finished and handed over to Anna.

There was a sudden spontaneous round of applause, which started with a few people on the back row but quickly engulfed the whole audience. Buoyed up by this, Anna stepped forward, suddenly excited to be here.

'Today, ladies and gentlemen, we're going to celebrate the old and new, the traditional and contemporary. We decided that there was more strength in working together than against each other. So Mr Knight and I would like to present our concept: Love Knight beer. Two beers, two processes, which we will sell side by side, leaving drinkers to make up their own minds and compare the two.'

Leo winked at her and she smiled, noticing quite a few members of the audience nodding approvingly. Suddenly she was flying – they could do this. 'Leo will take you through the marketing plan.'

Leo captivated the audience with his well-rehearsed presentation and Anna watched him, her heart filled with pride as he charmed each and every one of them. And then at last it was time to finish and present their final message, rounding off with the slogan – *Neither Wrong Nor Right, Love Beer, Love Knight*. There was another spontaneous round of applause, while Jakub and Karel poured glasses of beer and put them on the silver trays handed round by waiting staff.

The Ambassador came over to them.

'Very nicely done. I think the two of you could have a future in the diplomatic corps if the beer-making gig doesn't work out.' His mouth twisted in a discreet smile as he glanced over at the two brewers. 'I'm not sure Jaroslav could have come up with a better political solution if he'd tried. You do know he only secured the two of them to sponsor the programme because of their bitter rivalry. He set them up, telling each the other had signed up, when neither of them had. But I think you've outdone him. Smart move. I guess we'd better try the beer now. Ladies first.'

One of the waiters served up three glasses of Anna's beer and she held her breath as the ambassador and Leo lifted their glasses. She couldn't care less what His Excellency thought, but her insides squirmed as Leo took his first sip

'Congratulations, Anna Love. Sunshine in a glass. Bloody lovely. I'm so proud of you, Anna. This is seriously good beer. Light, floral but with a smooth, smooth depth of flavour.'

'Thank you.' She turned quite pink with pleasure. '

A server approached and Anna took a glass of Leo's beer. She sniffed and then tasted. He watched her and only she would have known from the carefully indifferent expression on his face how much her opinion meant to him. She took a second sip, keeping a straight face and didn't say a word. Sometimes it was fun to tease. She took a third sip, raised an eyebrow and tilted her head to one side.

'What? You don't like?' Leo's face scrunched and he glanced around the room, trying to gauge the reactions of the judges.

Her face broke into a smile. 'Well done, Leo Knight. You've nailed it. What an amazing depth of flavour. That is ... woody, hoppy, smoky. It's like being beside a warmth hearth in winter. I love it.'

'Seriously?'

She heard the need for reassurance in the doubtful pitch of his voice.

'Seriously. It's good. I couldn't choose between the two.' She smiled up at him. 'Glad I'm not one of the judges.' Over Leo's shoulder, she could see them sidling out of the room with their clipboards.

'Oh, God, this is it,' she said, her head swimming a little. She had to clutch Leo's arm. 'They're off to make their judgement.'

'I feel a bit like the Pope,' said Leo, with a jaunty smile. 'With all the cardinal fellows going off to vote.'

This irreverence bought a grateful burst of laughter from Anna and the ambassador's wife, who said dryly, 'I think the prize is somewhat different.'

'You do know it doesn't matter,' said Anna. 'Now we're an official team, it's a win-win.'

'I know,' said Leo, 'but I want that official, industry endorsement. If these guys like it, we're okay. Otherwise two Brits making beer in the Czech Republic … I don't know. If one of them is award-winning…'

'Stop fretting, Leo,' she told him. 'It doesn't matter. One of *our* beers will be at the Beer Festival. Lots of people will be drinking it. You said yourself it will be great publicity for Our Place.'

They decided that Love Knight would sound far too much like a sex shop and had settled on Our Place as the name of their joint venture.

After half an hour, during which Leo, much to Anna's amusement and the ambassador's wife's exasperation, had rearranged most of the eye-level Christmas decorations on the tree, the double doors opened and the judges trooped back in, handing a sealed envelope to Jaroslav, who promptly handed it to the ambassador.

Leo gripped Anna's hand as the ambassador strolled to his podium. 'I think, without more ado, I'll announce the winner. Everyone has been waiting long enough.'

He slit open the envelope and read the contents, a broad smile breaking out on his face.

'I'm pleased to announce that it is ... a tie. Both beers win and will both feature at this year's Christmas Beer Festival. Congratulations, Miss Love and Mr Knight.' He lifted his glass of beer. 'To a wonderful collaboration, a marriage of the old and the new.'

Leo scooped Anna into a hug and kissed her soundly. 'Congratulations, Anna, love.'

'Congratulations, Leo.'

'Told you we could do it,' he said with a cocky wink that made her burst out laughing at the outrageous lie. Irrepressible as ever – and she wouldn't change it for anything. They were in this together and the future in Prague looked very bright.

Acknowledgments

I arrived at Václav Havel airport with my agent, Broo Doherty, in May 2022, somewhat anxious about the trip ahead. We were meeting my editor, Petra Lásková and editor in chief, Tereza Lebedová, for the first time and we'd be spending the next few days in their company in Prague.

Fast forward four days and the four of us, plus their colleague from Grada Slovakia, lovely Janka Turnová, were all in tears at the prospect of saying goodbye. The trip cemented some wonderful friendships and reminded me of the value of having friends around the world. It reminds us that we have more in common than our differences.

On that first trip, I met so many lovely people and received an incredible welcome from the team at Grada, readers, bloggers and the bookstore staff at Knihy Dobrovský where I signed books for an incredible three hours. I can't thank all those that waited in line enough. I also visited the British Embassy and I'm very grateful to Nick and Erica Archer for hosting a very special day.

Since then I have been to the Czech Republic several times and as I flew in last time it felt a little like coming home. In May I spent a week starting in Prague before visiting Brno and touring South Moravia before crossing the border into Slovakia.

This book is my love letter to Prague and all my lovely Czech readers and the friends I've made there. I'd also like to say a big thank to all my readers in Slovakia, who gave me such a wonderful welcome in Bratislava this year, where I signed books for three hours in the Martinus bookshop. The welcome I received from readers there was unbelievably warm and generous. I was also treated royally by the Grada Slovakia team, Alexandra Janogová, Dominika Miklošíková and Janka Turnová.

Special thanks go to Michaela, @radsi_knihu, for lending me her name for this book and for her friendship and support and to @zdenka_mevedi, the lovely blogger who also lent me her name (the real Zdeňka is much nicer than my Zdeňka). Thanks also go to Kirstina @thebookfly for all her support and chocolate treats! A huge thank you to my brilliant translator, Lenka Čurdová whose skill at translating at speed is quite incredible and very much appreciated.

Huge thanks to all the bloggers, instagrammers, reviewers and readers that share my books, send me lovely messages and show the love – it is so appreciated and I'm so grateful to each and every one of you.

Even bigger thanks to all the team at Grada, especially Lida, chauffeur extraordinaire and all round wonderful person – it was a delight getting to know you.

Biggest thanks go to the gorgeous Petra Lásková and Tereza Lebedová, who have championed my books in the Czech Republic and made them such a huge success over there. Ladies I absolutely adore you and it is always a privilege to spend time with you xxx.

And yet more thanks to my amazing UK editor, the legendary Charlotte Ledger, who trusted me enough to write a book about Prague this time and to my agent and travel partner in crime, Broo Doherty, for looking out for me and supporting me when I'm having a wobble.

And I'm sorry if this is running into Oscar territory, but I also want to thank to my running buddy, Ruth, who provided the inspiration for the scene on Charles bridge when she told me it was where her husband Giles proposed to her.

There are also so many people behind the scenes that bring a book to publication, so another heartfelt thank you to each and every one of them.

There is never a day where I'm not grateful to all the people, from readers to members of the publishing team, that have given me the chance to make stuff up for a living. I am living the dream and loving it.

ONE MORE CHAPTER

YOUR NUMBER ONE STOP

FOR PAGETURNING BOOKS

The author and One More Chapter would like to thank everyone who contributed to the publication of this story...

Analytics
James Brackin
Abigail Fryer

Audio
Fionnuala Barrett
Ciara Briggs

Contracts
Sasha Duszynska Lewis

Design
Lucy Bennett
Fiona Greenway
Liane Payne
Dean Russell

Digital Sales
Lydia Grainge
Hannah Lismore
Emily Scorer

Editorial
Arsalan Isa
Charlotte Ledger
Jennie Rothwell
Tony Russell
Emily Thomas

Harper360
Emily Gerbner
Jean Marie Kelly
emma sullivan
Sophia Wilhelm

International Sales
Peter Borcsok
Ruth Burrow

Marketing & Publicity
Chloe Cummings
Emma Petfield

Operations
Melissa Okusanya
Hannah Stamp

Production
Denis Manson
Simon Moore
Francesca Tuzzeo

Rights
Helena Font Brillas
Ashton Mucha
Zoe Shine
Aisling Smythe

The HarperCollins Distribution Team

The HarperCollins Finance & Royalties Team

The HarperCollins Legal Team

The HarperCollins Technology Team

Trade Marketing
Ben Hurd

UK Sales
Laura Carpenter
Isabel Coburn
Jay Cochrane
Sabina Lewis
Holly Martin
Harriet Williams
Leah Woods

And every other essential link in the chain from delivery drivers to booksellers to librarians and beyond!

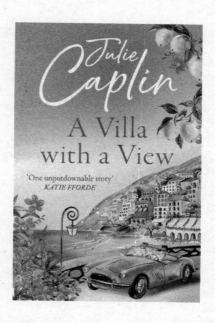

Discover a sizzling summer romance set in the Amalfi coast.

Lia Bathurst had always dreamed of escaping to the white sandy beaches and turquoise blue seas of the Amalfi coast – but that dream hadn't included meeting her real father. A father she had never even known about until a few weeks ago! Yet here she was, standing outside the gates of a gorgeous pink villa being refused entry by the insufferable – and insufferably handsome – Raphael Knight, her father's business manager.

Available now in paperback, ebook, and audio!

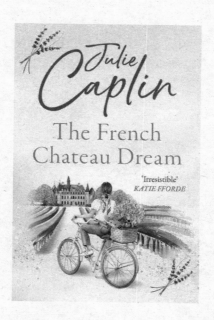

You are invited to a summer of sparkling champagne, warm buttery croissants and a little bit of je ne sais quoi

With a broken heart and a broken spirit, Hattie is in need of a summer escape. So when an opportunity comes up to work at a beautiful, stately chateau in the Champagne region of France she books her flights quicker than the pop of a cork.

Romance is the last thing Hattie is looking for but then she wasn't expecting gorgeous Luc to stroll into her life. Hattie starts to wonder if a holiday fling – or maybe even something more – might be just what she needs.

Available now in paperback, ebook, and audio!

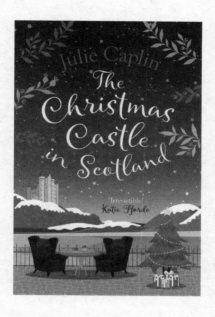

Escape to the snow-peaked caps of the Scottish Highlands and a romance that will melt your heart...

Izzy McBride had never in a million years expected to inherit an actual castle, but here she was, in the run up to Christmas, Monarch of her own Glen – a very rundown glen in need of a lot of TLC if her dream of turning it into a boutique bed and breakfast was to come true.

But when Izzy's eccentric mother rents a room to enigmatic thriller author Ross Adair and the Scottish snow starts to settle like the frosting on a Christmas cake, it's a race to get the castle ready before they're all snowed in.

Available now in paperback, ebook, and audio!

371

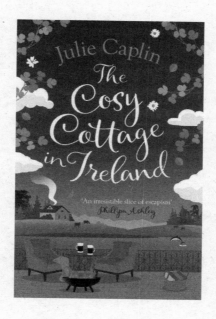

Snuggle up in your favourite armchair and take a trip across the Irish sea for comfort food, cosy cottage nights and a heartwarming romance…

Talented lawyer Hannah Campbell wants a change in her workaholic Manchester life – so she books herself a place at the world-renowned Killorgally Cookery School in County Kerry. But on her first night In Ireland, sampling the delights of Dublin, Hannah can't resist falling for the charms of handsome stranger Conor. It's only when Hannah arrives at her postcard-pretty home at Killorgally for the next six weeks that she discovers what happens in Dublin doesn't quite stay in Dublin…

Available now in paperback, ebook, and audio!

YOUR NUMBER ONE STOP

ONE MORE CHAPTER

FOR PAGETURNING BOOKS

One More Chapter is an
award-winning global
division of HarperCollins.

Sign up to our newsletter to get our
latest eBook deals and stay up to date
with our weekly Book Club!
<u>Subscribe here.</u>

Meet the team at
<u>www.onemorechapter.com</u>

Follow us!

 @OneMoreChapter_
 @OneMoreChapter
 @onemorechapterhc

Do you write unputdownable fiction?
We love to hear from new voices.
Find out how to submit your novel at
<u>www.onemorechapter.com/submissions</u>